OLIVIA'S ISCA WHISPERS

Philippa Varney

Cover design by: SVA
Original charcoal artwork by Philippa Varney from roman sculpture Jeune Femme. Photo: Topsham Estuary, Devon

To all who are loyal, inquisitive and kind

*Lives of great men all remind us
We can make our lives sublime,
And, departing, leave behind us
Footprints on the sands of time;*

HENRY WADSWORTH LONGFELLOW 1807-1882

CONTENTS

FOREWORD

Ancient Rome and Isca (modern day Exeter) - Two cities. What are their connections?

Olivia makes monumental discoveries as she is embroiled in mysteries surrounding spies, stolen paintings and family secrets are uncovered.

Olivia's Isca Whispers

CHAPTER 1

'What Is Precious Is Never to Forget..'
The Truly Great
Stephen Spender

England Buckinghamshire 1968

From his hidden vantage point on top of the crumbling stone wall, the tall boy raised his black curled head slightly as he saw, set amongst trees and parkland, Blackstone Manor School all shut up and quiet. His hands clung to the tufts of weeds, and his bare knees scraped against the rocky ledges. His eyes were screwed up as he noted the many gables and roofs rising from the school. He scanned quickly the double-fronted stone house in the foreground. It was intriguing but not like the more extensive deserted manor further away. His short life experience had been the cramped terraces and alleyways of East London, but he was very familiar with the old churches and, more interestingly, their old roofs in the borough where he had lived. He knew the potential of what he was now surveying. His bright blue eyes narrowed, and his lips curled into a knowing smile.

As his heart rate quickened and his breathing deepened, his right hand instinctively moved to his left wrist, and he twisted rhythmically the black cords tied around his wrist. The familiar tightening stabs quickly brought his mind back to the scene before him. A crunching of gravel caused him to duck rapidly as he caught sight of a girl leading her dog towards the fields behind the house. The people who lived there must be the family of his new headmaster. His keen eyesight and hearing had heard and seen enough for now. Sebastian Routledge jumped down from the wall. His feline actions kept him close to the ground as he slunk away. Seb was an observer of people and situations, quick to react to anything advantageous or with risks. His mum had recently gathered him up and rushed away from London to live with her sister in Beaconsfield. He had witnessed personally the raw hand of his mother's many men friends and learned rapidly how to act out a part for his own advantage. His quick mind, new contacts and the ability to turn his charm and intelligence to his benefit had made it possible to pass the entrance exam to Blackstone Manor. He was a day pupil, because of his aunt's influence and money, from the beginning of term. Seb felt his future was about to change for the better, he just needed a few good accomplices plus his own clever manoeuvrings, and he would be made.

Olivia Hadleigh sat across the table from her best friend, Amanda Waverley. This was a special occasion for Olivia. At 11, having tea all on her own, just because Mandy liked her and had called her a best friend. Olivia, though felt a cloud of sadness draping itself over the afternoon. Mandy was her idol at school. She was pretty and petite. In fact, to Livia, just perfect in every way. She knew all the answers to the algebra questions that were still a fog to Livia, and above everything, she was going to be a famous ballet dancer. Mandy had passed the Royal Ballet entrance exam at White Lodge Richmond. She had undergone the intensive week-long course and been accepted for the following academic year.

They had been close friends since starting out at junior school together. Olivia was tall and skinny; her hair was fine and long, in disarray most of the time. Today she had fought with an elastic band and tied her straggly locks into a high ponytail, slightly skew-whiff, but to Olivia it would do, almost central.

She was part of a family of five. They were all different characters. Her mum, Bridget, 'Briddy' had been brought up in Oxford, where her father taught at one of the colleges. Bridget's mum had inherited a bookshop from her family, and Olivia's father, Richard Hadleigh, had met Bridget whilst an undergraduate at Oxford. He had started to visit 'Quills' frequently, where he had become acquainted with their marvellous section of antiquarian books and the equally appealing, young Bridget. They had married after a long courtship and the intervening second world war, along with Richard finishing his doctorate in Latin and Ancient History. Subsequently, Richard had been given the post of Head of Blackstone Manor School, Beaconsfield, where they had lived in the headmaster's house for the past seventeen years and raised their three girls, Imogen, Tatiana and Olivia. Olivia, the youngest, usually felt ungainly and awkward unless she was scrambling over the Chiltern Hills with Ruby, her cocker spaniel. This gave her enormous time on her own to conjure up exciting adventures and romantic encounters whilst developing a keen interest in the natural world around her.

In contrast her friend Mandy, an only child, was neatly dressed, extremely polite and always looked just like the porcelain dolls sitting perfectly in the window of the doll's hospital shop in Beaconsfield High Street. In the photography shop window next door, Mandy's portrait was placed, centrally, pride of place. An example of the perfection of a young ballet dancer about to embark on her career in London.

The young girls had sat together on their first day at junior school, and Mandy's neat, methodical italic handwriting had been a source of wonder and an eyeopener to Livia's uneven style, which all too often depended on her moods of imagination. It was a spidery scrawl most of the time, which changed its slant from left to right daily. Some days she felt like a writer from the 16th century, with embellished tails and strokes. The first few words usually showed great artistic promise, but the storytelling took over. Therefore, sadly, her legibility soon deteriorated as the intensity of adventure took over.

The Singleton Park Girl's School they attended also expected them to learn to use a fountain pen expertly. This had become a source of added mishap and sloppiness. However, Mandy and Livia, an unlikely pair, had a tremendous mutual passion for conversation, history and reading books. They shared an interest in languages and found they enjoyed their French and, recently, the new Latin curriculum. They could sit together for hours in the window seat of Mandy's bedroom reading her latest collections of Anne of Green Gables, The Flicka trilogy, the Little Women series, What Katy Did (and didn't) Do Next, progressing to Dickens and Forster, early on in their youth. As Anne Shirley would say, 'they shared a kindred spirit.'

So this tea they had together was tinged with a sombre seriousness as Mandy would leave just four weeks after the summer holidays had finished. They both vowed to write and tell each other about their new lives. Livia wasn't too sure how her life was going to be different. She was stuck here in Beaconsfield and was to be moving up to the Lady Clara Backsley Grammar School, Chesham in September, where she knew no one. Mandy showed Livia the enormous trunk packed for boarding school with numerous items of clothing - the new school uniform and her ballet clothes and shoes. She had a new wooden pencil case that Livia had bought her. It looked plain, childlike and small alongside all the new pens and pencils, protractors, and other tortuous mathematical equipment Livia had never seen before and hoped never to have to encounter.

On this day, reality struck Olivia. Life seemed cloudy, unclear, misty and unfathomable. Amanda Waverley was growing up and leaving behind her childhood. Livia felt slightly awkward, scruffy and ungainly when they said goodbye. Mandy was smaller than her, but today it seemed as though she had grown to stand upright and confident as a person of responsibility. Having her vast trunk and lists of school regulations and uniforms, curriculums, timetables, new names and new friends she referred to. Livia said a few mumbled words:

'Thanks for the great tea; the scones were delicious. On Saturday, we're off to Aunt Geraldine's holiday home just for a week in Topsham, so I will pop up to see you before you leave.'

Mrs Waverley put her arms protectively around her daughter and smiled thinly, trying hard to disguise her relief. At last, this strange, awkward, gangly girl would be out of Amanda Waverley's life. She had decided then and there that Amanda would be fully occupied for the next few weeks. There would be no time for any more visits. Livia felt distant and chilled. She wasn't sure whether to hug and then just grinned and waved, holding back an unshed tear and a choking gulp in the back of her throat. As she walked up the gravel path from the house, she instinctively pushed her hands roughly into her denim jeans and stabbed her right foot at the loose pebbles. They shot across the perfect lawn, narrowly missing the new concrete water feature. She felt eyes burrowing into her exposed neck as she heard the front door slam behind her.

It just wasn't fair, life. Her whole life was falling apart, and her best friend was leaving her. What would happen to her? Going home to her condescending, mean elder sister, Imogen, 'Impy', who was beautiful, clever with a photographic memory for details, full of confidence, already knew which life course she was taking to enhance her acting career, and only had snide, insulting comments directed at Livia. The other sister, slightly dazed dreamy Tatiana, buried herself in linseed and oil paint, creating new dazzling canvasses each day in the garden studio she had taken over the last two years. Olivia wasn't even sure Tati knew which day it was, let alone that she had a younger sister.

Silently she got into her Dad's Austin Cambridge waiting on the road to take her home. The sun had been heating the dark shabby leather interior, so the familiar smell of warm homeliness encased her. Her dear, kind, unchanging Dad turned to her as she slid onto the worn shiny seats. He smiled at Livia and reached back to her, ruffling her hair slightly. He didn't speak but drove away silently. Livia snuffled in the back seat. Dad slowed the car, pulling over onto hard, compacted ground that the tractors had furrowed. There was just enough room for the vehicle to park before an old wooden five-bar gate. He turned to Livia and handed her one of his famous sizeable white muslin handkerchiefs. She took it without words and blew a large snort into the cotton cloth. With the corners, she wiped her eyes.

Her Dad wound down his driver's window, letting in the summer fragrances of new-mown hay. A single bee buzzed around his outstretched arm. Imperceptibly, Olivia became aware of the resonating sounds of summer. She leaned forward over the front seat and scanned the picture in front of her eyes. To her left, the meadow rose steadily towards Whiteleaf Hill. To the south, hills were densely covered with thick beech woodland. Tall majestic trees faded to misty greys in the far distance. There was a churring jerky call from a couple of whitethroats in the scrubby hedgerow nearby as they came into view to investigate the human presence. The sun shone onto the car's bonnet and bounced off a dazzling reflection. The air almost sparkled as a peacock butterfly's iridescent blue and yellow eyespots flickered past, alternating its colours from vibrant oranges and blues to camouflage browns. All of this reminded Livia dreamily how privileged she was to live in this glorious stretch of unspoilt land. Those few minutes of quiet reflection brought a soft change in Olivia's feelings. Her father's silent but warm companionship and the calming atmosphere of the natural beauty surrounding her changed her mood, and she felt a deep sense of hope and a revitalising spirit. She looked across to her father; he hummed a tune to himself.

'You know Dad, you really are great! Why is it just being here, looking out and taking a few minutes staring at all this? I feel almost better? But there is a very big But....Do you think Mandy will forget me? Will I ever have a best friend again?'

.... Olivia just wanted to know. What did he think?

There was a moment's breathing space before he replied.

'You see all those trees in the distance. When I first came here with your mother, it was an open area, no more than

just lots of small saplings; there were big gaps between them. Seventeen years ago, it was beautiful then. It's changed and grown. A few older trees have been cut down, but new ones are growing all the time, becoming dense and verdant. There's a wide variety of wildlife, they have made homes there, and each year it's a delight to come up here to see how it's developed and enjoy its new splendour. The new growth adds to the old, and benefits come from this natural progression.'
He smiled at Olivia,

'I think you are doing alright today. You've had a good time with your friend.'

He paused.

'Mandy will always be special, and you won't forget her. She will have lots to tell you in her letters, make new friends, and their lives will enrich yours. You too will sprout out, and your young branches will take on leaves and fruits, which will grow and reach out to others. You trust me, I know.'

He paused.

'Come on now, We've got some serious planning to do for the holiday in Topsham. We need to sort out the paint box and easels. I've a new sketch pad for you, and this year it would be good to take some photographs so we can capture all the moments across the estuary and paint when the weather is not too good. So let's get going.'

Olivia knew the moment had passed. Dad always gave her word pictures to help her visualise answers. At eleven years of age it didn't always make sense, trees and leaves, friends and future. It all seemed so foggy, the future unsure. One thing she knew though was she did feel better, hopeful and contented. Yes, the holidays were upon them, and Aunt Geraldine's Topsham house was just the best place ever for boating along the estuary, exploring the Haldon Hills with Ruby and generally dawdling around the streets of old Topsham.

The next few days were spent helping to pack all the luggage for the holidays to Topsham. Dad tinkered with the car, checking the oil and brake fluid. The once-a-year check that the screen washer was filled up was Olivia's chore. The old tin jug from the kitchen store was kept just for this purpose. Livia searched in the pantry; she knew it was right at the back. It had definitely been used this time last year. Dust and old spider webs were disturbed as she rummaged around. The telephone rang shrilly in the hallway. Jars and tins seemed to be stacked against her answering it swiftly. Olivia loved to respond, so with much clattering and banging of utensils, she shot out of the kitchen pantry and grabbed the receiver.

'Good afternoon, Hadleigh household, Olivia speaking,'

'Oh, my dear. It is you, Olivia; you sound so efficient and grown-up. Aunt Geraldine here. How are you, darling girl?'

Before Livia could take a breath to reply, her aunt's voice took command.

'Now I want you to inform your mother I must be in London on Friday. Uncle Juno has a conference, I'm to join him for the weekend, so I will be only at home tomorrow. Be a darling and tell your mother that tomorrow is the only day she can come to collect the keys for 'Gung Ho'. Do, do, come with her, Olivia. If you come around 10.30, we can take the pooches over the back lane together. So did you get all that, darling? I will prepare a light lunch as well. It will be an absolute hoot to see you. You will come too, won't you?'

She reassured her aunt that the message was written down on the hall stand notebook, and she would take the note directly to her mother in the garden. Olivia dearly loved Aunt Geraldine. Excitement and intrigue surrounded her life. With snippets of family conversations and Livia doing her own poking about it, she had pieced together an exciting and mysterious life story of Aunt Geraldine. She was her mother Bridget's sister-in-law by first marriage to Bridget's eldest brother, Archibald Hamilton-Jones. The more senior family members always raised their eyes whenever Archi was mentioned. He had been what everyone called the 'black sheep of the family. What that actually meant, Livia had no idea. She hoped to find out, though.

There was some mystery surrounding the infamous Archi. His sepia photographs showed a tall, fair-haired young man with sharp, piercing eyes over heavily hooded eyelids. He had a slightly Teutonic, proud look with chiselled features and a high forehead, always in flying gear or at the wheel of an MG K3 Magnette sports car. He had met Geraldine in 1931.

The Hon. Geraldine Ingram-Spires had been a young, flamboyant, flame-haired debutante. In 1920, she was presented at Buckingham Palace with all the other young aristocratic belles of the day. Her first season had been a round of extravagant parties, meeting the few remaining eligible gentlemen of the day, so many young men had been lost in the Great War. But Geraldine, unlike many of her contemporaries, did not just want to 'bag a rich husband' and retire to a country estate. She was educated and spoke fluent German, French, Italian and Latin. Her mother 'Lavinia Ingram-Spires', the aspiring intellectual and socialite, encouraged Geraldine to travel and experience as much cultural enlightenment as she could in the four years she was sponsored by her family.

Geraldine travelled first to Italy. She toured the galleries of Florence, Rome and Venice and stayed at homes of former aristocratic families and politicians her mother had been connected with. The Corsini in Florence, the Ruspoli in Rome, and Count Montifiore Grenadino Battista in Frascati. She was exposed to many political ideologies and learned much of her future useful talents in diplomacy. Aunt Geraldine had led a life Olivia only dreamed about. Her travels further took her to Paris in the mid-20s, where she met and made friends with Peggy Guggenheim and was introduced to many avant-garde artists and liberal thinkers of the day.

At this point, Olivia's history of Aunt Geraldine was a bit patchy. The previous information she had joined together throughout 5 or 6 visits to her aunt in Little Missenden was all she had. Therefore Olivia was eager to continue her conversations and discover the next episode in her aunt's colourful life. She longed to hear more about the Count and

Countess in Frascati. In Olivia's fertile mind, she had conjured up the grand exotic world of Italian aristocrats and their mysterious ancient castles. Yes, she was curious to know anything she could about Count Montefiori Grenadino Battista. All she knew was that he had a magnificent collection of Italian renaissance paintings. The name rolled off Olivia's tongue as it whirled around in her head. Livia felt like an investigative journalist. In fact, she had kept a small black notebook of all the information she had gathered. So tomorrow would be a day with well-posed questions and carefully disguised interest in the years just before the second world war. What assignments had Aunt Geraldine been involved in, what was her job, and where had she been trained? How did she meet the scandalous Archi? Where did he disappear to? Had she been a spy?

The following day, Livia hoisted Ruby into the dilapidated Morris Mini Traveller. The double doors at the back were lopsided and just about stayed closed when slammed with great force. Ruby loved to stick her black and white speckled head out of the sliding back windows and gulp at flies as they trundled along and took the short journey to Aunt Geraldine's house. It only took about twenty minutes, the sun was shining, and Livia and mum chatted away companionably about the latest books they were reading. Briddy had always encouraged reading books together with Olivia. Sometimes they read the same book concurrently, so there was much discussion about the storyline and the main characters. They both liked to guess how the plot would develop. Briddy had done the same with her grandmother and her mother too. She knew the lively times she had enjoyed as a young girl and encouraged Livia with the same enthusiasm. Briddy was a wise woman. These times spent together discussing plots and other people's fictional lives gave her an insight into Livia's thinking, and thus, she was able to draw out gently her daughter's personality and encourage and, cautiously, direct her development and growth to a mature, confident young person. Livia had strong opinions, a keen sense of justice, and a sharp mind. This often relayed into her tongue taking over, and words tumbled out of her mouth before her brain had engaged to fully appreciate the impact of what she said. Briddy would tell Olivia the many times she had put her foot in things as a young girl, her embarrassing situations and the grand faux pas she had made. All of this contributed to Livia growing in confidence and being well-prepared for the next few years of growth, both physically and emotionally. Along with the ups and downs of sometimes just plain cranky thinking.

As they approached the house along the driveway. Aunt Geraldine's two cocker spaniels, Blue and Digger, raced out of the open front door. Livia slid back her window and waved, shouting.

'Coooeee, boys, we're here.'

At this point, Ruby yelped and nearly leapt out of the side window. Briddy slowed the car down and parked a few yards to the left of the main entrance. Misbourne House was a Georgian box, in the sense of being a cube, beautifully proportioned, with mellowed red brick facade and two deep bays on either side of the double doors leading to the entrance hallway. Aunt Geraldine had told them it was built in 1729 for a wealthy merchant who made money with the East India Company, trading spices and silks. Since Aunt Geraldine had lived there for six years, she had filled the house with her own collections from her travels. The rooms were lined with bookcases containing many rare and valuable antique editions. Throughout the hallway were paintings crammed onto every wall space. It was like walking through different eras in time. Individual pieces of 18th-century antique furniture were placed beside sofas and armchairs by Marcel Breuer, Le Corbusier and Eileen Grey, which wouldn't have looked amiss in an art deco house of the 1930s. The whole place was a feast for the design senses. The contrast of high ceilings, deep-set sash windows, and the views out to the pond area and kitchen walled garden gave its occupants and visitors a sensation of being well looked after. Always too, Aunt Geraldine set a rich casserole simmering in the Aga for lunch, its exotic aroma wafting through the house. Very welcoming as they entered through the front door into the hallway.

'Come here, my dearest Olivia. Ahh, Yes, you have shot up again. As I thought, you will be tall and slim, and....'

She gently held Livia's jawline in her right hand and, as if surveying a delicate piece of porcelain, said

'Yes, you have your mother's good bone structure. You will develop into a handsome young lady.'
She turned away and picked up her notebook.

'First on the agenda, coffee in the library, my daily, Mrs Smallshaw has kindly started the brew, and I will just go and tell her we are ready for it now. You both go through, be with you in a jiffy.'

Aunt Geraldine seemed to glide off towards the kitchen. As she strode along, the softest fabric folds drifted, trailing behind her. This, probably, was because she wore a long cashmere wrap over her silk trousers. The two garments seemed to drape together and just float around her statuesque body.

The coffee was delicious, not the usual powder-in-hot water type they had at home. This smelt like the aroma in the big department stores they visited once a year in London, a mixture of expensive perfume and rich dark coffee grains, freshly ground, decanted from a stainless steel pot, then a generous serving of fresh cream. Aunt Geraldine was the best hostess, having picked up crumbly ginger biscuits from town, and no one ever complained about dunking biscuits in this house.

Whilst Aunt Geraldine and Briddy talked together about their gardens and family news. Livia mooched around amongst the bookcases looking at various authors she hadn't seen before. Next to the bureau were diverse art books displaying collections of new photographic galleries and their exhibitions. Alongside this was a maroon leather portfolio tied with black cotton laces. Livia tugged at one of the laces, and it parted the folds. She lifted the front cover. A few sketches of hands and feet drawn from different angles emerged; some completed, others just the outline. Carefully moving the thick papers, she scanned through the sheets and saw other subjects, in pencil and charcoal, animals, women's faces, hands, ears, and elaborate hair arrangements dated June 1927, Paris. There were other sketches of buildings, arches, doorways and castellated walls. These were different from the life drawings, much more defined, unusual perspectives. Some looked like the building was exploding outwards or shooting off at an angle to infinity. She couldn't decipher the handwriting but noted PennAmerica 35; Livia was fascinated. She sat quietly, just following the lines. Her aunt gently laid a hand on her shoulder and softly said:

'What do you see, Livia?'

'I see an explosion of such energy, amazing shapes and rooms. It's fascinating. almost like we're in outer space. How would this house be suspended on nothing?'

'These were drawn by a man of immense vision. He was a friend of mine, a great innovator and a world-renowned architect. He gave me these drawings many years ago. I have been reviewing them and cataloguing them. I have collected so much stuff over the years. It's now time I took stock of what I have. I have also mislaid a few items; important I locate them.'
Her aunt, for a few seconds, looked anxious and distracted.

'Now let me see, Ah yes, Would you like to help me, to make an inventory....?'

Olivia was immediate in her answer.

'Well, yes, but when?'

'I've just mentioned to your mother that maybe when you return from 'Gung Ho', you could stay over here four days and assist me. Let's see, it could be a week on Monday. You will be home on Saturday, and I could pop over and pick you up Monday early. Let's say precisely 10.30 a.m. would allow us to start just before lunch. What do you say?'

'Oh, Yes, please, it would be so interesting. There is one slight snag. Would it be possible to bring Ruby? She's very well behaved. Well, most of the time, probably better than me?'
Aunt Geraldine smiled.

'Yes, she's always good company for Blue and Digger. They can root around the orchard together, no problem.'

Olivia was over the moon. A whole four days with her aunt, she would have ample opportunity to explore this vast house and what a great time for filling in all the missing history pieces of her aunt's mysterious past and the first husband, Archi. Olivia's sense of mystery and inquisitiveness had been piqued too by the sudden anxious look on her aunt's face when mentioning something missing that needed finding. She might also get to see the ever-elusive Uncle Juno Spitzer, the owner of Holstein Spitzer pharmaceuticals. The writing in her notebook would have to wait until her stay after the holiday.

The next couple of days seemed to drag by for Livia. She tried so hard to pack a small suitcase with all the things she might need for every type of weather expected in Devon. To Livia, though, a couple of corduroy trousers, a good thick woolly jumper and a swimsuit along with one summer dress seemed to be all the essentials she would need for clothing. For her, the principal requirements were her tools. Sketch pads, biros, pencils, charcoals, notebooks and the new Kodak Instamatic her Dad had given her as a holiday present. Plus, tennis rackets and welly boots for traipsing around the damp woods near Gung Ho. This was quite a task to squash inside a battered reinforced cardboard case with dodgy hinges. A hefty bounce on the suitcase, and everything apart from the racket was secured inside. Mum always took all the extra underwear and toiletries, so Olivia was all set, ready to leave early on Saturday morning. It was the customary holiday ritual for Dad to oversee the car's packing as each family member brought various bags, cases and an unending stream of extras. As usual, Dad couldn't believe how much stuff four females needed to take for a short trip of one week. The constant huffing and puffing never dissuaded them from insisting he cram it all in.

The drive towards Devon took most of Saturday. It was a family tradition unless, for absolute emergencies, they kept driving and only stopped every two hours. So, weary and crotchety, they arrived at Topsham in the early evening.

All of Aunt Geraldine's possessions were impeccable, and so too, Gung Ho. She had told Livia the name came from a Chinese word meaning 'enthusiastic' and 'work together harmoniously'. It certainly lived up to its name. Built around 1750, the house fitted into The Strand perfectly. The white stucco facade dazzled in the late evening sun. Its deep sash windows intimated an invitation to sunny and exciting times to be had inside. Aunt Geraldine always provided a vast wicker hamper of food for their arrival. She called it the 'Good Ration Supplies', and Mr and Mrs Babbage from the post office checked the place was aired and cleaned through.

To Livia, the most beautiful parts of the house were views of the River Exe and its small moorings where a light boat, the 'Topper', was kept. The first couple of days, it rained continuously. There was a constant pong of wet dogs in the house as Livia still took Ruby on waterlogged walks along the estuary and through the muddy reeds. She loved to watch the wildfowl and the curlews pecking and turning over the dirty sand. The damp, misty rain never bothered Olivia. It gave an atmosphere that fed her fertile imagination as she conjured up stories in her head.

Tati stayed in her room and painted. She came down for meals but seemed to have a wild and distant look in her eyes and, when spoken to, hardly raised her head, absentmindedly talking of 'light and dark'.

'Have to get it down on my canvas. Must get back; the paint will deteriorate.'

She would quickly grab some bread and cheese, with mum passing her a tray of juice and fruit to take away to her room and her masterpiece. Impy seemed happy to laze in bed until mid-morning, then lounge around and read all the glossy magazines she had brought along with her. Richard and Briddy luxuriated in the quiet time they could have in one of the large sitting rooms facing the Exe. They shared a passion for companiable reading together, and holidays at Gung Ho offered them this. Richard wallowed in the ancient histories of the Roman era.

Poets' and scholars' tragedies and plays were a source of constant joy. He lived through their battles and laughed out loud at the comedies. Briddy read and re-read her favourite classical writers, Joyce, Hemingway, Tolstoy and on a lighter note, Austen and Elliot. She loved the tones of old England that Thomas Hardy helped her travel through. The excitement of Victorian intrigue in Wilkie Collins's literature. Thus the first few wet days were spent with everyone indulging in their favourite pastimes. On Wednesday, everything changed. The sun rose and shone across the estuary. Livia was awake at 6:00am and saw the startling red streak across the horizon as the sky changed to soft peach and burst into a brilliant light of sunshine against the bluest of blue skies. As she looked out of the window, the contrast of the rolling grey clouds of the last three days was breathtaking. She leaned out of the wooden window and just breathed deeply.

The next few days of the holidays were spent walking by the Exe, sitting in the sun, doing family picnics, and eating all the goodies Aunt Geraldine had provided. During those remaining times together, Tati left her paintings and seemed more like her old, younger self. She laughed a little and joined in with family games. The sun brought colour to her pale face, and she remembered to eat and enjoy just being a young girl of sixteen. Impy draped herself over the shingle and posed in the sunshine with copious amounts of Nivea suncream smoothed into her perfect body.

Dad took them into Exeter on Friday afternoon and walked down by the Quay. The previous year, a lot of work had been done to turn the derelict warehouses into a newly opened nightclub. Impy was instantly attracted to this and asked if they could stay until late to see this place when it opened. She wheedled and whined, stamping her feet in anger at not being allowed to go alone and wait for the evening in the city, slamming her bedroom door when they arrived back at 'Gung Ho', shouting out loud:
'You people have ruined my life. I never do anything exciting.' Briddy and Richard looked knowingly at each other and

distracted the girls with a trip on the River, so by the time it was getting late, they suggested a quiet meal in one of the restaurants they had passed on the way back to Topsham. Imogen sulked all evening.

So the holiday came to its conclusion. 'Gung Ho' had appeared to have succeeded in bringing them a semblance of harmony and rest as a family. Only Imogen refused to cooperate, grumbling and protesting at the unfairness of her life with them all. She insisted they would 'all see' when she made her own way in the future.

Livia's enthusiasm for staying with Aunt Geraldine the following week was significantly increased by her thoughts on the subjects they would discuss and the art to collate. The long journey didn't feel fatiguing; she felt no car sickness, even when she read her novel. Only a fluttering sensation in her stomach growing with a sense of excitement for the coming week at Misbourne House.

The boy lay on his back in the deserted gardens of Blackstone Manor. A smile crossed his handsome face, his eyes glistened, and his thoughts assimilated as the black cord systematically, methodically tightened around his wrist.

CHAPTER 2

'...To Strive to Seek to Find and not to Yield.'
Ulysses. Alfred, Lord Tennyson

England, Little Missendon 1968

With only a few days to go before Livia was due to stay with Aunt Geraldine, the unpacking and sorting out a bag to take to Misbourne House with relatively clean clothing was no mean feat. Briddy worked hard to help settle everyone back into their lives at The Lodge, Blackstone Manor.

Tati removed herself and her paints to the studio shed in the garden. It hardly seemed she had ever been away. Briddy would go to the studio each evening, and Tati would be covered in paints and oils, sometimes indiscriminately spraying the paint everywhere or sitting squat on the wooden floor gazing intently at a plain canvas. Briddy would remark on her work and try desperately to engage Tati's interests in things they had been doing during the day, the weather, the pet dog, and tonight's meal. Tati remained distant, and on the second day after their return from holiday, Briddy had to physically raise her from the floor and lead her home for their meal. Briddy took her food, and when the wind howled, and the rain pounded the fencing and clattered the garden pots around, she took a woollen shawl and, without Tati even noticing, wrapped it around her bony shoulders.

That night they seemed to enjoy time together. Dad related funny stories he had heard from his brother John, the local GP, who always had a tale to tell when he had been on his rounds. Even Tati came out of her reverie to join in with the laughs and ravenously ate the chicken and mushroom pie mum served. Impy, too, seemed to join in the family banter. She was hilarious as she imitated the amusing character Uncle John had encountered that morning. Briddy felt a sigh of relief. Her daughters tonight appeared to be relaxed. Livia roared with laughter at Impy's impersonation of the frantic husband, his wife in labour, chasing the doctor up the street in his pyjamas. He had two angry toddlers wailing in his arms. As he ran, he tripped over the hens (they had escaped from the coop) and dropped one of the children in a muddy puddle. All this happened as the next-door neighbour's Jack Russell terrier tore at his pyjama seat and removed a fleshy chunk from his rear end. The poor doctor needed to figure out who to treat first.

Before sleeping, Briddy spoke to Richard of concerns over Tati spending so much time alone with her paints and seeming to be in a world of her own. She didn't feel it was healthy for a young girl of just sixteen not to have friends or be more connected with others. Richard was drifting off to sleep as Briddy spoke but mumbled he would have a chat with her tomorrow after Geraldine had been to pick up Olivia.

Aunt Geraldine was one of those people you could absolutely rely upon. She had said her arrival would be at 10.30 am, and her sleek MG 1100 drove up the drive right on time. Olivia was waiting outside on the front porch sitting on her battered suitcase with Ruby lying at her feet. After saying goodbye to the family and placing her bag and Ruby in the tiny rear seat, they were away.

The short drive to Missenden seemed to whiz by for Livia as they chatted about the holiday at Gung Ho and Aunt Geraldine outlined the sequence of the cataloguing they would be engaged in over the next few days.

Firstly they had to list all the paintings displayed on the walls. Secondly, they would look at sketches already placed in portfolios and label any not having clear identification. A leather-bound folder had been bought for this purpose and together they could enter all the dates, names and details. They would also try to do an inventory of the furniture. This was something Livia really looked forward to. She had never been into every room in the house and knew this was a rare opportunity for having a good old poke around. The task seemed enormous to Livia, but knowing how orderly and efficient her aunt was, made it all the more likely they would be able to accomplish everything. As her aunt would say, "all tickety boo".

They began their cataloguing. Livia noted points down as they walked around the house. Aunt Geraldine relayed the history of her time in Paris in the 1920s when she had become friends with Leonce Rosenberg, an art historian and collector. Having helped Geraldine appreciate Cubist and Abstract Art, she bought a small collection of now-famous artists' works. Names such as Andre Derain, Jean Metzinger, Henri Leger. Aunt Geraldine spoke with a great understanding of this genre of artwork. In two small oil paintings, figures outlined in black and brightly coloured in blue and orange, two small birds were entwined together in the bottom right-hand corner. Olivia picked them up. Her eyes fell upon the black signature. Picasso.
'Wow, Aunt. Are these by Picasso?'
Geraldine's face clouded over. After a deep breath, her eyes scanned over the paintings. Her words came out very deliberately.
'Yes, Olivia, these two are originals.'
She explained they were part of a collection of four small works. The two she had were the only ones known to still be in circulation. Geraldine covered them over and quickly turned her attention towards larger paintings, architectural in form. These were by Charles-Edouard Jeanneret; Livia asked who he was.

'Ah yes, he became a good friend of mine, his famous name is Le Corbusier, he was an architect living in Paris who became closely connected with Amedee Ozenfant they collaborated together to produce some paintings, beautiful works of art.' See here these are two works by Amedee. I have placed the works of a similar genre together. Can you see their relationships, Olivia?'

'Yes, they are all blocky and exaggerated; some features don't look real. Their eyes and noses seem to be sometimes in the wrong places.'

Her aunt smiled and encouraged her to look at the small pieces of sculpture on marble plinths.

'See here too. This is in the modernist style by Constantin Brancusi. I met him whilst he was with Peggy Guggenheim in Montmartre. We frequented the cafes and what times we had together. Always lively. Heated conversations on art, politics, music, and philosophy. People came and went, and Peggy was a great source of encouragement to the down and out. Today I wish I had paid closer attention to their work and collected more pieces. However, I have happy memories of those bohemian days in Paris before the second world war and its horrors.'

Aunt Geraldine moved along the corridor of the hallway. She passed her right hand over the frames of these pictures, caressing over memories and friends. She then turned decisively to face Livia.

'Come, let's move on to the Italian pieces. These were collected whilst I was in Rome. What year would that be? Maybe in 1926, this first one is a still life by Georgio Morandi, and here these etchings are by Giovanni Fattori, and this small oil is by Silvestro Lega.

Now we must start another page for the sketches in the portfolios. Come, let's go into the library. You go through and find the maroon folder. It's on the desk. I will go and sort out some refreshments we could do with them. We've been on the go for two hours.'

As Geraldine moved out of the room, a high-pitched shrill bell rang in the hallway. Livia noticed her aunt pick up the receiver and immediately speak in Italian.

'Pronto'

Livia would have loved to dawdle and listen to the conversation. The lilting sing-song tones of her aunt's Italian. She decided to learn this beautiful language, one of the to-dos in her little black book. Her keen hearing caught the conversation as it occasionally changed to English. She heard smatterings of … 'Interpol….Ah, two, only two…. detective Horley….Lucien Van der Berg….Montefiore… … This woman, she must have moved around freely. We need to know who she was.' The conversation was lost in rapid Italian words.

Livia padded through the library, where she had previously found the sketch folder. It was still in the same place on the vast, gleaming wooden desk, along with numerous books and writing equipment. A large antique bronze lamp lit the reading area. The walls were covered in golden yew wooden bookcases. Some shelves were behind glass cabinets, while others were open and reached high towards the ornate plastered cornices. A carved wooden library ladder with rolling castors and polished balustrades was a beautiful feature of this room dedicated to the leisure and pleasure of reading. On the deep rich oak floors were Aubusson rugs, incorporating delicate floral imagery with heavy architectural borders. No doubt it originated from the same time the house was built.

The coloured spines of the books and their variety was alluring, heavily suggesting antiquity. Olivia quickly realised she would be easily distracted if she started to explore the shelves. Just one of the few authors she already knew stood out, Dorothy Sayers. There were four with their original dust covers in pale yellow. Livia couldn't resist the urge to have a peek inside. 'Gaudy Night', 1935, Dorothy L Sayers, first edition. It was in perfect condition; she turned the pages and was immediately drawn to the first chapter. She didn't notice her aunt's entrance with the tray of tea things and only looked up to the chink of china cups.

'Oh Aunt, how lovely this book is. It's one I haven't read. May I borrow it to read later before bed?'

'You may, Olivia, please don't spill any tea; it's rather precious. A good friend of mine gave it to me. Take it to your bedroom now. It will be safe there. Then we can have our tea and get on with the folio listings.'

When Livia returned, the tea things were ready, and Aunt

Geraldine had already opened the folder with two neat piles, compiled and prepared to catalogue. There was no mention of the telephone call, and Livia dared not to ask at this time about it. Livia drank her tea and started on the first group. Her aunt went through names and dates as they compiled the inventory. It seemed to Livia that many of the sketches were her own aunt's work during the 1930s. There were numerous letters, some in Italian and French, these were bundled together, and Aunt Geraldine skimmed over their classification, dismissing them as 'pre-wartime, jumble'. She did, however, hover over a couple of small faded photographs and sketches. One was a woman and child, and the other possibly an angel; a few notes scribbled in Italian. After examining these more closely, Geraldine put them in a small leather case separating the sketches from the letters into the various compartments of the folder. Her aunt spent a lot of time inspecting the more extensive drawings Livia had seen before and handling them with great care.

'Olivia, these are the sketches you remarked on previously as 'exploding buildings'. They are perspectives and conceptual works of architectural drawings for a famous building that architect Frank Lloyd Wright designed in America. I was in Pennsylvania on behalf of my work for the government. In 1934 I met Frank and he gave me some conceptual drawings, which I treasure. They say so much of the mind of that great man, his expertise. Imagine having the vision to create this from your thoughts and having the insight and skill to complete it. True genius.'

Olivia wondered if this was the time to ask a few discreet questions about 'Uncle Archie'.

'So in 1934, you were in America. Were you there on your own? It must have been an exciting time for you.'

'Yes, I was sent along with a delegation of other English people until late 1935. There was growing tension in Europe over Hitler's re-arming of Germany. President Roosevelt was concerned that America would remain neutral. The British government wanted the support of America. It was a delicate time.'

Livia waited a few seconds and proceeded cautiously.

'Were you married then to Uncle Archi?'

'No, No, we were good friends. He was a dashing young RAF pilot, and we were involved in similar work. I saw him on and off during those couple of years and felt madly in love with him. Swept along in the moment of romance and the exciting work we were doing. We sometimes had to pretend we were someone of another nationality. I had to take on the persona of different professions. One day I was a journalist for a few weeks, and then I would have to be a nurse or a secretary for a government official. Being constantly watched, observed I took meticulous notes of everything I heard and saw. Timekeeping was of the utmost importance. Our life or one of our colleagues depended on the strictest adherence to being at a specific place at a precise time.

Archi and I were married in late 1935 when I returned from America. We had a fantastic holiday. Whenever he was home on leave, he would whisk me off to some hideaway in the Cotswolds or Devon. I became fond of south Devon, and my parents left me the house in Topsham near Exeter. Archi and I lived on the Thames at Datchet in a riverboat. Sounds romantic. Frankly, it was cold and terribly damp but close for us both to be near his RAF station and my work in London. The war years came along, and I was sent on missions to France.'

Here Geraldine paused. She ran her hands through her hair and passed her fingers over her furrowed brow. As she shifted her weight, Olivia noticed an almost imperceptible wince from her aunt.

'I was badly injured in France. I don't remember much of what happened. I think I was unconscious for a long time. Hidden by the resistance in an Abbey, then secretly brought back, recuperated. Things had changed so much. A lot happened painful things. I bear the scars.'

The air was heavy with tense emotion. Olivia sensed that there was so much more to tell in that short summary. Not for this moment, though. To be noted in her black book that evening. Geraldine continued:

'Archi went away and was stationed for a long time in Egypt. We were apart a great deal during those years. Busy with our own lives, just short snatched letters. The war changed us all; he met his second wife, Joan. She was a relative of his RAF friends from Rhodesia stationed out there.

Those years were strange. People lived unnatural lives. It was easy to deceive and be deceived. The camaraderie of working closely together in life and death situations, long separations from family, and real mundane life caused us to behave in ways that brought consequences, so often the outcome was sad. War is a terrible thing.

Livia, don't ever think it was glamorous. We were numbed by death and loss. Working in a vacuum devoid of feelings, accomplishing our latest assignment. We didn't have time to grieve. I was part of a secret organisation set up to infiltrate enemy lines and disrupt the Axis powers' strongholds as much as possible.

Now that's enough about that. My ex-husband Archi was another matter. I have never seen him after Egypt. There were unpleasant exchanges between us. My parent's lawyers dealt with the divorce. He never returned to England after the war. As far as I know, he was given employment with family farming concerns of Ian Smith in Rhodesia, he married that woman Joan and I believe has been involved in various businesses and politics for that regime, ever since.'

Her voice became strained, and Livia could see deep pain had cast a shadow over her once brilliant green eyes. There was silence in the room for just a few seconds. Gathering her composure with a deep breath she slightly raised her elegant chin. Her words came out sharp and brittle.

'Last year, Rhodesia claimed independence from Britain. I fear no good will come of this. What will ensue can only be a time of great tension and possibly a bloodbath. There is no good news for the white man who has lived off the rich pickings of that beautiful country and taken its resources for their own gain. '

She turned towards her niece and, looking her straight in the eyes, said softly:

'In life, Olivia, there are always consequences for our actions. It's a scientific fact, 'cause and effect' in the natural world and our personal lives. What we do and say affects not just ourselves but others too. Take to heart this fact. You will be guarded against some of the sad pains that come to many. Teach yourself to analyse your situation and make lists of pros and cons. This phrase is taken from the Latin, 'for and against.' I've made it a rule to do this with most decisions, along with trying to foresee possible outcomes. There will always be unforeseen occurrences. Refrain from letting the fog of a busy life cloud your crucial choices. Seek to wipe away unnecessary obfuscations before actions.'

Olivia looked wide-eyed and bewildered.

Geraldine laughed out loud.

'Oh, my dear. If you look the words up in the dictionary, all will become clearer.

Become like a sleek well-equipped sailing boat. Able to weather the storms of life, you will be mentally and emotionally prepared for the many challenges you will face with fortitude and resilience.

You are growing up quickly, Olivia, don't be surprised at being unsure or confused. When you become more aware of yourself that you have many changing moods. They will seem to overpower you. Sometimes you will be ecstatic with happiness, and then the next second you will feel in the depths of despair. It's all part of growing up. Do recognise, though, that you,and only you, have control of your emotions, keep them in check, don't always let out what you're feeling straight away, and enjoy your youth, but never become overly self-absorbed. Look around you outside yourself. The more you add to others' lives, the more you will be content. Analyse consequences and come to conclusions.'

A light breeze breathed air through the open sash window and the early evening song of the birds echoed through the room. Aunt Geraldine looked down at the desk and folded her hands lightly together.

Olivia went over to her aunt, placing a hand on hers.

'Thank you, dear Aunt, for letting me be here with you.'

Aunt Geraldine smiled.

'One thing, I do know, my dear, yes, each day is to be enjoyed and faced with courage. Today is a good day. We have accomplished much. Tomorrow we will list the furniture and some of my jewellery. But now I think you and I need a good gallop across the fields with the dogs. Uncle Juno is not home this week, away in Dusseldorf, so I think we will splash out and have a good old nosh up at the little Chinese in the next town. How about that?'

'Oooh, sounds fab.'

Olivia stood up and dashed off to the kitchen, where the three dogs were snoozing on the cool flagstone floor. Immediately they all stirred up in a medley of sniffs and much wagging of tails. The dust rose from their flapping bodies and with a few yelps, they followed Livia and her aunt out of the back door chasing each other over the kitchen garden path and out through the iron garden gate. The atmosphere was still warm, and gnats rose in front of them. The dogs snapped and gulped the air. This was just what they all needed, the dogs raced ahead, and Olivia ran with them, throwing sticks and letting her long limbs go with loud whoops.

That evening Livia felt like a grown-up. Here with Aunt Geraldine in the 'Fen Ying' Chinese restaurant. The walls were covered in a deep red flock wallpaper and slim silk paintings of Chinese men and women serving tea. Some depicted mountains rising from misty landscapes and brightly coloured plump birds resting on branches of blossom trees. This was all new to Livia. She was transported into another time and place. The music playing was soft and lilting, and there was a faint sound of a waterfall in the background. Aunt Geraldine asked what she would like to eat.

'Well, I've only had 'boil in the bag' Chinese food before, so I don't know what to say. I like chicken, vegetables and rice. Oh yes, and those crunchy, crispy, savoury crisps. Mum says I can eat anything. and I will certainly try it. Whatever you have, I will too, please.'

Aunt Geraldine called over the waiter, who appeared to know her well. Mr Chung Manchu bowed to her and asked how Mr Spitzer was. They exchanged pleasantries, and he recommended the crispy duck and various side dishes of vegetables, dumplings and rice.

The food came along piping hot, and Mr Manchu, with a flourish, lifted the bamboo lids from the dishes. To Livia, the aroma was fragrant and inviting. They both had forgotten how long ago it was since they had last eaten, and engaging in all the cataloguing work along with the refreshing walk with the dogs had worked up a keen appetite. Mr Manchu discreetly returned after some time and enquired if everything was satisfactory, he was also interested to know who this young lady was with Mrs Spitzer. Aunt Geraldine introduced Olivia and told him she was helping her sort all her books and things. Livia was a great help. He looked at Olivia and said.

'There is a Chinese proverb that says, 'If you want happiness for an hour - take a nap. If you want happiness for a day - go fishing. If you want happiness for a month - get married. If you want happiness for a year - inherit a fortune. If you want happiness for a lifetime - help someone else.'
You will be a happy lady.'

He bowed slightly and left them. Aunt Geraldine explained to Livia that Mr Manchu had come from Hong Kong, where he had been a teacher, still had an extensive library, always liked to discuss literature and had become good friends with her and Juno over the last five years. He was a kind man who took good care of his wife and two daughters. They now all worked hard in

the family business. At the end of the meal, Mr Manchu brought his two girls along to give sweets out and to be introduced to Olivia. Olivia smiled shyly at Mo Choo and Ying Yue.
Aunt Geraldine thought the girls' names were delightful. And remarked.

'Lovely names, girls, what is their meaning? I know you put great store by choosing names full of significance?'

Mr Manchu smiled.

'Yes, Mrs Spitzer, Mo Choo means 'free of sadness' so named after the death of our first child. Ying Yue was born in the nighttime when it was a full moon. Her name means 'reflection of the moon.'

Both of the girls smiled and looked slightly embarrassed. Mr Manchu carried on further with his conversation with Aunt Geraldine. Olivia shyly asked them.

'My name is Olivia. I think it means Olive tree, which is less meaningful than your name. Which school do you go to?'

'We are at Lady Clara Grammar in Chesham, we've been there for two years, and our English names are Harmony and Suzie. We're called by these names at school. We much prefer it.'
Olivia immediately told them she, too, was going to Chesham in September. They promised they would look out for her and then told her all the many activities they were interested in. Harmony, the eldest, was keen on History and Art, whilst Suzi preferred running, hockey and swimming. They were enthused about the indoor and outdoor facilities at Chesham.

Their father shook Mrs Spitzers' hand and beckoned Olivia to say goodbye. Aunt Geraldine was pleased to see the girls all getting along and the coincidence they would all be together at school the following September. Livia told her aunt about the loss of her friend Mandy, who was off to Ballet School, and she had been fretting she wouldn't be able to make any new friends. Tonight she felt reassured. At the end of a busy long day, Olivia felt heartened and encouraged. So far, she had learned more of her aunt's history, she had been enlightened into the world of fine art, and to top it all, there were great possibilities ahead for the autumn term at Lady Clara Backsley Grammar School Chesham. Somewhere also was tingling in her mind, the beginning of a new mystery involving an Italian telephone conversation.

The following day Olivia awoke to the piercing sound of a shrill telephone ringing out in the hallway. Her aunt was quick to answer. Again a conversation in fast-paced Italian ensued. Livia was sure she recognised Montefiore and Van der Berg's names. She took out her notebook and wrote down any parts of the conversation she could remember. Fortunately for her, Geraldine's voice was shrill and carried up the sweeping staircase through her now slightly open bedroom door. When the conversation ended, she continued piecing together all she knew about the letters and sketches her aunt had placed in the folder. Two small cloudy photographic copies of paintings, 8 inches by 12 inches, one of a woman and child, the other an angel, and notes along with the names of people, could they all be connected? Livia silently closed her notebook. She would wait and see when an opportunity arose to ask questions or even have a peek inside the leather folder.

For the next couple of days, Livia was surrounded by the world of antique and modern furniture. The house contained exquisite chairs and side tables dating to around 1750. Two such chairs her aunt showed her were purported to be made by Chippendale. They examined the bases, and Aunt Geraldine showed Olivia the cabinet maker's marks neatly etched into the underside along with holes where the furniture had been supported whilst on its carriage from the London workshop in St Martins Lane. She said this was as good as a signature for verifying the authenticity because Chippendale never signed his work. There was also a copy for Livia to look at 'The Gentleman and Cabinet Makers Directory'. Published originally by Chippendale in 1754 of his designs and details of the furniture he made. Livia devoured this book; it fascinated her. To see similar real-life pieces in her aunt's house was a sheer delight.

The books and furniture were like an overwhelming heady experience for Livia. Her interest in history had always been there, but now to see history come alive in the form of actual physical examples was genuinely thrilling. There were some small pieces of ancient Roman artefacts in a glass cabinet. These were labelled in the casement. Looking at them together, Livia just asked one question after another. Their age, where they were from, and how they came to be collected into Aunt Geraldine's care? Livia was enthralled by the jewellery that had come from Pompei and Herculaneum. She had so many questions about the people. Who might have worn the ornaments? Who was Augustus, Julius Caesar, Tiberius, or Nero? Where did they all fit into the timelines of history? Her aunt watched Livia's response to all she was learning. The delight on Livia's face made Geraldine smile. She was seeing all her treasures in a fresh new light.

She took out of the case a gold ring and bangle. In Latin, 'Claudia Acte' and 'Nero' flowed around the bangle. Small round indentations were chased between the words. The ring also was gold and heavily embossed with vine leaves and what appeared to be 'bees' circling around the words 'Columel...Villa Avernus... Villa Alba' Geraldine wrapped the jewellery in soft tissue and placed them in Livia's hand.

'Here, take these. Let them be the start of your historical collection. Do some research into the pieces. Find out what the words mean, and try and date them. You will have such fun exploring the past.'

Livia's eyes widened, and her smile broadened as she gave an enthusiastic kiss on Geraldine's soft cheek. She had ancient pieces of her own and would guard them forever. That night she took out her notebook and drew as clearly as possible the bangle and ring along with the inscription and a big question mark with the words. Who, When, Where?

Livia went to bed dreaming of emperors, palaces, statues and golden ornaments.

Geraldine let the dogs out into the kitchen garden. The scent of mint and rosemary rose as the dogs brushed past the plants. The night was warm and still. The scuffling sound of the dogs rooting amongst the shrubs broke the silence. She sighed contentedly to herself. A slight twinge in her stomach reminded her of past pains. She dismissed this quickly. Today had been a good day. Then suddenly, catching her unawares as if out of nowhere, an old, forgotten, restless agitation buzzed inside her bones. Was it excitement? Where was this energy coming from? Thoughts of adventure, travel and discovery swirled around her brain, a need to make plans. The seed of an idea formed, setting in motion events that would profoundly affect Olivia's whole life. She paced up and down, carefully planning and plotting a journey combining enjoyment and investigation. The trip of a lifetime. There and then, her itinerary was formulated. On that Wednesday evening, as Livia slept. Geraldine telephoned her sister-in-law, Bridget.

Bridget had just sat down to read 'Woman's Weekly' when the telephone rang. She waited a few moments, but no one else seemed to respond. No one seemed bothered to answer, so Briddy took the call. The light was on in Richard's study, along with the gramophone playing his favourite Chopin waltzes as he made preparations for the new school term in two and a half weeks. Tati, unusually was asleep in her bedroom, and Impy was soaking herself in the bathroom listening to a crackly transistor radio and the Beatles playing out loud and clear 'Hey Jude'.

'Good evening, Hadleigh household, Bridget speaking.'

'Hello darling, Briddy, it's me, Geraldine. How are you all?'

'Very well, thank you, is everything ok with you and Livia?'

'Yes, Yes, Better than Ok. We're having a splendid time. Your Olivia has such thirst and enthusiasm for the Arts and History that I'm almost exhausted. She asks such thoughtful questions and just soaks up everything. She has a fascination with Ancient Roman history. I've shown her one or two items I have collected over the years. We are getting along famously with the cataloguing and having a wonderful time together.

Now I want to put something before you. I have yet to mention this to Olivia. I want to take Olivia to Italy for a short break next week. Specifically Rome and Pompei.

As her aunt, it will be my treat entirely. You and Richard will not have to consider any of the expenses.

Now before you answer, I have thought this through. Livia could stay here until Saturday. We will drive up to town and get all the necessaries needed for this spontaneous trip and stay over in London for a couple of days, then take a flight to Rome from London Airport, I mean Heathrow (all these new names for places). We could return the following Saturday, and she would be home on Sunday, giving her a whole week to prepare for her new school. Of course, you could pop Olivia's passport in the post.

The experience would be mutually beneficial. It would give me the greatest pleasure, and seeing all the charms of Rome and Pompei through her eyes would be such a joy. This could also help Livia to make decisions regarding her future courses.'

Bridget was flabbergasted. Her mind was racing; what a fantastic opportunity for Olivia. Geraldine seemed to have thought of everything. She would be thoroughly competent to take her daughter. In fact, she felt a sense of relief immediately. The trip would be with Aunt Geraldine and not a supervised school trip. What would Richard say? She smiled to herself; no problems there. He was all for his girls experiencing anything to do with history and culture. They could never have afforded such an expedition. Yes, she would be totally in agreement with the vacation. She replied:

'Well, Geraldine, you are one for springing things upon us. You know it sounds amazing. What a wonderful opportunity for Livia. Italy has been her dream of all the places she has wanted to go. It sounds like she has a newfound interest in ancient history too. Richard, I am sure, will be all for it. He would jump at the chance himself if he had half a moment. It's been a long time since his student days of poking around ancient monuments. Give me this evening to broach the subject with him gently. I will call you in the morning, and if everything is ok here, you can talk to Olivia. She is going to be so excited. And Geraldine, just, well, thank you for being every girl's perfect aunt. Speak to you tomorrow morning. Lots of Love. Good night'

After leaving the phone, Briddy took a few moments for herself. What a surprise for Olivia, this unexpected travel. She laughed, seeing the enormous excitement her youngest daughter would have tomorrow. With a broad grin on her face, she went straight to Richard. He was delighted and didn't take a second to agree to the expedition to Rome. The next day during their evening meal, they told Impy and Tati that Livia would be away for a little longer with Aunt Geraldine. Tati took no notice and drifted off to her paintings. Impy was more curious and wheedled out of Briddy all the details. The outward show of envious interest from her was the fact Livia would be in London for a few days before her excursion, probably buying up all sorts of beautiful things to take with her and staying at some swanky hotel, which she would have appreciated much more and had much more benefit.

The most annoying thing for Imogen was that she could not vent her jealous wrath on her little sister and so just resorted to stomping around the house and annoying everyone else with her histrionic dramas and shrieks of blind rage.

Only the boy outside, sitting on the old stone wall, stared as he witnessed the alluring girl shouting and moving from room to room through the open windows. He watched as she flung open her bedroom window and shouted out a loud screech of fury.

'Olivia Hadleigh, I hate you! You just wait and see. I will get even one day. I will.'

He watched for some time, twisting and tightening the black cord around his wrist. Thinking, staring and planning.

Meanwhile, at Misbourne House, to Olivia's young and

uncluttered mind, she was swept along by Aunt Geraldine in a state of dreamlike awe as the whole expedition took place with ease, jubilant agreement, and clockwork military precision as only an 'Aunt Geraldine' could organise.

CHAPTER 3

"I thought I knew everything when I came to Rome, but I soon found that I had everything to learn."
Edmonia Lewis.

Rome Summer 1968

The afternoon sun shimmered a transparent vapour from the tarmac as they arrived in sweltering heat at Aeroporto Internazionale di Roma-Fiumicino 'Leonardo da Vinci.' The taxi raced through the mayhem of the busy streets of Rome, passing famous buildings and fountains. Livia half expected Sophia Loren or Audrey Hepburn to pop out of the elegant shops or be part of a film shoot by the Trevi fountain. The car screeched to a halt outside Rome's central Hotel Du Cale. Livia looked up at a luxurious marble colonnaded edifice, built like a palace. The receptionist, Mario, welcomed Geraldine like a long lost friend as he conversed with her in Italian, handling all the paperwork and passports and giving their key to the porter. He handed her a brown envelope. Geraldine tapped it with her index finger before placing it in her leather folder.

Their room was spacious, ornate, and like nothing Olivia had ever experienced before other than when she visited stately homes and viewed the rooms from afar. The views from the balcony overlooked the Colosseum. This monumental building was backlit by a vivid deep blue sky with dark clouds accenting its golden glow. Aunt Geraldine had provided Livia with a new suitcase and clothes for their trip and a set of vivid books that would help answer some of Livia's questions she had foreseen would come up. Whilst Livia settled in and unpacked her books, Geraldine went to the telephone with the brown envelope. A rapid conversation ensued in Italian with notes taken down by Geraldine on the papers she had taken from the envelope. Olivia just carried on discreetly with her unpacking until the conversation finished. She knew her aunt would speak in her own good time if she needed to learn more. Geraldine placed the papers back in the leather folder. A brief look of pain passed across her eyes as she leaned forward. Olivia had seen this before. The moment passed; Geraldine shook her head and, raising her shoulders, she sat tapping her pen as she looked out of the window, deep in thought. She turned to face Olivia; her serious look changed to a broad smile.

'We have a busy few days ahead, my darling. We are going to have a wonderful time. So much I want to show you. I may have to make a few telephone calls in the early morning, but it will not interfere with our trip. Now I think our first night in Rome means a special Italian meal. Then an early night, so we will eat in the hotel's restaurant tonight. Can you be ready in fifteen minutes?'

Olivia did not need any further urging; she could be ready in five.

The next few days were life-changing for Livia. Reading the many books gave her a glimpse of what was coming. The sights of Rome were astounding. The Colosseum, the Arch of Constantine, and Palatine Hill above the Tiber river. Grand palaces of emperors had stood there. In Livia's imagination she conjured these up from the fallen ruins. In the Roman Forum, Olivia visualised the political and religious life entertained there, along with all the hustle and bustle of courts, market traders and meeting places for discussions and intrigues. They walked a little along the Via Appia Antica, one of Rome's most ancient roads. How many famous and infamous characters had passed over those stones?

Each day they returned to their hotel, footsore and heavy

with heat and tiredness. The refreshment of a cool shower and early evening meal made the sweetness of deep sleep the medicine that enabled them to awaken, ready for the next day's exertions. Two days of their stay were spent at Pompeii. Aunt Geraldine knew from previous visits, the best way to see Pompeii and understand the significant sights was to hire a guide. Francesca was young, energetic and always ready to explain and answer the stream of questions pouring from Livia. They started at the Port Marina and looked at the Forum, where Livia imagined trade, commerce, and politics being wrangled by men in an ancient epoch. Alongside the Forum was the Grain Store, where many of the plaster casts of the victims of Mount Vesuvius' destruction were starkly displayed. Nearby was the Calidarius, a hot water bath equipped with all the bathing facilities Pompeians would have needed. Following along Via dell'Abbondanza was the Amphitheatre, one of the oldest buildings of its kind in the world, where vicious battles with wild animals had taken place, and 20,000 spectators watched on. On their way back toward the Porta Marina gate via the Necropolis, beautiful tombs and gardens lined the route. They passed by the Villa Dei Misteri with its exquisite frescoes. Names of long forgotten people were inscribed fading on the stones. These monuments made a deep impression on Olivia. So many real people had lived similar lives to herself and her family, they cultivated the land, reared children, ate, drank and enjoyed the entertainment; lived and died. What stories could be told of their thoughts and deeds?

As Olivia wrote her diary each day of the places they had visited and the names of people chiseled on the stones. She became increasingly aware of the lack of a woman's hand in the inscriptions. The scholars wrote about life, battles, poetry, festivals and gods. There were transaction details, exchanges, and bequests, but these were men writing. Something was missing; the women's thoughts. What was life really like for the women of Ancient Rome? The wives of leaders, their slave women, their daughters, the mothers of emperors, aunts, and grandmothers. Olivia's interest was stirred as she pondered these thought-provoking questions in her fertile young mind. Halfway through their trip in the early evening, Geraldine received a telephone call. Rapid Italian conversation rattled along, the envelope appeared, and further notations were made. Her aunt replaced the receiver.

'We have a day out tomorrow away from the city. We will visit one of my old friends at his Villa in Frascati. The Count and his wife, they have invited us for lunch.

I knew them in my mid-twenties. It seems so long ago. Yes, we were all so young and carefree. The war came along; Monte worked so hard to preserve many treasures from the Nazis. I never told you, well, many works of art were secreted away within his Villa, in underground tunnels dating back to Roman times. He had contacts from the Netherlands and France and was a go-between among the allies and many Jewish families. The Count had most of his treasures in the main house but hundreds of stored items in the passages. Many of them were discovered and stolen by the Nazis. Some have been recovered and repatriated, but a few exceptional pieces are missing. We keep in contact, and our ears are open for word of any appearance in the galleries. You may have noticed the envelope I was given when we arrived. It had some interesting new information about a couple of fifteenth-century portraits which may be surfacing. So we will have lunch with the Count and look at his records and any information he has.

You will find his villa extraordinary, Olivia. It has a remarkable history, built in the late sixteenth century in the most fabulous Baroque style, ornate grand garlanded pillars— the most elaborate stucco decorations. Don't feel intimidated by its grandeur. It might look like St Paul's, but dear Monte and Caterina are the most enchanting people you would ever wish to meet. I think you will love them and their gorgeous palazzo.'

Olivia's heartbeat quickened. She was enthralled to be involved in a real live hunt and mystery for missing artwork, along with the opportunity to visit an Italian aristocrat and his Villa Battista. Her ears quickly picked up on the name Montefiori. She was sure this connected to the phone calls she had overheard back at Missenden. She had guessed her aunt's involvement in something secret. Olivia's own little book of secrets and questions she slipped into her bag as they prepared for their trip the following morning.

Villa Battista stood high up in the Alban Hills just outside Frascati, two hours from Rome. Although only a short distance, their taxi driver had to keep stopping as the further they were out of Rome, the more rural it became. Just around one tight bend, a herd of slow-moving cattle and the need for the friendliness of the Italians to converse with each other slowed the journey further. It gave Livia time to watch and listen. She marvelled at the clean, cooler air away from Rome, imagining all the noble families leaving Rome, visiting their villas in the hot summer months. They must have travelled the same route as she was taking. Slow-moving with their carts, luggage, families, slaves and animals. Passing returning traders with their produce and livestock to market in Rome. What stories these roadways and rocks could have told? Marching armies of centurions, sweeping along. Maybe returning to Rome with their spoils, stopping off at villas along the way. Renewing friendships and acquaintances. Establishing their own lands and properties.

They rounded the next bend in the road, and the magnificent Villa Battista appeared before her eyes. Her curiosity had already been aroused but in no way prepared her for the jewel of a palace before her. The gates alone were over twenty feet high, with ornamental cones planted atop the two towering pillars on either side. Fountains spewed water into a deep ornamental pool fronting the main entrance and a five-storied facade of pale pink stucco. A large cylindrical domed tower stood central to the vast solid portico, whilst dramatic scrolled wings swept symmetrically on either side. The scene was framed by a thickly wooded hill to the rear, fading to a hazy horizon of tall chestnuts and poplars in the far distance.

Olivia half expected a liveried footman to formally open

the grand door. Instead, a tall elderly, handsome-looking man with a smiling suntanned face and greying swept-back tousled hair stood in the entranceway. He opened his arms to Geraldine, kissing her on both cheeks. Holding her at arm's length, surveyed her with a warmth of friendliness and genteel approval. He looked across at Olivia and similarly welcomed her, all the time smiling and speaking with a rich Italian accent.

'Come, come, my dear, dear friends. You are most welcome. My dearest Geraldine, so long, so long. Ahh, too long.'

His repeating words for emphasis only increased the sincerity and emotion behind his feelings. He turned towards his wife, who smiled warmly. Her eyes were deep brown, contrasting with her white hair swept elegantly back. A very slight drooping of her mouth towards the left side barely changed her face's symmetry as she spoke. Nothing, however, could detract from the softness of her kindly eyes. Olivia had never noticed how the eyes and mouth could smile together; Countess Caterina had this ability. She stood tall, elegant, and erect and only when she turned to take them through the vast hallway did Olivia notice her carrying a slim wooden cane. Hardly perceptibly, she walked with a slight limp, leading them through to a beautiful salon looking out to the rear across gardens and parkland. The long windows were ajar, with overhanging sun canopies providing shade from the dazzling Italian sun. They walked out onto the balcony, where seating and refreshments were laid out. The Count took Olivia by the arm across the terrace and showed her the distant views, describing points of interest to her whilst answering the myriad questions she had about the history of the house, his ancestors, and to her most keen interest, the Roman ruins lying beneath the house and valley below.

Geraldine and Caterina watched on as Olivia completely monopolised Count Montefiori. He found her a most avid student, and her light, engaging manner and her questions delightful. Soon forgetting she was just a young girl, she made it easy for him to expound on his favourite subjects. He was surprised at her knowledge of her surroundings and the history of his Roman ancestors. As they leaned against the stone balcony, he pointed out to her the tented area in the distance where an archaeological dig was going on. This explained the chipping and banging intermittently heard in the valley. The University of Rome were investigating Roman mosaic floors, recently uncovered. Distractedly engrossed in the activity below, Olivia leaned forward between the ornamental planters. As she squinted against the sunlight, two men carried crates and lifted objects up to the light. Her attention was so engrossed in the dig that nothing the Count said was heard. Suddenly, the nearest planter to where she was standing dislodged. With an almighty crash and clatter, it bounced, cracking and splitting as it hurled downhill, narrowly missing one of the men working there. One of the dark-haired, dusty-looking youths raised his arms and shouted something in Italian. His voice echoed around the valley. Olivia dived down instinctively behind the stone balustrade. The Count waved to the workers and replied loudly back in Italian. With many gesticulations and what appeared to be heated arguments, a short interchange between them eventually seemed to calm the situation. Seeing no one was injured, the workers raised their arms, and promptly their heads disappeared again into their work.

Olivia felt like she wanted to die. She had disgraced herself, and a priceless ornament was now smashed to smithereens, scattered into a thousand pieces whilst bashing the pristine gardens below. Someone had nearly been killed, a very loud argument had taken place, and now the potential wrath of the Count and Countess Montefiore would be all directed at her. She buried her head onto her knees and burst into tears. A cool hand patted her head, as she heard the Count say.

'Ah Olivia, my dear, have we not all at some point in our lives wished we could roll back time, relive a moment when we could have changed something we did or the position we placed ourselves in? Come now. I should have made sure those old pots were more secure. Look down the valley. No one was injured. No damage was caused, just an old pot I should have replaced some time ago.'

Olivia looked up gingerly towards this kindly man. She felt small and childish, hot and embarrassed. However, from their easy free expressions, the Count and his wife reassured Olivia she should not give a second thought to this minor mishap in their eyes. The Count busied himself, helping Olivia stand up and dust herself. He handed her a huge white handkerchief with a beautifully embroidered blue motif, MGB in the bottom corner. Not for the first time had a cloth from a kind-hearted older man been given to comfort her. He swept his hand to one side when she tried to hand it back.

'No, no. You keep it, Olivia; you never know when it may come in useful.'

Raising both hands in the air and laughing loudly, he turned towards Geraldine and his wife.

'This young lady has taken me over and captivated me, all the interests we have in common. I think we are going to be good friends, Olivia. However, I have neglected my dearest friend Geraldine and my most wonderful wife.'

As he spoke, he laughed again and gently took Olivia's elbow. He was not the only one captivated. She just followed his lead toward the older ladies. They did not appear in the least to feel neglected or unhappy. Geraldine, her leather folder opened, talked away in Italian to Caterina, with their heads together, studying the letters, reading glasses perched on the end of their noses. Both talked animatedly, writing onto sheets of paper.

The Count smiled as he watched two of his favourite women engrossed in the papers and documents. Caterina felt the intensity of his gaze and raised her eyes to his. She nodded to him and said.

'It is my turn to have the company of our young friend Olivia. You have monopolised her for long enough, Monte. Come, Olivia, I want to show you the marvellous views from our belvedere.'

Olivia did not miss the knowing look her aunt and the Count exchanged as Countess Caterina elegantly raised herself and took Olivia by the arm, directing her firmly back towards the large open doors leading onto the hallway. Olivia knew this signalled her aunt to discuss the missing artwork.

The spiral staircase up to the high belvedere was steep and narrow, the countess took her time pausing at intervals, pointing out places of interest through the tall thin slit windows. The views from the top were panoramic. The room was bright, and a large telescope was positioned out of the open window to the west. Caterina invited Olivia to a look. She gradually adjusted the lens and scanned the surrounding valley. Her attention was caught by a shining metal reflection. She focused more closely and saw the trowel of one of the workers as he deftly removed soft earth around a colourful blue patterned mosaic. He shifted his dark curly-haired head over the ground, and the view was lost to Olivia. She carefully turned the focus handle and looked over his shoulder. His fingers swept at the soil and dust. It was as if she was beside him for a moment, seeing the blues and ochres of a woman's head appearing out of the grime. Olivia watched, transfixed. Suddenly the young man turned his head towards her and looked directly into the lens. It was the same dark-haired young man from before, that had narrowly missed being injured by the dislodged ornament. Olivia jumped back. She swung the telescope away in the opposite direction towards the horizon, her cheeks burning and her heart racing with an overwhelming feeling she had been discovered.

They stayed some time looking out across the hills. Caterina was an endless source of knowledge when identifying the many birds around. She picked out a distinct pair of golden Orioles, the male's striking golden body and the bird's black wings contrasted against the bright blue of the sky. To Olivia's surprise, the sound of a double hoop alerted her to the most exotic bird she had ever seen, the Hoopoe. Its crested crown of feathers fanned above its head, and its bold stripes added to the bird's glamour. The sounds echoed through the valley as they watched on. After some time, Caterina took Olivia down the winding staircase, searching for Geraldine and the Count. They were both sitting relaxed, enjoying a sparkling drink. She just caught the tail end of their conversation.

'So Geraldine, it could have been one of many. The house was a hospital. We had many young doctors here too. The Allies set up a field hospital when Rome was captured. The Germans were coming and going up until that time, but these photographs, at last, form a definite picture to be distributed, more added clues to help us.'

It was apparent to Olivia that they had completed their discussions. She noticed the leather folder was bulging with added documents. Also carefully placed on Geradine's knees was a stained and worn red book. Immediately, the Count sprang up from his seat and arranged cool drinks for them all.

He invited them to a concert he had arranged the following week. Professor Gambocelli and the archaeological team had completed most of the work on the mosaic and were arranging to transport their findings to the Sale Della Croce Greca over the next two weeks. There was to be a grand concert in the Villa's gardens for them all. Geraldine looked across at the pleading in Olivia's eyes.

'That would have been most generous of you, Monte. Unfortunately, our trip to Italy must end on Saturday. If the school holidays had not been coming to their end, we could have extended our stay. Olivia is starting her new school, and I have promised her parents that she will return to make all the preparations. My husband, too, will be home on Sunday. I really must be there for him.'

She looked fondly towards the Count and Countess.

'It has been too long since we have seen each other. Now, we must not lose touch again. The trail seems to have opened up again. You have given me fresh hope, and the sketches and photographs now are much more definitive. The book too, Monte, a clear picture of what we are looking for. I may have information soon regarding the portraits.'

She patted the folder and placed the book inside her case.

Olivia's eyes had spotted the old book, and her intuition told her she needed to explore its contents. How she wished they were staying longer. Then she remembered the young man she had nearly decapitated, and she giggled to herself. It may be a good thing to return to England on Saturday. The embarrassment of having to explain herself would have been excruciating. Her cheeks burned with the thought of the situation she had avoided.

As the taxi sped away up the long drive from the Villa, Aunt Geraldine looked across at Olivia's reddened cheeks.

'You do look flushed, Livia. Is everything OK?'

Livia lifted her head up and blew out softly through her lips.

'Yes, thanks. I just remember everything that's gone on today. I feel slightly embarrassed by the 'pot incident.'

She giggled out loud. Her aunt, too, laughed.

'Oh, Livia, if I were to tell you some of the crazy things I've done in the past. The scrapes I've had to escape from. One day we will have time together, not just collating all my bits and pieces but also going through the high jinks I've had over the years.'

Olivia looked at this sedate, elegant older lady styled in the latest fashions. She blinked as she caught a raised eyebrow and a sparkling twinkle in those green eyes. There were stories yet to be told, and Olivia was meant to be there when the time was ripe for them to come out. She beamed at her aunt and laughed out loud. She felt safe and secure here. Her inner turmoils and fears, not understanding, not knowing, vanished. The outside scenery looked bright and clear, and the future felt hopeful and exciting. Aunt Geraldine relaxed and laughed. Turning to Olivia, with one eyebrow raised and half a smile on her lips, looked her directly in the eyes.

'Olivia Hadleigh, there are a lot of adventures we are going to have together. I may even make you sign an 'official secrets act'. What goes between us stays between us......unless... it is a matter of life and death. Only then are secrets revealed. Come now, we will shake hands on that. Our word is our bond.'

CHAPTER 4

'False face must hide what the false heart doth know
Macbeth. William Shakespeare

Beaconsfield late summer 1968

The late summer sun lengthened its rays into mellow autumn hues. The trees changed, scattering their crunchy golden leaves, and the air dampened into the early morning fog. Everything was changing.

The Hadleigh household altered too. The girls each took new journeys in different directions. Imogen went away to London, having secured a place at the Royal Academy of Dramatic Art. Much to Briddy's relief and related connections, she was able to stay for the first year at her cousin's house in Camden, just a few stops on the tube from the studios.

Tatiana caught the train each day to the Art College in High Wycombe and, by some miraculous means or other, seemed to find her way home each night in a dream-like state of semi-consciousness. Briddy and Richard had spent the last few days of the holidays taking great interest in her person and equipment. Gently Richard had coaxed her along to discuss her thoughts and concerns. Waiting with long moments of empty silence for Tati to form her opinions into words and expressions. He knew she had only one interest in life, her art, and she would always struggle with interacting in social settings with people she just did not relate to or even care about. Richard encouraged, cajoled and gently tried to give her advice. Tati occasionally looked at him as she fidgeted and twiddled her fingers together.

'I must carry on with the painting now, Dad, got to go.'

So concluded the genuine concern Richard showed Tati towards the next stage of her career in 'the Arts'.

After all the excitement, intrigue and adventures in Italy, life in Beaconsfield for Olivia was mundane and almost sleepily boring. There was one excitement. The opening of her packet of Roman jewellery, holding it up next to the open window, the late low sun intensifying the deep yellow of old gold. As the light faded, she moved under the anglepoise light, examining the markings closely. A new project was just beginning. She placed them on the window sill. The flash of her camera captured the words engraved in the dusky evening light. Livia settled down into bed, tired. She kept her eyes on the beautiful gifts her aunt had given her. Then as her eyes became heavy, she fell asleep. Not only had the flashlight caught her photograph perfectly, also the boy hiding in the bushes, watching, had seen everything.

She spent the Monday of the last week before the new term traipsing around the school uniform shops and stationers for all her equipment. Burrells, the outfitters, had run out of the school ties, so they had to go to the shop her father's school used in Windsor. Fawley's was an old-fashioned place with a distinct smell of mothballs. As you pushed open the glass door, the tinkling sound of the brass bell overhead rattled away. Glass cabinets contained all the generations of school wear needed for numerous establishments in the home counties. Olivia was sure the assistants were as old as some shields and plaques displaying centuries of honourable schoolmasters and their illustrious famous pupils. Mothers with their children lined up to be measured and cajoled into oversized blazers and coats.

They sat waiting their turn on one of the benches provided. Olivia daydreamed, watching the people, noticing little things from the corner of her eye. Two gangly girls pinched their little sister until she screamed; the mother turned and smacked the bawling child, shushing it to be quiet. She noticed a ginger-haired scrawny boy wiping his fingers across the glass drawers, pulling out two silk school ties, and hiding them in his trouser pockets. Livia stood up to speak, but at that precise moment, Briddy grabbed her hand and moved them along the bench nearer to the waiting shop assistant.

As Olivia turned back, the boy had disappeared and, no doubt, had the ties. Her mother spoke to the lady sitting next to her and found out she was a near neighbour, Avril Courtney, a constant chatterer. In five minutes, Briddy was told the circumstances of her poor sister's son, Sebastian, who was now living with them and being a 'near genius' had passed the entrance exam to Blackstone Manor, so was being kitted out with all his uniform. Just as she paused for breath, out from the changing rooms came the dark-haired young man, dressed from top to toe in Blackstone uniform. When Avril discovered Briddy was the headmaster's wife, she became increasingly annoying in her prattle and fawning all over Briddy. The boy immediately summed up the situation. He quickly took charge, realising his aunt was not favouring him by ingratiating herself with Mrs Hadleigh. He gave his most charming smile, then gently ushered his aunt towards the sports department. Briddy breathed a sigh of relief. Olivia watched as the young man showed impeccable manners toward his most irritating aunt. She was impressed with his calmness and patience but disturbed by something unnerving in his tone. It was as if he were playing to a stage audience. He seemed very aware of the many eyes watching him. Everything was correct but almost too good for a young man of maybe fourteen years. His handsome face, piercing blue eyes and confidence were striking. Many of the young plump spotty girls were watching him, nudging each other, slightly drooling over this good-looking boy turning heads as he moved around the shop. Olivia, after a while, found it all a bit strange. This boy, Sebastian, was well aware of his audience and appeared to be playing a game. He looked innocent, nonchalant and oblivious to the attention he received, but each move he made seemed to be planned. This young man was all too aware of the impact he was having. Olivia shrugged her shoulders, turned her back away from him, and kept her eyes fixed on school ties. She did not notice, as he left the shop with his aunt, the backward glance he made towards her and her mother, his actor's face changing from affable to slightly menacing.

That last few days of the holidays, Olivia roamed the fields and Eatonwoods near their home with her spaniel Ruby. The late sun still had warmth, and the ground was dry, with little rain that week. She could sit amongst the brambles reading and throwing sticks for Ruby. The path taken was well-trodden and hard. Running along, her foot caught in some roots and, stumbling headfirst, fell into some nettles. She got up and saw a small black swinging shape dangling amongst the bushes hanging from the trees. She called Ruby over; they sat quietly together as she looked into the dark space ahead. Ruby sniffed the air, her nose lifted, sitting motionless, her nostrils flaring. She, too, had spotted the swinging dark shape. Ruby barked. Livia held her collar as she strained to dive forwards. Holding her tightly, they scrambled through the bushes towards the hanging form. Ruby barked again and lurched as overhead hung the swinging dead body of a black crow dangling from a black cord. Olivia shuddered. What was it there for? Who would have done such a thing? The bird was too high up for her to reach. There was a sharp crack of twigs over to her left. Ruby jerked in the direction of the sound and then growled. Livia felt cold and chilled. She thought she heard her name, for a voice hissed out loud.

'Olivia'

She put Ruby's lead through the collar and pulled her away from the scene, quickly running towards home as dark clouds blotted out the late afternoon sun and a rumble of thunder sounded in the distance.

When she arrived home, she put her head around her dad's study and waited for him to speak. He swung round on his old captain's chair, raising his glasses onto his head, placing his pen on the desk.

'Well, the wanderer has returned; good job just before the rain. Having a good time?'

Olivia moved into the study and, sitting on one of the wooden crates stacked on their side, leaned forwards resting her chin in her hands. She told her dad about the dead crow she'd found in the woods. The noises they had heard, along with Ruby's reaction. Why would anyone do such a horrid thing?

Richard thought for a moment or two. It was only one bird. It could have gotten tangled in someone's wire, blown by the wind. Or maybe some nasty person didn't like corvids. He told her not to give it another thought.

'You stick to the open paths, Livia. There are always a few odd characters around. Come on, I can smell something good from the kitchen. I'm just going to put this marker away, and I will be along to join you and mum.'

As always, Olivia felt reassured and comforted by her dad's words. Still, the voice she had heard, her name, hissed. That familiar fog of not understanding, inner turmoil, and uncertainty returned and crept over her like cold, damp fingers encircling her mind. She closed her eyes and shook her head. Repeating to herself the words.

'Reason and logic, not blind clouded emotion. It's just a feeling, not reality. Go away. Now!'

Olivia ran towards the dining room, focusing on the upcoming family meal.

Richard slowly closed his study door with a feeling of unease. This was the third instance brought to his attention of strange deaths of animals over the last two weeks. His brother had come across a kitten strung up in someone's back garden while doing his rounds. Mr Symons, the caretaker at the school on opening up the bike shed for the new term, had found behind the locked shed door the skeletons and feathers of three dead birds all tied up together with a stack of stubbed-out cigarettes nearby. He decided to keep his eyes and ears open for any more unexplained events or strangers loitering in the area and make a call to the local constable. There may have been more unexplained animal deaths in the area. On top of all this, the school roof was leaking.

The rest of the week was quiet, apart from a lively conversation on the telephone. Geraldine had called to say she had the photos developed of their trip to Italy and was coming over the following afternoon to show them to her. She also had some news about the missing artwork.

When Geraldine arrived, Briddy could see Livia longed to be alone with Geraldine, so she took herself off into the garden for half an hour, sweeping up the fallen leaves. Eagerly Livia watched as her aunt brought out the battered red book.

'Right, straight to the point, Livia. We've been able to locate a couple of photographs of the missing paintings. We only had the two rough drawings from Monte's descriptions until now. We have these now. Very dark and poorly photographed. The originals would have been painted in vibrant blues, reds and gold. Here, The Madonna and child, a small panel painting 8 inches by 12 inches by Masaccio, and a matching panel in tempura also believed to be by Masaccio of the angel Gabriel. These were taken by a French photographer in 1879. The paintings were incidental to other photographs he took of the Villa. But see here, it clearly states the long-lost paintings by Masaccio dating back to 1420 in the Villa Battista. Monte has only just come across this old book. It is such a find.'

Olivia looked closely at the faded black and white photos for some time, then said.

'So, what's the next plan of action to find the paintings?'

Her aunt smiled to herself; Olivia wanted to be fully involved in the hunt for the missing paintings. She explained the photos could now be circulated amongst the various agencies searching for lost works of art the Nazis had stolen. Her contacts at Interpol working from the Netherlands would be invaluable now they had these photographs. Olivia produced her little black book. She looked sheepishly at her aunt. Geraldine was pleasantly surprised to see Livia's enthusiasm and orderliness. Livia quickly covered the first few pages. Making a new list of anyone involved in the inquiry. Names, dates, organisations.

Geraldine was happy to supply all she knew. Suddenly the pieces slotted together. Words Livia had heard from patchy telephone conversations now became real people. Inspector Horley from Interpol and his colleague Lucien Van der Berg, the Dutch art specialist. The trail had gone cold for over 10 years, but now with the photographs, there was every possibility new evidence would come to light. Someone would have seen those pictures at some point since their disappearance. Olivia asked to take a photograph to keep in her notebook. The more people had a clear idea of what the paintings looked like, the more likely they would find them.

The photos were developed overnight at the Gallery photo shop in the high street, but to Livia's disappointment, the pictures of Masaccio's Madonna and Gabriel were none too clear. Only a hazy dark shadow of a woman and child and an even more indistinct image of a dark shape appeared in the second photo. The manager, Mr Castle, noticed Olivia flicking through all the photographs and spending time on the two dark and indistinct ones.

'Some lovely scenes of Italy I noticed you've taken photos of. Sorry, the two you have there are so poor.'

'Yes, they are pictures of photos from an old book. Is there any possibility of enhancing or enlarging just these two? Would it make any difference?'

He took them from her with the negatives and held them up to the light.

'Well, maybe, the photos are hazy, but I have a few techniques that sometimes enhance what's on the negatives. I could have a go. Give me a few days, and I'll see what I can do.'

To Olivia, it didn't matter. She had more material to put in her notebook. She researched the artist Masaccio and found a yellowing old book in her father's study. 'Lives of the artists' by Vasari. In the section under Masaccio, she found mention of lost works of panel pictures in tempura. She wrote everything down in the black notebook. She returned to the photographers at the end of the week. Mr Castle was intrigued by the photos, his new techniques had brought out the shadows and contrasts, so the pictures were now much clearer. He spoke to her of his familiarity with Italian paintings and, with his interest in photography, he had toured many art galleries and taken hundreds of photos. He asked if she knew what these two pictures were. Olivia explained they had been lost for many years, and the photos had just turned up in an old photography book. Mr Castle scratched his chin. He picked up the pictures and took them over to the window.

'You know, I can't be absolutely sure, but they seem familiar to me. Well, at least this of the angel. Someone has shown me this picture or a photograph of it before. I've seen it in Italy. During the war, I was a photographer for the RAF taking significant photos for the allies. We marched with the Americans from the south towards Rome. I was wounded and looked after in a field hospital, then shipped back to England. Let me think; someone has shown me this picture before. I'm so sorry; so many confused memories. Bodies battle the heat, then the cold of winter. I will have to give it some thought. I might have even seen it in one of the galleries in Italy.'

Olivia weighed up her situation. Here in front of her was a man who had been in Italy during the 2nd World War. Appeared to know a lot about art. He was an official photographer in the British army, and now there was a possibility he had seen one of these paintings. She decided to tell him what she knew. He listened intently to her account of the stolen paintings, their visit to Villa Battista and Count and Countess Montefiore and the new piece of photographic evidence that the panels had existed and been at the Villa.

'You know what, I think I was in the hospital at this Villa you are speaking about. It seems too much of a coincidence. I remember seeing this painting whilst I was injured and cared for at this Villa. I am trying to remember seeing something hanging on the walls, though. The walls were ornately plastered, but no paintings. How is it I remember a photograph though of this painting? I am so sorry. My memory. I was severely concussed for many days, and then all I remember was; returning to England by ship. I remember an American ship called the 'John J Meany' hospital ship. We were all piled in from Naples. In fact, most of the officers, doctors and nurses from that hospital were with us on the boat. I remember being helped by a kind doctor with a limp. Funny how some things stick in your mind. The hospital was disbanded. We were the last of the patients to leave.'

Olivia felt sure there was more to this story than she could get that day. She thanked Mr Castle for all his help and said she had enjoyed hearing about his life and experiences in Italy. She would get her aunt to call by with the book containing the photos of the two paintings. Seeing them could jog his memory. He said it had made his day talking to her, and he felt excited to know they could be on the trail of the lost paintings. Her aunt would be more than welcome. He assured her he would look up all his old albums and see what he could find.

The afternoon sun was low, casting long shadows, and the air was chilly. Olivia hurried along the High Street, then left towards their house down the country lane. Deeply engrossed in all her thoughts, she hadn't noticed the young boy following her. Quickly crossing the road, he briskly walked ahead of her, turning into her lane. It now appeared he was coming towards her. He nonchalantly called as she approached.

'Oh, we met the other day at the outfitters in Windsor.'

Livia looked up into a pair of bright blue twinkling eyes. She remembered this boy, Sebastian. Something too flickered through her mind. Now, what was it about him she found unnerving? Today he looked amiable and slightly shy. Yes, she remembered noticing his changing faces, his ability to charm those around him. She tilted her head to one side. Well, he didn't look too bad today.

'Hello.'

Olivia felt embarrassed, she was not used to the company of boys, but she was a good judge of character and felt a bit uneasy with his over-friendliness towards her. He gave her a disarming smile but rested his eyes a fraction of a second too long on hers. Sebastian recognised the bashfulness of this girl. Revising his tactics immediately, he became the shy, innocent lost boy. It always helped the girls to feel sorry for him. No one could resist a lost person.

'Sorry I startled you; I'm just getting used to all the lanes hereabouts and trying to find the shortcuts. Getting lost, think it's this way. It's all so new and green. I'm in the right direction towards my aunt's house?

He swept his hand around him to gesture toward the fields and woods. Then looked over the hedge with his hand on his forehead.

Livia felt annoyed she wasn't feeling kindly towards this stranger, who, she reluctantly admitted, was lost.

'Your aunt, Mrs Courtney, I think I know where she lives. Carry on along this lane. You will come to High Street. I'm sure you'll know where you are then. Once you leave the main roads, it can be a bit confusing.'

'Ah, I've gone in a bit of a circle today, thanks. I will get used to this road, mainly going to school daily.'

He stepped to one side around Olivia and raised his hand in a goodbye gesture, strolling towards the main high street. Olivia was puzzled. How strange he professed to be uncertain of the way home, yet he knew full well he was on the road to Blackstone School. The light was starting to fade now, and Olivia always found this short stretch of country lane unsettling. Beyond the thick hedge, she heard the cracking of twigs and light running feet. A small dark figure disappeared across the road in front of her. She hurried on towards home, deep in thought. Again her thoughts went back to the day's discoveries regarding the stolen paintings, her conversation with Mr Castle, his stories of the war, evacuation and injuries, and loss of memory. She decided she would have to stop being so negative about the boy Sebastian. Having read too many mystery books made her suspicious of strangers. She dismissed him from her mind.

Once home, Olivia telephoned Aunt Geraldine with her news about the photographer Mr Castle. Could there be a link to the lost paintings with this man? He had told her he had been at the Villa when it was a hospital during the war. Her aunt told her to keep all this information to herself. She would pass on the details and go to see Mr Castle herself. Gently warning Olivia not to get any more involved at the present. Try to concentrate on the new school she was going to on Monday. Make lots of new friends and enjoy every opportunity placed before her.

That night, Olivia looked over her school uniform and packed her satchel together for the following morning. She glanced over to where she had left her Roman jewellery. To her utter shock, it was not there. She spun around, bent down on hands and knees and swept her hands across the rug. Jumping up, she knocked her ornaments off the dressing table. The bangle and ring were not found. Crouching looking under the bed, an awful dread overwhelmed her. She had left her bedroom window open all day. Where were her treasures? She dare not tell her parents of her foolishness. No, she would find the missing items herself.

Olivia was distraught. Not only had her jewellery gone missing. It was all her fault; she felt wretched, a complete failure. Her stomach gurgled, butterflies were doing somersaults and gymnastics. As she fell onto the bed, she felt strange tinglings, her body changing, her limbs awkward. She would have done anything to avoid Monday morning and the new school. If she buried her head in her pillow long enough, perhaps everything would stay the same. The jewellery would reappear. She would remain the same; nothing would have to change. Her pillow soaked up her tears and muffled her howls of anger. Gradually she lifted her head up. Why was she the only person in the world feeling so miserable and hopeless? Did anyone else feel like she did? Was she so alone, embarrassed wretched and useless?

There was a slight scratching at the door of her bedroom, and as it opened, a small black shiny nose appeared, then a trembling body of fur and a quivering happy tail waved at her. Olivia had to smile and admit to herself not everything was changing. Ruby stayed the same. She never noticed any difference at all in Olivia. Livia smiled and ruffled the wavy fur on Ruby's ears. She felt the silkiness on her fingers, the brightness of those doleful eyes, and the way the warmth of Ruby's body on her cold toes was soothing and familiar. The minutes passed, and the feelings of desolation disappeared just as quickly as they had descended. Olivia looked around the room, what had just happened? Nothing dramatically had changed, only her mood. She sat, considering for a moment. Were mood and feelings affected by thoughts and actions? If distracted from yourself, could you alter how you felt? Remembering her aunt's words.

'There are always consequences for our actions. It is a scientific fact, 'cause and effect'. Analyse the consequences; one moment, we will feel ecstatic, and the next, in the depths of despair. All part of growing up.'

Olivia sighed in relief. Perhaps this experience was going to happen to her more frequently. She sat up, determined to make a list. She would copy Aunt Geraldine, analyse consequences and actions, 'fors and againsts'. Her aunt had always kept busy and active, not just concerned with herself but interested in the world and others outside of her own circle. Olivia came to a decision from that day forward. No more self-pity.

When the morning arrived, Briddy struggled with Olivia's hair, plaiting it into strict braids aided by lashings of setting lotion, the oversized blazer drooped on her shoulders, and the straw boater plonked reasonably straight on her head. She almost felt prepared for the days ahead.

They set off along the country roads towards Chesham. Briddy related to Livia her first day at high school in Oxford and lightened the mood with a couple of funny stories about the odd teachers. Livia felt a growing churning in her stomach, and all the funny stories in the world didn't stop her from feeling sick or wanting to rush to the bathroom. Her mouth was dry, and her hands were clammy. Tears welled up in her eyes. The minutes passed, and her mum kept talking. Livia knew she just had to breathe deeply to suppress the impulse to vomit. She wound down the window, and the cool fresh air swept over her face helping her to gulp away the sensations of the morning's breakfast rising towards her throat. As she inhaled steadily, her nerves calmed, and her mum's voice returned to her hearing.

'Here we are, darling. You just do your best and have some fun, Livia. Bye Bye now.'

Livia gave her mum a quick squeeze, picked up her satchel and walked down the long gravel driveway towards her foreboding future.

CHAPTER 5

'There's no art To find the mind's construction in the face'
William Shakespeare. Macbeth 1.4

England Buckinghamshire 1968

Lady Clara Backsley Grammar School was a converted, large, red-bricked, Victorian mansion that had recently been extended with a square modern block housing the science department and new swimming pool facilities. The high-pitched chatter in the playground increased as more and more girls mingled and shrieked as they found someone they knew. It was apparent who the newer ones were smaller in height, dressed in new oversized uniforms. Shiny leather satchels crisscrossed their small backs, light, empty and rattling with pens and pencils. A few huddled with friends who had come from the melting pot of schools around and about. Livia stood watching, listening for the bell, a coach arrived, and girls poured out, swelling the numbers waiting and pushing them all closer together. Livia was jolted slightly forwards into another girl much more petite than herself. The girl's hat was dislodged and fell sideways onto the ground, revealing the most beautiful glossy long black plait Livia had ever seen. Livia bent forwards. Picking up the boater, she extended her hand.

'So sorry, I barged into you, here; let me dust the hat down. Isn't it weird wearing a hat? My mum had a job finding one to fit me. They were all so enormous. Anyway, we made it. By the way, my name is Olivia. Everyone but the teachers call me Livia.

I rattle on a bit, but I'm feeling dead sick and nervous, and I talk too much when I'm a bit jumpy.'

The young girl with the beautifully plaited hair giggled and stared nervously through her large deep brown eyes at Olivia, she looked even more terrified than Livia, and her voice came out squeaky when she spoke.

'I'm Ranjita. I'm scared stiff of being here. My mum and dad made me come to this school. Thanks for helping with the hat.'

Livia felt the start of a familiar camaraderie. Someone else felt the same way she did and was happy to express it. The bell clanging caught their attention, and the mass of young girls moved forward toward the entrance door. Livia felt the presence of a small hand clinging to her satchel. They were so tightly packed together that she could not see behind her but had the strange feeling her new friend Ranjita would not let her out of sight.

Mrs Fallows addressed the new girls and told them their Form classes were arranged alphabetically by their Christian names. M-R was signposted to follow Mrs Thomas. The hand on the satchel still held on tightly as Olivia and Ranjita followed Mrs Thomas and the fourteen other girls towards their classroom.

From that first day forward, they became the best of friends. The petite little girl from Slough, with a unique head for mathematics and Livia, the tall gangly chatterbox, whose big heart and insatiable appetite for history and Latin, became inseparable.

Ranjita and Livia's friendship widened out to Harmony and Suzie. After a couple of days, they arranged to play tennis with them after school. Suzie struck at the ball with a formidable force. Her forehand was impossible to return. The two sisters together were powerful opponents. Tennis, at first, was a slow game for Ranjita and Livia. The two sisters giggled together, and after a lot of whispering and Chinese banter, they soon adjusted their natural skills and offered to swap sides with Ranjita and Livia giving them the benefits of pairing with one of them. After a couple of weeks, all four of them shared in scoring points against each other, and it was only the onset of bad weather that stopped their weekly fun on the tennis court. Those few weeks the four girls spent together firmly forged their friendship. Suzie and Harmony laughed, Livia talked, and the shy, timid Ranjita learned a lot. They joined school clubs, art and sports groups, and the newly formed drama society. Their headmistress had arranged for a production of Macbeth from the Blackstone Manor Boy's school to be shown before the half-term break. Olivia was intrigued and curious to know more from her father. She tried every way to extract the details. He just smiled and said it would be a surprise and an extraordinary production to look forward to. He would say no more.

After school, for tea and cakes, the four friends often went to Olivia's house. One afternoon they were walking with Ruby across the fields. All of them chattered about their families. Livia made jokes about her strange sisters, particularly the older, theatrical Impy. She made them all laugh as she took off scornful faces and bossy ways. Pointing and strutting around as only Imogen would do. Reciting chunks of pieces from familiar plays. Then Livia posed as Tati, vague, vacant and distracted with her pretend brush and easel. Ranjita found her shyness fading away. As her confidence grew, she opened up to them about her family.

When Ranjita spoke about her younger sister Sukdeep, known as Suki. Her whole face lit up, describing details about her sister's face, beautiful hair, and smile. She stopped abruptly in her tracks, her large brown eyes filled with tears and softly said.

'Suki cannot walk or talk.'

The others became silent as Ranjita carried on, describing how she loved to take her for walks around the garden in her wheelchair. Suki could follow with her eyes. Ranjita knew she was smiling, though no one else would admit this. Suki was now ten. Ranjita sighed. Not knowing what would happen to Suki the older she got. Her father and brothers said they had arrangements in place. She looked anxiously at the other girl's blank faces as if they would be able to answer her questions.

Nobody knew what to say. Olivia broke the silence.

'We could visit your house sometime during the half-term break, we could all go with you for a walk with Suki, make her laugh a bit. Keep her well wrapped up and just chatter around her.'

Ranjita's large brown eyes seemed to open up more expansively. With a sudden look of terror. Her voice was hoarse and barely audible.

'I should not have told you about Suki. My father, my brothers.'

She gulped and whispered.

'No one, no one knows about Suki.'

Ranjita sank to the ground. She started to shake and closed her eyes as tears rolled down her cheeks. The other girls had never seen someone so frightened. Olivia felt she had to say or do something for this poor distraught friend.

Thoughts raced through her head. What would mum and dad have done? She leaned forward and put her arms around Ranjita, gently cradling her in her arms. The other two girls stroked her head.

The moment's intensity was broken by Ruby, who wanted in on the big hug and leapt onto the girls, barking and licking faces. They all ended up in a heap on the damp grass. Ruby bounded off into the woods.

Olivia turned to her little friend.

'We won't say anything. Come on, we've got to catch up with Ruby. Your dad will be here soon to pick you all up. Race you to that oak tree in the clearing. Guarantee Ruby's gone under the brambles.'

For culturally inexperienced young girls in matters far beyond their years of understanding, Suki was put out of their minds for that moment.

Ruby had disappeared under the briars, which meant they had to take a route around the bushes to get to where she was heard barking. The ground was boggy, squelching as Harmony and Suzi raced ahead, with Livia pulling Ranjita behind her.

Poor Ranjita tripped over the uneven roots. As she fell, she badly grazed her knees. Then to Olivia's horror, there in the middle of the clearing was that same familiar sight she had seen a few weeks previously. A large hanging dead crow, swinging from black twine high up in the oak tree. This time, fresh blood dripped from its feathers, and as it swayed, it twitched. Harmony and Suzie held each other and looked on with disgust. Ruby leapt up towards the crow, then sensing a new smell on the ground, followed her nose along a few feet towards a heap of twigs and ash. Olivia quickly attached Ruby's lead. The ashes and cigarette ends were piled together. The ground beyond the ash was churned with deep tracks from some heavy vehicle that had recently been there. Next to the ash was a small penknife and a few shaved shards of wood and black cord. The air was heavy with the smell of diesel, and a strangely sweet, woody odour caused Livia to wrinkle her nose and feel a sickness in the pit of her stomach. Ruby yapped then, sniffing the air, barked loudly. Remarkably Ranjita appeared the most composed, even though she had tripped and her knees were bleeding.

'This is not a nice place to be, that poor bird. Someone has been here recently. I think we should get back to your house Olivia. I don't like it here.'

As they turned to head home, standing watching them, was the boy Sebastian. His eyes scanned the girls clustered together. His mouth parted into a dazzling smile as he looked at them kindly. He looked beyond them towards the crow and the pile of cigarette ends.

'Oh my goodness, that's not very pleasant. You poor girls, I was just on my way home, cutting across from school and heard you all in here. The dog, barking, wondered what was going on. Are you okay?
You're not, are you?
Come on, I'll walk with you back to your house, honestly, no trouble. I'm sure I've seen an old tramp poking around here. You never know who might be around.'

As they all started to walk away, two boys about the same age as Sebastian appeared, coming from another direction. Trailing behind them was a much smaller boy, scruffy ginger-haired, with his hands in his tatty jeans pockets. Sebastian waved to them and shouted out:

'Hi there, I was just helping these young girls back to their homes. Well, Olivia Hadleigh's home.'

He stressed the word 'Hadleigh'. The older boys sneered at him, pushing their hands into their pockets. They stood, arms folded and feet firmly planted in the squelching mud, blocking his path. The younger boy caught up and bumped into the back of the older ones, nearly pushing them into Sebastian. He glared at them, prodding them in the chest.

'See you both tomorrow at school.'

His voice lowered.

'Get Squirt out of here fast.'

Sebastian stared hard at the boys and then brushed them aside. Turning towards the girls, he beckoned them on in front. Olivia hurried forward. She wanted to loiter in the boy's company only as long as necessary. As she glanced back, one of the boys pushed a packet into Sebastian's pocket as they moved away. The ginger-haired boy went to speak but was dragged away quickly. The path home was just a few hundred yards ahead, and Sebastian made a great deal of being their escort, appearing to take care of them. He mainly focused on little Ranjita, who looked a bit shaken up.

They arrived at the open kitchen door of their house. Sebastian helped Ranjita inside and immediately went for cold water and a cloth for her knees. Briddy appeared; she stopped as she saw Sebastian and looked at Olivia.

'Oh, this is Sebastian. He walked us back from Eatonwoods. Ranjita fell on the roots.'

The kitchen had become very crowded as Richard Hadleigh entered the back door.

'What's all this commotion? Thought I had left the schoolroom.'

His eyes glanced over towards Sebastian. His face became

stern.

'What are you doing here, Routledge? You left your drama group some time ago?'

For the first time, Sebastian seemed unnerved, then, regaining his usual confidence, nodded towards his headmaster. Explaining after drama practice he happened to be taking a shortcut through the thicket when he found the girls. He quickly made his excuses and left speedily through the back door.

After the parents had collected the girls to take them home. Richard took Olivia to one side in his study. He had the stern look of a school headmaster about him as he seated her opposite the other side of his desk.

'So tell me, Olivia, what was that young man doing in our kitchen this afternoon? How do you know him?'

Olivia began to puzzle over how they had all ended up together. She had definitely not invited him along with them. She absolutely did not like or trust him, yet somehow, he had wheedled his way into her life on several occasions. An anxious sick dread filled her stomach.

'He was there in the woods when we found another one of the dead crows. Ruby was making a racket. The other girls were a bit scared. Ranjita had fallen, and he offered to help us home. It was a bit strange for him to be there. Two other boys turned up, no three— a small, scrawny ginger-haired boy. Sebastian seemed to order them away from us. He just took over.'

She shuddered as she remembered the package that had changed hands. Her brows furrowed as she raised her eyes towards her father. Should she tell him what they had found in the woods? What was it about this boy she feared?
Glancing towards the window, Richard continued.

'I'm keeping my eyes on this Sebastian and his group of friends. Apparently, I hear from his drama mistress that in this production of Macbeth he's excelling. However, this group of boys turn up whenever there's a bit of a disturbance. Routledge looks pretty personable when he's in adult company and always has a good excuse for his actions. Nevertheless, I want you to steer clear of him, Olivia.

And you say another dead bird was hanging in the woods, and these other boys, what were they doing there?'

'Yes, half-dead, poor thing—twitching, swaying on the black cord. Then Ruby sniffed out a pile of ash, cigarette ends, a penknife and black twine. That's when Sebastian appeared.

I think he was watching us. Then the other boys turned up.'

Olivia hesitated. With wide anxious eyes, she carried on.

'One other thing, I'm sure they put a package in his pocket. He brushed them aside and took over, helping Ranjita get back home. Ruby was going mad, pulling at the lead, barking, sniffing at the air.

There was a strong smell in the air. The same one we get when the lorry comes to deliver the coal. The ground was all churned up too.'

Richard turned towards Olivia.

'You know, don't worry about all these dead animals and this boy Sebastian. Just keep clear of him and his company. In fact, I don't want you to go into Eatonwoods and the thicket with Ruby for the present. Until this business of the dead animals and a few other unexplained things have been sorted out.

Now, I've a couple of phone calls to make before dinner. Let mum know I will be along in about half an hour.'

Olivia dawdled outside the study door as she heard the phone click. She heard him ask for 'Detective Brockett'. The conversation was muffled. She only caught snippets, but enough to know that something was under investigation at the school. Dead animals, cigarette packages, and Eatonwood were mentioned. There were minutes of silence, interspersed with the words 'leaks and lead missing'. Then finally, she heard her father say.

'Okay then, I will see you tomorrow.'

Her mind raced over the events of the last few days. She thought back also to the missing items of Roman jewellery. She would have one last scour of her bedroom. If she still couldn't find them. Livia would report it when the police came the following day. She quickly ran up the stairs and, taking the black note pad started a new page at the back, writing out as many details as she could remember. The name Sebastian seemed to connect with all the unexplained occurrences. Her Father was suspicious enough to ask her to avoid him. She wrote in large letters - Lead and leaking roof. The ginger-headed boy, was he Squirt? Where had she seen him before? It came back to her. The school ties at the outfitters, the scruffy boy smearing the glass cabinets, shoplifting. Was something happening at the school?

Livia, too, was intrigued by the mention that Sebastian was involved with the Macbeth production. Her headmistress told them they would all see the play at Blackstone School. She shivered as she thought of Sebastian. His ability to act out a part, so charming one moment and the next, cold and calculating. What would his character expose about his hidden capabilities if he were in the upcoming production? The call of Briddy to dinner broke her line of thought. Snapping the notebook tightly shut, she left it for a later, more in-depth study under the covers before sleep. One last look for the bangle produced nothing.

The next day, Saturday brought a police car to the house. Olivia watched from her bedroom window and then sat on the stairs hoping to hear the conversation. To her surprise, her dad called her into his study. Two men were with him. One of them, facing the window, blocked out all the sunlight. She saw the back of a broad-shouldered, rain-coated man. He turned and looked down at her. His glasses accentuated the dark staring eyes. Olivia half expected him to clap her in handcuffs and cart her off to jail. His voice, however, was totally at odds with his intimidating appearance. He spoke with a soft lilting Scottish accent and smiled at her. His thick bushy eyebrows raised above the rims of his spectacles with surprising independence from each other.

'I'm Detective Inspector Brockett. I understand you are

Olivia. Been some funny unexplained things going on recently. Your Father has told me you may have seen things that could help us with our investigations. Now, young lassie, I understand you were in the woods yesterday. Tell me what you saw there?'

Olivia looked across at the two policemen and her Father. He nodded for her to speak.

'Well, I was in Eatonwoods with my three friends and my dog Ruby. She ran off and started barking from the thicket, so we all traipsed through the mud and there hanging from one of the trees was a semi-dead crow. It wasn't completely dead this time, just like I saw a few weeks ago. Ruby went mad, leaping up, then darted off again, sniffing a scent along the grass. I followed her. There was a pile of cigarette ends and some black twine, and the turf was churned up all around us. I grabbed Ruby, and then this boy we've met before, Sebastian, turned up and offered to bring us home. He helped Ranjita as she had fallen over. We came home.'

'Was there anyone else around that you saw in the woods?'

'As we were leaving, two boys who knew Sebastian Routledge appeared from the trees. They came over to him. I think they gave him something, he put it in his pocket. Oh yes, and a smaller boy, I've seen him before, scruffy ginger-haired he turned up, bumped into them. No one else was around. We tried to get home as quickly as possible.'

Richard spoke:

'Routledge was in my kitchen when I arrived home. He made some excuse about cutting through the woods to get home. I know he left the school drama practice at least an hour before. Goodness knows what those boys had been up to in the woods.'

The inspector with the independent animated eyebrows turned back towards Olivia.

'Well, thank you, Olivia, for all your help. Is there anything else you want to tell us?'

Olivia took a deep breath, looking anxiously at her Father and continued:

'It's my Roman jewellery. It's gone missing from my

bedroom. The other night I put it on the window cill and took a photograph of it. Now it's nowhere to be found. It was a present from Aunt Geraldine. It was to be my new project. Finding out where it came from. Dating it and discovering who the inscriptions were about. I left my window open. I feel awful.'

The inspector raised his eyebrows and looked kindly at Olivia.

'I will have a little word with your father about this new incident. Don't you go worrying about this matter now. A few items have been recently reported missing from kitchen window cills and open bathroom windows. We take everything seriously. You let me have copies of the photographs of the jewellery, and then I can put it all on record. We will deal with the school first today.

Let the wee lassie go now, Mr Hadleigh. My sergeant, Conway, and I would like to visit the school with you and the caretaker. You can show me around. We need to look at the roof. Saturday will be a quiet time, Yes?'

Richard turned and unhooked the school keys from the wooden board. Olivia was trying her hardest to think of an excuse to go with her father as she watched them walk up the driveway. She glanced around his study and saw two Yale keys with labels on the hooks. Written in large scrawly letters, 'Bike Shed' and 'Attic Rooms'. She grabbed them along with her old duffel coat off the hall stand and waited a few moments at the back door, hoping to give them all time to be inside the school before she arrived, allowing her to follow behind without being detected straight away. She hoped to creep along to listen and then, if she was seen, she had the excuse of bringing them the keys they might need. The large entrance door had been left open at Blackstone School.

Olivia slipped into the hallway. The imposing oak staircase with its sweeping balcony stretching around the first floor never ceased to make her feel small. The familiar smell of pencils and stale cabbage filled her nostrils. She craned her neck, tilted her head to one side and then paused to listen. Where were the voices coming from? She could hear her father's and the soft Scottish accent of the inspector coming from the upper corridors. Olivia bounded up the stairs stopping at the landing to focus on the direction of the voices. If she could stay within hearing distance, just close enough but not too near to be detected. She could work out what was being said. There was a metal clanking as something scraped across the wooden floors. Then clearly, she heard her Father.

'So, these are the buckets we had to temporarily put out to collect the water. See the staining on the ceilings. It must have been dripping for at least two weeks before the term started. With all the rain we had in early September. Someone has been busy taking the lead systematically. We only noticed the damage when we opened up these rooms. We will have to go up through the attics onto the roof behind the parapets to show you what's missing. The insurance assessors are coming out on Monday. If you follow me, there's a narrow back staircase we can all go through.'

Olivia immediately grabbed the moment, if she followed them up the staircase, that would be her best opportunity to offer the keys, and if she was quiet, maybe she could discreetly follow.

'Cooee, Dad, it's me, Livia. I thought you might need these keys to get into the attics.'

The inspector looked at Richard before turning to Olivia with a wink.

'Ah, you're a bonny wee lass, one step ahead. That's always a good place to be in life. I could do with someone like you on my side.'

Olivia beamed as they took the keys from her. No one appeared to notice as she followed behind onto the flat roof. Richard pointed to the bare places where vast folded pieces of lead had protected the gables. Twisted, thin metal strips remained where the large flat sheets had been cut from the roofing planks and pulled away. The inspector whistled as he surveyed the bare wet wooden boards exposed and darkened by the rain.

'This is a substantial theft, Mr Hadleigh. No wonder you have those huge leaks now. It looks like they used some kind of shute over this parapet to send the lead down this back way. The stonework is all damaged. Ahh, they even left a few tools. Conway, bag these up. I'm not hopeful as it looks like this work was done a few weeks ago, but you never know, we might still have a fingerprint or two.'

His eyes followed the shallow tracks of churned-up grass as he leaned over the stone parapet. He pointed ahead.

'We need to get down there and look at those treads. I guess someone used a wheelbarrow to transport the lead towards those woods and then met up with a heavy transport vehicle. Conway, get forensics on to it. Where does this rear entrance lead beyond those trees, Mr Hadleigh?'

'Well, that's the back of the school, kitchen stores, and that leads to a track. We often have cross country along that route, so it goes through to Eatonwoods, then there's access to the lane and back towards the main road.'

'We will bag up all this stuff here and be on our way, for now, Mr Hadleigh, unless there's anything else you can think of that could help us?'

As the inspector spoke, he looked from Richard to Olivia and fixed her with a firm gaze. Olivia had been scanning the roof. Walking close to the damaged parapet, she had caught sight of tufts of black twine attached to the rough stonework. Was it worth mentioning, or keep it to herself? She decided to speak up.

'I'm not sure if it's anything, but you see all these tufts of black twine. I think it's the same, like the black thread I saw the first time I found the dead crow. It was all tangled up in this kind of twine, and then just the last time we came across the dying crow, it was tied up with the same cord. There were pieces of it by the ash pile in the woods too.'

The inspector beckoned to Conway, who packed the threads into an evidence bag. The two policemen took themselves and their bags down the narrow stairs. Bumping and squeezing through the narrow passageway. Olivia wanted to giggle as she saw the tops of their heads disappearing and bobbing, along with lots of huffing and puffing. Plenty of jottings for her notebook after this morning's discoveries.

Her black book already had three lines of enquiry for her fertile mind. Firstly the history and mystery surrounding her aunt and her long-lost uncle Archie and his possible nefarious activities in South Africa. Secondly, the missing Masaccio paintings were the most thrilling, as she now had a photo of what to look out for. Now the third investigation close to home, unanswered questions about this strange and unnerving person Sebastian Routledge, the package, the black twine, and the stolen lead from the school roof. Her missing jewellery. Olivia shuddered. This could prove to be the most dangerous and scary. She thought of the great strength of her Aunt Geraldine, being sent on secret missions, clandestine spying, had her life started to take an unexpected new turn? Could she be uncovering a mysterious crime or finding something that had been hidden for years? Her mind raced along with the butterflies somersaulting happily in her stomach.

One week after the visit of Detective Brockett, Richard was informed that arrests had been made and lead retrieved. A large lorry had been confiscated one foggy dark night, travelling very hesitantly and slowly along the A4 towards London. The back lights had not been working, and a routine stop by a police motorcyclist had caused two shady characters to leap out onto the grass verges and attempt to run for their lives. The more portly of the pair had fallen over as he tried to climb a gate, and a very agile and keen young constable, quick to react on his first arrest, had grabbed him by the scruff of his neck and flattened him to the ground in a bold rugby tackle. Not knowing why the pair had been so quick to run off had alerted Constable Havers to call for backup.

Flashing lights and two police cars soon arrived. The filthy white van was in deplorable condition. The rear left light was smashed, the number plate held together with wire, and upon opening the creaking back doors, it was evident a vast, heavy stash of lead in various states of age and condition was why the van had been travelling so slowly. The snivelling mud-stained and very winded man Havers had flattened now protested his innocence. He had no idea of what they had been carrying.

'I'm just a driver.'

So the unravelling of the missing lead case began. Further arrests were made in London as the two squirming delivery men opened up about their accomplices amongst the criminals and gangs of east London. The daily tabloids carried articles on the Newnham gang operating from East London for a couple of weeks, with photos of various members, their families, and wives and girlfriends. It was to be sometime before any of the Hadleigh's understood the full extent of the theft, the dead animals, and maybe never the school's full involvement. However, one thing happened: there were no more thefts of lead from any roofs in the Beaconsfield area and no more occurrences of deaths of crows or kittens. There was no sighting of the stolen Roman jewellery.

These events coincided with the most outstanding performance of the Blackstone Manor Boys' production of Macbeth. Sebastian Routledge took the part of a sinister but electrifying Macbeth. Every nuance of emotion he portrayed, from evil murderer to lover and manipulator of others' fates. The drama teacher acted as his conniving wife. All eyes were drawn to Sebastian. If not in awe alone at his acting, there was a spine-chilling fear; it was all for real. Not only did the girls at Lady Clara Backsley Grammar school get to be transported, terrified and spellbound at the evening's theatrical spectacle, also, members of the public were invited. A celebrated art critic from a national newspaper was there, Barney Grey. He lived in Beaconsfield, and that same week, Constance Grosvenor, director of the National Theatre, was staying over with her family. Hence this insignificant town production hit the national newspapers, and very quickly, Sebastian Routledge was whisked away to begin a new life and possibly freedom from further investigation into his association with criminal or cruel activities in the sleepy town of Beaconsfield. He was given a full scholarship to the Royal Arts Academy for his next four years of schooling, with every prospect of continuing to be signed up for national productions.

 Richard Hadleigh heaved a massive sigh of relief as he sat in his office, running his fingers through his already greying hair. The boy Routledge was gone, no longer his worry or responsibility. His school had been preserved from scandals regarding its pupils. They had been well compensated for the stolen lead. The roof was repaired, and the boys all seemed to settle down. Feelings of fear amongst them had quieted. Even young Edward Squires, the ginger-haired scruffy 'Squirt,' had settled down to his studies with a new sense of confidence about him. The boys he had followed around, and previously appeared to be scared of, now seemed to have a new respect for him and no longer bullied or pushed him. He had newfound respect shown toward him. Whatever it was, Squires knew about them, they cautiously kept their distance. One turn of his head with a fixed stare, they quickly ran in the opposite direction.

Most nights over the dinner table, Richard passed on to the family any new information he heard from the police. On one of these nightly discussions, her dad browsed through the paper. He suddenly jumped up and whistled out loud.

'Well, look at that. Isn't this the mother of that Routledge boy? Marrying a Mr Harry Newnham of Penge, South London?'

Olivia rushed over behind her Father.

'Where, let me see, Dad. Oh my goodness, she looks similar to the woman we saw in the shop buying ties. Yes, it is her. Wow! the connections with the Newnham Gang dad. That horrid boy, his mother. I wonder if we will ever know? '

That night holding her pen to her cheek, balancing the little black notebook on her knee, she smiled to herself and placed the photo of the new Mrs Newnham and newspaper cutting inside the pages marked 'The missing lead and bird investigations'. Sebastian connected.

So one of her mysteries she could successfully bring to a conclusion or a temporary halt in the investigation. Yet, she would leave a couple of blank pages just in case. A big question mark was still placed over the words Roman jewellery. That mystery was still clouded over with unanswered questions.

CHAPTER 6

'There are so many little things which make life beautiful.'
Happiness
Ella Wheeler Wilcox

Beaconsfield, Slough and Amritsar. 1968-1974

The trail of the missing Masaccios went distinctly cool over the next few years. Aunt Geraldine had spoken with the photographer and was convinced that if his memory had been more precise, they could have tied up more evidence with the Villa Battista, the missing paintings and their disappearance during the war years. All that Geraldine could get from Mr Castle was a copy of a black and white photograph of him on crutches with three other men all smiling on board a ship leaving Naples. The kind doctor, a Dutch officer and an American friend he made whilst onboard the repatriation ship. Geraldine took the battered photograph and turned it over; the names David, Stan, Luc and Manny were written in smudged ink. She scrutinised the photo again and asked him which one he was. Scratching his head, he puzzled:

'I wish I had a better memory of those events as we were evacuated from the hospital. Sorry I can't be more helpful. That's me, David, Stan was the English doctor, Luc the Dutchman and Manny, our American friend.
Every time I see the photograph of the stolen Masaccios, I'm sure I have seen them.'

Geraldine didn't think she would get much more helpful

information from him. Then it struck her a question he might be able to answer:

'Who was the person taking the photograph Mr Castle?'

He smiled at her with a dreamy look in his eyes.

'Ah, please call me David. That certainly sticks in my memory. One of the nurses. She was beautiful, elegant, and brilliant, not your standard nursing auxiliary. Venetia Bourne, we were all in love with her. None of us got anywhere with her. She only had eyes for the officers and particularly Stan, the doctor. I wonder what happened to her?'

Olivia frequently visited her aunt whenever school holidays came around, spending time together looking at Geraldine s collections and discussing art and history. Still, Geraldine always hesitated when the conversations slid towards her clandestine work during the war. Olivia sensed her reluctance to talk about the infamous and shady character of uncle Archie. The pages of the little black book remained blank but were never completely forgotten.

Olivia worked hard at school, Ranjita and her became inseparable. The winter months moved along, and Ranjita invited Olivia to her home. The family celebrated Diwali, and Ranjita desperately wanted to welcome her friend. Richard took Olivia to Slough, hoping to meet up with Ranjita's parents and to make sure Olivia was in safe company.

After the country lanes of Beaconsfield, Slough had long rows of similar houses. The Slough Trading Estate sprawled out in front of them, and turning off the main road, Richard found number 12 Farnham Common Close. It was a bay fronted 1950s semi-detached house, concreted up to the front door and decorated with flashing lights around the windows and porch.

Ranjita was seated at the front window looking out for Livia. She rushed to the hallway. Nervously standing behind her father and brothers, they opened the front door to their guests. Mr Singh was about sixty years of age. He wore a deep blue turban, and his three sons wore orange turbans. He respectfully welcomed Richard to his home and invited him in for tea and sweet cakes. Mr Singh spoke little English, so the eldest son Jamal translated. They talked of his work at the airport and Ranjita's school. The father was very proud of his children. He prompted his sons to tell Richard they would be moving house shortly to the outskirts of Slough. They were building a much larger home for extended family members coming to live with them. Jamal was at university and training to be a pharmacist. Sanjib was going to be a doctor. The younger boy Aasha who was about twelve, sat sullenly by his father.

Aasha folded his arms, glaring at the visitors; his right hand kept moving in and out of the folds of his sleeve. Olivia sat quietly beside her father. She noticed this movement, and suddenly, the older brother poked Aasha in the ribs with his elbow. A clattering sound and glint of shiny metal shot under the table. Aasha was restrained by his older brother whispering into his ear. He sneered at him and slumped back into his chair. Small sweet cakes were offered around, teacups passed along and Olivia bit into the square yellow cake. After the first sweet sickly taste, she crumbled it onto her plate. Livia looked around the room, longing to see Ranjita and hoping to catch a glimpse of Suki. The older women sat huddled together at the far end of what would once have been the dining room, now knocked through into the front room with the bay window looking onto the concrete and road. Richard quickly grasped that education and status were held in high esteem by the Singh family, and for the sake of the friendship of the two young girls, he spoke of his own work and years of study at Oxford University.

Mr Singh signalled Olivia to go over to Ranjita, sitting at the other end of the room with her mother and aunts. The older women of the household jabbered away in a strange tongue, conversing with each other, nodding, pointing and staring at Olivia. Ranjita took Livia to one side of the room, where brightly coloured posters of Indian gurus were displayed on the walls. She drew Livia towards them and spoke to Olivia in English with their backs to the others.

'These are the gurus of my family religion. Many of the women here bow to them in the mornings. I don't; I think they are just colourful posters. We don't really know what they looked like, the old gurus. I look forward to having my own choices about who I worship, but I must keep my voice low as my older brothers understand English well, and I'm not permitted to speak out against the family traditions. Let's pretend we are looking intelligently at the pictures. We can talk about other things quietly together. They will never know.'

She said all of this with a cheeky smile on her face. Olivia immediately entered into the spirit of the conversation. She longed to ask more about the boy Aasha because, sure enough, as she looked back, there, hidden beneath the low table, caught in the deeply patterned carpet, was a long thin dagger-like knife. Ranjita seemed to instinctively know what had passed and took hold of Olivia's arm and steered her away from the men and back towards looking at the wall posters. The warning look on her face was enough to signal to Livia this was not the moment to ask too many questions. Quietly they spoke together of their school and the exciting books they had read.

Along with a nudge, wink and a smile, she asked if Ranjita would like to spend some time at her house over the weekend. She loudly suggested doing some homework together. Ranjita was delighted and spoke in Punjabi to her mother, who looked anxiously across at the father. Olivia asked her father to ask permission from Mr Singh. He nodded his agreement and thanked Richard. He would drive over the following weekend with Ranjita, and she could stay until Sunday afternoon. Ranjita looked at Olivia, her eyes full of happiness, along with disbelief her father had agreed. She was bursting to let out a whoop of delight but somehow managed to contain her excitement. She was being allowed to visit a family outside her immediate relatives. Her mind raced with the possibilities and freedom for a whole weekend.

Suddenly there was a loud thud on the ceiling. The older women rushed out of the room and up the stairs. Ranjita looked at Olivia with wide-eyed fear in her eyes. She held her finger to her lips in a gesture of silence.

The following weekend was the beginning of some of the most enjoyable times for Ranjita and Olivia. They shared their hopes, fears and dreams. Forging a bond between them of understanding and friendship, they progressed together in their studies at school. Olivia found History and Latin more and more exciting. She excelled with a natural talent for studying ancient antiquities. Over the next four years, Ranjita spent one weekend a month at Olivia's house. Revelling in the lively freedom of expression the family mealtimes allowed. At first, she was shy and reticent, sat quietly listening as the family talked, contested and wrangled issues of the day and the world beyond. Gradually she found new confidence and enjoyed the encouragement given to debate with Richard Hadleigh about politics and women's rights. She became a keen conversationalist and formed solid opinions and logical thoughts on the rights of the vulnerable in society. Ranjita decided to champion the poor. She would study to become a lawyer. When Olivia was fifteen, her obvious choices for university were to study Ancient History and Latin. The two girls talked together about trying to get into the same university that offered their chosen courses. They both worked hard at their pre 'O' level subjects, and their school reports reflected the mutual encouragement they gave each other in their endeavours.

During the summer holidays of 1972, Ranjita informed Olivia her family would visit relatives in India for six weeks. Upon Ranjita's return, they would send off to all the universities to get prospective courses to attend the same university when they had completed their A levels. As young teens, this seemed such a long time to be parted. They both dramatically vowed to write and made an emotional pact their friendship would never die.

Ranjita telephoned Olivia the day before she was due to leave Heathrow airport. To Olivia, she sounded sad and spoke in a distant, quiet voice.

'I can't speak for long. I'm on my own now. There is so much going on. Jamal is taking us to the airport tomorrow. Aasha gets morose daily, and I think they have to medicate him to prevent his convulsions.'

Ranjita lowered her tone even more, and the increased urgency in her voice alarmed Livia.

'I spoke to Dad boldly yesterday about my prospects of becoming a lawyer and representing the family in international human rights in the future. I've never spoken up to him before on these matters. He just flew at me in a great rage. Livia, he raised his hand to my face; he silenced me. Told me to know my place and duties as a woman. For the first time in my life, Olivia, I fear my future. Please, please write to me whilst I am away this summer. You are my only friend and will be my lifeline. I have posted a card with a post office address in Amritsar. I may be able to collect my mail from there. I will send word when I can. Here the whole household seems to be in turmoil. We are taking so much luggage it's as if we are going away for months, not just weeks. Mum's spent a fortune on new suits for us all. Gifts for all the relatives in Amritsar, we will be dripping in gold. It all seems pointless when we could be helping out the less fortunate than ourselves. When will I ever be free of all the family trappings and inconsequential nonsense of tradition and duty? I can't speak anymore. There's a car arriving. They are all coming home. Olivia, please, please write. Goodbye, dear friend.'

The telephone clicked, and the call ended. Livia felt a sickening dread sweep through her stomach. What did all that mean? Ranjita sounded genuinely, deeply worried. Had her father really taken his hand to Ranjita's face? Livia ran to the mailbox to see if the card had arrived with Ranjita's forwarding address. The box was empty. In the meantime, Livia wrote in her diary all the events Ranjita had related to her. She then composed an upbeat letter of encouragement to Ranjita, which she would post just as soon as the address arrived.

Over the next few weeks, Livia posted five letters to the Amritsar postal address she had been sent. She anxiously awaited replies, but nothing came. On the sixth week of the school holidays, Livia telephoned the home of the Singh family in Slough, hoping for news of her friend's return. The number she dialled just had a continuous tone. Repeatedly the same long ominous tone occurred. Livia told her mum the entire account, from the first anxious conversation she had received from Ranjita to the last phone call to their family home in Slough. Her mum reassured her that there was probably some reasonable explanation. Maybe they had completed the move to their new house in Farnham Royal, they had been building for a few years, or possibly the line had changed whilst they were all in India. She would speak to Dad that evening, and they could drive over and pop a letter through the house door in Slough.

They arrived that evening at 12 Farnham Common Close. A different picture from the first time they visited confronted them. Now weeds grew between cracks in the concrete drive. Dustbins were piled high with rubbish. They walked up to the dusty, cobweb covered front porch and knocked on the door. An ominous hollow sound of emptiness echoed out. Livia stood nervously behind her Dad. The windows were all tightly shut, and the curtains pulled across untidily. Richard Hadleigh rapped the letterbox several times; he leaned forward, lifting it slightly. The hallway was piled up with letters and newspapers; there were no pictures on the walls. The hall stairway was bare of carpet.

'Livia, there is no one here; the house is empty. They must have moved to their new house. Let's try next door. They may be able to help us.'

They spoke to the elderly couple living next door. Mr and Mrs Abbott.

'We keep ourselves to ourselves. Not ones to interfere in other people's business. Nobody has been about for five or six weeks. Before they left such a lot of noise and drilling work, a significant new concrete patio was laid out. At least it tidied up that weedy garden, all overgrown it was. Then a big removal lorry came, took all day for the furniture to be uploaded. Sorry, don't know where they all moved to. Mr Singh had left with them all five or six weeks earlier. I think they had a big family wedding to attend in India. Mr Singh gave us a gift of Indian sweets before they left.'

Mrs Abott pursed her lips together, folding her arms and looking across at Olivia, she said.

'Nice young girl they had about your age, what was her name, Anita, or something like that, pretty girl, long dark shiny hair. Always spoke to us, spoke good English. Shame we couldn t talk to her Mum and Dad. The only girl in the family, the rest of them boys. All going to do well in the world, they said, the boys, I mean. Not much of a life for the girl, married off to someone they'd never met before, stuck out there in that hot country. Well, must be off now, got to get the dinner on the go.'

Mr and Mrs Abbot closed their front door. The conversation had raised more alarm and worry for Olivia. What had become of Ranjita? Why had she heard nothing from her friend? Would she ever see her again? Was Ranjita the young woman who had been married off? Why had the Abbots said that 'Anita' was the only girl? What about Suki? How could she find the answers to these worrying questions? Her Dad saw the concerned look on Livia's face. It reminded him of a few years earlier when her best friend Mandy had left and gone off to London, promising to write, and after the initial first exciting letter, not a word was heard from her. Poor Olivia had a raw deal when it came to best friends. However, this situation was rather alarming, and Richard felt a strong obligation not only on behalf of his daughter but also in connection with the fate of Ranjita. He promised Olivia he would endeavour to find out what had happened. Reassuring her they might have to wait until the beginning of the new school term, as Ranjita would no doubt be at school on the first day and have lots of exciting news to tell her about her holiday and move to the new house at Farnham Royal. Olivia must not fret but be patient, and he would do all he could to get to the bottom of this mystery.

The first day of the term came and went, and no Ranjita

appeared. Olivia went to Mrs Fallows's office at the end of the lessons. She knocked on the door and waited, formulating how she would make her enquiries. Mrs Fallows's brittle voice called out:

'Come in. Ah, Good afternoon Olivia, do take a seat. What have you come to see me about?'

'Good afternoon Mrs Fallows. It's my friend Ranjita, she's gone missing. She went to India on holiday at the beginning of the holidays, promising to write to me. I wrote five letters, but no replies. I've been to her house in Slough with my father. It is empty, all shut up, the phone line is dead, and she's not shown up today at school.'

Mrs Fallows's eyes narrowed, and she pursed her lips. Placing both of her hands on the desk in front of her, said:

'Ranjita's family removed her from this school after the end of term.

You were good friends, I know. Did Ranjita not tell you where she was going to continue her education? I believe the family was moving house. I had communication with her elder brother. It was through him all the correspondence.

I can see Olivia; this is a shock to you. Let me consider what I can do. I have an address in London for her brother, and if he wishes to let us know where they have moved to, I will let you know.'

'Mrs Fallows, I am so worried. Before she left, she was scared for her future. Those were her words to me on the telephone. I've heard nothing since that night.

We had such plans together.

We were going to try for the same university.

She wanted to be a lawyer.

I know something terrible has happened.'

Olivia began to cry. She felt dreadful, small and helpless. Mrs Fallows knew Olivia was a well-adjusted sixteen-year-old teenager and knew her father, Richard Hadleigh, professionally. Looking now at this distraught young girl. Mrs Fallows, the sensible, strict, matter-of-fact but fair headmistress, felt a worrying concern. Keenly desiring to get to the bottom of where

Ranjita was now living and being educated. She rose from her chair and gave a box of tissues to Olivia.

'Now, Olivia, let's not jump to any rash conclusions. I will make my enquiries and promise to get back to you. You are clearly distressed. I am about to leave and want to take you home in my car. Come, it would be good for me to have a word with your parents too. Let's start the new term positively. Your last year was outstanding, Olivia, and it was excellent to hear you are thinking of studying Ancient History and Latin, my favourite subjects. There is a good course at Exeter University. I studied there many years ago before doing my master's and doctorate at Cambridge. Let me collect my things together. You go now, wipe your eyes, and you look fine. I will meet you in the staff car park in ten minutes.'

Mrs Fallows drove Olivia home and spent half an hour with Richard Hadleigh in his study. Later that night, Livia's father reassured Olivia that everything would be done to locate Ranjita. Her headmistress had connections and legal responsibilities regarding the whereabouts and safety of her pupils, and he, too, as Headmaster, had authorities he could turn to in assisting Mrs Fallows if she needed help.

The weeks passed by, and no news came about Ranjita. Harmony and Suzie asked every day if there had been any news, Olivia felt powerless to assist, but her father was always on the lookout to encourage her not to give up hope there would be some news soon. He told her he was pursuing enquiries, and so was her headmistress. At the beginning of the new year, a yellowed envelope came through the letterbox at the Lodge. Briddy looked at the foreign stamp and strange script printed over the top. It was addressed to Olivia; she took it straight away to her daughter.

Livia's heart quickened, seeing the familiar handwriting of Ranjita. She scanned the pages. It was dated November 30th 1972, and read:

Dear Livia

You will have been back at school and started the new year when you receive this letter. How I miss my old life in England.

There is so much to tell you; where do I begin?

When we left England on July 6th, I had no idea what was before me. We arrived in Amritsar, a hot, dusty, filthy place crammed with people and packs of dogs freely roaming the streets. Noise beyond belief.

Our family home is on the city's outskirts but in sight of the famous Golden Temple. The house is full of relatives. I still need to find out all of the relationships. I was taken to a part of the house where my grandmother and six aunts live. I was confined there for six days without seeing my mother, father or brothers. The only means of communication was the written log I kept each day. On the seventh day, my father came to see me with my uncles and another family I had not seen before.

Oh, Olivia, it was awful. I was introduced to a young man of twenty-five named Surinder. He was the son of distant relatives living in Amritsar. He was to be my husband, and it was decided we were to marry in six days. My father took me to a room on my own with my brothers and insisted I agree, and if I did not, it would disgrace my family, and I would have the most severe consequences. I pleaded with my brothers and told them of my prospects and hopes to be a lawyer, which would bring honour to my family. My father beat me whilst my brothers held my arms. I do not remember the next few hours. Kept in a darkened room, women came and attended to my raw wounds. My mother came and wept with me. She pleaded with me to obey the family's wishes as she had done when she was only fourteen. She said the boy was from a good family and I would be well cared for.

Olivia, I had no choice, no one to help me escape, and nowhere to go. I had to agree. We were married in a ceremony which lasted for three days. Surinder took me to the house of his mother and father. His sisters and their husbands and children all lived together. We have our own room, and I am treated well by Surinder. He works away during the week in the city. He is a dentist, so one consolation, I will always have good teeth. (I am trying to keep my sense of humour, Livia). I miss you all so much. I miss your family, the free conversations we all had, your kind mum and dad, and even Tati, weird but true!! Surinder finds it strange I want to be a lawyer. He wants a wife like his mum and sisters, stay-at-home women who cook and care for children.

My immediate family returned to England, apart from two of my brothers. They live somewhere in the country, and I haven't seen them since marriage. Olivia, I do not know where Suki is now. She did not come with us to India. I dare not ask where she is. I am afraid for her. Where is she? I weep for my little sister. I have to keep my thoughts to myself and my written log at the moment. I will not give up hope one day of fulfilling my dreams and finding answers to my questions. There is so much more to life than this. I have a burning desire to help others. These women here need a voice. I have seen more than what is offered here. Please, please, Livia, write to me often, keep me sane and hopeful, my dearest friend in the whole world. Ranjita. PS - I did receive all of your letters, but only now have I been able to go out and write to you. Send your mail to the mailbox you have already. All my love and friendship...

Olivia wept as she read and re-read Ranjita's letter. Her heart went out to her dear friend, she immediately took pen to paper and wrote a long letter, full of all the local news, school, Harmony and Suzi, her mum and Dad. Her concerns and worries, but above all else, wrote of happy times, the good memories they had shared, and the hopes they both still had. She felt a strong desire to keep her friend's spirits and aspirations alive and upbeat. She discussed these matters with her mum and dad. She spoke to Harmony, telephoned her Aunt Geraldine, and showed the letter to her headmistress. Even Tati was touched and said she would do a painting for Ranjita, one of hope and courage. They would mail it out to India along with letters and photos.

The unseen forces of friendship, loyalty and love from all these various people whose lives Ranjita had touched united them. She was spoken of often. She was thought of. She was written to and always remembered. The letters to and from India accumulated, and the tender bonds of affection and understanding grew more robust and enduring. The distance of thousands of miles, the power of tradition and culture, family allegiance and deficiency of learning never crushed or extinguished the belief and burning desires Ranjita held. She wanted to study law and use it to enhance the lives of others who could not assist themselves through lack of education, ill health or simply because of where they were born.

Over the next three years, Ranjita built up the respect of her husband. She cared for all her wifely responsibilities and took a keen interest in his dentistry practice. She spoke with him intelligently about his work and the politics of Amritsar, and she read avidly the newspapers each day. She joined the University library and devoured law, economics and books on politics. When Ranjita reached nineteen, Surinder's respect and high esteem had been well established. He saw her as a great asset to his own life and gradually grew to love this wife of four years. She surprised him, she made him laugh, and he enjoyed her articulate outspokenness along with her caring ways. He listened to her heartfelt concerns and saw they could work as a team. They could work for the good of their families and others around them. Ranjita was patient and waited for the right moment to broach the subject of her attending the University in Amritsar to study law.

CHAPTER 7

'Think where man's glory most begins and ends, and say my glory was I had such friends.'
William Butler Yeats

Beaconsfield, Amritsar and Exeter University
England 1975-1976

Ranjita and Olivia started their university education concurrently in two different cultures on separate continents. Ranjita's battles had been hard-fought - prejudice against her as a young woman, family traditions and hostility from the proud men in the family had been hard for Ranjita. If Surinder had not been won over and given his support, the resistance would have been too much for her. Then to her great surprise, the publicity and strong leadership of female prime minister Indira Gandhi had finally swayed things in her favour. Ranjita had won over her fiercest opponents within the family of Surinder.

That autumn, she began to study law at Amritsar University. To Olivia's delight, she had a short crackly phone call from Ranjita just before she left home, full of excitement and optimism. Both of them garbled away like it was their first day of school. She managed to jot down a long telephone number for a contact in Amritsar. Five minutes later, the line went dead. Livia beamed as she replaced the handset. Reflecting on the heroic challenges Ranjia had overcome.

Meanwhile, Olivia's biggest quandary had been to decide which one of two places to accept, Holloway or Exeter. She wrote to Ranjita, spoke to her mum and Dad, her headmistress and had a long conversation with Aunt Geraldine. The enthusiasm and passion that Aunt Geraldine had for Exeter finally was the point whereby Olivia decided this was the place for her. In Aunt Geraldine's words:

'It's an ancient city with Roman connections, small but not tiny. Loads of history to be investigated. Interesting and picturesque places close by. Many independent shops, the University campus is wonderful darling, in its own splendid grounds and safe. The archaeology and ancient history courses are second to none. There are many guilds and societies on hundreds of subjects and activities you can join at the university. You will find the people too, relaxed and friendly, a little bit slower pace of life than London, but you have your whole life ahead to travel and explore busier cities. Just enjoy your time and immerse yourself in learning and every opportunity that comes along. I have nothing but good memories of my time there. I know it was some years ago, but I remember Exeter City with a smile on my face and many fond memories.'

That was it for Olivia. Geraldine had confirmed this was the university for her.

The summer weeks before Olivia took up her place at Exeter, Imogen returned from London for a short break with the family. She swept in like a whirlwind. Everyone was made acutely aware that she was now a RADA-trained actress. Her voice and person never seemed to have time out from drama. She spoke with projected confidence and exuberance, and the whole family were mesmerised and slightly exhausted by her gestures and extreme facial expressions. Imogen had unflagging energy and was always looking for a new 'project'. Most of the family, after breakfast, hurriedly made their excuses and slunk away to avoid her over-enthusiasm. One morning Olivia was about to escape from the table when she felt Imogen's gaze resting on her face. Imogen stared at Olivia and then raised her hand into the shape of a camera lens. It was as if she had seen Olivia for the first time. She jumped up and took hold of Olivia's profile between her hands, squealing out loud.

'Well, I just don't believe it. It's incredible, my scrawny little sister.

Under all that fly-away hair, there's a reasonably grown-up face. Olivia Hadleigh, you need my help. Come upstairs with me immediately. Now. Come on, there's work to be done. Oh, it will be such fun.'

Olivia was half dragged and pulled up the stairs to Impy's bedroom. Pushed in front of the mirror, Impy frantically brushed the hair away from Livia's face. Imogen had a knack for knowing what looked good. She had a keen eye for what was photogenic, and with narrowed eyes, she realised this ugly duckling of a sister had turned into a stunning young woman. This was the first time Imogen had ever really shown Olivia sisterly interest, so she just sat back and indulged her older sister. Imogen sighed deeply. She decided something must be done immediately. A pair of dark green velvet trousers and a light muslin embroidered blouse were dragged out of Imogen's suitcase, much more feminine and colourful than Olivia was used to wearing. This, along with a clip that kept part of Olivia's hair off her face, and a gentle dusting of blusher and mascara, transformed the gawky schoolgirl into a gorgeous university student.

Olivia couldn't believe what a difference just drawing her hair back and wearing a bit of colour could make. Imogen was ecstatic in her theatrical way. She crowed about how clever she was. Working as a model to supplement her acting career helped her to know precisely how to enhance a girl's appearance. She clapped her hands, danced around, bragging about her incredible expertise, and emptied out all her unwanted last-season clothes for Olivia to try on and take with her to university. This was a new experience for both of them and highly enjoyable. They shrieked and laughed together. Imogen's showy, comic dramatics added to the fun, and for the first time, Olivia felt she had a sister whom she liked and had something in common with. The act of Imogen showing an unselfish interest in Olivia briefly awakened a mutual understanding and an awareness of what real sisters can feel for each other.

Olivia stopped looking down with intellectual disdain, and Imogen, possibly, for the first time in her life, felt the pleasure of unselfishly giving something to someone else. She was happy and experienced the warmth of genuine family affection without any need for pretence or artificiality; this affected her mood. Imogen was calmer, and for the whole of her final evening with the family, there was an air of peace and restfulness. Richard read the paper, the Hadleigh girls all chatted together, and even Tati seemed to respond to the changed mood. She sat with her sketch pad and pencil, looking intently at Olivia. The end result was remarkable. Tati had captured the laughter in Livia's eyes, along with the glints of light and dark in her shiny hair, tied back, revealing the handsome high cheekbones and slightly parted lips on the brink of laughter or conversation. Everyone praised Tati's work. It was outstanding. They could see she really was a talented realistic artist. Usually, her work had been abstract, incomprehensible to the family. Tati appeared to take all this to heart. Over the next few evenings, Tati produced numerous sketches of the family. Catching them when they least expected to be noticed. Disappearing at the end of the week to her studio for the following week to immerse herself in her newfound passion for realistic painting. Imogen returned to London.

Moving to Exeter took place as the air changed from warm summer dryness to autumnal misty dampness. A coolness in the atmosphere and familiar feathery waves of unease deep in the pit of the stomach arrived. The beginning of new terms, new schools, and expectant changes came on the first day of September. Livia stumbled across the black notebook, stuffed amongst old socks and knickers, as she packed up her belongings. Dusting it down and flicking through the pages of her scrawls, cartoons and unanswered questions, she remembered the mysteries still unsolved: the missing paintings, her stolen or lost jewellery, Aunt Geraldine's secret past and uncle Archie. She shrugged her shoulders and carefully placed it into her rucksack with a thoughtful sigh.

Livia had said a long farewell to Ruby. The short walk through the woods now took longer than those early years when Livia remembered the galloping puppy darting and diving at the squirrels and birds. Ruby was fifteen, and her brain told her to chase the rabbits, but her poor back legs were not up for it. Now mostly sleeping near the Aga, with a wag of her tail whenever someone came over to her. She had always been amicable from her early days as a bumptious bouncy puppy, ready for a scoot across the fields. So many glad and sad times, Ruby had been there for her. The secrets that Ruby had been told could have filled a book. Livia stroked her silky ears, and Ruby rolled onto her side and flopped her tail up and down. That last evening she didn't follow Livia out of the kitchen, just settled herself down again to sleep contentedly by the warm range. Livia was glad to have that final contented memory of dear Ruby sleeping soundly as she quietly closed the kitchen door.

Halls of residence for the first year were within the grounds of beautiful parkland surrounding the campus. Marden Hall was a purpose-built accommodation housing around one hundred students. The common area felt a bit like the first day of the school term when she met Ranjita, scary, noisy and unfamiliar. The letters to India were going to be full of all these new experiences. This time, there were males and females from different nationalities and backgrounds, no neat lines, no uniforms, and no whistles and bells. She noticed spare places at a table with two distinct, brightly dressed young girls. Sara Dimmick was dressed in jeans and a gaudy-coloured tie-dye tee shirt. She appeared to be London city streetwise and not to be messed with, exuding intelligence while studying Chemistry. Next to her was Alice Henry from Peckham. Her family had come over from Jamaica in the fifties. She had been born here and was studying English literature. Alice laughed a lot, dressed in dungarees and had a bright red swirly scarf tying back her unruly head of frizzy hair. When Sara found out Alice was also from South London, she immediately softened, and their south London accents broadened. Livia sat close by, listening and smiling as they jockeyed and bantered between themselves. Alice sensing Livia watching on, welcomed her into the conversation and chatted away. Livia spoke of where she had come from and her courses. Alice was the bridge between Livia and Sara, and after a while, they all exchanged jokes. The general noise in the hall was getting louder as more students piled in to eat. Three young men came with their meals and sat next to the girls. After listening for a few minutes without speaking, the guy sitting next to Olivia turned towards her and, hitching up his tortoiseshell, thick-rimmed spectacles, offered a limp cool hand to shake.

'Hello, where are you from? I'm Tom Westerway, Cookham, Berkshire.' sounds like a familiar accent, the home counties, yes?'

He spoke with an old-fashioned pronounced English accent.

'I'm Olivia Hadleigh, Livia. Yes, live quite near you, Beaconsfield. This is Sara and Alice. It seems we're all in the same Halls this year, no doubt be seeing a lot of each other.'

Tom blushed a deep beetroot red as the other two spoke to him. Alice particularly pounced on poor Tom, asking him many questions about himself. Livia watched on and observed that Alice had a great way of asking for information in a friendly, relaxed manner, and before they knew it, the other person had divulged their complete personal details. Tom explained slowly and hesitatingly whilst fussing with his spectacles, he was studying Archeology. The specs didn't really slip down, but Tom was clearly very self-conscious and hitching up his glasses was a nervous gesture because as soon as archaeology was the topic of conversation, he stopped touching his glasses, and his words flowed. Livia knew she was going to get on well with Alice. She would be a great person to have around when the conversation dried up or with someone shy. Definitely, a good friend to have on one's side. Sitting near them was a beady-eyed gaunt young man, Robert Grey. Studying journalism from Twickenham, his Dad was already a journalist and mum a newsreader on the telly. Robert also had a way of wheedling information; his eyes keenly watched and scanned the room. He missed nothing. The last person sitting with them was John Dixon from Birmingham, a law student. His words flowed articulately and, although a bit argumentative, would be a welcome comrade to fight your corner. John loved his food. His plate was piled high with pie and chips. When Sara hadn't finished her bread, he tucked into that too. She looked a bit taken aback but grinned at him and handed over the plate.

Robert said he was off to the local. Having already checked out 'The Chancer' just a short distance away on Union Road, if they all wanted to tag along. Livia suddenly felt grown-up. Was this what being an adult felt like? A tingly feeling of freedom made her feel giddy and slightly giggly as she looked at this eclectic mix of young people. She would be making choices about new friends, places, and opinions. She made up her mind she was going to grab and enjoy every second of this new life. Alice turned back with a grin. Livia was still sitting at the table.

'You coming dreamer?'

The Chancer was popular, noisy, and packed with young people crushed against the bar. Older-looking tutors and a few dishevelled local-speaking characters were seated at the few tables. Livia watched on as each of her new friends ordered. The girls had cider, balancing the spilling glasses high above their heads. They elbowed through towards a window seat, where a few other young people were talking animatedly. Everyone nudged up to let the new ones join them. Alice straight away asked about everyone. She was very sociable and made it easy for them to butt in on the conversations. John sat next to a plump girl from Reading, Susan Smith. Her round shiny pink face glowed, and two empty cider glasses were quick to be refilled. Her whole life story spilt out into John's right ear. Her Dad was a volume house-builder from Reading. She was the first in her family to attend university, so they expected great things from her. Dad had already given her a directorship in the growing family business. She was studying marketing and economics, her words jumbled along with the hiccupping and shrieks of laughter at John's unfunny jokes. She kept repeating how nice it was to meet John, someone else who didn't mind enjoying his food and letting it show, as she good-naturedly patted his stomach. He just laughed, winked and bought her another cider.

Next to Susan sat a slim auburn-haired man with a blonde, blue-eyed dainty young girl sprawled across his knee. They seemed to be besotted with each other. After saying hello, broad Scottish accents gave their introductions as if they were on University Challenge. Montgomery Cameron studied architecture, and Gabby Fitzpatrick fine art and sculptor. Edinburgh was their home city, but now they just loved the southwest. Soon to graduate, Gabby talked exuberantly, and without taking a breath, she gushed,

'Can't wait to finish at uni.'

They had such plans, loved Devon, and had persuaded her parents to set them up with a studio. They were getting married, and Monty would practice in the same place. Livia was mesmerised; something in the back of her mind reminded her of Impy.

Just as they had all finished introducing themselves. The conversations lulled, and Livia felt tired as she looked around the crowded room. Thinking about returning to her room, her eyes narrowed as she saw a tall young man a little older than the first-year students, approaching their group. He stood a head above them all, with tanned dark European looks, his black hair flopped over his eyes. Sitting next to Monty, he saw Livia and engaged her with his mocking bright blue twinkling eyes. He immediately held out his hand to shake hers. As his strong hand grasped hers, a delicate thong of cord brushed against her index finger. A sick foreboding swept over her. What was he doing here? She held his gaze steadily and withdrew her hand as swiftly as possible.

'Hello, Olivia.'

Thinking quickly, she replied.

'Sorry, do I know you?'

His eyes, for a brief second, flashed annoyance but just as swiftly returned to their alluring blue intensity of interest tinged with humour. Livia knew immediately who he was. That sick feeling gripped her stomach. She shuddered. Sebastian Routledge, the boy, had grown into a tall, handsome young man. Olivia looked away, mustering up the most disdainful look she could find. He persisted:

'It's Seb from your father's school, remember, maybe, four years ago. You were all a bit scared, and poor Ranjita had hurt her ankle.' True, I was only there for six months, left after the performance of Macbeth. I do remember you, though, and your young friends.'

He laughed gently,

'I do hope she recovered OK. It does seem an age ago. How are you and your family?'

As Olivia gathered her thoughts and listened. She made a decision. This young man was persistent and clearly wanted to be pally towards her. Her memories of his personality and that final night's performance of Macbeth sent warning bells through her whole body. She replied.

'Yes, Sebastian Routledge, I do remember you vaguely now. Let me see. A lot of things were going on that year. There was a big investigation by the police at my father's school. The lead from the roof was stolen. The performance of Macbeth and I believe we saw the pictures in the newspaper of your mother's marriage to someone well known in London. Amazing the memory for important details and so many things we can forget. Just as well.'

Olivia stood up, and although the room was noisy and crowded, that tightly packed group surrounding the window seat was quiet as they watched the tense scene before them. Two combatants, like preying birds eyeing each other. Who would break the tension? Alice took control.

'Well, we're off now. Come on, Olivia, all that unpacking to do. Night all.'

She stepped alongside Olivia and shuffled her towards the door. Monty and Gabby followed behind them, with Sara and Tom grabbing their coats. Alice slipped an arm through Olivia's as they walked briskly along. Sara took the other one. No one said anything, but Olivia felt her knees wobble as she was supported and half-carried by her two new friends. Closely followed by three more guarding her back.

That night's sleep came quickly filled with fitful dreams. Ranjita kept calling her. Olivia couldn't find her. As she saw her, she vanished, just out of reach, being dragged away by a dark stranger. She woke up staring into the dark room. Her dreams had unnerved her. She glanced around the room, relieved no one else was there. The next day her head was thumping as she lifted it from the pillow. A heady mixture of unfamiliar cider, new friends and bizarre dreams made it unforgettable.

Work took over Olivia as she settled into a pleasant routine of lectures, reading, research, and study. To Olivia, she was living the dream. Her course took her back to Egypt and ancient Sumeria and the languages and writings of these people. Mainly her fascination and curiosity for the lives of women and children grew. There was a lot of documentation regarding the warriors, scholars and rulers, who were all men, but Olivia wanted to delve into the possibilities of discovering how life was for women and children. It was like following a faint trail, sometimes non-existent, but the pale footprints were there. As the weeks went by, she became more and more absorbed and fixated on her quest to uncover facts and proof of ancient women's words. She attended extra lectures on humanities and the languages of Latin and Greek.

Reading the notice boards, a lecture was advertised by a visiting PhD student from Pennsylvania university Archeology department. The lecturer visiting was Theodore Davidovitz.

Olivia attended and was immediately hooked on the fascinating world of archeology concerning women and the findings of ancient Rome. After the lecture, Olivia made her way to the speaker and introduced herself. He warmly shook her hand. His hands were large, and the skin felt rough but far from unpleasant. His dark unruly curls were very distracting. There was something about him that seemed vaguely familiar. She was the only female undergraduate there that day, and he asked her about her interests in the subject.

Olivia had so many questions. He was only too happy to discuss matters with this young inquisitive, decidedly beautiful student. They sat relaxed talking for some time when suddenly Olivia realised everyone else had left and she had to be at another lecture. Theo looked intently at her with kind, grey eyes. He thanked her for her support and hoped they could meet again to discuss their mutual interests. He was in the second year of his research but was planning another lecture in a month. She would be most welcome. Olivia was now getting exceptionally late for her following class, so she just flew out of the theatre, her head buzzing with new ideas. Archaeology was intriguing and thought-provoking. Along with these thoughts racing through her brain, the beginnings of an interest in a certain tall, dark, slightly unkempt but handsome archaeologist brought the raising of her heartbeat and heat to her already pink cheeks. Where had she seen him before?

Olivia spent the next couple of weeks scouring the notice boards and hanging around the archaeology department, hoping to get more information about this subject and Theodore Davidovitz. She found a pamphlet advertising his following lecture and research program at Exeter with a brief history of his academic achievements. He had taken a BA in Archeology at Pittsburgh University and spent one year in Rome and Pompei, obtaining an MA in Archeology at Yale University and was now twenty-nine, studying for his PhD in Anthropology and Archeology. There was a short note about his family. His mum was a second-generation Italian migrant whose parents had come over in the early 1920s. Theodore had been named along with his three siblings after Presidents of America, Zachary, Woodrow and Dwight. His mother was fiercely proud of her American heritage and sincerely appreciated all the presidents and the constitution of America. Theo's father was of Russian Ukraine origins. They had been bankers and, sensing the changing situation for Jews in Russia in those pre-revolutionary years, had escaped in 1910.

Theo was nowhere to be found. He seemed to have disappeared. To Olivia's disappointment his lecture was cancelled and rescheduled for three months. A damp cloud of melancholy descended on her life.

One afternoon wandering around the university took her into areas she had not been to before. The Carr Hall block was empty and unfamiliar, the corridor long and dimly lit. Overhead she heard footsteps coming down the stairs, and her heart raced as a feeling of uneasiness quickened her breathing. Darting towards the lift. She frantically tapped the open button, as she entered, she felt herself being pushed forwards as someone leaned against her backpack. A long-forgotten woody odour filled the air. Instinctively moving forward she span around, as the doors closed. There in front of her was Sebastian Routledge.

'Hello Olivia, So good to see you again.'

All the boldness she had previously displayed towards him disappeared. She was frightened of this man; he smiled at her and touched her arm. She flinched and took a step back. He leaned against the lift wall with his head on one side, his blue eyes piercing, pupils dilated dark and staring. Looking at her, his eyes narrowed as his right hand moved towards his left wrist and appeared to be twisting a thin black cord between his index and forefinger. The seconds on her watch pulsated against her wrist, seemingly slower than ever. Suddenly, the lift stopped, the doors opened, and Olivia dived with all her strength out of the elevator and through the glass doors into the fresh air and busy walkway. She ran, without looking back, down the pathway across the car park. A large black Range Rover screeched its brakes, narrowly missing her as she stumbled and fell forward onto the gravel. The driver shouted, throwing his door open. The passenger, too, rushed over. A furious Robert Grey was driving his dad's car along with Sara. Livia was out of breath and couldn't speak for a few seconds.

'What are you playing at, you little fool? You could have been killed, tearing in front of me like that.'

As he bent down, he realised it was Olivia. He could clearly see she was in quite a state and was having difficulty just getting her breath. He gently took the backpack off her and offered a lift back to their halls. Sara helped her into the back of the car. She could see Livia was greatly distressed and sensed something was wrong. What had her friend been running from? Why was she so frightened? Robert started to talk in his interrogative voice. Sara placed a hand on his knee and shook her head discreetly. He nodded. Sara took Livia back to her room, sat her on the bed and handing her a mug of hot sweet tea said.

'Want to talk?'

Olivia let out a deep breath.

'Need help figuring out where to start. You will think I'm paranoid.'

Sara sat down on the chair and took off her jacket.

'Try me.'

'Well, Do you remember the first night we were all at the pub? A guy came up and sat with us. I was quick to put him down, and we all left.'

'Yes, you seemed pretty shaken up after seeing him.'

'He was living in Beaconsfield about four years ago. Went to my father's school and was often hanging around our house. He would turn up in the woods or in the lanes and try to talk to me. Other events were going on too. I found birds strung up dead in the woods and the unexplained killing of pets in the area. I had jewellery stolen from my bedroom, it was never recovered. At my father's school, there was a huge theft of lead from the school roof. The police investigated, and subsequently, a lot of arrests were made. The local newspapers did a story connecting all the theft with a London gang. This boy, Sebastian Routledge, seemed involved somehow, but nothing was proven. There was a lot of bullying at the boy's school. After giving the most spectacular performance of Macbeth, Sebastian moved away to drama school. He just disappeared, along with his mum. There was something about him that was quite scary to us youngsters. Strangely after he left, the bullying stopped. Then the next thing we read in the papers was that his mum was marrying Harry Newnham, one of the suspected gang leaders in the lead theft. I thought I wouldn't come across him again until now. He was in the lift with me over in the Carr Hall block. He only touched my arm. I just ran when the door opened. He makes my flesh creep. That's when I nearly got knocked over by Robert. Am I going mad, imagining it all?'

Sara looked seriously at Olivia.

'Where I come from, you quickly learn to be pretty savvy about characters. I'd say trust your gut instincts. If it doesn't feel right, it probably isn't. I've had to take a few hard knocks and learned a few 'tactics' along the way.'

Sara paused, then continued.

'Look, I hope you don't think we're a bit nosey. But, after that first encounter with 'pretty boy' at the pub, Robert was sure he'd heard the name, Sebastian Routledge. He's really into finding out who and what people are about. We could see you were a bit shaken up. He was bothering you, so Robert did a bit of digging. His Mum and Dad, people he knows etc. Anyway, this Sebastian Routledge has had a checkered past. Robert's Dad was the one who wrote an article about him after seeing his performance of Macbeth. He got a scholarship to Drama school, then left after a year, not sure why. Robert's still looking into what happened. Also, if there is a family connection with the Newnhams of Penge. I've lived in that area all my life. I know you wouldn't want to mess with that family.'

Olivia put her head in her hands.

'I was so enjoying our time here. Seeing that 'person' has

unnerved me. I do not want to be around him. I don't want to be involved in anything with him.'

She looked up and grinned at Sara.

'Perhaps you could show me a few of your 'tactics', Sara. I think I must be so green and naive to you. I need to get savvy and tougher, a bit more streetwise and not such a wimp.'

Sara looked seriously at Olivia.

'You're OK, Olivia. Here, put this in you're front pocket.'

She tossed a small paper sachet over to Livia. Olivia's eyes opened wider. What was this, some dangerous secret powder? It even crossed her mind that illicit drugs would so dull her senses that she wouldn't be scared of anything.

'You get any serious bad attention, just tear this open and toss it in their face. Don't go wandering aimlessly off on your own. Stick to your classes and with crowds. With some people, you don't want to cross them. If he's close to that family you mentioned, life can be difficult. You take care now. We will be watching your back.'

Olivia turned the packet over. A big black label marked 'capsicum powder' was stuck to the front. She knew immediately how hot that was, remembering preparing a curry using the powder and then accidentally wiping her eyes. She laughed out loud.

Sara laughed too.

'Come on, this twit will not stop us from having fun here. Alice can make an amazing curry with that stuff too. In fact, I can smell that pot cooking right now. We're all piling into her room tonight. Let go party,.... girl!'

CHAPTER 8

'..The shy sweetness of meeting, the same distressful tears of farewell-
Old love but in shapes that renew and renew forever.'
Unending Love
Rabindranath Tagore

Meeting Theo again Exeter

In the dusty darkening passageway, Robert's hand shook as he replaced the handset of the payphone. He had a lot to consider. His notebook bulged with scrambled information. Was he the only person now in possession of this news? He looked furtively around him, had anyone been nearby listening in? The public corridors were empty, just the echoing sound of voices in the distance. He had managed to conceal from his father why he had been so interested in that person. He knew it wouldn't be long before his dad pieced together his lines of inquiry and discovered why he was so inquisitive about incidents that had happened four years ago. A drama student was found hanging from the bannisters at her flat. A suicide note, 'she couldn't carry on.' The sudden disappearance of members of the flat, Seb Routledge being one of those students, his connections with the infamous Newnham family of Penge. Barney Grey had quite a story. His investigative research had taken him into the dark underworld of London's ganglands, theft, drugs and prostitution, and so far, the stepson's name had only been loosely connected. Robert knew more now. His father's story

would soon be released in the national newspapers.
He closed the notebook stuffing it into his inside pocket.

Robert was familiar with the layout of Carr Hall, having walked up and down the corridors for days. Checking outside from the courtyard for the window occupied by Sebastian. Today he passed down the stairs and stood outside concealed behind a large oak tree looking up at the lighted open window. A man's figure moved across the window and leaned out. A spark of light flashed, and a cloud of pungent smoke billowed. Robert thought long and hard. He remembered, with a smile, how they caught out Al Capone. Tax evasion, not the notorious other evil crime he had committed. Now was the time for his next phone call.

Over the following days, Carr Hall was cordoned off by the Police, and several arrests were made of students possessing cannabis. Sebastian Routledge disappeared from the campus. Members of the Newnham gang were arrested along with a large haul of stolen property, jewellery and silver trophies. Rumours were that the Police had been tipped off by an unnamed undercover journalist. A few days later, a full front-page article was published by Barney Grey. The web of human trafficking, prostitution and drug distribution was all unveiled and detailed.

Olivia longed to question Robert about his father's article. Each time she tried to approach him on his own, he shrugged his shoulders and gave her a wink whilst patting his lips. Sara, too, evaded all questions but reminded her to carry the 'secret powder' with her at all times, then roared with laughter. Livia had to be content to let things lie low, happy to know Sebastian was gone. It was sometime before the nightmares subsided, and slowly her anxieties reduced.

Then news came from her parents. Her Roman jewellery had been recovered, found, hidden amongst the haul of stolen goods from the Newnham gang in London and returned by the 'Inspector with the independent eyebrows'. One set of unidentified fingerprints was imprinted on the gold bangle. There were no police records of these prints, but they would be kept on file. Olivia was relieved to have it all given back to her. The black notebook was updated. A few mysteries were being solved.

Other than for cooking, Olivia's need for capsicum powder was fortunately never required during the next few months. Her student life moved into a steady rhythm, along with various new friends, new ideas, new foods to taste, and exploring this exciting city. Life was good in Exeter. Sara and Alice became her lifelong buddies. Alice often invited them to her room for Jamaican 'rice and ting'. On a one-ring electric hob, she miraculously managed to concoct a delicious meal like they had never tasted before. The sweet smell of chicken and rice wafted through the hallways and before they knew what was happening, the friends that had joined up on Olivia's first day all squeezed into Alice's room, enjoying a spoonful of Jamaican delights. With expanding waists, Susan and John seemed to relish any food on offer, enjoying the company of each other and a free meal anytime it was offered. Monty and Gabby, too, were generous in their returns of invites to all. They shared a sizeable Victorian terrace in the city with six others. They had a decent-sized kitchen, and although Gabby was useless at cooking, they both welcomed Alice knowing she would be more than happy to cook for them all. They provided the meat and vegetables while others took a bottle or two.

Those evenings were memorable, superb, and full of fun, debate and good-natured banter. Robert always had his notebook and sketchpad. They knew he secretly wrote down the odd things said for his future best-selling novel. As the alcohol increased throughout those evenings, secrets dropped out of slurry mouths and fuzzy brains. One night, it was suggested they would tell each other a secret about themselves never revealed before. Alice was pleased to go first.

'Well, I remember going with my friend Marni into clothing shops when we were nine. We got the shopkeeper to get all sorts of odd items out for us to look at, pretending our mums had given us a list, then leaving when the counter was full of socks, underwear, and stockings, always saying it was the wrong colour, and leaving just as they were beginning to get cross. We felt very grown-up.

Once or twice it got a bit too close for comfort. My mum saw us in Coopers the wool shop. We just upped and left. That poor woman over the counter, buried in a mountain of Fair Isle wools of every colour you could think of. My mum had to go in and buy eight balls of yarn. She had never knitted in her life. Did I get a telling-off that night! Was not allowed out on Saturdays for two weeks after that.'

'What about you, Sara? I bet you've some stories to tell?'

'Well, the only one I'm prepared to own up to is once concocting a chemical solution that exploded in the school lab overnight. As a result, half the prefab block was blown apart. Caused quite a stir, I can tell you.

The Police put it down to a faulty bunsen burner leak. Never owned up to it.

There is one other. In my shed at the back of our house, I managed to get a distillery going for my grandad. He always said it was the best gin he had ever tasted. It was great fun.'

Olivia found the eclectic mix of minds and personalities hilarious and bizarre. She watched such diverse individuals' interactions and noted how some changed and adjusted. While others remained fixed and set, and nothing would alter their immovable course. She felt hopeful and relaxed, with a tingling expectation of all that was happening around her.

April brought a few days of vacation to her parent's home. She looked at her familiar surroundings differently, as if wearing a pair of magnifying glasses. Everything had changed. The front door looked shabby, and her bedroom was cluttered with childish things. She noticed the stairs creaked, her bedroom windows were baggy, and the latch rattled. Her dad looked tired, running his hands through his greying hair more frequently; he looked anxious and drawn. The house seemed quiet and old-fashioned after the noise and random colourful conversations of young adults flexing their independent voices and ideas. The hues of grey, green and faded mauve blended into an atmosphere of old dusty cupboards and childhood memories. Briddy smiled to herself as she watched Olivia. Seeing something of herself when she was that age.

'You see it all differently, Livvy? Noticing things that never were so obvious. Widening your viewpoint. It's exciting, isn't it? So come on, let's have a cuppa together. Mug or cup?'

Sitting outside the kitchen door, an early spring sun warmed the stone seat. The birdsong and smells had stayed the same. The first cuckoo sounded. They both started and excitedly burst out simultaneously, like every year,

'Hear that!'

Through the thicket, a swathe of bluebells glowed intensely, blurring into the distance, following the ancient trail path of Eatonwoods. A nosey robin beadily looked at them, tilting its head jerkily as it perched on the spade a few feet away. Livia looked across at her mum. Briddy had seen it all before. Not always the rounded middle-aged homely woman, for she too had lived through the excitement, the anxiety, the trepidation, the discoveries. It had all been done before Olivia. How foolish she felt, but only for one second. Then it all babbled out, all the new experiences the friends. Even her terrifying encounter with Sebastian, the police raids and his disappearance. The engaging lecturer with kind grey eyes and rough, strong hands, her new interest in archaeology. The more she spoke, the more she realised. She had to see him again, Theodore Davidovitz. Even his name made her fascinated and inquisitive. Her colour heightened as her hair flopped forward, covering her embarrassment and shining eyes her mum had spotted.

'I remember the first time I met your father. We talked, or rather he talked. I listened. Someone with something interesting to say. This lecturer sounds interesting, Livia?'

With a sidelong glance at Briddy, Livia laughed, brushing off any comment. Then, changing the subject, she said.

'Is Dad okay? Is it the school or something else? He looks unusually distracted.'

Briddy looked down at the pebbles. She brushed an imaginary speck from her skirt.

'He's had a lot on his mind recently. It's not just the school. There's been a police investigation involving a family we all knew some time ago. I think you should ask him yourself. It's the house where the Singh family used to live in Slough. You need to prepare yourself for some unpleasant information. Go have a chat with him. He's in his study.'

The door to the study was slightly ajar as Livia drew near. The familiar scene of her father, glasses on the end of his nose, pen poised, poring over textbooks or manuscripts. Sunlight streamed through the half-opened window. His desk was in an orderly mess, knowing exactly in which pile he had placed what he wanted. Even the storage boxes were exactly as she remembered. The perfect place she had loved to squat on, waiting to talk to him as a child. He always swivelled his chair, and she felt like the only person he had time for in the world. Not sure why, but today she knocked softly on his door. He turned, a big grin on his face.

'Ahh, my big grown-up daughter, come on in.'

He opened his desk drawer and handed her a rolled-up tissue.

 'Your treasure returned, Livia, makes you wonder what life they have seen. Ancient and modern.'

'What a relief to get them back, Dad. I don't suppose the inspector told you any details?'

'Very little, I'm afraid, said there is still an ongoing investigation, but the photos we had sent of the missing jewellery were able to identify them as belonging to you, so he was able to release them reasonably quickly. He did say, though, that they now have on record a new set of unidentified prints lifted from the jewellery.'

'That is very interesting. '

'So, How is everything with you?'

He motioned towards the boxes and relaxed back into his chair.

'I've just been chatting with mum. Bringing her up to date with all my goings on.'

She paused and looked across at his desk. All the photographs, his girls at different ages, significant occasions, her first day at high school, the baggy blazer and boater crammed onto her head. She picked it up, along with a faded one of her with Ranjita on one of the weekends spent exploring the woods together.

'I remember that day so clearly. Mum dropped me off, and I met Ranjita. You had always said I would make new friends. She really was and still is such a good friend. We write about our new lives and our uni friends. I'm so glad to have known her. I admire her courage and her tenacity. She's a fighter and will make a fantastic lawyer.

Dad, is there something I need to know about the Singh family? Is Ranjita okay? Her last letter was about six months ago. Before that, I had one crackly phone call.'

Richard sat upright, folding his hands together, his face tensed. Olivia would never forget that moment he started to relate the events surrounding the Singh house in Slough. The clouds overhead obscured the sunlight. The birds stopped singing outside as Richard closed the window and began.

The house at number 11 Farnham Common Close had been vacant for over a year after the Singh family had left. Finally, it was sold by public auction, left in quite a dilapidated state. One year's growth of bindweed and heavy dusty pollution from the traffic covered the exterior windows. Very quickly, the property deteriorated. Then a new young family moved in. Gradually they renovated, and after a few years with an expanding family, they started to build an extension at the rear. Unfortunately, the enormous concrete patio was crumbling and had to be dug over. This is where Olivia's father paused. His face took on a grim look.

'The remains of a young girl's body were buried in the

disturbed concrete. The complete account has only just been made public, Olivia. The Police had contacted me, knowing I had made previous enquiries into Ranjita's whereabouts. Your old headmistress Mrs Fallowes was also involved. It appears it was the body of a young disabled girl. A family member of the Singhs.'

Olivia stood up aghast. She closed her eyes, covering her face with her hands.

'Oh no. Dad, Ranjita's younger sister Suki? She was disabled and kept out of sight all the time. Ranjita never saw her again after she left England. Her letters have always asked where she is. How did it happen? Is there any more information?'

'I'm so sorry to have to tell you all this. The investigation was extensive.

That poor young girl had suffered severe trauma to the skull. The father and mother fled to India with their youngest son. One of the brothers, still living here as a doctor, has been tried as an accessory to manslaughter and concealing a dead body. The case was heard about six months ago. I didn't want to burden you with all the sordid details. But it appears the youngest boy became aggressive and supposedly accidentally hit his disabled sister on the head. The family found her dead and concealed the body under a mass of concrete disguised as a new patio.

Don't you remember the neighbours we went to see who said there had been a lot of construction work just after the family had left for India?

It's all quite gruesome and grisly. I'm so sorry, Livia, you've had to find this out.'

Livia's complexion was ashen; she slumped back onto the seating box. Her heart ached for poor little Suki. But her pain for Ranjita struck like a dagger. The tears streamed down her face as she sobbed into her father's shoulder. She stayed still against him for some time. No one spoke, and gradually the light changed, the clouds overhead parted, and the final rays of the late afternoon sun shone through the window. Livia sighed and wiped her eyes. She would telephone that long number in India.

Try to speak with Ranjita about anything she could do to give her friend some comfort.

That night of April 13th 1978, the TV news was full of a bloody battle that had taken place in Amritsar. The Sikh-Nirankar clashed with traditional Sikhs. Sixteen people were killed in the violence. A wave of terrorism ensued from that day. Olivia persisted in trying to place her telephone call to Ranjita. Finally, her friend's voice was clear and confident the following day.

'I'm Okay, really, Olivia. Surinder and I are away from the violence.

It's been dreadful this past year. A fire has ignited in my belly. I am disgusted with my family, ashamed, and angry. I'm determined to fight for all the causes I feel strongly about. But, Livia, we must not give in to fear or oppression. When I have finished my law degree, my husband and I will return to England, and he wants to support me with a practice in International human rights.' The line distorted and buzzed.

'Ranjita, are you still there?'

'Yes, I have to go. There is not much time left allotted for this call. There is a curfew here; we are facing difficult times ahead, my dear friend. Write to me soon. Courage!'

Click and silence.

Olivia could only imagine how difficult life was for Ranjita. That short call had filled her with foreboding for the future. She pictured the diminutive, shiny-haired young schoolgirl, tenaciously holding onto her satchel. Those weekends of Ranjita opening up and debating with her father. Her strength of character had developed, and now. What a voice she had found, what aspirations, yes, what courage, what hope. Beautiful, inspiring words, worthless without actions. She took the photo of her and Ranjita and placed it in her black notebook. This day was to be remembered, marked as a turning point in her life. No more holding back, no more shrinking away from her fears. Every opportunity to make positive things happen had to be seized.

Towards the end of the year, Olivia was sitting in the grounds of Streatham college. She had taken the afternoon off and was sitting under a huge willow tree, half-reading, half-dozing when she became conscious of a shadow blocking the warm sun on her face. Opening her eyes and dazzled by the sun directly behind the person, she couldn't determine who this tall man was. As he stooped down and sat beside her, he said,

'Hey, Olivia? I was hoping I might see you again. It's been a long time since the lecture, and for all those questions you had about archaeology.'
He leaned forwards and handed her a package.

'I've bought you a book. I hope you find it helpful. I'm sorry not to have been able to give it to you before. I've had it with me for several months. Unfortunately, I was called back home,
but I'm here now for a month before the end of term, so there should be time for one more lecture. Will you come?'

Olivia noticed he looked drawn and tired, but she remembered the kind, endearing grey eyes when he looked at her. Would he disappear again before she had followed up on her questions? Was she to him just one of many hangers-on he had following his words and thoughts?

Whatever came over her at that moment, she did not know, but she did not hold back as her mouth opened. She saw clearly what she wanted.

'You look tired, but your eyes are bright and clear, just as I remember when I first met you.'

Theo smiled, his eyes fixing her gaze. Olivia took a deep breath.

'Theodore Davidovitz, I would like to spend some time with you, not just listening to your lectures.

I like you as a person. Yes, I really like you. Now, if you think I'm crazy and want me to come and listen to your lecture, and I'm just another girl student, I will accept that. But this is a very big but. I've missed you, and I think the more I get to know you, the more I will like you. So if there is the slightest chance, you would be willing to?'

Before Olivia could utter another word, Theo leaned forward and kissed her adorable mouth ever so lightly. Drawing away, he said.

'Yes, the same. Miss Olivia Hadleigh. I think we need to spend a lot more time together, starting right now. It doesn't have to be all talking, though.

When I first met you, I was right in the middle of a paper I had to finish. You were a distraction to me, in my mind, most of the time. Unfortunately, I had to return on a family matter to the States. I was delayed longer than I had hoped, but I did finish a necessary piece of work. I didn't know your address or, even whilst in America, your surname. You were just that girl I couldn't get out of my mind. Interesting and interested in all the things I'm interested in.

Come on, we have a month from now to make up for the lost time. I want you to come down to the Quay with me. Let's walk along the towpath toward Exmouth. It's a beautiful afternoon.'

Olivia picked up her canvas book bag, popped her sunglasses on her head and let Theo take her hand towards the river.

Every afternoon at the end of lectures, they walked along the river Exe. Theo loved the river and expertly pointed out the names of the birds wading in the estuary. She was pleased to know it was 'curlews' that were the familiar birds seen from holidays spent at her aunts house.

They often explored the narrow back streets of Exeter and visited small galleries, searched along the Roman walls and traced the wool merchant's ancient pathways. Theo showed her parts of the city with his expert eye, showing evidence of Roman fortresses and mounds.

Towards the end of that month, Olivia took him to Topsham. 'Gung Ho's white facade glowed in the afternoon sun, its windows like blinkered eyelids, all shuttered up. The overhanging wisteria had entwined around the side pathway, concealing the gate onto the estuary. Olivia stood looking, smiling, as she grabbed Theo's hand.

'Come on, Theo, there's something I want to show you. We can get around and over the gate.'
They clambered over the side wooden gate and along the towpath to where 'The Topper' was moored. Livia shouted out, pointing.

'Isn't she just gorgeous?'

Olivia remembered the combination for the lock, which gave a satisfying click when it released the rope from its rings. Theo took over and expertly manoeuvred the boat across the water. Olivia watched him with a surprised quizzical look.

'You are so good at this?'
Theo laughed.

'Ah, my family. The Davidovitzs have lived in Pittsburgh State for decades. There, parks flank wide rivers, and we've a cabin on the banks of the Allegheny River. I've spent most summers with my brothers rowing and messing about in the rivers.'

Theo talked as he rowed, about his life in America, schooling, family, and how he had spent his thirteenth birthday with his uncle in Rome. His mother's family were still there, and his uncle Ernesto had been a great archaeologist. He had spent many summers in Italy with his uncle on archaeological digs. That had been the beginning of his great interest in Archeology, and he had known then that was what he wanted to be and do. Discover the work and lives of our ancestors. Like Olivia, he tried to understand their feelings, desires, needs, motives, and emotions.

They talked for hours, so attuned were their thoughts that often, before one could finish their sentence, the other knew what they were going to say. Finally, as the sun was setting, and the early English summer evening brought a distinct chill to the air. Theo rowed back to the mooring, and secured the boat. He suggested they have something to eat on the Strand before returning to the city. Theo put his arm around her slender shoulders, and Olivia rested her head against his chest with a deep sigh. As they walked along, Olivia knew he would soon return to Pittsburgh for the summer recess. For eight weeks, she would not be seeing him; she felt sick inside. She could not imagine her life without this kind, thoughtful, exciting, gorgeous man.

Would he come back? Was this the only portion of the time they would have together? Was he too old for her? Did he view her as too young for him? Olivia knew he was her soul mate, and she did not ever want to let him go away. This time though, she determined not to be the one to initiate stating how she felt. He had to do or say something. Was it the American way to be laid back? Was it his way of letting her down gently, going away, hoping she would cool off? He was so committed to his work and finishing his doctorate that maybe they would get together in a couple of years. She would have finished her BA, and he would have completed his PhD. All these thoughts flashed through her racing mind. She felt tense and agitated. Then just as they were nearing the busy bar. Theo stopped and gently turned her to face him. His eyes were bright, and searching her face, he hesitated. Stroking her hand, he said.

'I can't stand this, Livvy.

I can't leave you here in England. I love you, Livvy. This summer, someone else will snatch you up. You are the only person I have ever met that I can talk to about anything and everything. We have the same interests, and we love the same outdoor pursuits. I want to spend every moment I can with you. I can't wait another two years before I finish my doctorate and your BA is completed.'

He moved closer, wrapping her tightly in his arms and whispered into her ear.

'Marry me.

Come with me to America for the summer; we could stay at my parent's cabin on the Allegheny, return in the fall, rent a house here in Exeter, and finish our studies together. I have a small legacy from my grandmother. So if we're careful, we could manage on that.'

Olivia almost collapsed. Her legs were like jelly, her breath left her, and if Theo had not held her so tightly, she would have fallen over. All her concerns of five minutes ago evaporated. This was her man for keeps.

'Have I rushed you, honey? Take your time.'

'No, No, I mean no, you're not rushing me. Yes, Yes, please, please marry me as soon as possible.
Theo, I love you.'

CHAPTER 9

'Not a whisper, not a thought,
Not a kiss nor look be lost,'
Lullaby
WH Auden

England and Pittsburgh USA

That summer evening, when Theo and Livia made their plans to spend the rest of their lives together, was just the beginning of a mad and hectic whirlwind before they married. Livia's parents were at first amazed and alarmed. Finally, however, Theo and Livia went to visit them, and Theo won them over with his thoughtful, intelligent mind and deep love for Olivia. In fact, it was not long before most of the Hadleigh women were a little bit in love with him. Only Tati appeared to not have any interest in anyone or anything. Her sunken cheeks and transparent skin gave her a haunted and vague appearance as she looked vacantly on. Then shielding her eyes from the sunlight, she slunk away to her studio in the garden.

Richard and Briddy both took time with Livia and Theo separately. Then, having reassured themselves about Theo and being content that Olivia was wholly settled in her mind and heart, they both agreed. Get married without any fuss. As there was so little time to arrange a large wedding, it was decided that upon their return from America, they would have a celebration on the grounds of Blackstone Manor, when all the family could be present.

The next person to be satisfied was Aunt Geraldine. She spoke with Theo on her own for some considerable time, ushering him off into the garden and interrogating him for over half an hour. The Hadleigh women watched on, pretending not to be looking from the kitchen window. There looked to be a highly animated conversation going on, with mainly Aunt Geraldine taking the lead. She sat Theo on the wrought iron garden bench whilst she paced to and fro, pausing with her hands on her hips as she allowed him to answer her stream of questions. Only Olivia occasionally noticed her aunt put her hand to her stomach, and a look of pain passed over her eyes. This quickly was replaced with a stream of further questions for Theo. Poor Theo looked like he was being put through the third degree. First, he ran his fingers through his thick dark hair, then as the minutes passed, he stood up and warmly took in both his hands Aunt Geraldine's outstretched hand. Finally, they returned to the house arm in arm, where three pairs of enquiring eyes stared at them. Aunt Geraldine was the first to speak.

'Well, all seems to be settled, so far.'

She looked with fondness at Olivia.

'This young man Theodore Davidovitz loves you very dearly. You will make a good match for each other's minds and hearts. However, there is just a slight hitch to your marriage. You are British, and Theodore is American; a few hurdles must be overcome. Fortunately for you both, I still have some clout and influence at the Home Office, with whom I am frequently in close communication. Therefore I have told Theodore of all the relevant documents, i.e. birth certificates, passports, student identifications, visas etc., that are needed to process speedily your licence to marry before you go to America. All will be well with any luck and a great deal of active persuasion. Let's say the wedding can take place in four weeks.

Now Theodore, let me have your documents asap, and Olivia, I'm sure you can rally around now and give me yours. Then, I can start the ball rolling tomorrow morning. In fact, there's a couple of old cronies I can telephone tonight.'

Livia looked astounded at how her aunt had taken charge of everything and seemed to know exactly what to do. Theo seemed very quiet and slightly bewildered, looking with awe at this formidable woman, who gathered everything she requested with military precision and took off in a flurry of hugs and goodbyes to set her battle plans in motion.

The marriage licence arrived on the 1st of July. The wedding took place on the 7th in Exeter. It was a small affair, most of their friends from the university had all left for the summer break, and only Aunt Geraldine and her husband Juno were present for the short ceremony, along with a tall, distinguished gentleman who seemed to be a great friend of Aunt Geraldine. He watched all the proceedings, acted as a witness, and disappeared in a black limousine driven by a chauffeur when it was finished. Theo and Olivia hardly noticed anyone else there. They were just so grateful to be married. The small wedding party of four went back to the Topsham house Gung Ho. Uncle Juno and Aunt Geraldine stayed briefly for a light champagne lunch of lobster, fresh fruits and Devonshire cream. Discreetly leaving with the least amount of fuss. The older Spitzers left the newlyweds to themselves with the warmest affection and best wishes that only people with deep love and understanding could give.

The next three days and nights blurred together as they buried themselves inside 'Gung Ho', and a pleasing harmony grew as they shared their love of each other and gradually emerged on the morning of Tuesday to walk together barefoot on the warm stepping stones, down towards the moorings. 'The Topper' was as they had left it a few weeks earlier, and Theo rowed the little boat leisurely along the river. His eyes swept over Olivia's out-stretched long limbs and face that glowed with a permanent hint of a smile. Livia closed her eyes. As she mused, she tried to recapture and ingrain in her mind the seconds and hours they had spent here at Gung Ho. Those blissfully ecstatic first few days began the voyage of their lives together.

Their first literal 'voyage' was on Friday afternoon. The flight from London to Pittsburgh took around eight hours. Theo's family had paid for the tickets and had given them first-class seats. The treat was the most comfortable seats and room to sleep and enjoy a meal together. Olivia and Theo talked almost nonstop about his family and life as a youngster growing up in Pittsburgh. The little information Livia had already was only from the back of the pamphlet advertising Theo's lectures whilst at the university.

Livia was fascinated with Theo's childhood when at the age of thirteen, he had a visit to the Italian side of his family, the Gambocellis. His uncle Ernesto Gambocelli had worked with many fellow archaeologists on the site in Pompeii from 1950. So Theo's first trip to Italy was an adventure into the world of ancient history through the eyes of his fascinating uncle. He had accompanied him most days of the three-week trip to Pompeii and Rome. New discoveries were still being made. Theo's face lit up as he remembered his joy with his brush and trowel, trailing behind his uncle, his 'zio'. He laughed with Livia as he recalled every boy's dream of a dusty dig and the excitement of finding coins and fragments of pottery as his 'zio' interpreted and described the ancient meaning of the words and pictures. Livia told him about her first visit to Rome and Pompeii with her aunt when she was eleven. The excitement of visiting the Villa Battista, the Count and Countess Montefiore. The missing Masaccios. It all seemed so long ago, yet the memory and excitement of following the trail persisted with Olivia.

Theo scratched his chin and looked intently at Livia.

'Tell me, when you were at the Villa Battista? Was it the summer of 68? Was there by any chance an archaeological dig going on at the time? Uncovering the mosaic floors? Do you remember a massive pot crashing into a boy?'

Livia suddenly felt a realisation flowing over her.

'Oh no, Theo. This can't be true.

Were you there? The pot fell down into the site. Was it you? The dark curly-haired young man, shouting, looking up at us in the villa.'

They both started to laugh.

'I remember seeing a mass of blonde hair disappearing behind the balustrade just after the pot had nearly knocked my head off. '

Olivia choked a laugh.

'I nearly died of embarrassment. The Count was so kind and reassuring, and I had broken one of his, probably priceless ornaments and all he did was give me his handkerchief and tell me not to worry.

Afterwards, I went up to the top of the Belvedere with the Countess and looked through their telescope. I spied the top of your head as you were examining some fragments. You turned, and in my foolishness, I thought you had caught me looking at you.'

Theo smiled and stroked the stray hair that had fallen over her beautiful eyes.

'I wish I had met you then, we could have been in love for longer. I remember the sunlight flashing in front of me and turning to see the reflection of a glint of something high on the rooftops. It was you all the time.'

Livia gently prodded him in the chest.

'Theo. I was eleven! All arms and legs with wild stray hair. I'm so glad we didn't meet until now. It was a near miss, though. I don't mean the pot either. The Count invited us to stay over for a grand concert you were all attending. I did so want to be there, but we had to return. Imagine if we had met then, I would have been mortified to have known you were the person I had nearly decapitated.'

Theo squeezed Livia's hand and promised to take her to Rome again the following year. He would show her the Battista mosaics. His thesis involved more research that would also involve an extensive visit there. This would fit nicely with Livia's second and third-year studies as she moved from ancient Egyptian and Sumerian histories to Greek and Roman history. Olivia squeezed Theo's arm and kissed his cheek, exclaiming:

'I just can't believe it. Finding you, and that you actually liked me too. You've married me, and we just love the same things. I've always found it hard to fit in, feeling a bit gawky. Not many people like old things, you know Latin and the Romans. It's never been hard to talk to Dad, Mum, or Aunt Geraldine. She's encouraged me all my life. She's shown me artefacts she's collected, given me precious Roman jewellery and educated me that there's more to life than Little Missenden, the big outside world. Oh, Theo, I have so much I want to learn.'

Olivia sat back in her seat for a few seconds. Theo could sense there was more she wanted to say. He waited.

'Theo, I've meant to ask you, what did my aunt say to you in the garden back home? '

He smiled to himself, then said,

'She's an extraordinary woman, your aunt. She asked about my family history, dates, names and places. Where did my folks live in Europe during the second world war? History of my grandparents' before emigrating to the USA. She also wanted to know about my financial status and what my political leanings were.'

Olivia glanced at Theo, feeling incredibly embarrassed at her aunt's questions.

'It's Ok, Livvy, honey, I've nothing to hide. Your aunt cares so much for you and your future; she needed to be sure I wasn't a subversive revolutionary waiting to live off an heiress.

I'm not particularly interested in following the political shenanigans of the day. In fact, very often, I don't vote. To tell the truth, I've usually been up to my waist in a dusty dig, piecing together the history and misdemeanours of ancient civilisations. Sad that today's leaders still haven't learned not to repeat history by doing exactly as our predecessors have done. Don't tell my mum, though, as she's very patriotic.'

He said all this with a wry smile.

'After all her questions, your aunt seemed to quickly make up her mind that we were well suited and immediately swung into action, helping us to make it all possible. She's amazing, if not a little scary. I think if I ever don't treat you well, I will have to escape to some remote island, change my whole identity and live as a recluse. Because Aunt Geraldine would track me down and be sure to submit me to the most terrifying tortures before having me exterminated.'

Olivia looked wide-eyed at Theo, and only when he broke into his usual good-humoured laugh did she see the funny side of his story. Theo drew her close to him despite the protruding armrest between them.

'Olivia Davidovitz, don't you worry. I've promised you I will love you and take care of you. Of course, I'm going to lash things up a few times and make a few blunders. I might forget dates and be late sometimes. But you are precious to me today and, like my chosen art, will grow more precious to me as the years go by. Aunt Geraldine will never be chasing me because I will always be by you, loving and treasuring you.'

Olivia sighed contentedly and relaxed into his warm embrace.

Because of the five-hour time difference, they arrived in Pittsburgh early evening. Theo's mum and dad were waiting for them as they entered the exit lounge. Sofia Davidovitz was a tall, dark, handsome woman of fifty-one. Although expertly enhanced, her hair still had the same colourings as Theo's. Her eyes were dark and, upon seeing her eldest son, immediately lit up with the same laughter in them as Theo's reflected. She ran to Theo and hugged him, kissing his cheeks and patting his dark curls, then lifting her head away. She surveyed his face whilst holding him close with both arms.

'Ahh, my Theo, you look so handsome, so well, so happy. Your mama is happy. Now your little wife, come come, we must all meet her. Oh, Olivia, you are beautiful, elegant, just as Theo described, ah, such a wonderful couple, my grandchildren will be so cute and delightful.'

She took Olivia's face between her hands, kissed her forehead, and kissed each cheek very lightly.

'Benjamin, come here, see what a wonderful daughter-in-law

we have.'

Benjamin Davidovitz was tall like Theo. He still had a thick head of dark, well-trimmed curly hair slightly greying at the temples, his face was tanned, and his eyes were kindly and grey like Theo's. His smile beamed a welcome to Olivia as he held out his hand, and he took Olivia's and enfolded it between his warm solid hands. He hugged his son, giving him a loud clap on his back, then turned to Olivia.

'Well, it's sure good to meet you, Olivia; we've heard about you on the telephone from Theo. In fact, that's all he's talked about these past three months. Way back in the fall, we knew there was someone he had taken a shine to, couldn't concentrate on his work, and was in a rush to get back to England when his business here was done. So you are very welcome to be part of the Davidovitz tribe. Hope you'll stay with us tonight before setting off to Rivertree. Now come on, folks, let's get you and all your luggage in the automobile. Just about two hours upstate to home.'

The drive out of Pittsburgh headed north towards Endeavour, followed a straight motorway initially. As they left the city outskirts, the landscape changed from urban to rural, taking them through wooded areas and long stretches of road with few houses. Each homestead seemed to have lots of land and trees surrounding it. The evening light soon darkened, and just after two hours, they reached the Davidovitz home around nine o'clock. The house was a white clapperboard wooden-style family home. The deep entrance steps went up to a large verandah with overhung wooden eaves. Lights illuminated the drive as they pulled into the approach way.

It had been a long and exhausting day. Theo and Livia had been awake now for over twenty hours. The Davidovitz family quietly showed them to their room, where they just fell into the bed, and sleep engulfed them. When Olivia awoke the following day, it was around twelve noon. She could faintly hear Theo's voice downstairs. He had already showered and was talking with his parents. Livia stretched out and surveyed the room. She guessed this must be the guest room. They were in the eaves of the house on the second floor. Three oversized, gabled windows looked out from the front of the house; to the rearview, there was an eyebrow dormer. The whole room was panelled out with wood, painted brilliant white. The floor-to-ceiling shelves contained books on interiors and wildlife with a few tastefully chosen pottery pieces in shades of coral, deep turquoise and terracotta. The curtains were a duck egg blue gingham check, and the wooden floor was covered in thick blue and white rugs. The room felt like a beach house, refreshing and calm.

Livia enjoyed the drowsy feeling of dozing between sleep and wakefulness, tingling with a desire to take a look out of the windows. Theo had left one of the front windows slightly open. She could feel the heat from outside steadily raising the temperature in the room. Unfamiliar birdsong filled the air, a warbler and a distant hoot of an owl, strange in broad daylight. Livia was puzzled, not sure she heard correctly. There was no sound of traffic, lots of birdsong and the low whining sound of a heavy electric saw in the distance.

She grabbed her wrap, tossed the bedclothes to one side, padded across the cool floor to the front window, and opened it wide. The hazy view to the West was of dense pine forests, and she could just see the outline of the road they had travelled the night before, sweeping away to the far right, away from the house in the distance. The shallow window to the rear looked out toward the national park and acres upon acres of forests. The vast Allegheny River views and the beautifully rugged, unspoilt landscape swept beneath her gaze. The next few weeks would be exciting, a land she had never visited, exploring, rambling and generally messing about on the river. Olivia spun around out of her reverie and, within a few minutes, was showered and dressed, feeling a heightened sense of keen anticipation of the day's activities and breakfast that her stomach reminded her was long overdue.

As she walked down the broad wooden staircase towards where the voices were coming from, she noticed all the paintings of previous presidents placed on the walls along with sports trophies, college and school photos of four smiley young men with distinct dark curly hair and grey steady eyes of the Davidovitz family. She entered the kitchen, and six pairs of eyes stared at her briefly before breaking into smiles and a mixed animated outburst of 'hey' and 'well hello'. Theo quickly took over and put his arm around Olivia's waist, feigning an exaggerated over-protectiveness.

'Now come on, guys, let me introduce you to my lovely wife, Livvy, Mrs Olivia Davidovitz, your new sister.'

He stressed the word 'sister,' winking at his younger brothers and holding Livvy very securely with both arms surrounding her slim frame. Livia giggled and gave them all a big grin. His mum shrieked with laughter, and his dad rounded everyone up to sit around the kitchen island where he had prepared brunch for them all. Livia was used to being surrounded by women in her family who were often strange, unpredictable, temperamental, moody and not always communicative. However, she was fascinated by the mix of boisterous good humour, noisy banter, and often clumsiness of these handsome men. A lot of food, a mug of coffee and a puddle of juice all ended up on the floor when two solid young men grabbed the jug of orange juice together.

Sophia pretended to clip them around the ears, raising her eyes as she handed them a cloth and stood over them, arms akimbo, whilst they mopped up the mess. Then, she turned to Olivia and said:

'These two are my twins, Zachery and Woodrow, both at the university in Pittsburgh studying, I hope, very hard to be doctors, and this is my baby, Dwight, on a sports scholarship to Michigan University.'

Young baby Dwight looked the biggest and tallest of all the Davidovitz offspring, standing over six feet four and broader in the shoulder than his older brothers. Sofia walked around the table and hugged Theo, ruffling his curls.

'And my big son Theo, your mama is so proud of you, the

international archaeologist. You have such a clever husband. I have read all your articles published in the American Journal of Archaeology and have them all stored and catalogued. Olivia, I will show them to you.'

As the meal progressed, each brother asked Olivia questions about herself, her family, where she lived and her work on ancient studies. They were a lively, intelligent group of brothers, each with their own individuality, and it was evident they cared very much for each other. Finally, Theo's dad cleared all the meal leftovers and started washing up. His wife, too, left all the younger ones to talk together. Sofia beckoned to Olivia to follow her.

'I have something for you. I've been putting it together for some years now. See, it's for you to keep. You will have some interesting conversations with Theo over it.'

She gave Olivia a large folio and, as she pressed it into her hands, said:

'It's of all the important and less important but humorous occasions in Theo's life, photos of his old relatives. Great-grandpa and mama his baby days and growing up years.'

She flicked through the leaves. There were faded black and white photos and brown sepia ones of dark-haired, handsome smiling faces. The clothing spoke of a time many years ago, and even the fuzzy images evoked a feeling of warmth and cloudless skies. The Italian Tuscan landscapes shimmered in the background. Sophia pointed to one of these.

'Ah, that's the family farm near Frascati. That's my brother Ernesto with Theo, many summers they spent together digging. We were so poor as children, but one thing I do remember is those tomatoes and zucchini.'

She laughed as she fondly stroked her hand over the familiar faces.

'You must get Theo to take you to visit them all, the Gambocelli's. I've lost track of how many of us are still alive, but the house and farm are still there. Fascinating site and history connected with all that area. You would find it interesting. A lot of the ancient Roman scholars and nobility had villas there. There is a legend that the wife of the conqueror of Britain lived and died in that area. It's never been excavated, but I remember as a child finding coins and small relics of bygone days.'

Sophia looked wistfully out of the window, briefly lost in her memories. She then turned to Olivia.

'Anyway, you have this. Keep it safe now. You will have some fun looking through it together.'

Olivia thanked Sofia and gave her a hug. She was intrigued and longed to speak further to her new mother-in-law. To open up the album and have answers to questions brimming up in her mind. But they had to be on their way to their honeymoon at the river house. Theo was already loading up the pickup truck his dad was lending them. Sofia had prepared a carton of food along with blankets and linen. She assured Olivia that the river house near Tidioute was well stocked, but it would be best to take fresh linen as they hadn't been to open it up for a couple of months, and there had been a fair share of rain in May.

The short drive to Rivertree House meandered through the national park. Substantial black cherry trees stood stately, with underplanting saplings and wildflowers filling the air with a herbal fragrance. Occasionally a white-tailed deer darted out of view, and so many birds Olivia had never seen before. Theo promised they would go hiking together and said that at the cabin, there was a well-stocked library of books on the birds and the history of the region from the early days of logging to the present-day controversial mining of resources.

Rivertree House was something more than the 'cabin' Olivia had imagined. It was nestled by time amongst the trees, almost invisible behind the canopy of branches outstretched like limbs cradling and concealing it. Olivia felt a strong connection and blurring of the building and the trees. It was as if the trees owned the house and had somehow grown together. Built some hundred years ago and owned by the family for the last thirty years, it was mainly dark hardwood and stonework. The front looked like a double-fronted family home with a third-storey gable directly above the main entrance. However, the rear was where the house took on a unique charm. This side of the house stood amongst the tallest cherry and birch trees which shaded its overhung wooden verandah on the first floor. Above this were the bedrooms, all having leafy views through the trees, each with adjoining decked balconies for what promised to be lazy days of relaxing, taking in the slow-moving river and its many changing vistas. The land dropped softly away towards the river, a gentle grassy slope down to the landing deck.

The languorous days they spent at Rivertree, on the river, hiking in the woods, loving each other, picnicking and dipping into the calm river, deeply etched unforgettable moments into their lives together. They spent hours silently reading on the occasional rainy morning, then Livia would sometimes watch Theo without him realising, writing and researching his work. She liked to see his profile bent over his desk, the way a stray curl or two bounced out over his forehead. Then he ran his fingers through his thick dark hair, stretched his arms above his head, and resettled himself back in his studying pose. He would pace up and down as he read, stopping and pondering, then, as if a eureka moment came to him, would quickly return to the desk and rapidly write intensely for the next few minutes.

Olivia knew that Theo's next year would mean extensive work on his paper, so she resolved to be as understanding and patient as possible. His time would be wrapped up with his work, and she, too, would throw herself into her studies, knowing they were working together for the same goals and aims in life. The weeks flew by, and the last day of their time at Rivertree came. Two people tanned, relaxed and recharged, locked the doors of Rivertree and began the next stage of their trek home, first to say goodbye to Benjamin and Sofia, then the long flight home to London.

They stopped for a short overnight stay with Richard and Briddy at Beaconsfield, promising to return for the long-awaited family celebration during the autumn break. It was just Briddy and Richard at home that weekend, and for a fleeting moment, Olivia noticed her mum's slightly drawn features even though she smiled at the newlyweds. Maybe it was her realisation that her mum was getting older for the first time. She was the same age as Theo's mum, but the contrast was noticeable. She looked fifty-one years, her hair was greying, and the lines around her eyes seemed more prominent than the last time they had seen each other. There were moments when Olivia caught a glimpse of her mother's eyes. They looked sad. To Olivia's relief, Richard was always at Briddy's side, and it did not go unnoticed how he squeezed her hand and put his arm around her as they waved goodbye. That weekend wasn't a moment for quiet, confidential talking time together. So she resolved to keep in touch each week by telephone and cheery letters. She felt so lucky to have parents who put no pressure on her or made her feel guilty about not seeing more of them. She knew they loved her and only wanted the best for her, and now Theo too.

CHAPTER 10

'A thin wet sky that yellows at the rim,
And meets with a sun-lost lip the marsh's brim...
The wild goose, homing, seeks a sheltering,
Where rushes grow, and oozing lichens cling.'
'Marshlands'
Emily Pauline Johnson

England Exeter, The river Exe and the Marshes 1977

Life in Exeter was hectic. A new influx of students meant all were searching for somewhere to rent before the beginning of term. Although Aunt Geraldine had assured them they could stay as long as they liked at 'Gung Ho', their preferred choice was to find somewhere closer to the university.

Finally, a week before the new term, they secured a light, sunny two-floor apartment in a tall Georgian townhouse on Colleton Crescent. It had been a complete fluke that they heard about this through one of Theo's colleagues who just happened to know a retired doctor who owned the whole property and, as he was recently widowed, wanted to let out the top two floors. Fortunately for Olivia, Theo fitted the criteria perfectly. Dr Compton instantly approved of the young archaeology tutor, himself proving to be a quiet elderly, private man. Reminiscent to Olivia of the way the Count had welcomed her to his Villa in Italy. Tall and slim with a slight stoop and a noticeable limp. He was always impeccably dressed in a linen suit, shirt, and tie, and as he shook their hands, he inclined his head as if with a slight nod. These older men were of the same generation, well-mannered with minds full of life and experience, having lived through two world wars and seen significant societal changes.

Olivia was curious to know more about Dr Tristan Compton, or as Theo would have said, she was 'just plain nosey'. She secretly wondered what his collection of books would tell about the man and his life. When he knew Theo's subject and interests, he showed them his extensive library and welcomed Theo to use it any time, keen to leave them to come and go as they pleased. Olivia, looking eagerly over Theo's shoulder, shaking her head up and down, beamed a huge smile, showing her keen interest in browsing.

The house had never been professionally divided into separate accommodations, but it did have one large room on the first floor with three sash windows facing the Exe and a large bathroom and separate toilet at the rear. Above this, two spacious bedrooms and a closet shower room with the most glorious views over the Exe towards Haldon Hills. The doctor was happy to divide the large bathroom with a partition wall, making a compact kitchen. He even agreed that a door at the top of their stairs would be a good idea for privacy.

The doctor was a soundless neighbour. So quiet that very often, Olivia was slightly startled when she found him in the hallway at the bottom of their stairs. Then like a shadow, he would disappear quickly into his library. Unless it was Theo, then a conversation was started, and they both vanished into the library deep in discussion on a historical or archaeological matter. Dr Compton was a learned man in these subjects, which Theo found more than helpful when he needed another mind on the angle he was taking with his thesis. The doctor told them the collection of books on art and jewellery had been his wife's passion. She had studied and travelled extensively, collecting art and amassing her own books.

Olivia's second year at university proved to be more demanding than the previous one. Perhaps it was the distractions of married life, loving and caring for another person. Or the full intensity of more deadlines and essays to complete. Nevertheless, her subject matter that year fully engrossed her interest. The Romans, their literature and the birth of the empire were fascinating to Olivia. She read many classical writings in Latin and was enthralled when translating the ancient text into English. She imagined living in the era with the people. However, she became increasingly disappointed at the non-existence of writings from ordinary people. She read books written by modern-day historians on their hypotheses and suggestions of what life had been like for the everyday women, slaves and children of the citizens of Rome. A lot of what she read was supposition and hearsay. The actual ancient written writings were all by scholarly men and usually slanted towards their selfish views of love, war, wine, slaves, and women.

Theo and Livia had many lively discussions on the anthropology and culture of these ancient civilisations. Theo was most interested in this field of science and its interrelationship with archaeology. He did not read Latin like Olivia, although he could easily decipher Egyptian hieroglyphics and understood Greek. For Olivia, it was a dream to have such a source of experience and knowledge beside her. If Theo did not know all the answers to her questions, he very soon came up with a resource or avenue of information that could point her in the right direction, and Dr Compton's library soon became an invaluable study room for both of them.

Tristan Compton's habits quickly became evident to Olivia's keen eyes. Every Monday morning, he went to the local library until noon. On Tuesdays, his cleaner came, so he went out for five hours exactly. A car drew up outside on Wednesday afternoons, and he was driven out until his return at precisely six o'clock in the evening. He was generally home on Thursdays and Fridays after his cleaner had finished in the mornings, then out until the early evening. Olivia's life was a whirlwind of expeditions and relaxation over the weekends; hence she did not follow the doctor's routine on Saturdays and Sundays. Knowing that he was out all Wednesday afternoons, the opportunity to explore the library uninterrupted was keenly anticipated. She found her old black notebook stashed away and decided now was the time to open it up to new discoveries and maybe even find a few answers.

The wet mist from the estuary rose most days and left watery droplets on the long sash windows and a dripping moist fog on the panes inside. With its wall-to-wall, high bookcases and ochre paintwork, the library had thus appeared shadowy and dark. It always felt like dusk was approaching in that room. The fogged windowpanes clouded the sun's natural light. Today was different. The air was dry; the sun had shone all morning. As Olivia opened the library door, shafts of sunlight beamed onto the glossy wooden floors. She had only ever been aware of bookcases lining the walls of this vast room. Now she noticed spaces between the tall, dark casements. The walls were crammed with paintings and curios. Some with ornate gold frames, portraits, and dark landscapes. A couple of still-life pictures with bowls of fruit and glass water pitchers, exquisitely lifelike, caught Olivia's attention. Many frameless paintings were higher up. Oil paint on dark boards made it hard to distinguish the subject matter. The watercolour paintings of harbours and seascape scenes stood out bright and were clearly preserved behind their glazing. There were box casements of butterflies, iridescent blues and yellows. Giant black beetles, and a collection of bird eggs, all with minute labels listing their type and name. Books that had previously looked brown and shabby transformed as the gold tooling on the old leather spines glistened and changed the room into a magical emporium of colour and texture, and for Olivia's inquisitive fingers, a strong desire to touch and open. She moved along the cases. Familiar titles jumped out at her. Many Aunt Geraldine also had collected. Her eyes rested on three particular shelves, large complete volumes of encyclopaedias. Books on anthropology, Egyptology, Roman architecture and art. She stopped in her musings as she turned her head on its side and noticed a large, reasonably recent book dealing with Roman jewellery. Tightly wedged into the shelf after a bit of wiggling it slipped out, the dust puthered up, tingling her nostrils. She settled down onto the battered deep leather sofa, turning the book's pages, entering into her world of Roman antiquities. Suddenly a photograph showed the similar bangle given by her aunt. Livia sat upright. She thumbed through the references. Claudia Acte, mistress to Nero. Could her bracelet be something from this woman? Time stood motionless for Livia. Only the heavy clock chimed each hour as she delved into the encyclopaedias and various reference books, all following the trail of Claudia Acte. She read:

'Claudia Acte: Unknown date of birth, slave girl probably to Nero's young wife, Octavia. She was taken by Nero when he was 17 years of age (AD 54), and she was probably 16, to be his mistress. He gave her freedom and intended to marry her. Agrippina the Younger intensely opposed the marriage, considering Claudia to be beneath their royal lineage. This caused a rift between mother and son. Little is known of her later life, but it is thought Nero continued to view her as a friend and sought her stabilising counsel along with bestowing great wealth and property to her. She is spoken of in the works of Tacitus and Suetonius. Acte outlived Nero and funded and organised Nero's funeral, one of the few faithful people. In the words of Suetonius, "his funerals cost two hundred thousand sesterces[...]. His mistresses Egloge and Alexandria and the concubine Acte deposited their ashes in the funeral mausoleum of the Domitius, which stands on the Field of Mars…".'

Livia paused and took out her notebook, copying what she had just read. Was she on the trail of Claudia Acte and emperor Nero? Excitedly she started to imagine the possibility of Emperor Nero of the first century making a gift to his mistress and that she could now have such an item. There was still the other mystery, the writings on the ring. Where had she written the inscription down? Thumbing through her notebook, she smiled as she saw all her notes and headings.

1. Aunt Geraldine - life with Archie. His nefarious deeds in South Africa. Injured French resistance at the Abbey. What were her scars? Where? What happened?

2. The Stolen Roman jewellery. 'Claudia Acte - Nero' 'Columel....Villa Avernus.... Villa Alba

3. Lead Leaking Roof, dead animals, Seb. R.!!!

4. The Masaccios. The angel Gabriel and the Madonna and Child. On panels 8 x 12. Photos attached.

There it was, section 2. Now to start filling in the blank spaces about the jewellery and begin a few more lines of inquiry into anything to discover about Claudia Acte and the incomplete words Columel, Villa Avernus and Villa Alba. Where had she seen the word Columel before? She was distracted from her thoughts. As she lifted her notebook, a photograph wafted onto the floor, the hazy picture of the missing Masaccio. Olivia studied it closely next to the sunlit window. Her eyes wandered over the numerous paintings and exhibits tightly packing the spaces between the bookcases. High up above the picture rail, two small dark panels stood out amidst the brightness of the watercolours and iridescent butterfly wings. Olivia caught her breath. She held the photo up towards the panels.

At that moment, a car pulled up outside, and the clock chimed. The photograph fell to the floor along with her notebook. Quickly gathering her notebook and slipping the books she had been studying back into the bookcases, she plumped the cushions back into their orderly places and quietly closed the door to the library speeding up her stairs as the key in the lock to the front door turned. Racing up the stairs, her thoughts darting and diving to conclusions, her heart pounding. Had she seen something like the missing Masaccio hanging on the library walls? She slumped into a chair and opened her notebook, flicking through the pages to look again at Madonna and Gabriel's photo. It was not there. Frantically looking, she shook the book upside down. The picture had gone.

Remembering when it had floated onto the floor. Olivia was sure that after examining it, she had firmly placed it back into the notebook. She gasped, in her hurry to get out of the library; it must have slipped out again. It had to be retrieved. She could not let Dr Compton know it was hers before identifying if he really did have the panels. If he found it, there was a faint possibility he would not recognise it. In her mind, she quickly went through their conversations and was sure they had never discussed Masaccio, missing paintings, Nazis or Count Montefiori.

Then an idea came to her. Olivia headed to her small kitchen and started to fling open cupboards and drawers, hunting for ingredients. Sure she could manage baked scones and a fruit cake, although baking had never been her best skill. But the cake turned out superbly, delicious-looking golden and shiny and the fruit did not sink heavy to the bottom. When Theo arrived home that evening, he was thrilled to smell the delicious aroma of baking, which his wife had not ventured to do since they married. Livia was nowhere to be seen, only a brief message with a love heart and a big. Enjoy them! on top of the freshly baked scones.

 Olivia had carefully carried the cake down the stairs. Patting her pocket to make sure the 'lost earring' was safely hidden away. She took a deep breath hoping her nervousness was not evident. Knocking softly on the rear kitchen door, she called:

'Dr Compton, it's me, Olivia. Would you like a bit of homemade fruit cake for your supper?'

He opened the door and smiled as he placed his hands together.

'That's very kind of you, my dear. I hope you have had a pleasant day.'

'Yes, Yes, thank you. I was doing some research for my dissertation. "The Lives of Real Roman Woman". You have such an extensive library. It's a delight to look at all the books. There is one slight problem, I was twiddling with my hair and accidentally pulled one of my earrings out whilst I was in the library, which might have fallen between the sofa cushions. Can I look at the floor in there?'

'You go ahead, put the main light on. The sidelights are not very bright in the evenings. Would you like me to assist you?'

'Oh no, you enjoy the cake. I will have a good hunt around. Have a lovely evening.'

Olivia sighed in relief as he closed the kitchen door, and she shot into the library. Her eyes scanned the floor as the bright light lit up the darkened room. Remembering where the photo had initially fallen, she knelt down and ran her hand over the deep-piled Persian rug. She took the cushions out of the sofa. It was nowhere to be seen. Then looking at the base of the bookcases, she noticed each had gaps in the middle, where the woodwork was raised from the floor. Peering down amidst the swirls of dust, she glimpsed the photo. What could she use to pull it out? Her hands were not slim enough, and it was just out of finger reach. Her eyes spotted the thin fire poker on its stand. Grasping it, the pan and brush rattled, clattering onto the hearth. Only a few seconds left before the doctor came in to see if all was well. Olivia grabbed the poker and swept it under the bookshelf. The photo shot out along with a great ball of fluff and dust. The library door opened as she pushed the picture into her back pocket and pulled out the second earring.
Looking at her dishevelled hair and very red face were Dr Compton and Theo, both with puzzled looks on their faces.

'You Okay, honey?'

Olivia lifted her earring up before them.

'Yes, look, I found it. It must have rolled under the bookcase. Sorry for all the noise. I couldn't reach it, so I used the poker, and all the lot came tumbling down. Well, thank you, we must be having our dinner now. Good night'

Livia grabbed Theo's arm and ushered him up the stairs, closing their top door firmly before sinking to the ground with one almighty sigh of relief. Theo looked at her enquiringly:

'What's been happening, Livvy?'

She poured two large glasses of red wine, and they sat down, looking out across a sunset of deep oranges and reds. Resting her head on his shoulder, she said:

'Where do I begin.'

Olivia explained all the discoveries she had made that afternoon. Firstly, the account relating to her jewellery. Theo nodded and smiled encouragingly.

'There's something else, but I'm not sure I'm right. I have never told you why we went to Count Baptista's Villa, have I? My aunt was involved in discovering and repatriating stolen art that the Nazis took from the Jews during the second world war. The Count and her were working together on two particular pieces that disappeared from his house. When we visited him, he found a photograph in an old book that identified them more clearly. Aunt Geraldine gave me a copy of the picture. I had it enhanced and reproduced by the photographers in Beaconsfield.

Theo, Mr Castle, the proprietor, recognised the paintings from way back during the war. But he had been a patient at the Villa when it had been a field hospital, just before returning to England. He could only remember some of the details.

Anyway, for over seven years, the trail had gone cold. Nothing has come up, and the photos have been circulated amongst Aunt Geraldine's contacts.'

Olivia paused, her eyes as big as saucers. She whispered.

'Until today. Theo, I think they are in the library downstairs. The missing Madonna and Angel Gabriel. I had the photograph in my notebook and was examining it by the window when I looked up. I'm almost certain they're on the wall between the bookcases. Two dark painted boards 8 x 12 side by side.'

Theo looked carefully at the dark photos. Ran his fingers through his thick curly hair and read and re-read Olivia's notes. She then explained what happened next, pretending to lose her earrings, searching under the cases, and hurriedly getting upstairs. She watched and waited.

'The common sense side of me says: let's not get involved, leave it to the authorities. We need to be sure they really are the lost panels. Let's sleep on it tonight. Tomorrow when we go to the university, you ring your aunt and see what she thinks. I don't want you to go into the library Livvy nosing around until we have more information from your aunt. Promise me you won't.'

Livia nodded. She was so excited, a little scared, but buzzing in her head to pursue this new lead.

The next day, after Geraldine had calmed Olivia down and comprehended amidst all the jumble of conversation, the full import of the possible discovery. She decided that she would visit them. Stay at 'Gung Ho' for a few days and get to know Dr Compton better. Olivia must invite him to dinner with Geraldine and leave the rest to her. She would be known as a 'Lepidopterist' with a keen interest in his collections of butterflies.

Olivia knocked gently on the downstairs door. As it opened sharply, the doctor smiled invitingly. Startled at first, Olivia jumped back, quickly saying:

'I hope you enjoyed the cake. Theo and I wondered if you would like to come and have supper with us one night over the weekend. I have my Aunt Geraldine coming over to stay at her house in Topsham at the weekend. She is a collector of all sorts and particularly a keen Lepidopterist. I hope you don't mind me telling her what a wonderful collection you have of butterflies. She's coming for supper on Saturday evening would you join us? Aunt Geraldine would love to meet you.'

The doctor looked puzzled for a split second, and Olivia saw just a glimpse of sharpness in his eyes before he answered her.

'Your Aunt Geraldine, you say? We may have a lot in common. Very interested in the moths and butterflies? Let me see, just one moment whilst I check my diary, step this way.'

Olivia followed into the inner passageway. A door clicked open and light flooded from the large rear windows. The doctor opened a drawer in his desk and looked through the pages of a thick diary. He then put it on the bookshelf above his head alongside a long succession of similar leather-bound books.

Olivia scanned the spines of each one noting they were all dated in order going back over many years. He followed where her eyes rested, and she quickly averted her gaze to the window.

'What a beautiful view you have onto the garden. The wisteria and orange blossom together. They must have a history to tell, so mature looking. They are beautiful.'

'Yes, it was my wife's work of many years. The gardener now keeps it under control.

Saturday evening, supper, you say. Yes, that would be most acceptable. I rarely have guests nowadays, and it's not so easy for me to climb the stairs. I have one thing to ask.

He patted his left leg.

'Come and have supper with me here, I have a good supply of fine wines, and together with your skills in the culinary field, I think we would make a good table together. Shall we say 7 pm Saturday? I won't take no for an answer.'

Olivia quickly thought this new turn of possibilities through. It could work out better than she had anticipated. The conversation would undoubtedly lead to 'butterflies' and his collections in the library, which would be accessible from his dining room. She smiled and held out her hand.

'It's a deal, 7 pm Saturday, and I will provide all the nibbles, food, etcetera.'

Saturday evening arrived, and a battered but utilitarian Jeep, its canvas dark covers flapping in the wind, backfired and parked outside. Out jumped Aunt Geraldine. She had dressed to match the persona of someone slightly obsessive about their interest in butterflies and definitely not in their appearance. Her usually sleek, chic red hair was a mass of unruly curls, dishevelled and messy. She wore a pair of canvas dungarees and half-moon tortoiseshell spectacles on the end of her nose, with a coarse jute tote bag casually hanging over one shoulder. As Olivia answered the door, she clapped a hand over her wide-opened mouth. Only as Aunt Geraldine flashed her familiar bright green eyes warningly at Olivia. She suppressed her gurgled laughter. Never had she seen such a changed appearance in her dear aunt. 'a supreme actress and mistress of disguise'. Olivia was enchanted by this new person. The slightly distracted, one subject-focused, academic field worker specialising in butterflies and moths. She had even adopted a stoop and stiffness to her neck so that as she turned, her whole body turned, and her head had a nervous twitch. Olivia quizzed her aunt about her health. Was she in pain? Did she really have a shake and feel all stiff? Geraldine laughed.

'My dear girl, this is the disguise.'

They went upstairs and closed their door firmly as Theo hugged the new 'Gerry,' as she was called. From that moment on, they all played a part in the act that Geraldine had prepared. She immediately went into leadership mode. Geraldine brought them all under control and briefed them on how the evening would proceed. To Olivia, this was highly amusing, the look as opposed to the person. No surprise shown at her portrayal of the obsessive, slightly wandering, forgetful middle-aged butterfly enthusiast.

Dr Compton met Geraldine. She hooked him in as if caught in her vast delicate Aerial net. It was Gerry and Tristan from that hour onwards. Geraldine invented a whole new life history about herself whilst extracting from the doctor snippets from his life during the war and his work in Italy. She even found the name of the area he had worked in and the ship he was repatriated on, the American ship John J Meany. More and more, his life fitted into events that had led up to the disappearance of the Masaccio paintings. No mention was made of Count Montefiore or the Villa Baptista. In one brief moment, as he reminisced, he mentioned the name of his good friend David the photographer. Geraldine was careful to appear as disinterested as possible in art and never spoke of disappearing paintings. After food and drink interspersed with the two of them and their mutual interests, the invitation to view the collection of butterflies was very swift in coming. Tristan led the way. With Gerry fumbling behind him, she took out her magnifying glass and asked to step onto the library ladder to look closely at the casements. He apologised for not bringing them down. His leg made it impossible to climb the step ladder. Theo offered to bring them down. Geraldine immediately said:

'No! I want to get up close on the ladder. Please do not dislodge them. The movement may damage them.'

She took out of her bag a headband with a bright torch attached to the front, along with her notebook, camera and magnifying glass. Gingerly with false hesitancy, she climbed the steps. Her head twitched slightly, and the light bobbed up and down. All eyes followed her up. Olivia's part in the proceedings now took over.

'Dr Compton, I was looking at your books about Roman jewellery the other day. I think I may have a clearer understanding of the origins of a couple of pieces I have collected.'

'Now, Olivia, please, you must start calling me Tristan. We are all coming to know each other so well.'

The desired effect occurred. The doctor's eyes and attention moved to the other side of the room where the Roman history books were shelved. Theo placed himself alongside Geraldine to steady the ladder, blocking site of her from across the room. He then took out of his pocket a flashlight. Shining it onto the paintings alongside the casements, Geraldine clicked her Polaroid camera and photographed the Angel Gabriel alongside The Madonna and child. The light on her head remained fixed. It did not wobble or tremble for those few moments. All the time, she had the remarkable capacity to carry on a detailed conversation about the types and species of butterflies whilst examining the panels closely. Olivia distracted Tristan, and Geraldine had, within those few minutes, photographed and developed her pictures. Her character slipped briefly as she jauntily stepped off the ladder's bottom rung. Her eyes shone sharp and bright, her head held high without a twitch. Her sparkling green eyes narrowed as she looked across at Olivia. Something incredible had been discovered.

CHAPTER 11

'A beautiful body perishes, but a work of art dies not.'
Leonardo Da Vinci

Exeter 1978

Tristan had not missed the change in Geraldine's demeanour. The excitement in her eyes and the straightness of her posture. Her head no longer shook.
Geraldine turned to face Tristan.

'Your collection is remarkable. You have so many beautiful things here. Your specimens and also your artwork are exceptional. Tell me, how long have you had the two panels above the butterfly casement? The small dark paintings.'

Olivia took a sharp intake of breath. Theo took hold of her hand, squeezing it tightly. Tristan craned his neck towards the pictures; his eyes narrowed, and his mouth contracted as he peered upwards. He scratched his head and then pointed at them.

'You mean the dark brown pair? Never really noticed them that closely before. They must have been put there when we moved here in the 50s. My wife, Venetia, was an art collector. They must have been in the satchel that came back with me from Italy. I believe she had a few paintings in it. She did all the arranging of the artwork. My cleaner just uses a long-handled feather duster to keep them all clean. Why do you ask?'

Geraldine was now her usual calm, capable persona. Theo and Olivia stood still, with shallow breathing, transfixed as they watched the unfolding performance.

'I want to show you something. Can we go back to the dining room table?'

Tristan led the way, his uneven steps resounding on the wooden boards. He sat straight-backed at the head of the table and placed both hands out in front of him. Geraldine arranged the magnifying glass and the newly developed instant photos alongside the enlarged pictures of the Masaccios from the old book. The doctor's eyes scanned from one to the other. He picked up the magnifying glass, examined his paintings closely, and then the enlarged photograph. He sat back in his chair and covered his face with his hands, massaging his temples slowly. Geraldine laid out the photos David Castle had given her on the table. The four young men on board the 'John J Meany'. The Villa Baptista, from the front of the formal gardens, as they would have been in 1944. Two photos showed army vehicles, red cross ambulances parked in the driveway, and nurses in the garden with the wounded. Tristan picked up the pictures and turned them over; he nodded. The magnifying glass hovered over the image of a tall slim nurse pushing a wheelchair. He closed his eyes and gently placed the eyeglass and photo on the table.

'So many memories. I was there, the Villa Baptista. The Nazis put me in charge of looking after the allied wounded, just before the Americans arrived. This one is of us onboard the repatriation ship. We forged firm friendships. The nurses too, but Venetia stood out. She was different, elegant, artistic, and intelligent. She was moved around a lot visiting other hospitals. Only sometimes with us at the Villa. I wondered if she was some kind of resistance worker. She appeared to have her secrets and was fluent in four or five languages. She was with us on the repatriation ship. Then when we disembarked, we lost track of each other. But she gave me a satchel, the medical corps bag she wanted me to bring home, and she would collect it from me later.

I didn't hear from her for six months. Then I got a phone call from her out of the blue. The rest is history. A whirlwind romance, married within the year. We settled here in Exeter, and after my parents died, I bought this house. Venetia started to arrange the paintings then. I was so busy setting up the medical practice. The surgery was in Southernhay West, so I wasn't always around in those early years.

What does all this mean? I fear what you are about to tell me is not good news.'

Geraldine sat down and paused as she looked out of the window. Turning to Dr Compton, she said:

'These two panels, The Madonna and Angel Gabriel are paintings that are part of a collection housed at the Villa Baptista, the property of Count Montefiore Baptista and his wife, Catherina. They are by the 15th-century artist Masaccio and have been missing from the Villa since the Nazi occupation. These are the panels you have in the library. Interpol has given me the authority to seize works of art and return them to their rightful owner. Here are my credentials, and this is the leading investigator based in the Netherlands, Lucien Van der Berg.

Tristan looked at all the paperwork. His hands were shaking.

'I had no idea about the paintings. Lucien was with us in Italy. Look, he's in this photograph with us, David, Manny and myself. You say he's in charge now.

All these years have gone by. Venetia kept secret where the paintings had come from. I never questioned her, and now it's too late.'

He sighed.

'She died last year, short illness, a brain tumour.

I wonder what else she kept from me.'

They all sat quietly for a few moments. Geraldine started to speak.

'Tristan, there is something else, this time, it could be good news. You have some framed sketches in ochre and black ink, faded, of a women's features. Mouth, eyes, and nose and there are delicate posed hands. The writing is in mirror antiquated Italian. They may be works of significant importance.

I have only ever seen similar work in the Windsor collection.'

Olivia shrieked.

'What, are you saying, they're by Leonardo da Vinci?'

Geraldine placed a hand over Olivia's.

'I don't know for sure, but I would very much like to take them away to be verified. I am cautiously very excited.'

Tristan looked bewildered.

'First of all, I have stolen works of art in my possession, and now these drawings could be an even more extraordinary find. What is going on? Venetia had so many pictures. We need some experts to assess what I have on my walls.

Let me get you the bag they were wrapped in. A medical bag, but also something of Venetia's in our early days together. I kept it as a reminder of all we went through.'

Over the next few weeks, Geraldine verified the photos of the panels with colleagues in London and Amsterdam. The slowness of communications meant it was over a week before all could be finally agreed. The dark wooden panels were the missing Masaccios. David Castle was again interviewed, and more of his photographs were examined. The mysterious, beautiful nurse was identified as the wife of Tristan. Venetia Compton. Stan was recognised as Tristan, the doctor with the limp on board the ship. At David Castle's interview, his recollections became more lucid, the mystery was pieced together, and the hazy understanding of the past came into focus. The panels had never been taken by the Nazis but by the beautiful Venetia, collector and thief of renaissance art. Her disguise as a very competent nurse and her fluency in German, Italian and French enabled her to travel in Italy and France, nursing the wealthy and gaining access to private collections of artwork. During the turmoil of war with families, homes and possessions disrupted, it had not been a difficult task for her to secrete away one or two objects and artefacts of significant antiquity. People had been more concerned for their lives than their treasures.

The Masaccio paintings, after a lengthy appraisal and

processing of red tape and bureaucracy, were finally returned to the Count in Italy. Olivia had followed the whole story and was constantly being updated by her aunt. Tristan had also been involved all along the way. His interest in art had been ignited. Each day he talked with Olivia about the progress of the investigation. They became close friends. His face no longer bore the weight of sadness, but his eyes lightened; new interests and pursuits changed him. He pulled down all his old diaries and started writing a memoir of his exploits and travels with renewed enthusiasm.

As the Masaccio case was brought to a satisfactory conclusion, another intriguing page opened up with the finding of the black and red chalk drawings of a woman's features. Additional pages containing extensive notes and lists in antiquated Italian were found when the frames were fully opened. Some pages were just drawings, but one specifically had descriptions alongside the sketchy face looking across the Tuscan Hills. The excitement was intense. Geraldine took care of the sketches and then enlisted experts at one of the leading London auction houses to identify the age of the works, the artist and the possible subject. The Surveyor of the Queen's Pictures, the Royal Collection, Sir Oliver Shepherd, was a great friend of Geraldine. He took the sketches and spent many hours analysing their authenticity and comparison with similar works by Leonardo de Vinci held at Windsor. The art world was in a frenzy. The likeness to the eyes and mouth of the Mona Lisa was remarkable. Never before had any sketches or drawings for this painting ever been uncovered. Were the drawings just casual sketches or, more excitingly, preparatory sketches for this much more significant work of art? Sir Oliver introduced Geraldine to his good friend Jane Robson, curator of the Print Room at Windsor. She was initially sceptical, believing Leonardo had completed thousands of drawings but very few related to his paintings. These new findings were remarkable. However, still, there were numerous questions to be answered. Where had the drawings come from, and how had Venetia Compton gotten hold of them? What was their provenance?

Poor Olivia longed to pursue the investigation, but her studies at the university had to take precedence over following the life and past of Venetia Compton. Until further information could be revealed about where Venetia had been during the war and how she could have gotten the drawings, the sketches remained tantalisingly unverified. They were returned with encouraging but non-committal reports from various experts.

News of the sketches leaked out naturally to friends. The newspapers and journalists got hold of the story. Tristan felt slightly bewildered by all the interest and, in the end, posted a notice on his front door, banning any more journalists from knocking or bothering him. He gave the name of his solicitors as the place for further communication. Robert Grey was not deterred, and being a friend of Theo and Livia, Tristan felt entirely comfortable with this inquisitive young man. Behind the scenes, Robert took up the search into the life of Venetia Compton nee Bourne and her wartime travels through France and Italy, nursing and 'collecting'. He often dropped by and soon became friends with Tristan. In their discussions, Tristan showed him his diaries which went way back many decades. As they started examining these, amidst some of the dusty volumes were slimmer notebooks, very similar to school exercise pads. These were all in the written hand of someone other than Tristan. Immediately he recognised his wife's meticulous italic writing.

Dates, accounts, places and sketches were all there. Together they catalogued them in chronological order. A most revealing account of Venetia's travels, adventurous life, and all her collections began. From the tatty yellowing paper emerged codes and maps. A jigsaw of journeys and places. Venetia had cared for the sick and vulnerable but used her knowledge of their ramblings for her own use. Drawing out of her patients' secret hiding places for their treasures, she had written down dates next to sketches of objects she had found. Robert came across the account of a journey in the autumn of 1944 through the

Loire valley. He started to read it out loud as he pieced together the trail.

'SATURDAY: I came upon the Chateau in all its glory of bygone days. Its reflection in the river perfectly mirroring to me a double vision of its once magnificence. The white of its exterior dazzled in the sun. A quiet stillness surrounded it. Days of bombing had produced gaping gashes, the facade damaged by the pounding of hundreds of bullets. The stained glass and roof of the chapel were devastated, small fires burned in the distance. The Garconnet and Minimes tower virtually obliterated. I could not waste time reflecting on past glories. I had so little time to find the entrance to the tunnel. The enemies had retreated, and the allies were fast approaching. I was only one day ahead of them. The once-secret passageway between King Francis and L. Years of neglect had left the area covered in ivy and undergrowth. My map was clear, though. The letter taken from Lilly Eliades, now would be my reward, the dressmaker Mathilde's letter to her mistress Marie Caroline and Duke de Aumale at Orlean House in Richmond. Will I find the drawings?'

There was a blank page, then overleaf the following words in bold capital letters.

'I HAVE THEM.'

Tristan drew closer to Robert. They both looked at each other in astonishment. They peered at the handwritten pages. What was this place that Venetia had visited in France, in the Loire valley? She mentioned drawings, L and King Francis? Tristan tugged at Robert's sleeve and said:

'Come on, let's go into the library, bring the notes with you. We need to unearth what this place referred to is. The Chateau, The Garconnet and Minimes tower. Who is this Lilly Eliades? The Duke de Aumale and where is this Orlean House in Richmond?'

Tristan spun around and virtually ran towards the library. Robert smiled as he tried to keep pace with the limping half-skipping older man. How fortunate for them both, rows of encyclopaedias were available to them. So, began hours of painstaking research into the life of Leonardo da Vinci and King Francis. Tristan pulled out the encyclopaedias, and with Roberts's help, they extracted all the information they could. He read out loud.

'King Francis had installed Leonardo in the Chateau Clos Luce close to his own Chateau, The Amboise. There had been a secret underground passageway made to meet and continue their friendship whenever they wished. After Leonardo's death, his assistant Salai sold the 'Mona Lisa painting to King Francis. Leonardo lived at the Clos Luce for four years until his death in 1519. Leonardo's drawings, writings and compositions had been entrusted to his executor Francesco Melzi and upon his death to his son, a lawyer.''

'This is interesting, Robert. We need to know who told Venetia where to look. Could drawings of preparatory sketches for the Mona Lisa have been left at the Chateau Amboise or the Chateau Clos Luc in the secret passageways? This Lilly Eliades, what is her connection? Maybe she is still alive?

The only person I know who can help us out now is Geraldine. If anyone can trace this Lilly Eliades, it is her.'

Geraldine was definitely the person with all the connections and was soon hot on the trail of Lilly Eliades. Sadly Lilly had died sixteen years earlier. She had been a wealthy philanthropist and art collector. Living at Thames River House, Twickenham from 1927. Her son Christopher was more than happy to communicate with Geraldine. She gently drew out of him his mother's connections and interest in Orlean House. He was delighted to talk about the many exploits of his mother and stepfather.

'Mother bought part of the adjoining property, the remains of 'Orlean House', just before it had been demolished. The 'Octagon Room' and the stables buildings were designed by James Gibbs; they were the only part remaining. The larger house had been the last residence of the Orlean family, the Duke de Aumale and his wife Marie Caroline, who had lived at the Chateau Amboise in the Loire Valley before being exiled to England in 1852. Queen Victoria had been their friend and given them Orlean House as a gift.

Ma was a collector of all sorts. While renovating the Octagon Room, she found all kinds of artefacts, papers, small ornaments, letters, sewing needles and dressmakers tools. Many went missing. Why are you interested in my mother and her collections? '

Geraldine explained that they were trying to trace whether a private nurse had ever been employed by the Eliades family to care for Mrs Eliades at any time.

'Yes, actually, there was a nurse who came for three months. Ma was very ill with nervous exhaustion. After she had purchased the adjoining property, extensive renovations were made. Along with all the demolition work by the gravel merchants. My poor mother suffered severely from her nerves. Then this beautiful tall, elegant nurse came. My mother was sedated, and the nurse cared for her every need. I didn't see mother for some weeks.

Gradually mother recovered and then spent a few months recuperating in the South of France. The nurse went with her, mother returned after a couple of months, but sadly nurse Bourne did not. What a stunner she was, handsome face and dazzling smile. I was twenty and madly in love with her.'

Geraldine sat back in her chair and held the telephone receiver tightly with both hands. She calmly thanked Mr Eliades for his help and firmly replaced the receiver in its holder. Her eyes darted towards her notes, and picking up her pen, she quickly wrote down everything that had been said. Excitement buzzed through her body. The Masaccio case had been solved, but now another more intriguing and potentially explosive revelation was opening up. At that moment, Geraldine made up her mind. She quickly packed an overnight bag and left a short message for Juno and her housekeeper, then telephoned Tristan. 'I'm on my way, can't speak over the phone.'

Within an hour, she was speeding down towards Exeter. The

rain poured, and the monotonous swish of the windscreen wipers pounded out a beat coinciding with her heart's rhythm as it slowed and calmed. Her ability to plan and strategise in her mind whilst involved in physical activity was now working overtime. Despite the torrential rain, the journey time flew by, accomplishing travel and a well-formulated plan of action as she drew up outside the Colleton Crescent house.

Tristan and Robert had been waiting in the front living room, constantly looking out for the arrival of Geraldine. As the street lighting was switched on, Geraldine arrived. Her familiar smile and bright eyes instantly encouraged Tristan to speak:

'Come on in, my dear, what terrible weather you've driven through. Robert has just gone to fetch fresh tea. Here take a seat. Now tell me, your curious, quick phone message, that you were on your way. Well. We have been on tenterhooks all afternoon. What is your news?'

Geraldine sank into a huge leather armchair. She sighed, a contented woman with a smile broadly spread across her face.

'Lilly Eliades was a woman of some property and art collections in Richmond. She owned the Octagon Room, the only remains of the Orlean House in Richmond.

While in England, Duke de Aumale and his wife Marie Caroline lived at Orlean House after leaving their home.
The Chateau Amboise in the Loire Valley!
The Chateau is where King Francis had lived with Leonardo, not a few hundred yards away in the Clos Luce.

Now the account has become very interesting. Lilly Eliades was nursed by a beautiful tall, elegant young lady named nurse Bourne. They both went to the South of France, where Mrs Eliades recuperated for two months. Christopher Eliades said that his mother had at some point owned items she found in the Octagon Room as she was renovating it. Marie Caroline's maid, Mathilde, had kept letters, paperwork, ornaments, and dressmaking tools.

The letter from Mathilde may have been the one Venetia referred to in her diaries. Lilly was often sedated and may not have always known what she was saying or doing.'

Tristan's face paled, and he sank back into his chair. He looked tired as he finished her sentence.

'Venetia must have taken the letters from this sick woman.'

The realisation and sadness of the moment were interrupted by Robert with the tea tray. Geraldine sat quietly; Robert looked first across at Tristan then, with furrowed brows, tilted his head enquiringly towards Geraldine. The clock ticked, the rain beat hard against the windows, and they drank their tea silently. Suddenly Tristan sat up.

'Of course, why didn't I think of it before? Let's go and find the medical corps bag. The one that had concealed the Masaccio panels I brought back from Italy for Venetia. There is a pocket at the back; I have never examined it. Come on, Robert, help me up.

That evening the rain stopped, and a watery low sun gleamed clear and bright, briefly illuminating the old letters on the dining table. Moulding and spattered with foxing marks, the papers were dusty and faded. But the discovery in the pockets of the medical bag was no doubt the missing letters from Mathilde, the dressmaker, to her mistress Marie Caroline. Geraldine's command of the French language was quickly put to good use, and she read and translated the words clearly to them all.

Mathilde had been left in France as the family escaped to England. She spoke of her work, listing the dresses and various clothing she had stored away along with mundane concerns she had for the family. Then as the pages were unfurled, she wrote about the drawings.

'I have taken it upon myself to carefully conceal in the Chateaux tunnel your most precious drawings Madame, along with the writings and their explanatory notes of the landscape surrounding Lisa Del Giocondo.'

Tristan thumped his hand down onto the yellowing pages. Geraldine jumped, and Robert threw his hands in the air and whooped.

'Here are the letters that Venetia must have used to find the hidden drawings. This mention of Lisa Del Giocondo the 'Mona

Lisa'. We have a paper trail that links all the missing pieces, and we have the preparatory sketches by Leonardo. What do you say, Geraldine?'

Geraldine looked at Tristan and beamed as she hugged him. Robert wrote hastily in his notebook as he tried to contain his shrieks. The dining room door burst open, and Olivia and Theo looked in amazement at the scene. Books piled high in disarray, and scattered papers filled the dining table. The room glowed with the last rays of the red sun beneath the storm clouds above the horizon.

Three faces exuded excitement and childish joy. Their shouts and laughter rippled through the air. Olivia rushed forward, trying to make sense of what was happening.

'What have you found? What's happened?'

All Geraldine could do was a point at the letters, gasping.

'It's all there. The drawings are genuine, and this is incredible.'

Tristan sat down, his shoulders sagging, catching his breath. He threw his hands in the air and shouted.

'Get the champagne, Robert, two bottles. Here take these keys, cellar door, first on the left in the hallway.'

Their home became a hub of students coming and going. With all the public interest in the sketches, various societies or journalists would drop by to interview anyone familiar with the Leonardo drawings. After the initial excitement and discovery, it became apparent to Tristan that the pictures' responsibility, security and guardianship were far too much for him to care for. The pleasure that the friends at Colleton Crescent had enjoyed, touching, holding, inspecting and gazing with awe at such glorious treasures, had been a reward. They all agreed they had to be viewed and appreciated by a much wider audience.

The drawings were finally transported and donated to the Victoria and Albert Museum. They would be available without charge for the public to view and loaned annually to the Louvre in Paris.

The excitement of discovering and uncovering antiquities had taken hold of them all for the past few months, and it took great effort to return to concentrated study. Theo immersed himself in his archeology papers, sometimes staying late at the university to have some solitude from all the friends that dropped by now frequently at 'Tristan's' open house. The rejuvenated doctor loved to be involved with all the younger crowd, keen for discussion and debate. Montgomery and Gabby were frequent visitors. Tom was always on the lookout for Theo and anything archaeological. Another young man Felix Gander also joined their set, he had enrolled on the archaeology course along with Tom, and they had both signed up to work on a dig the following summer in Syria at the site of an ancient temple near Ain Dara. Theo had written about this site after previously spending six months there. Hence Felix and Tom were happy to draw from his first-hand knowledge all they could before going to the site. Sara and Alice enjoyed the company of these 'historians' too. But, of course, Alice was always welcome. Wherever she went, her 'chicken rice and ting' went down a treat too. Susan and John were now a pair, getting plumper by the day, following wherever the excellent food was, and stimulating debate. John loved the argument and very often played devil's advocate provocatively. He liked to test his abilities to turn controversy and dispute his own way. He would make a very clever lawyer. At most of these gatherings, Robert Grey turned up too, notebook always on hand, jotting down the rhetoric and behind-the-scenes gossip from student life. They all begged him to make sure to use different names when he wrote about them if he published his scribblings.

On rare occasions, Theo and Livia had time to themselves. They crept down their stairs, closing the front door as quietly as possible. Then out onto the crescent and down the steps to the estuary. The leisurely walks along the Quay, investigating the fascinating brick arches where once merchants had stored their goods, were exciting times. They loved to poke around the empty warehouses and then meander along the footpath towards Exmouth, away from the hubbub of student life, research, debate and people. They would often just stroll in silence, breathing in the clean, fresh air, watching the water birds ducking and diving. A few times, they cycled all the way through to Topsham and right onto Exmouth. Even in the winter when it wasn't raining, the views were spectacular, the bright blue against scudding cloudy skies, the peace and silence restorative. Just dog walkers, fellow cyclists and a few local joggers frequented the pathways. They explored the marshes around the nature reserve. Olivia loved how Theo always knew the names of the birds they saw. She slowly recognised the Teal, Avocet, Curlew and black-tailed Godwits with their long spindly legs and pointed beaks. Theo took an interest in their habitat and seemed to know so much about them. Every day was an education for Olivia as she drank in the information. Like a thirsty plant for moisture, she thrived and blossomed.

On warm days, they sat amongst the high grasses on Topsham's side of the bank. Looking out across the marshes, watching the ducks and waders feeding in the shallow wetlands, reminded Theo of the area around Rivertree, his home in Pennsylvania. They often spoke of their dream to live somewhere like this when all the years of student life could be behind them. They talked of having a family and their own home. For the first time in her life, Olivia thought of babies, lovely gurgling little ones like Theo. Theo reminded her that all he remembered of his younger siblings were sick and wailing. Then his mom and dad chasing them around to get them to bed. Livia laughed and reassured him with a playful push not to worry; she was willing to wait just a little longer for her dream of baby Theo and the many others to come along.

CHAPTER 12

'The Wonderful hope and expectancy of my heart.'
World Voices by Ella Wheeler Wilcox
New York: Hearst's International Library Company

Exeter and Rome 1979

Would life ever be the same again at Colleton Crescent? Day trippers walked by, staring at the tall windows, pointing and peering. Photographers leaned against the railings pretending to take pictures of their companions posing. The frenetic interest in the Da Vinci sketches was unprecedented. However, like most sensational stories, headlines one day are very soon superseded by another mystery, scandal or catastrophic world disaster. That year's excitement and Colleton Crescent's notoriety gradually tempered down. New stories took over the paper's headlines. Tristan quietly carried on writing his memoirs. Robert came less and less, working hard with his studies and research to complete his degree. Theo, at last, had the peace to complete his thesis from home.

Often in a dreamlike state, Olivia could not shake off her restless reverie of feeling slightly apart from reality. Her mind would not settle back into her studies. Edgy and unsettled, she drifted around the apartment, wistfully looking out the window across the estuary. All she could think of was when Theo would return and the happiness she was enjoying in those early months of marriage. Bizarrely vivid thoughts of renaissance Leonardo da Vinci kept floating into her imagination. She had been distracted by Leonardo da Vinci for too long. She took hold of a duster and vigorously started wiping down the cupboards. Pulling out a long drawer, her eyes rested on a forgotten tissue package. Her fingers unfolded the crisp creased layers revealing the gold bangle and ring Geraldine had given her. Running her fingers over it gently, the gleaming gold of ancient Rome glistened as she turned it over, heavily embossed with vine leaves and 'bees' circling around the name 'ColumelVilla Avernus'. Ahh, still the question of what this signified. Could she demystify the past lives of real people from the Julio Claudian dynasties? Was this what she needed to get back into formal research and study again? The gold turned through her fingers. Simultaneously Olivia's mind whirled into motion, and more importantly, her quest for answers ignited. Olivia's heartbeat quickened. They had to go to Rome that summer. She would renew her old friendship with Montefiore and Caterina at the Villa Battista in Frascati. Olivia had always been curious to see the returned Masaccios in their place at the Villa.

As soon as Theo's paper was published, he was invited to speak at the Society of Antiquaries in London and the British Archaeological Association. Following international reporting of his work on Ancient Roman and Greek archaeology, offers came from European universities. Olivia said nothing. She still had one more year to complete her degree but wanted Theo to choose alone his teaching post. She was happy to complete her degree wherever he was appointed.

Word got around that Theo was being headhunted. At Exeter, Professor Arthur Digby soon heard that Theo was considering taking up a position at another university. Swiftly he offered him a post in the newly established Anthropology and Archaeological Sciences department for Ancient Roman studies. Olivia secretly hoped and prayed Theo would take the position. She tried her hardest to disguise her enthusiasm for staying in Exeter. To her delight, Theo accepted the teaching post at Exeter.

Spring slid into summer unannounced, with only the sun higher, amidst endless days of rain and the south-westerly blowing the tall rushes across the estuary, sometimes at right angles to their upright pose. Their silks and tassels blew in the breeze.

Summer break arrived, and the long-awaited trip to Rome. Rome heaved with traffic and tourists but kept its ancient charm for the two intrepid explorers. For one precious day on their own, they revisited famous sites they had both known in their teenage years. Their next few days were a hurly-burly mix of all the Gambocelli relatives eager to get to know Olivia. They were embraced into a lively and affectionate family of uncles, aunts, and numerous exuberant children. Phone calls came into the Rome house from the Frascati side of the family with hospitality offers if they could make it out there. Theo was hesitant. He knew he had three days of work commitments in Rome. Olivia immediately picked up on the Frascati connection.

'Oh, I could go, Theo. I meant to get in touch with Monti and Catherina in Frascati. If I stay one day here in Rome at the Museo Nazionale for my studies and research. Then I could visit relatives and friends out in Frascati. Is that Ok with everyone?'

Smiles and nudges all around confirmed how happy all were that this tall, energetic and beautiful young woman was willing to visit the Frascati Gambocelli's. Everything was taken out of Olivia's hands. Transport, accommodation, food parcels, enough for a three-week expedition, and hugs and kisses from all accompanied the short trip to Frascati in two days.

Olivia's day exploring the library threw up some interesting thoughts. Researching the noble women of the imperial days, she read Latin writings of Seneca, Suetonius, Tacitus and the poetry of Ovid. Gaining insight into the mind of the ancient men of Rome but very little into the concerns and feelings of Roman women. She dug out snippets of information on women of poetry Sappho, Erinna and Sulpicia. What few lines of poetry or epigrams remained were by male scholars writing about women, with their interpretations of love, tragedy, death, life and families. These writings extensively referenced ancient times' male political and social history. The women mentioned appeared well-read and had an insight so tantalisingly suggested that Livia visualised the possibilities of revealing more and making it the central theme of her dissertation. In the evening, Theo and Livia discussed their research and findings. Whether unearthed literally from the ground or from the many pages of ancient manuscripts, their lives were enriched by these lively discussions, which often led to more questions than satisfying answers.

South of Frascati, high in the Alban hills, the breeze and clear air were a welcome change from Rome's odour and hectic pace, where noise, traffic, and intense heat sapped energy and blurred its ancient beauty. The Appian Way out of Rome, now a modern congested road, allowed Olivia time to contrast it with the travellers of centuries ago. Long before these tarmac roads. She imagined the cobbles and flagstones. The loud clattering of iron wheels on hard stone gradually changed to dusty tracks as they approached the Alban Hills in the distance and the Grand Villas of the noble families as they visited for the summer months, maybe to a more relaxed bucolic way of life amidst the rural landscape and farming communities. Seeing the Gambocellis farm added to the ambience of a bygone rural time.

The wheels screeched amidst the dust and scattered pebbles. The old house hid its elegant splendour behind a high terracotta crumbling wall. Through the open windows of the taxi, Olivia breathed in the scent of wisteria and jasmine. She glimpsed ancient twisted limbs encircling a veranda and balconies along the front of the Villa. A cockerel scooted across in front, its life saved for one more day.

Theo's Nonna, Francesca Gambocelli, stood at the open shaded door. She smiled and greeted Olivia. Her bright black eyes surveyed with interest, and her head nodded approval as she beckoned Livia in through the opened oak doorway. After the heat of travel, the cool, shuttered rooms wafted a refreshing, uplifting fragrance of lavender and beeswax. She was led across a marble entranceway into a circular hall. The stairs wound upward, in two directions, onto a galleried first floor. Light flooded in through an octagonal cupola above the top of a domed ceiling. Olivia almost lost her balance as she walked with her neck leaning back, staring up at the ceiling. There were murals painted all around. Scenes of trees, flowers, birds and deer, and men and women seated under arbours of entwined flowing vines. The plasterwork was peeling and fading to soft hues of blues and greens. Suddenly a young woman's voice shouting startled Olivia from her thoughts. Splashes of paint sprayed above as a metal container crashed to the floor. In the far corner below the balustrading was a wooden scaffold. On top of the platform was a young person leaning out, balancing pots and brushes on a tray in one hand, with the other holding a pointed trowel. Nonna turned and spoke rapid Italian to the girl gesticulating from the scaffolding who replied:

'I am so sorry. Yes, I will be down immediately.'

Her head disappeared, and with her feet pounding on the rickety ladder, she landed on the marble floor. Olivia saw a petite young woman dressed in paint-splattered dungarees with her black hair tightly bound up in a red cotton scarf. Her height and stature at first resembled a young girl. However, as she moved and spoke, confidence and energy showed clearly she was much older and in complete command of her situation. She beamed a smile at Olivia and held out her hand. Realising how much it was covered with paint, she withdrew it hurriedly, wiping it on an oily rag. Olivia laughed aloud, thinking of her sister and all the paint regularly splattered over her hands and hair. She extended a friendly hand.

Nonna Francesca, with great dignity, introduced her.

'Signora Chiara Fortuna. Conservator and restorer from Studio Fortuna Roma.'

Olivia immediately felt drawn toward Chiara and her work. They shook hands, and without restraint and her usual exuberance, Olivia asked numerous questions and commented on the frescoes, the history and the methods used. Nonna stood back and, after a few minutes, coughed, interrupting them. They both turned, simultaneously apologising. Nonna Francesca raised one hand and, smiling at them, said.

'No matter.'

She swept her hands into the air and, in a commanding voice, said.

'You young people, stop this chattering. You must both now come with me. Signora Fortuna, you go and clean up. We will eat on the terrace, and you and Olivia can continue your conversation and mutual interests over refreshments. I can see you both have a lot to talk about.'

She spoke sharply, but her lips half smiled, and her beady black eyes twinkled mischievously.

The afternoon passed with lively conversation, as Olivia and Chiara soon realised they had so much in common. Chiara had a wealth of historical knowledge of the area around Frascati, and as soon as she knew of Olivia's research into first-century Roman women, she was quick to speak of her recent findings. She was restoring artwork on walls and stonework of old buildings that reflected the gardens from ancient times.

'I have been reading the writings of Lucius Columella; his twelve volumes of Husbandry. The descriptions are lovely, referring to flora and fauna adorning the gardens in the first century.

There is a beautiful chapter on beekeeping; it's almost poetic. Columella was employed by the elite of Roman society to work on the land surrounding their sumptuous Villas.

I agree with you, Olivia. Noble women must have been involved in organising and administrating all the work. It's so long ago that nothing has ever been preserved of their writing and personal thoughts. Columella himself had villas nearby.

His works mention Ardea, Carseoli and Alba, all near Rome.'

Olivia's brow furrowed.

'One moment Chiara, this name Columella. Where have I heard this before? When you said, Alba. The two seem connected to something that's buried in my brain. I do wish I could remember.'

Olivia stood tapping her forehead.

 Nonna Gambocelli watched, listened and nodded to herself. She started to laugh.

Startled and slightly embarrassed, Olivia turned and apologised for chattering solely to Chiara.

'It is no matter, my dear. To hear you young people talk of my ancestors with such interest warms my heart.

You do know this land was once in the ownership of nobility? Columella may have designed gardens on this very land. If the layers of earth could be dug up, who knows what secrets would be uncovered. They all came here from Rome for the summer months, senators, poets, governors, the wealthy rulers with their families. Villas and farmsteads were built all in the foothills of the Alban Hills. As the local farmers, today dig the soil, often fragments of Roman times are dug up. I have a collection of old ceramic and coins. '

Olivia's eyes looked intently at this handsome old lady. What else could she glean from her?

'Nonna Francesca, has there ever been an archaeological dig organised here?'

The old lady shrugged and sighed, but her eyes darted towards Olivia's face.

'Bah, they come, and they go. This official and that bureaucrat. They poke around, take measurements, and photographs. Then they appoint new professors and new chancellors, and the government changes. Occasionally we get letters. I have collected many over the years.'

She looked up and laughed again, raising her eyes and shrugging her shoulders.

'Italy is my country of birth. I love my country. It has a rich heritage, much of its treasures buried beneath centuries of soil. Today, layers of bureaucracy, legal wrangles and new laws' have piled up to slow the progress of ever uncovering some of these treasures.

I say, All the best to anyone who can get the permits to start a dig or even find the department to issue them. It's all a great mystery to me.

Come with me. I will show you my 'unofficial finds' I know nothing about their history myself.'

She looked furtively over her shoulder, then tapped her forefinger to her lips.

They followed her to the rear of the house and up another flight of stairs onto a back landing. Nonna Francesca unlocked a tall double-doored armoire. She pulled out drawers. Each held cracked fragments of dusty pottery, but beneath the flaking and cracks, bright colours, a bird's feather, a sprig of flowers, the paw of an animal, a man's hand, a jigsaw puzzle with many pieces missing. Olivia lifted the pottery pieces and then moved the trays around. Beneath them were more artefacts, metal shards, an earring, and what looked like coils and rings. A treasure trove waiting to be uncovered, history to be discovered. Chiara, too, looked closely at the artefacts. She pulled out a small magnifying eyepiece from her pocket and turned a metal bauble in her fingers. She read out loud.

'Villa Julian, Gracaen. Tiberius. What is this referring to? The reign of Tiberius? I would love to investigate further, he had a villa built in this region?'

She picked up a dull brown coin.

'This coin, see the distinctive head of Nero. Amazing to think these span eras of emperors.'

Olivia leaned in to look closer. Chiara handed her the eyepiece and the sestertius.

'Wow, imagine how old this must be, Nonna Francesca? Have you ever shown these to Theo? This is fascinating stuff you have here. '

Nonna Francesca sniffed and shrugged her shoulders, saying she had often looked at the pieces with her children and grandchildren. They had played with them. With so many fragments often appearing, they only viewed them as pretty coloured ceramics and old bits of metal. Everyone was busy with their own lives and interests. She carefully closed the drawers and relocked the door. Putting her head on one side and narrowing her eyes, she looked seriously across at Olivia for a few seconds. Leaning in towards Olivia and raising one eyebrow, she spoke quietly under her breath:

'Come again, Olivia; when there is more time, you are all welcome to look and see what you can uncover. Maybe it's not just rubbish.'

She paused and then said.

'Keep in touch, write to me about what you find. I know I am an old woman, but I still like to read. I have my library.'

She tilted her head to one side, hesitating. Should she say more?

'I may not understand your world, but I do want to hear about history. '

She patted her forehead.

'There is more to tell up here. Come back soon with Theo.'

'Oh, we will. We're hoping that next year we will have more time to visit for longer. It's been such a busy year, and this visit is almost over. Theo is still in Rome, finishing his work. I have to go tomorrow to see some friends I met many years ago at the Villa Battista. Then it will be back to Rome and home on Saturday. It's been too short. My mind is buzzing with ideas and so many questions to be answered. I think I will be the 'forever student and researcher'. So much to explore. It's all so tantalisingly close by.'

Olivia's stay overnight with Nonna Francesca and her new friendship with Chiara ended quickly. Chiara gave her address and details to Livia, promising to correspond with any information she could find in the Fortuna archives. Olivia fingered through her black notebook, which still had half the blank pages left from when she had used it as a teenager and started writing an investigation page. With bullet points:

- Alban Hills, Villas of emperors, Villa Julian, Gracaen Tiberius. The metal bauble with Nonna Francesca
- Possible dig for Theo!
- What the Fortuna archives will produce?

• More questions for Nonna Francesca? What does she know?

As she turned the pages, her eyes fell upon the drawings she had done of her Roman jewellery and the wording, 'Columel Villa Avernus Villa Alba.

'That was it! The name is Columel. Could it be Columella? Chiara had mentioned Alba too. Was there a connection? Could her jewellery be connected to Columella? What was the Villa Avernus? Where had it been? The digging had to continue. Could she get her hands on a copy of his writings?

From her balcony, she watched the sunset, turning from its dazzling brilliance to a red-orange orb as it dipped beneath the horizon. Darkness descended quickly, no street lights for miles around. Only a distant glow from Rome's direction some thirty miles away. The stars sparkled in their numberless millions. The warm night breeze lightly fluttered the muslin drapes behind the half-closed shutters, drifting into the room a heady scent of jasmine and rosemary. No traffic sounds, just the chirrups of cicadas and an occasional dog barking across the valley. Olivia slept dreaming of a young girl in her linen tunic roaming through the Hills, her slave girl following as they skipped and ran. Breathing in the same fragrances, hearing similar noises that she was, on land that had only changed by layers of earth, time, people and ravages of weather.

A short journey the following day took Olivia south to the Villa Battista. As the taxi approached the entrance, her thoughts returned to when she was a teenager. Again the beauty of the Villa and its surrounding countryside took her breath away. The tall gates were open already, and to her delight, the fountains were still spouting out high fantails of water. She smiled to herself. How kind of Monte and Caterina to welcome her with this display. Even the taxi driver slowed and softly said, 'Oh Mama mia' as he saw the magnificent house and water spewing high before them. He looked more closely at Olivia through the rearview mirror and nodded to himself as he sat more upright and passed a hand over his slicked-back hair.

Monti and his wife had been looking out for Olivia. The door opened immediately as the car stopped outside the main entrance. The taxi driver sped around to open the door for Olivia. She reached out and shook his hand, smiling as she handed him the payment and asked for his return that evening. He nodded and bowed slightly as he agreed, delighted to see the Signora at 9 o'clock.

The sight of Monti and Caterina, some eleven years older, brought a wave of emotion to Olivia. She had only been their visitor for one day at the Villa, but she had never forgotten their kindness. The investigations into the lost Masaccios and the letters passed between them had formed a close friendship with these dear people. Now to see them again, still handsome and elegant. Monti, a little bent over and Caterina, now in a wheelchair, brought tears to her eyes. Her mind returned to their hospitality, kindness and understanding of the youthful folly she had shown.

'My dear Olivia, welcome, welcome again after all these years.'

Monte held out both hands to Olivia and held her close. His wife, too, kissed her warmly on both cheeks.

'We have a lot of catching up to do, and of course, you must see the panels restored and placed in their original positions. All thanks to you and Geraldine.'

That afternoon was full of laughter and intense conversations. They covered the years together. Olivia's student days, her marriage to Theo. Laughing at the coincidence of Theo being the young archaeologist Livia had nearly decapitated with the falling stone pot. Monti and Caterina were enthralled to hear about the investigations into the missing Masaccios and then finding drawings lost for centuries by the great Leonardo. Monti was astounded. He kept shaking his head, repeatedly asking about the sequence of events leading up to the verification.

'This is most intriguing, Olivia. I am just overwhelmed. My

memory is not as good as it used to be, but I remember the days when the house was used as a hospital. I recall the nurse, well she was outstandingly beautiful.'

He looked across at Caterina and placed his hand over hers.

'We both remember her. Ahh, a very clever woman, it seems, an actress with many skills. Tell me again how you verified the provenance of the sketches?'

Olivia repeated the events, realising that the years had brought memory loss for Monti and Caterina. Nonetheless, she was happy to relay what she knew repeatedly. Livia discussed her recent research with them, her visit to Nonna Francesca, and the restoration work Chiara was doing. It made them happy, and each time she concluded, they smiled and shook their heads, clapping their hands together. Monti's eyes lit up:

'Ahh, that has always been a passion of mine. Restoration and then to discover what those clever ancient women really thought. Some of the Caesars' well-known or somewhat notorious wives are written about with such arrogance and condescension. Let me know what you find, Olivia. You mention the works of Columella. I, too, am familiar with his writings. I probably have some volumes of 'De le Rustica' in my library. I remember volume ten, the one about beekeeping. Extraordinary. I must have a look at it,

in fact, I have a couple of books I can give you. Written by gentlemen explorers in the late 18th century. The language is very archaic, but there might be a glimmer of a reference you could pursue. Some of those men had bizarre thoughts but were well-educated travellers searching for truth. There may be some reference to their findings.'

Olivia was immediately keen to see the books. This could be the breakthrough she needed.

Two young women arrived and attended to Caterina in the afternoon and during their evening meal. They wheeled her into the dining room and discreetly took her out when she needed assistance. When on their own, Monti said.

'You can see we have excellent care. Camilla and Rosa live

here with us now. We will never have to leave this house. Our nephews and nieces have arranged it all. We will always be here. You are welcome to visit anytime, bring your husband when next you come to Rome. Perhaps you may write to me a little about your life and discoveries. Then there is some hope of me remembering this beautiful day.'

He looked at her knowingly with humour in his eyes.

'You are just beginning. You never give up, I can tell. Your enthusiasm and zest for life have been invigorating today. Yes, write to me about what we have spoken of, and I shall enjoy reading it repeatedly.

Now when Camilla and Rosa come back, we must have a photograph. The grown-up Olivia, along with us two. I will get the carers to send you a copy.

The books too from my library. I will go and get them. Take them with you when you go.'

Olivia said her goodbyes to her dear old friends. They smiled and laughed and kissed her, with Monti's parting words not to forget to write, dismissing from her mind a feeling of sadness at leaving them.

On the journey back to Rome, Olivia opened up the dull yellowed pages of the gold-leafed books Monte had given her. 'A Gentleman's Travels' by Reverend Horatio Goodstanton and 'A Roman Trail' by Quinton Longstaff. Both proved to be quite wordy and tedious reading. Olivia was familiar with Latin, but reading the long-winded writings of 18th-century explorers took a while to adjust. She was determined to persevere. The possibility of gaining more evidence of essays from ancient women spurred her. Suddenly a passage sprang out of the pages of the book by Quinton Longstaff.

'From my long extended walk through these densely covered Alban hills, valleys and vineyards.   The land dropped before me, and the great lake glistened far in the distance. Amongst the foliage,   I stumbled on a jagged rock. Days of scraping away the lichen and moss followed, and a flat stone emerged. Words weathered and hardly legible in Roman Latin were inscribed. It seemed to be poetry.

'I gave voice to with my stylus.'

P Graeci of A P..ius

My husband, my judge and my ………

What great injustice I have borne at the hands of my rulers.

I rest at last

Was this a tomb? The hand of a noblewoman of Rome?'
The book then described the birds and flora that he could see. No doubt his main interests took precedence over this potential ancient tomb. Olivia looked up and held the book tightly to her. She gasped. Where was this place the writer spoke of? Travelling through valleys and vineyards and looking from high vantage points to a vast lake.

That familiar tingling sensation came over Olivia when something new was about to happen. The haze starting to lift. Tantalising facts, so near but out of apparent reach. Again another turn in the quest for knowing the lives of bygone people. She placed an envelope from her bag in the book, writing in pencil. Where, when, what? A woman of Rome? Resolving to add these words to her notebook. She closed the volume firmly, sighing with a big grin, which remained until she met up with Theo.

On their last night in Rome, they ate in a trattoria Theo had discovered in one of the lesser-known back streets behind the university. Candles at each small table lit the dark interior. Only one table was unoccupied. The others were filled with families and their lively young children. Laughter and noisy voices mingled with the chink of glasses and crockery amidst the delicious smells of pungent wood-smoked meats, roasted garlic, and oregano. The food was hearty. The wine was deep red, flavoured with a taste of complex berries and a hint of cherries and liquorice. Olivia looked across at her handsome husband. She raised her glass and smiled, her eyes sparkling with expectation. He caught that look he had seen before, very recently.

'Come on then, what's your news, what are you plotting? I can see it in your eyes, honey.'

'There's so much. I feel alive and refreshed. I have so much to tell you, Theo. We have to return here soon. Your family in Frascati, your dear Nonna Francesca. Do you remember the large cupboard come dresser she has upstairs? All the little drawers were packed with bits of pottery and metal pieces. It's just waiting to be investigated. Have you ever tried to dig in the land around the house and farm? She showed us a coin with Nero's head on it. Inscriptions too from some sort of Villa and Tiberius name and another too. She hinted at so much.

I met Chiara Fortuna, who told me about Lucius Columella, an ancient writer and gardener. I must get a copy of his work. Do you know Chiara? There could be a connection with the inscriptions on my jewellery.'

'No, not personally, but Studio Fortuna is very well known. They are well respected and have years of archived pieces and records of their restoration work. I knew my grandmother had commissioned them to assess the work needed on the frescoes. Generations of their family have worked on restoration and conservation, and they can trace their family trade back to Renaissance times.

So you enjoyed meeting my Nonna? Quite a character. Don't be misled by her appearance or that she 'knows nothing'. You want to see her library. As a young girl she only had primary education, but her father collected books and encouraged her to read. She is basically self-taught, but her knowledge of the geography and history of the area is incredible. She made sure my mum went to school and encouraged her interest in art, ensuring she had the best education possible.

She keeps up to date with all the news in the archaeological field too. My uncle Ernesto, I know, values her views.'

Olivia looked astounded. She shook her head in amazement.

'That is so interesting. I will keep in touch with Nonna

Francesca; I wondered if she knew more than she was letting on.'

Olivia then sat quietly, thinking for a few moments. Her eyes narrowed as her forefinger tapped her lips. Theo watched as he imagined the cogs of her brain clicking away; something was about to emerge if he just waited.

'There's something else, and I'm not sure if it's connected. The Count at Villa Battista gave me two books written in the 18th century by explorers of the region and surrounding area. I haven't managed to read them all, but there's this one passage that talks about uncovering a tomb with inscriptions. The writer suggests 'like the hand of a woman'.

I have so much buzzing around in my head, so many loose ends. There could be some connections. Firstly my jewellery and possible relationships with Columella. Then the wording on your Nonna's fragments, and now this book mentions a tomb 'somewhere in the Alban Hills.'

Olivia had not taken a breath as she recounted her thoughts with infectious excitement. Her eyes were bright, and her cheeks pink. Theo reached across the table and took her hand.

'It's intriguing. When we get home, collate all your information together. Then we will assess all the possibilities, and it could be worth another journey out here. Incognito this time, giving us a chance to explore the area before we raise an elderly Italian lady's expectations.

If there is anything to be found, there are many red tapes to go through, making it official.'

He caressed her hand, bringing it up to his lips to kiss.

'And Livy, don't ever lose that passion you have. I love you.'

CHAPTER 13

'While just the art of being kind
Is all the sad world needs.'
Ella Wheeler Wilcox -Voice of the voiceless

Topsham 'Gung Ho'

In early July, Richard, Briddy and Tati came to visit at Gung Ho. Olivia was shocked to see again how tired and worn her mother looked. Tati was listless and more vacant in her expressions than ever before. Olivia anxiously waited for the right moment to speak with her mother.

Walking along the Goat Walk, arm in arm, relaxed with a gentle breeze blowing from the estuary, they reminisced about family holidays they had spent in previous years. Childhood companionable memories flooded back. Briddy slowed down, her breath laboured. Olivia gestured towards one of the benches facing the river. Maybe this was the right time to speak; she gently squeezed her mum's arm.

'It's so good to have you staying here, and lovely for you and me to have a bit of time on our own. You seem weary mum, how are you really at the moment?'

Briddy caught her breath and then turned to Olivia.

'Yes, Livia, I am weary, some days completely worn out. Maybe it's me, just getting older. Your Dad is still wonderful; he works so hard. There's talk he may retire in a couple of years. We've saved hard with having the house included with his job. We hope to get ourselves a bungalow by the sea, go back to our love of reading, writing and walking together. That would be nice to look forward to.'

She paused and looked down at her hands and sighed. Olivia placed a hand over her mother's.

'Mum, there's something else, isn't there? Can you talk to me about it?'

Briddy looked up with tears, scanning her daughter's face.

'It's Tati. I don't know where to begin.

She was travelling each day to art school in the beginning, always a bit absent-minded. Her tutors loved her work, though, and considered her unusual temperament. She had four years and just about managed to keep it all together.

Since then, she's become more and more reclusive.

Something happened on her way home one night. In her last term at the college, after her final exhibition. She was later than usual. I heard the door open as she came in, then running feet up the stairs and her bedroom door slam behind her. I waited; she never came down to supper. So, I knocked on her door and went in. She was sitting on the floor, with her arms wrapped around her, staring out vacantly. Her dungarees were all dirty, wet and muddy. Her face was scratched, and her hair hung in damp, messy strands. She started to rock and just repeatedly said. 'I should have saved her. I ran and ran.'

Briddy took a breath. Olivia reached out and silently took hold of her mother's clammy hands.

'At college that afternoon, Tati had found her best friend, Claudia, strung up from a beam in one of the old classrooms.

The police, interviews, funeral, and social services. I can't begin to describe what your poor sister went through, and she's locked herself away ever since.

Do you remember when you used to come home? Didn't you notice her appearance deteriorating?

Some of her paintings too. They're so dark I feel despair just looking at them.

There is something else, too. Tati will not eat. Livia, I am worried she's going downhill. She won't come to the doctor with me, and I can't get close to her. She's so far away inside herself.

Bringing her here for a holiday was significant coercion by your father and me.

Tati is twenty-five, and I'm at my wit's end to know what to do to help her.'

Olivia put her arms around her mother and spoke softly.

'Thank you for telling me, mum. You are so courageous, but it's too much for you to cope with all on your own. I didn't realise how bad it had become. This trauma that Tati's been through, I had no idea. What does the GP say? Have you spoken to him?'

'Well, he's quite old, and it's a bit awkward, he says she's over eighteen, and he can't do anything unless she goes in to see him herself.'

Olivia thought for a moment, then said:

'You know what, because there is such a vast university here, I'm sure there's a counselling department, especially for people suffering similar challenges as Tati. I will find out where young people get help at the uni. There may be a specialist counsellor that could give us some pointers. Theo may know the department heads catering for these issues.

I'll come and collect Tati tomorrow and take her out. We'll go for a walk along the Quay. Nothing too strenuous. If she's up to it, we'll visit one of the art exhibitions held in the disused units. See if I can spark any interest in her. There's also a foodie market going on, local produce, I'll get her to help me shop for some bits, and then you all come back to our place in the evening, and we will have a bit of supper together. How does all that sound?'

Briddy's face softened, and the sun on her pale cheeks produced a pinkish glow. Her own pale green eyes looked hopefully into Olivia's earnest face. The tears spilt silently out of her tired eyes.

'It sounds good, we can but try. Thank you, Livia.

You girls are all so different, each special in your own way. Impy, the actress, in life and on the stage, super confident, has an unbelievable memory for details, and so independent. Tati is a brilliant artist. Wrapped up in another world, doesn't have a clue how to live. Then you, my youngest, Aunt Geraldine's favourite, always inquisitive. Seeking intrigues and mystery solving. A little bit nosey.'

She smiled as she touched Olivia's nose.

'It's good you probe and question. All grown up, married, energetic and a problem solver, so warm and affectionate. You're helping me now.

I still have so much to learn from my grown-up daughters. Thank you, Livia.'

That night, Livia told Theo about Tati. He listened, then holding up his hand, he started to rifle through a stack of papers.

'I knew I had been given all sorts of manuals from the university regarding the different departments and social services available for the students and tutors. They might be able to point you in the right direction, even if it's only a listening ear, which could be helpful. Here's a couple of telephone numbers to call.'

Livia did not hesitate to call one of the numbers that evening. Mrs Hutchings was a good listener but let out a big sigh after Olivia told her everything.

'I really feel for your poor mum and dad. They sound like really good people. Reassure them that they are not on their own. We increasingly see trauma and anxiety problems in our students, which emerge as eating disorders, addictions, and self-harming. As Tati is not a student at the university, it would not be possible to give advice personally. However, I can send you a few pamphlets we distribute to students. I'm happy to post them to you.

There are organisations' addresses and a series of questions to help the sufferer to establish the extent of their needs.'
Olivia twisted the telephone cable in her hands. Running her fingers through her hair, she said:

'Mrs Hutchings, what can I do? I don't know where to start.'

'Olivia, be her friend, ask her about the things that she loves? Draw her out, don't say too much yourself. The most important thing your sister needs at the moment is kindness, then listen, listen and listen some more.'

She promised to post the pamphlets the next day, wished her well and hoped to catch up with her during the next term.

Livia managed to coax Tati out for their day together. For the first time that holiday, Livia realised how thin and gaunt Tati had become. She wore baggy denim dungarees, and Livia tied a bright red and white bandana around her wild rose golden hair. Her head felt bony, and her hair patchy and thin. The headband looked cute on Tati's head, and once or twice Livia caught a slight look of interest in those haunted, vacant eyes. They set off from Topsham along the footpath. Livia realised Tati would not be strong enough to walk the distance towards Exeter Quay so headed towards the railway station and caught the local train the short distance to St David's. As they stepped off the train, Tati grabbed at Livia's coat; her hands were shaking as her eyes wildly scanned around her. Olivia gently took Tati's arm and tucked it reassuringly into her own.

Olivia spoke quietly and calmly about life in Exeter. Mentioning some of the friends they had and their diverse interests. Tati kept her head down. Livia talked about Gabby and Montgomery, her sculptor work and his training as an architect. Tati raised her head. At last, a breakthrough, thought Livia, making a mental note to take Tati to visit Gabby and show her the studio.

They ambled alongside the Exe towards the Quay, which today was bustling with a farmers market. There were numerous cheese stalls and produce from around the local area. The market holders were keen to have their wares sampled, and as Livia tasted them, Tati, too, accepted a bite. Creamy Camembert and Stinking Bishop clearly were her favourites. Street musicians played flute and guitar, and a young woman sang country songs. They crossed the bridge making their way towards the brick arch stores. Olivia drew Tati along to the one containing a temporary exhibition of artwork from students at the university. The arches were once the storage places for cargo merchants traded on the estuary. A few were locked up and disused, but one or two had been converted into quirky shops.

They entered the dark cave-like interior through the double doors. It was as if Olivia had turned a light switch on in a darkened room, the effect the art exhibition had on Tati. She immediately moved away from Olivia and began touching and staring at the exhibits, talking to the students about their work. Sitting on one of the high stools next to the makeshift countertop, she soon gathered a group of men and women, all very similar to Tati, young, attentive and obsessed with the various art installations and styles under discussion. Tati was asked about her work, and one young man, taller and even thinner than Tati, with a shock of thick auburn hair and a face covered with an even deeper shade of red facial hair, stutteringly, discussed with Tati his sculpture work made up of intricate figurative wire designs. He only had one on show in the arches that day which had been sold. It was an owl placed in a position as if it were about to pounce on its prey. The details were complex, and the tangled wire added tension and excitement to the piece. Tati was transfixed.

Olivia stood quietly to one side, watching her sister start to unravel and express her words and thoughts to this tall ungainly artist. An idea sparked in her head.

'Hello'

She held out a hand to shake with the tall young man.

Tati jumped in.

'Livia, this is Jason Grimshaw; he's the artist who created this masterpiece, isn't it wonderful?'

Olivia stood back and observed the work of art before her.

'Yes, I've been standing at a distance looking with awe at the amount of detail you've put into your work. It must have taken a considerable time to complete; I know how long Tati takes with her artwork.

My husband and I are at the university. I'm still a student, and he's a lecturer there. We live just up on Colleton Crescent above the Quay.

Look, this might seem a bit odd to a stranger. But I'm popping home now. Tati and the family are coming up for supper this evening, so I best be getting back to prepare. You're welcome to join us if you're still in Exeter. We're an informal lot but love anything to do with art, archaeology and history, and we love to have a good old chat about all sorts of things. So, if you fancy a quick drink and a bit of supper?'

Tati looked pleadingly at Jason and said.

'That would be great if you want to if you're not rushing off anywhere?'

Jason grinned at Tati, nodded at Olivia, and stutteringly replied he would like that.

Tati looked at Livia and then back at Jason, suddenly seeming to have a rush of confidence.

'I tell you what, Jason, why don't I help you clear up here, and then we could walk up to Olivia's when you've finished. Together, so you know where she lives?'

Livia left the budding new friends with a bounce in her step and a slight feeling of optimism.

When Richard and Briddy arrived, Livia quickly briefed her mum and dad on the new friend of Tati's that was due to join them very shortly.

Just before Jason and Tati arrived, Livia quickly called Gabby and Monty to invite them over. Theo had invited Tristan also to join them. Their long chat that afternoon had convinced Theo he would get along well with Olivia's dad, Richard.

The upstairs rooms that evening were filled with laughter and lively debate. Sitting apart from all the loud conversations, Jason and Tati sat on the floor by the bookcases, engrossed in looking through art books. Olivia stood to one side and looked at her family and dear friends together. Tati and Jason's heads appeared to touch. Their unruly, frizzy mops brushed against each other like cobwebs strewn between two willowy stalks as they talked and nodded. Tati took no notice of Jason's hesitant stuttering, her eyes looking up at him, silently encouraging and patiently waiting to hear all he had to say. After a while, his voice became more assured; Tati, too, opened up, keenly attentive to the personal interest she was receiving from someone whose thoughts were like her own.

Livia noticed that Jason had a huge appetite for food but drank no alcohol. Everything he was offered he heartedly tucked into. His slim frame belied the fact he ate so much. As they talked, Jason ate, and quite absentmindedly, Tati mirrored his eating. Livia and her mum knowingly looked on and kept a steady supply of cottage pie and kidney beans for the two skinny young people. Richard enjoyed his conversations with Dr Compton, who insisted on being known by his Christian name to them, 'Tristan'. He had brought two bottles of vintage red wine with him and, when they were emptied, slipped away downstairs with Richard to replenish with a fresh supply. The smile never left his face, enjoying the lively company and good food for the first time in a while. After all the excitement of the lost paintings, the Leonardo sketches and writing up his memoirs had subsided, Tristan had wondered if he would feel so alive again. His home was now afresh with the sounds of laughter and young people. His contribution to the excellent wine made him feel, at last, after a long period of grieving and being slightly sorry for himself, this was something worthwhile. He could be part of living, breathing, participating and giving of himself again.

The evening western sun set over the estuary and flooded into the room through the deep sash windows. Not only was the light altered gradually to a golden yellow hue, but friendships started to glimmer. Tati leaned her head against Jason's shoulder. Tristan and Richard shared another bottle of wine and good-humoured stories of patients and students. Theo was engrossed in discussions with Monty, pointing out of the window, looking through binoculars towards the south east at something they had spotted in the distance. Briddy, Gabby and Livia were feeling slightly giggly and drowsy, having consumed two bottles of the excellent vintage from 'Dr Comptons' wine cellars between them. The cheap plonk that had been the tipple of their student days would not be satisfactory again. Changes would have been imperceptible to strangers, but there was an atmosphere that night - the air was warm, and conversations were close and confidential. Gabby closed her eyes and curled up in an armchair next to the window like a cat. Briddy smiled across and took Livia aside into the kitchen.

'Livia, what miracle has happened to Tati? I can't believe this young man Jason, do you know him? Is he a local artist? Who is he? Gabby, too, is such a pleasant person. She's arranged to have Jason and Tati over tomorrow evening. Could we be seeing a turning point? It's just finding something unique that grabs a person's interest, and it seems to be Tati's love of art and sculpture.

I'm a bit tipsy, a long-forgotten, pleasant feeling.
I've not seen your dad so relaxed. I think he has a new chum. Why don't you and Theo bring Tristan over to us in a couple of days to 'Gung Ho? Call us when you think it would be the best evening.'

Livia gave her mum a wobbly hug, glad that she and Theo could tumble into their bed upstairs and not have to find a taxi home as Briddy and Richard had. Jason had parked his car a few streets away and, after arranging to pick Tati up in the morning to help him the next day, left, thanking everyone and giving a big hug to Tati, Olivia and Briddy. Tristan said his goodbyes after exchanging telephone numbers with Richard. Gabby and Monty stayed longer; she was now fast asleep in the armchair. Theo made coffee for himself and Monty, seeming like they still had lots to talk about. Monty had his sketchpad out. Busily drawing as Theo looked over his shoulder. Livia said her goodnights and left them all to it.

In the early morning, Theo crept into bed beside an already deeply sleeping Livia. He was exhausted, but his head was buzzing with ideas and schemes he longed to share with Livia; The timing needed to be better. He would wait until she had graduated before setting out his plans.

Over the next few days, Jason and Tati became inseparable. Tati was taken over to Moretonhampstead on the edge of Dartmoor, where Jason's family lived, and he had one of the barns for his sculpture work. It wasn't long before Tati became part of the family. Jason's mum Pam took it upon herself to fatten up this scrawny friend of her son. She was an expert in making cheese and cream from the dairy attached to the farmhouse. So every afternoon, whilst the two young artists worked away in the studio, she supplied them with fresh scones and clotted cream. Jason never batted an eyelid when his mum appeared. He just worked and ate and ate some more. Even in that short week, Tati's sunken cheeks padded out, and her once-vacant eyes shone again with interest in life and food. Jason's family had a cottage industry on the farm. Pam worked the dairy and had a growing farm shop selling the produce from local farmers, dairy, arable and pastoral. Jason's Dad, Jim, and his youngest son Ryan worked the dairy farm together, whilst the oldest son Ash was a master builder.

The holidays ended too soon, but Tati decided to return the following month. Jason wanted her to stay and work alongside him in his studio. Feeling fond of Tati, Pam sensed the growing friendship and suggested she work in the shop with her when they were busy and lodge at the farmhouse. She needed assistance, and after showing Tati, the intricacies of cheese making, she was sure she could be a great help to them all.

So began Tati's new life, cheese making, baking and enjoying her food again, without needing any pamphlets and counselling. Jason and Tati continued to consume vast amounts of his mother's home cooking. Whilst Jason remained tall and skinny, Tati filled out to fit her dungarees. Her skin glowed with the mild fresh summer air, and her hair thickened up and grew long and wildly out of control. She had an area in the barn to continue her painting, and her interest in sculpture was encouraged.

Jason and Tati spent hours watching the wildlife on the moors. They collected photographs of birds in flight and resting, feeding and nurturing their young, then transposed them into Jason's wire sculptures. Tati painted and designed from the wild and natural landscape around them. After a few months, Pam and Jim realised that the two artists' work looked good. They could extend the shop area to an artists' studio for people to see the work and then sell some of it. Ash stopped by and saw that a substantial extension would be needed to house the new enterprise. Although he was an excellent builder, he knew architectural plans and planning permission would be granted before commencing work. Tati got in touch with Livia, and Monty was engaged to oversee the architectural project.

Whilst Tati was out at Moretonhampstead, Livia and Theo's lives quickened pace in Exeter. Theo was busy setting up his new department. With the recent influx of students, he was now fully involved in university life and politics from the other side as a lecturer. Livia got her head down in her final year as they silently worked in the same room on different sides for many hours without speaking. Aware of the other's presence, a brief word of encouragement, a shared cup of coffee or a late glass of wine before bed was all they needed to maintain their steady harmony of love and continued growing friendship.

Tristan was regularly in their company and showed a keen interest in the work of Theo and Olivia and very often asked. How's the young red-haired sculptor getting along with his work?

The student art exhibition had been in one of the arches owned by Tristan. Historically the units belonged to owners of The Crescent, and traders had used them for all sorts of business of varying degrees of lawfulness. He still owned two of them and enjoyed letting them out to the student exhibitions for a nominal rent. Therefore he took great interest in their work and future prospects.

That final third year was hectic for the group of students that had started life at Exeter together. Suddenly realising their finals were looming, they had much work to do. Which meant an awful lot of cramming and endless sleepless nights. The partying and pub visiting quietened down a little. Sara and Alice had worked hard all along, so it was no surprise they both received first-class honours degrees. Sara was offered a post at the pathology lab at Exeter hospital. She was delighted to be able to stay in Exeter. Alice had started writing short stories about life in and around Devon and received a job in London, promising she would keep in touch. They would all miss her delicious food and suggested returning to Exeter and opening a 'Ting' restaurant if the writing didn't succeed. Tom and Felix also decided to stay in Exeter and do their Masters. They had formed a close bond with Theo and often visited him for help and advice before setting off that summer to different digs, Tom going to Syria and Felix off to Turkey. Susan returned to her home town of Reading to take up the directorship in her dad's growing property company. It wouldn't be long before John Dixon followed her to become the managing director's son-in-law and lawyer. Family connections with the BBC and his father's journalistic colleagues had secured a plum job for Robert Grey as the assistant art editor of a leading newspaper. No doubt, too, he was fully ready to produce his first novel and maybe even had the next two lined up for publication; Robert never let out of his sight his little black notebook.

Olivia worked very hard in that final year. Her desertion took precedence over curiosity in further chasing the history of her jewellery. All she had time for was to place an advertisement in a national newspaper for a copy of the works of Columella. Finally, a reply came from a professor at Cambridge who had done a translation into English. He offered to send her a copy. The photocopied work arrived but was left in its brown envelope as life and anxieties over exams crowded out further reading.

Aunt Geraldine arrived at Topsham just after Olivia had received news that she had received a First Class Honours degree. Theo celebrated with her before driving her to spend a long weekend with her aunt at 'Gung Ho. He had insisted she went and promised he would be fine for two nights without her.

Aunt Geraldine and Olivia hugged and laughed like two school girls. They then walked along the estuary path, talking and taking in the sun facing the estuary. Geraldine was now a sprightly seventy-eight-year-old woman. Her mind was still as keen as ever. She was interested in Olivia's thesis on Ancient Roman women and their untold stories. She asked Livia: 'Tell me what your plans are now?'

'I'm tired, but I so enjoyed the research and writing. I may work for an M.A. Not immediately, though.

I need to go back to Rome and Frascati. The book Monte gave me. I read passages about finding a tomb, gardens and land around where Nonna Francesca lived. I would love to walk through and find out where that young man was when he saw a tomb.

I still have so many unanswered questions. The Roman jewellery. There's more to uncover on Nonna's land. A lot more to Nonna Francesca too. I have a photocopied volume of the works of Columella I haven't even unwrapped.

Theo and I. We need a rest. Time for each other.'

'I can see you will go back to Italy Olivia. You and Theo together.'
Olivia smiled and shyly looked into her aunt's knowing eyes.

'There's something else too. I know I have to wait a bit, tread gently with Theo, I'm not sure he's ready yet. But I do so want a family.'

She closed her eyes tightly and grinned.

Geraldine patted her hand.

'Come on, let's sit for a while in the garden. Over here, in the shade. Pull up the loungers. I have something to tell you. '

Olivia pulled the chairs closer together, and she lay alongside her aunt.

' I haven't told you before, Olivia, but now is the time.

As you know, I have never had any children of my own.

You have always been special to me. You have worked hard and shown me your deep interest in antiquities and the arts. Do you remember when you helped me compile the inventory of the contents of my house at Little Missenden? Yes, there was a reason for that, Olivia.

There was a trust set up for you. You would receive money from the bulk of my estate to be used by you at age twenty-one. You will be twenty-one very shortly. When I die, the remainder of my possessions and property will pass to you and any children you have.'

She placed a thick manila envelope into Olivia's hands.

'This document contains all the information relevant to the trust and my lawyers' letters.

I hope to live much longer, Olivia, but I want you and Theo to benefit now.

When I first met Theo, I had a lot of questions for him which he satisfied. I had to make sure he wasn't going to do anything stupid, and I made it quite clear that I had persons in place to watch that he behaved correctly towards you and any children you had. I told him then that you would inherit my estate eventually, and I also told him about the trust money you would receive at twenty-one.

You are to make use of this money now. I am confident that you both deserve it and will use it wisely. I don't believe in unnecessary secrecy over money and intentions; that's why I'm dealing with all these legal matters now. I have enclosed a copy of my will too. Juno entirely agrees with me and the bequests I have made. We both have our own independent assets.'

Olivia sat staring and open-mouthed after the speech her aunt had just made. She was overcome with emotion towards her dear aunt. As she took hold of the paperwork, she said:

'Aunt, I had no idea. This, this, Trust and the Will and everything, I feel overwhelmed and emotional. I can't think of a time when you won't be here. It's too sad. What will I do without you? You've always, all my life, been here or at Missenden. It's too much.'

Aunt Geraldine briskly took charge of the moment.

'That's enough sadness, Olivia. I am very much alive today. I am here for a great deal longer. These were not meant to be my dying statements to you. We will not speak of death again. I want you to enjoy the benefits now. You may choose to buy a house or whatever. Please let me have the pleasure of seeing you and Theo not forever struggling in the first years of your marriage.

So can we please now be happy and light? If you're game, I have the most beautiful bottle of Dom Perignon vintage on ice in the fridge and lobster tails we can chew on together. This will be our little celebration, and later on tonight, Theo is coming to take us out for a meal before he whisks you off home to 'Isca'.'

'Just one more thing. Don't give up on your investigations Olivia. Find out more, about the land in Italy. The jewellery and read Columella.'

CHAPTER 14

"What you leave behind is not what is engraved in stone monuments,
but what is woven into the lives of others."
 Pericles

Exeter and Topsham, 1980

When Theo picked up Aunt Geraldine and Livia from Topsham that evening, he was amused to find his young wife giggly and slightly tipsy. She wagged a pointed forefinger at him as she hiccupped and wobbled into his arms.

'Theo, you have known all along. My aunt's intentions were to give me this inheritance. I can't believe it, and you kept it from me.

Oh, Theo, we've had such fun together, my aunt and I. We've nearly drunk a whole bottle of something delicious and bubbly. Now I feel pretty squifferly, or something like that.

She doesn't want us to struggle along in the first few years. Theo, can you believe her thoughtfulness....I do love her so very much......We can enjoy our lives whilst she's still with us... we could have a place of our own to live.

Theo, you have a secret smile in your eyes, something else you have been keeping from me. Come on, why are you laughing at me?'

Theo spun Olivia around and gave her a crushing hug.

'I love you so much, Mrs Davidovitz, especially when you gabble and it all spills out of you. I'm not laughing at you mockingly, just happy at your enthusiasm and appreciation.

Imagine receiving the interrogation of your life. Yes, I knew of the inheritance, but I had been sworn to secrecy. In fact, I nearly spilt the beans on the aeroplane when we first visited my parents. You asked what your aunt had said to me in the garden at Beaconsfield, and I remember telling you that....Yes, I remember the exact words.

'Your aunt cares so very much for you and your future; she needed to be sure I wasn't a subversive revolutionary, waiting to live off an heiress.'

Fortunately for me, you never picked up on the bit about you being 'an heiress'. Phew, that was a close thing.

Yes, there is something else, Livvy honey, but let's wait until later. Your aunt must be wondering where we are and waiting for her dinner. I'm taking you both out. I've found a cosy pub on the edge of Dartmoor. Monty recommended it for fresh local food, it's a good drive, but maybe you two will have a doze on the way. You might need it. Come on, let's find your aunt.'

Aunt Geraldine was lying on the sun lounger, her right hand resting on her stomach with her straw hat slightly askew but covering her eyes. Her mouth was wide open, and she was sleeping, with a slight bubbling sound emanating from her throat.

'Ahh, look, Theo, she's dozed off. I'm not surprised; we have had such a good afternoon in many ways. It's a shame to embarrass her by disturbing her just yet. Let's leave her for a little while.'

Olivia pulled him over to the edge of the garden where the tide was low, and the mudflats were covered with wading birds.

'Theo, do tell me what the other secret is. You know me, I can't wait?'

They sat down on wicker chairs overlooking the Exe, and Theo told Livia about a discovery he had made with Monty some weeks earlier.

'We were bird watching and came across an abandoned house all boarded up, set back from the estuary among the reeds and overgrown trees. It's on the other side from here.'

He took a deep breath.

'Monty has since done some digging around at the local planning office. It's part of an estate in dispute, the family hadn't lived in the house for years, and it hadn't been sold because of subsidence. A lot of work had been done to try and underpin it. They wanted to sell it, but no offer was accepted. There were apparently two brothers and two sisters who could not agree. One of the sisters lives in America, and another in Switzerland. The years have rolled by, the house becoming increasingly dilapidated, sinking further into the marshes.'

Olivia was starting to look slightly alarmed. Theo nervously raised his hands.

'I know it sounds horrendous and maybe way too big a project for us, but I've been over it with Monty, and the views and position are terrific. It needs a lot of work, but with the right experts, Monty is cautiously optimistic.'

Theo's eyes dreamily glazed over. His voice lowered almost to a whisper.

'It feels like it's lain unnoticed and undisturbed for years, surrounded by the water, the birds and the trees.'

He paused, coming back to reality and shook his head.

'Realistically, it may be necessary to demolish the whole thing and start from scratch. Or, with a structural engineer and a good architect, it could be saved and renovated.

The more Theo spoke, the more Livia felt his enthusiasm and sense of adventure. A project they could do together. Aunt Geraldine had said she wanted them to get their own place.

She stood up and looked out across the water. In the distance, tassels and silks of the reeds swayed. The soft rustling sound intermingled with the Curlews whistling and burbling as they waded on the mud flats.

Livia wanted to go then and there to look it over. Theo said it wasn't practical to go that night, but they could see the location clearly if they went into the loft bedroom. Livia was up and ready in an instant. She grabbed a pair of binoculars off the hall stand,

and together they raced up the two flights of stairs. Theo looked out towards the south west and, focusing the lenses, soon found the top of one of the gables of the old abandoned house. He drew Olivia in front of him, and, pulling the top sash window down, they looked towards the old house. The evening summer sun had yet to set. The air was still and calm. Forever the romantic, Livia could visualise herself looking out across the water, seeing the various birds that Theo had helped her to know, the Oyster Catcher and the Curlew with its long slender curved beak, along with the numerous varieties of ducks. Ducks had all been just ducks until she had seen the differences between the comical Northern Shoveler, Tufted Duck and the Shelduck. The minutes passed as they gazed over the beckoning reeds and the ever-changing light on the water. Theo tapped Livia on the shoulder.

'Look, my love, your aunt, she's waking up. I can see her feet moving at the end of the lounger. We had best go down now. Let's talk to Geraldine and see if she knows anything about the old house there. She's had 'Gung Ho' for years, and she may be able to shed some light on the house and its owners.'

That evening was special. Theo was the perfect gentleman towards aunt Geraldine. The place where they had their meal had been an old coaching inn during the seventeenth century, it sat right on the road with deep sash windows, and the entrance floor was covered with well-worn grey flagstones. To Theo, it was how all Americans imagined quaint England to be, low-beamed ceilings and sloping walls. Added to the perfect warm atmosphere, the food was delicious. It was all from the local farms. Livia recognised the name of the farm where Tati was working, 'Wraybrooke Halt', a supplier of beef and dairy products. Olivia waited patiently for Theo to mention the old house to her aunt. They had spoken about almost everything else but the burning questions she had. Then to her surprise, her aunt asked Theo if he had plans to move and get their own place. She looked directly at him and said.

'You are both still young, and it's a busy time for you, Theo, at the university, setting up your new department.

I have certain regrets, not many, but I wish I had met Juno when we were younger and had a family together in our youth. Sadly the person I married when I was young was not around enough for that.'

She looked across at Olivia and, squeezing her hand, said.

'I have had Olivia to give my personal love and attention to, and it has been a delight to see her grow up. Seeing her happily married to someone who loves her and shares the same goals and interests intellectually gives me great pleasure and satisfaction. You are well-matched, and that is not said without the insight and knowledge that comes with old age.

Now, I hate giving advice, but just this once, indulge me. I will take advantage of this situation when you both feel benevolent and generous toward this old lady.'

Geraldine raised her head slightly and paused for just a short moment. She knew the impact this would have. Their attention was gained. She continued:

'Don't leave it before having children. Have them whilst Olivia is young and strong. I've seen many old career women have their children, worn out and stressed from too much business and high expectations of perfection. Waiting for the right moment to have children.

Grow with your children, build your house with them around you, let them see this young love you have, and make it a foundation to resolve to stick together and grow all of you together. Let your children see you love each other, fall out and disagree sometimes. Above all these everyday things, let them see you both yield and forgive each other. Keep the same goals, overall purpose, and just one more thing, as you oblige me by listening. Don't take over to the next day the previous disagreement you had. You are both excellent talkers, that's good. Communication is the lifeblood of love.

I would be delighted to see the next generation of young Theo's and Olivia's before I'm too old to bounce them on my knees. There that's my speech done. You may not be aware, but there is a little selfishness involved in what I have just said......

Theo and Olivia looked at each other, burst out laughing, and hugged Geraldine. Theo said:

'Well, Geraldine, I don't think even my own mother could have put it quite that way. One thing I am sure of, though, is she is going to love you. When she's over, you must come and spend some time together.'

He looked across at Olivia and then said:

'This is the time to tell you about a project we are considering. In fact, we both would like your input and local knowledge.'

Theo described the old house on the estuary, where it was, and all the preliminary investigations he had pursued. Geraldine sat for a moment thinking hard, with her mouth set slightly askew and lips pursed together. She listened until Theo had finished, then said:

'Yes, I know the property. It was lived in and owned by John Barnham. He built the house with his wife when they had had a successful career in the paper mill business. They could not have their own children but adopted four babies, no tell a lie - originally, there were five. All were adopted from various orphanages. This was all during the late forties and early fifties. I didn't know them that well then, as I didn't visit 'Gung Ho' so often. My parents came down a lot more, and I remember my mother being shocked at all the goings-on with those children.

John and his wife were very wealthy. They had several paper mills and adopted the children later on in life. They had some altruistic ideas of helping out the needy. However, they, unfortunately, had no idea about the family backgrounds of those children. I remember one of the girls from Vietnam brought over during that terrible war. What horrors that poor child must have seen. I think she was five when they adopted her. A tragic story that was. Being a different race from the others, she was bullied all her life, sent away to boarding school, and came home in the summer holidays bewildered and introverted. Sadly when she was twelve, she hung herself at school. It was awful. Another of the children was from an orphanage in East Germany, only a baby when he came, a strange dark-haired arrogant little boy, all I can remember of him was throwing stones at our boat when we rowed past him on the river. Then there were the twins, a boy and a girl, babies too when they came.

I believe the twins never slept well, up all night and tearing around all day. Lastly, there was another girl, I remember her, a fair-haired bonny baby. She grew up and moved out as soon as she was eighteen, telling them she would find her real parents. Poor Irene Barnham, fortunately she had the money to employ nannies.'

Olivia looked shocked, but her attentive wide eyes never left her aunt's face. Theo listened with an open and thoughtful mind, weighing her words carefully as she spoke. Geraldine continued.

'Sorry to only be relating tragedy. Irene died before John. She became frail in her older years. Then John was left on his own with the twins. The boy grew extremely tall and stayed home, and the girl never worked. After John died in the late sixties, the other children returned, and that's when all the legal battles started. None of them cared about the house, and I believe other relatives were involved too. The children had been left the house and some small legacies, but the executors of the Will were two older uncles. I remember one of them who had control of the finances of the paper mill business. Let me see what his name was, ahh yes, Rupert Barnham. Very strangely, he came to visit us once at Gung Ho. He had known Juno in business years before and discovered that we were at Topsham over the summer months. A pleasant man, Juno and him got on well. That's about five years ago now. He told us about some of the accounts I have just related to you. It's very true, too, that the children could not agree on a fair price for the property. They tried to renovate it themselves, unsuccessfully. I think they just couldn't come to any agreement, so it's just been left to deteriorate. With the wind, rain and salt air on the coast, it doesn't take long for properties left empty to fall to pieces. Also, the ground near the estuary is very marshy, not stable at all, parts of it are purported to be dangerous, there's talk of quicksand, and now the birds and wildlife have taken over.'

Olivia looked very downcast and said.

'It doesn't sound at all like a good project to me. I was so hopeful, and now all you've told us, I think it sounds fraught with problems. I haven't seen the site, only from your upstairs loft window, but with the legal issues alone plus the state of the ground and site…What do you think, Theo?'

'Thank you, Geraldine, for telling us the background. At least we know how the situation has arisen, whereby the property hasn't been sold and is bogged down in family legal issues.'

Theo laughed.

'Yes, as well as in the mud.

I've been to the site with our architect. Just looking purely at the site's position, its situation is ideal. Now the legal issues are another matter. They sound complex. We would have to consult a good lawyer to determine what we can do and a geotechnical surveyor for the land issues. For the house, we need a well-qualified structural engineer. They can give us a report on the feasibility of demolition or restoration. It is an enormous project, and we will have to weigh the costs, financially and emotionally. Are we able and willing to sacrifice time and energy? We have a lot to talk over, Livia. It's been a most enlightening evening.'

Geraldine could see that Theo was thinking carefully and soundly without being needlessly swayed by the emotional pull and romantic dream of living on the estuary. She had time to think before she volunteered the following statement.

'Go home, think about what you would like to do next. Theo, take Olivia to look over the site. I know it's accessible from the lane off the main road going towards Powderham. It's all overgrown, but you can get a feel for the site. After you've both had a good talk and looked over the land, come back to me if you feel you want to take it further. Rupert Barnham may still be around, and Juno could ask him if there are any possibilities for the property.

However, I don't want to build up any false hopes for you. First, decide if this is what you want to do.'

Geraldine was aware of the dampening atmosphere that had descended over the evening.
She rallied herself and, with an upbeat lightness to her voice, chuckled out loud:

'Come on, my two most favourite young people in the world. So many possibilities lie ahead.

Another adventure I may have a small part in?

Thank you both for a beautiful meal. What an evening we've had. I feel exhilarated by our lively discussion, good food and excellent wine.

She leaned forward conspiratorially to them. Her eyes narrowed, and the green sparkle in them glistened as she looked at Olivia and Theo. Olivia felt the air lighten, and her heart skipped a beat. The familiar elation of the thrill of the chase swept over her.

The drive home was quiet, each mulling over their thoughts. When planning and plotting her strategy, Aunt Geraldine felt a surge of energy invigorating her thoughts. A renewed strength reminded her of times when she had controlled situations and manoeuvred operations on behalf of her government department. She smiled to herself as she wondered what Olivia and Theo would have thought about this elderly lady and the previous covert and dangerous missions she had directed and brought to many a successful conclusion. The deep familiar pain in her side twinged as memories flooded back. So many thoughts to keep to herself.

Theo drove steadily back to Topsham. He looked back through the rearview mirror and saw Geraldine with her eyes closed, smiling to herself. For just a brief moment, a thought crossed his mind. What hidden depth there was to this elderly, refined lady. He was most grateful to have her as an accomplice, not an adversary.

Olivia's thoughts were in turmoil, but she remembered when she had been younger, her father's kind advice to take a day at a time, not to rush things and to soundly plan ahead carefully. She looked across at Theo and put a hand on his knee. She felt calm contentment and a tingle of a thrill at future prospects. This man she loved more each day, their plans, working together.

Over the following weekend, Olivia and Theo visited the old site on the estuary. It was hard to even see a house behind all the overgrown trees and foliage. Theo helped Livia over the rusted iron gate. They struggled for a hundred yards through an overgrown driveway with self-seeded beech and birch trees blocking the pathway. The trees made it impossible to see the house until very close up. It was overgrown with green ivy and lichen. Shrubs and bushes were sprouting out of the chimney pots. Part of the roof was missing and as they approached, pigeons cascaded in a flurry from the broken roof timbers.

They climbed over brambles and stinging nettles at the rear of the property, where a half-collapsed balcony spanned the whole of the first-floor rooms. Most of the upstairs latticed windows were cracked and the ground-floor ones boarded over. The main front door was of weathered oak and looked as if it would survive even if the old house collapsed around it. There was a dilapidated, ornate conservatory to the right of the main house, and part of the sidewall fissured with cracks. Building materials covered in overgrowth were stacked against the left of the house, and dripping moss grew over that sidewall. The whole building looked depressingly damp and crumbly.

Turning her head towards the water, the ground dropped gently amidst the reeds and marshes. Olivia's spirits lifted as the sun glistened on the still surface of the river Exe.

They both explored in silence, then sat together on an old broken wall, just looking at the view and watching the water birds swooping and diving. The only sounds were the rushes whispering in the breeze and splashes as the waterfowl landed and waded amongst the reeds. A pair of linnets trilled and sang amongst the overgrown bushes, the pretty red of the male distinct from the beige-brown female. A heron waded in the distance amongst the bullrushes, motionless for minutes, then a quick dart of the bill and a splash, as a wriggling silver grayling caught the light.

Theo placed his arm around Livia, drawing her closer to him and said in her ear as he pecked her soft lobe.

'Well, what do you think? Would you ever be tired of the view from here?'

'Oh Theo, it's just so peaceful looking this way, so quiet. It reminds me of your home when we stayed at Rivertree. This way, the view is marvellous, but that behind us is just a sad decaying wreck of a place. What did Monty say when he came, did he think it would ever be possible to restore it?'

Theo blew out his cheeks and raised his eyebrows. Exhaling, he said:

'He was concerned about the substructure. We walked a bit closer to the water's edge, and it's pretty boggy, meaning the house foundations are not on stable ground. That being the case, he had the idea to demolish the house and build further back towards the lane. Here we could make a natural deep lake using reed-beds and lots of sympathetic planting to bind the subsoil. The wildfowl will love it, and so will we for swimming!'

Olivia looked directly into Theo's eyes and searched his face.

'Have we decided, Theo? Let's go ahead to the next stage. Could we get an approximate site value before we contact the estate? Monty may know an agent that could give us a valuation. What do you think?....... I'm getting excited, Theo, but I'm trying to be realistic with a hint of optimism.'

Theo gave Livia a kiss on the side of her cheek and agreed yes, in principle, it's a good idea to get a valuation. He would call Monty when they returned home.

Over the next week, a valuation was arranged and sent to them through the post; they both thought it seemed very low. Would the estate be happy with such a low offer? Theo and Livia relayed to Geraldine their decision to contact the owners. She was glad to help out through Juno's previous acquaintance with Rupert Barnham.

Within two days, a meeting was arranged with solicitors Grantham Cooper in their Southernhay offices.

Rupert Barnham was a tall elderly gentleman of eighty-two years of age who quickly got down to business. He told them the estate had been in dispute for some years, but one of the beneficiaries had recently died. This had left three siblings who were now more willing to come to an agreed sale as soon as possible. They decided that three independent valuations would be satisfactory, and then Theo and Olivia would make an offer. Theo stressed that they would have to spend considerable money before making their offer. This would include various surveys on the land, applications for conditional planning approval for either renovation or demolition and new build permission. Therefore, all these factors would be reflected in the offer they finally made to purchase the site. They would need confirmation that before they invested in seeking permissions and surveys, they would have a conditional binding contract with the sole right to purchase, subject to planning approval.

Rupert smiled at Theo. He placed his hands together in an arch resting his finger on his chin as his eyes looked from Theo to Olivia. He then inclined his head with a nod toward his lawyer.

'You are an astute young man Mr Davidovitz. I will have my lawyers make up the necessary paperwork. I wish you both well. That place deserves a happy life. I may visit you when all is renewed.'

They all shook hands, and the slow-grinding wheels of the English legal processes and the even slower cogs of the planning departments were set in motion. The months passed, and the geotechnical survey confirmed that the house needed to be demolished with the new structure built on higher ground nearer to the entrance lane. After much wrangling with planners and conservationists, a sensitive plan was drawn to make a natural lake where the old house stood. The new home was planned with its frontage to the lane being of a traditional double gabled two-storey exterior and the rear to be of three storeys with the upper two levels having balconies on raised piers overhanging the ground floor rooms. The old original weathered oak door was to be preserved and helped to reduce the look of a new house without character. After a lot of tweaking from his original conceptual modern glass and steel look, Monty was given the brief and honed it into a home that fitted and blended into the surroundings in a tasteful but adventurous design. The views were maximised, and Olivia fell in love with their new house. The stone and bricks would build a shape. This was all exciting, but something more rewarding was giving her a sense of peace and serenity. She had discovered that the unseen, invisible, gave greater contentment than the visible, tangible in front of one's eyes. Her eyes shone, and a clarity of vision and insight overwhelmed her with joy. She loved and was loved. She had hope and had experienced true friendship.

Hidden from sight, too, new life had begun. The tiniest little one conceived and developing, unknown and secret for a few more weeks, was fluttering inside her.

After the site's purchase, the old house's demolition went ahead speedily. It had been decided that after the old house had been razed to the ground, the first process would be the siting and building of the new house some one hundred yards from the previous one. The lake would be excavated once they were in residence.

That summer, whilst Olivia blossomed, and Theo lived in a state of anxious suspense. They both enjoyed the excitement of a new baby on its way. The house took shape, and as soon as the glazing was finally in place, it felt like theirs. The apartment at Colleton Crescent had been their home for some time, and they both were sad to leave. They would miss Tristan too. What adventures they had all shared together. The discoveries, the paintings and the friendships that had grown between them. Tristan had become like family. He had taken a keen interest too in Tati and Justin and their work.

Before Olivia and Theo left Colleton Crescent, Tristan approached Olivia. He had a business proposition. His storage units on the Quay were disused and empty. He wanted to sponsor a permanent art gallery, exhibition area and saleroom for the new artists. He also wanted to donate some of his art collections for the public to view. He looked at Olivia with a hint of sadness in his eyes.

'Venetia would have been so happy to know that some good came of all her collecting.

She just loved beautiful artefacts. I can't believe she was all wrong. Only some of what she collected was dubious. It was a driven compulsion.'

He took a deep breath and smiled.

'Tell me you will consider it? The young people too, your sister and her young man.'

Olivia was astounded. She had been thinking for some time of an outlet for herself, one whereby she could spend time with the baby, encourage Tati, and have an enjoyable occupation.

Although now eight months pregnant and about to live in a new house that would need much organising and arranging, Livia spoke with Theo about the art gallery. Olivia had all the answers. She had made up her mind. She would manage the gallery most of the time from their new house, only being on site a couple of mornings. The rest of the time, Tati, Justin and a recently returned Alice would be there more often.

Those summer weeks were busy and hectic but filled with friends and enjoyable work. The new gallery started to take shape. Tati and Justin came to the gallery three days a week, and Alice was there every afternoon, so there were only two mornings when Olivia was on her own at the gallery and then

Tristan often popped by for a cup of coffee and a helping hand. He brought small pieces of artwork and his antique collection of butterflies. Being very quick to reassure them all that they were legitimately gained. Olivia secretly thought he wanted to be there more often and was sure he called whenever Tati and Justin were there. He loved the interchange with young people and was very forthcoming in his encouragement and support.

Alice took on the flat at Colleton Crescent and often had relatives and friends to stay over. Tristan could not be happier seeing his house full of this young and eclectic mixture of people. Alice continued to cook delicious meals, with Tristan often given a tasty dish to eat for his evening supper.
The gallery, however, needed to be faster in picking up interest from locals. People were cautious and suspicious; Alice, Tati and Justin were different, not locals.

Tristan suggested a small coffee and cake service onsite. The smell of freshly baked cakes and good quality coffee might entice a few into the gallery. Exeter Quay took some time to accept the new culture, colour and fun those disused warehouses needed. The locals were still slightly nervous about venturing in. They just strolled by, looking to see what was new and bizarre. Something more was needed.

CHAPTER 15

Something hidden. Go and find it...
'The Explorer' Rudyard Kipling

Exeter 1981

Baby Floria arrived early in August. Theo could never get used to the wonder of this tiny little person he loved instantly. Gone were all his fears and memories of childhood when his brothers had taken over his life with noise, crying, clattering, and bumbling behaviour. Olivia just smiled to see the transformation of her sometimes distracted, forgetful husband into a father who just loved to be around pacing the floor at night. She watched as he opened the doors onto the balcony humming to Floria, showing her the birds on the estuary. He was back earlier each day from the university and often worked from home preparing his lectures. If Floria was awake, he wanted to be there, not missing one moment of her growing and changing each day.

Most weekends, their house was full of extended family. First came Olivia's parents and then a surprise visit from Imogen. She looked thinner. Her eyes, heavily outlined in dark kohl, accentuated her long lashes and large green eyes, giving her skin paler transparency. Her whole appearance was arresting. Occasionally a sharpness and hollow look swept across her face when she was not smiling and exaggerating her theatrical poses. Impy's manner, though, had not changed. Making her grand entrance dramatically with broad gestures and exuberant praise for Floria. She fawned over Theo and made a point of ignoring Olivia. Along with her came bags and parcels with expensive gifts of dresses and coats, all in impractical colours and fabrics for her niece, kitting her out for the next couple of years. She cooed and cuddled Floria, quickly handing her over as soon as the baby bellowed and went red in the face.

Olivia loved to see all the family; it felt like years since they had been in one room together. Tati and Justin announced they were getting married the following Autumn. Tati was transformed, never plump but decidedly filled out in all the right places. Her skin and hair glowed. Justin had shaved his unruly red beard away, revealing a handsome earnest face. He still looked like a gaunt renaissance artist, with delicate bone structure and sweeping auburn hair flopping over his face but a new self-assurance was plain to see. He rarely stuttered, and whenever he spoke, Tati stood beside him, adoringly hanging on his every word.

Aunt Geraldine and Juno arrived at Gung Ho in early September, becoming frequent visitors, offering to babysit whilst Olivia and Theo had an evening out together. This turned into only an hour at the pub on the Locks. Theo and Livia were on tenterhooks the whole time away from Floria, constantly checking their watches. When finally the hour was up, they rushed home to find Geraldine comfortably seated in an armchair with Floria fast asleep in her arms.

Such were those early days of parenthood. Highs of anxiety tempered with contentment and happiness. Sleepless nights, weary days, colds, sneezes and high temperatures in the night then all normal in the day. Inexplicable crying and red cheeks, followed by a tiny white speck of a tooth appearing as a release for all that yelling. Bubbles, dribbles and smiles, which grew into hearty chuckles, made each day for them something that added to their appreciation of every moment of life. The photo albums grew, and letters and pictures flew across the Atlantic to Theo's family, who planned a visit as soon as possible.

Olivia was away from the gallery for six weeks after Floria was born. Then news came that the gallery was not doing so well. Towards the end of September, Olivia could stay away no longer. Baby Floria was bundled into her pram and spent a couple of afternoons sleeping contentedly at the back of the gallery as Olivia poked around, thinking up new ideas for a relaunch. Occasionally, people dropped by to browse, but few purchased anything. Alice was there full time with the coffee machine and small kitchen now installed. Tristan had asked permission to convert his two storage units into one with a large arch between the two spaces. Monty had been consulted, and a complete refurbishment of the inside was proposed. Olivia had big plans for the interior. The gallery would have a complete overhaul and a new official opening. Monty followed her one afternoon, making suggestions and listening to her ideas.

As she paced up and down, her fingers picked at the old whitewashed stone walls. They had been left untouched. She closed her eyes and then spun around towards Monty. He jumped as she enthusiastically said:

'That's what we need. A lined interior. White milky etched glass in large panels floor to ceiling, covering the uneven surface. Then backlighting. Could it be colour altered for exhibitions?'

Olivia moved around rapidly, waving her arms and pointing.

'We could install a wired system to hang the exhibits without touching the glass panels.'

She stood silent, her eyes narrowed as she held her index finger to her lips.

'We need to feature something antique and grand as a contrast.'

Olivia tapped her forehead, sifting through her brain's filing system.

'I've got it! The glass Murano chandeliers.'

'Sorry Olivia, what are you talking about?'

Monty looked bemused.

'I spotted them years ago at my aunt's house. Magnificent fluted gold chandeliers, there's a pair. They must still be in the attics. I'll get straight onto Aunt Geraldine. I know her she will be thrilled to be part of it all, and she'll definitely lend them to us.'

The arrival a few days later of two wooden crates created quite a stir amongst the public watching the commotion. That side of the Quay had not seen such busy interest since the great galleons of the 17th century had plied their trade, when Exeter Quay had been a hive of industry with merchants, sailors and customs officers boarding the vessels that came from far-off lands.

Four strong helpers gingerly carried the precious cargo into the gallery's centre. Everyone helping that day was stunned by the exquisite beauty and detailing of the two chandeliers. Each had ten flutes in clear crystal glass with a deep gold trim surrounding the frilled edges. When they were finally, very carefully, installed and the lights switched on, the whole effect was stunning. The contrast of modern glass panelling and meticulous antique Italian craftsmanship gave a world-class finish. The exhibits sparkled. Olivia and Monty stood back with the widest grins on their faces.

'Well, I'll give it to you, Olivia. You will be having commissions from the London galleries when they see this. Those chandeliers make it top-notch.'

Olivia stood outside, looking in.

Only one thing was missing. The gallery had to have a name.

Alice, Monty, Tati and Jason had many ideas as the banter went back and forth. Tristan spoke very little in the lengthy discussions, his eyes downcast. Olivia watched his face as different ideas were suggested. Then a thought crossed her mind. She decided to take the baby for a walk along the estuary and asked Tristan if he would like a stroll with them. She offered her arm as they walked along the sunlit towpath together. After a few minutes, Olivia spoke.

'The gallery Tristan. All the exhibits you've donated from your own collection will be here for a long time. You could alternate them with different artefacts on a regular cycle. It's your legacy, your brainchild.'

She squeezed his arm.

'I've given this a great deal of thought the new name for the gallery.'

She turned towards him.

'Let's give tribute to Venetia and the beneficial contribution she's made. Why don't we call it 'The Tristan & Venetia Collection'?
A celebration of your life together, the happiness you shared.'

Tristan looked up at Olivia, took out a large white handkerchief, and loudly blew into it, quite overcome with emotion.

With the gallery's refurbishment completed and 'The Tristan & Venetia Collection' sign in black lettering applied to the windows. They all stood outside, Tristan repeatedly exclaiming he couldn't believe what he saw. The old familiar white handkerchief frequently dabbed at those bleary wet eyes.

Unknown to Olivia, Aunt Geraldine had also arranged for the two little Picasso oils to be sent down to be exhibited. Olivia was thrilled until she realised the extra security needed. After last-minute discussions, a security alarm system was installed, especially for the paintings. They arrived in sealed glass cases with red signs on the backs. 'Danger, do not remove this card and backing.' These were placed in glass-topped display cabinets at the gallery's rear. The publicity surrounding the display of the Picassos was extensive. Bringing great interest from potential clients and art lovers all around Exeter and beyond. Olivia couldn't thank her aunt enough for letting them have the paintings on loan for the opening. Geraldine sensed Livia's nervousness.

'I've checked out the security system myself, and it's excellent. You're not to worry now, and I also have my own personal safeguards in place.'
Olivia looked questioningly at her aunt.

'Never you mind what they are. You will just have to trust me.'
Geraldine changed the subject, hinting that more of her treasures could be displayed in the future.

Saturday, 2nd January, was set for the open evening. Local papers, artists, the TV and any media people they contacted were invited. Olivia got in touch with their old student friend Robert Grey. He was now working for a leading national newspaper in the art critics division. He was more than happy to do a short write-up after being suitably impressed with the striking interior of the gallery. Even Imogen brought down half a dozen people she knew involved in the media and fellow actors, beautiful people surrounding her.

Olivia took little notice of the crowd with Imogen. But one tall, dark, handsome man with piercing blue eyes behind his dark shades and sharply trimmed beard watched her. He closely surveyed all the faces, exhibits and alarm systems. He leaned against the rear wall next to the Picasso exhibits. His fingers instinctively twisted the black cord around his wrist. Imogen leaned towards him and placed a casual hand on his lapel, offering him a glass of champagne. He tilted his head and declined, kissing her on both cheeks and whispering into her left ear. She lowered her long eyelashes and smiled. Mouthing to him.

'Yes, later.'

He silently made his way through the pressing crowds without looking back. As the entrance door opened. Olivia turned, feeling the cold night breeze gush in. All she saw was the back of the tall, dark man leaving. Her stomach tightened, and her brows furrowed; momentarily, a familiar odour passed under her nose. Then it was gone. She shook her head. Scanning the gallery, people, faces, laughter and voices intermingled. Theo caught her gaze, questioningly staring at her anxious white face; he moved towards her.

'You Ok, Honey? What is it?'

She took hold of his arm, with her head on one side and took a deep breath.

'It's nothing. It's passed now. I felt strangely familiar anxiety. Something came back a feeling, an odd sensation. I smelt a musky odour. I don't even know what it was. I'm Ok. I'm overtired and over-excited. Or too much champagne. It's been a busy few weeks. This evening too, has been a great success. Theo, let's leave, go quietly home. I love you.'

The opening night was a huge triumph, gaining national coverage for the city of Exeter and the growing art scene in the southwest.

The gallery became a hub for people to gather for exciting discussions and uplifting cultural exchange. The attraction of the excellent coffee and delicious cakes only added to its success. Olivia was highly praised in several prestigious design magazines for her innovative interior. People often just came to see the gallery itself, with the exhibits being a secondary reason for visiting. However, word got around regarding the quality of the work displayed. Six months after the new opening, the gallery was making a profit. Justin and Tati were taking commissions for their work, and Olivia was spurred on, looking for new and exciting pieces to display and sell.

As the early spring rains decreased, the house on the estuary started to settle into its surroundings. Newly planted saplings and trees grew. Their leaves opened and gently enfolded and caressed the house. Memories of Rivertree in Pennsylvania and Olivia's first experience there flooded back. They and their new home were being established. It was becoming their own. They kept uncovering hidden plants and beautiful old trees that had been smothered by the brambles and ivy. A Tulip tree and a delicate Mimosa started to thrive again. Underneath brambles and weeds, they found a large slab of concrete. The remains of an old building crumbled around the perimeter. Cracked plant pots and rusty garden tools were rotting in the undergrowth. An old brass tap rusted tightly jammed shut stood lopsided and entwined with ivy. The work and efforts of Mr and Mrs Barnham, their love of rambling roses and clematis became clearer. Just by the tap were two small stone tablets covered in moss. Scraping back lichen, the names of Boozie and Hamper were uncovered, and two paw marks were embedded into the stonework, with the words inscribed,

'Not just walkers, but our friends, happy times, never forgotten.'

Livia trailed her fingers over the stones and thought of Ruby and their many happy hours walking the Chilterns. Ruby had been her friend. Smiling, she thought of all the things Ruby had been told. The injustices and frustrations she had confided, the plans Ruby had heard about. How strange to think of Mr and Mrs Barnham traipsing over this land similarly with their two dogs, maybe when their children had been small playing in these gardens. Almost speaking to herself and breathing out, she mouthed.

'What a relief, the Barnhams had recorded some happy times at this house.'

During the midterm break, Theo set a date with the contractors for the excavation of the lake. Interested in any dig that went on, he laboured hands-on for a week with the workmen. Rubble from the old house had been left on-site to help stabilise the ground. As the digger removed cement and old bricks, the land became boggier. On the sixth day of the excavation, with the heavy machinery stationary and the workmen off-site, Theo rose early, poking around in the trench. His spade lifted clods of earth, unearthing round metal pieces that looked to his trained eyes like coins. He stopped immediately. Turning the coins over in his hands, the more he looked and examined them, the more he realised they were ancient. He scanned the trench. Without thinking, he swept his muddy hands through his thick hair. His boots squelched deeper into the mud; he found himself unbalancing, swaying as the suction on his feet drew him further into the trench. With an almighty stab with the spade, he levered himself onto the dryer bank, falling backwards, mud and coins spattering everywhere. His heart was pounding, his thoughts racing. He sat upright, grabbing one of the coins.

Saying out loud:
'What have we here?
In my own back garden, coins artefacts, more coins?
Oh my goodness!
Wow.'

Standing upright, he paced up and down, carefully looking at the area where he had found the coins. His eyes surveyed the whole site, taking in the closeness of the estuary. He rushed back to the house, grabbing his camera and binoculars. He photographed the area where he had displaced the objects. Theo was torn between his strong desire to examine the buried artefacts more closely and the archaeologist within him, to be patient and follow all the guidelines of a serious 'archaeological excavation site project'. He would have to record the horizontal layers of the surrounding area and anything found at the same level as the find. Against his better judgment but moved by his natural curiosity, he took one of the mud-covered coins, carefully wrapped it in a cotton cloth, and placed it inside a plastic specimen bag.

Theo was curious to examine the artefact more closely before he spoke to Livia. Taking it into his study, he cleared a space on his already cluttered desk. Books and papers tumbled onto the floor.
Moving the magnifying glass and lamp onto his desk, he removed the coin from the cloth, and as he did so, it glinted. Placing it for a short time wrapped in the fabric revealed that it was gleaming, shining, solid gold. He put it beneath the lens, moving it around, examining it from all angles. Immediately the profile of Emperor Claudius immerged. He had seen this coin before in an Australian collection. As he gently rubbed it, the inscription around the head stood out clearly.' Ti Clavd Caesar Avg Germ Pm Tr P' This coin was minted around AD41-42. His mind raced over his recollections of Claudius as emperor when Britain had been conquered in AD42. The person that had dropped this had been somewhere in this vicinity. It wasn't just a lowly sesterce of little value, but this was the money of pure

gold and would have only been used by someone of high station.

Theo ran his fingers through his muddied hair. He had to show this to Livia. He blew out a loud whistle as he contemplated the meaning of what he had discovered. They could be sitting on a Roman archaeological site. Exeter City had been the site of a Roman Fortress built possibly around AD50 when Vespasian had come and conquered Exeter. Some excavations were done in the city after the second world war bombing, which had caused large craters to reveal Roman settlements and thus enabled a study before rebuilding and new construction took place. To Theo's mind, though, he quickly grasped that this coin could predate the Exeter occupation. Was there going to be evidence of some kind of trade or Roman dwelling hidden under the bog here in his own backyard? The cautious scholar in him was reminded.

'Whoa, Theo, slow down, get the facts first, let's not jump to any conclusions.'

Nevertheless, his mind raced on. As a respected archaeologist, he could take complete control of this find and subsequent investigation. It could be a research site for his students. Tom and Felix would jump at the opportunity.

He sat back in his swivel chair with his hands behind his head, thinking, planning. Theo didn't hear Livia come into the study but felt her arms around his chest as she rested her head on the top of his hair. She pulled back as the mud stuck to her chin. Theo spun around and plonked her on his knee. Where had he been? He smelt of fresh sea air and damp earth.

'I have something to tell you. See here what do you think this is?'

He drew the magnifying lens down at an angle facing her and placed the coin nearer to her.

'Wow, it's a coin with the head of Claudius on it, Theo it looks like gold. Has someone sent it to you for examination?'

Theo smiled and said:

'Well, you are not going to believe this, my sweetest Livvy, but this was in the trench in our back garden. I was poking around in the mud, and this came up. It's unbelievable. There's more, too.

 Do you know what this could mean?

Here, we may have an ancient Roman site on our land. …. It's just incredible, an archaeologist's dream…..Livia, I'm going to cordon off the area, stop the contractors from further excavation and get a team from the university to sift through a section at a time.

Come on, I want to show you.'

Olivia was mesmerised by the coin and Theo's revelations. Her jaw dropped, and she was speechless, but only briefly. Her senses returned as she heard the baby chortling and banging her toys against the cot sides.

'Yes,….yes, I do want to see it. Let me grab Floria. She's stirring, we can't leave her, and I will get so distracted and won't hear her from the bottom of the garden. Oh, Theo, this is so exciting.'

Livia ran out of the study and up the stairs calling Floria. The baby gave her mum a big smile, dribbling as she gnawed on the side of the cot. Livia swept her out and danced around the nursery, whooping and singing. She quickly changed Floria wrapping her in a fleecy suit. The morning sun had yet to take the chill out of the air. The smell of coffee brewing wafted up the stairs. Theo had already cooked eggs and bacon. He had hastily filled two mugs of coffee and wrapped the eggs and bacon in toasted bagels. Livia quickly mashed up a banana for Floria as she munched on a crust. They couldn't stop talking about the incredible find. Theo went into full archaeologist mode giving Livia directives and information on the procedures, equipment and scheduling for a dig. She stood back, marvelling at his knowledge and enthusiasm for his subject. She thought she had seen the best in him at his lectures, but now this was another side. Theodore, 'the man in charge of his own dig'. A thrill ran through her spine. She was going to be there alongside the whole procedure. This would be the ride of her life, the unravelling of history, unearthing secrets buried for nearly two thousand years, touching objects that had passed through the hands of ancient living, breathing humans like themselves.

Theo carried Floria, and Livia followed. She could see where he had already placed string and stakes around the trench. He pointed to other objects that could also be metal coins. She asked him many questions: Why couldn't they just take them out and dig deeper? Theo explained the need to look at the layers consistently around each found piece. The context was as important as the find; they would have to widen the sifting of this layer before they went deeper. Everything would have to be photographed and catalogued with a detailed mapped grid of the whole site.

He looked back towards the house.
'We need somewhere to catalogue everything and site hut too for storage and weather protection.'

Livia, dreading the thought of their new home being invaded, remembered the concrete slab they had uncovered.

'The concrete slab we found the other day. It must have had a building on it at one time. That would be ideal for placing a site hut. There's that old seized up tap too. We could get it repaired for a supply of freshwater.'

Olivia was relieved to see Theo quickly head off toward the old concrete floor, calling her.

'It's a great size. Perfect base for a temporary office and hut. I'll get a plumber onto this old tap too. We could have a petrol generator down here during the day for electricity and heating, until we can fix up more permanent power.'

After discussing all the practical things, they returned to the house to make phone calls and arrangements. Digging this time would be very different from the one they had done months before.

The large wooden hut panels arrived and were assembled and ready for the office and storage area by Wednesday. A huge white tent was erected for the field workers to sort, sift and protect against Devon's varying weather, rain, storm and sunshine in any twenty-four hours. The setting out of the dig took two weeks before Theo was satisfied everything was in place. Theo had busily but discreetly got in touch with persons he knew to help with discoveries as and when new things came to light. Felix Gander and Tom Westerway soon became permanent members of the team. They had decided to keep the project as confidential as possible, only speaking with people who would not alert the press.

Olivia watched all the preparations and started feeling a quavering apprehension. Theo sensed Livia's growing tension. The solution came by making another entrance gate further along the lane for future visitors and workers to enter the site. He cordoned off their garden so the archaeological site became separate.

They even installed a radio system whereby when Floria was asleep at home, they could hear her. When she was awake, if they were in the trench, she was in her playpen out in the fresh air, with a plastic bucket and toys copying her parents.

Livia and Theo spent many afternoons together meticulously sifting and sorting. They unearthed numerous coins, all very similar to the original ones found. Then on the third week of standing knee-deep in waders, they hit something big. Theo was reticent to proceed. Carefully scraping away some of the mud, he outlined the structure. He stopped, raising his right hand sharply. Wheels emerged, metal bolts and panels, and large animal bones tangled amongst the frame. The grime was thick, sticky and slimy and was like working blindly through black treacle.

'Livia, stand back. This is an upturned crate or cart of some kind. We can't do this on our own. We will need the heavy digger, an overhead crane, and a winch.
It's too dangerous to continue. We need the manpower of Felix and Tom.   Let's just cover the mud with the tarpaulin sheet.'

The two-day wait went by agonisingly slowly. The south-westerly blew, and the sun shone, adding a much-needed dryness to the air and the land. As dawn broke on Saturday, frenzied actively started again. The heavy machinery dug around and under the structure. Felix steered as Tom helped Theo with the winch and crane. Olivia kept away safely, peering through her binoculars from the kitchen window.

Theo was conscious that exposing anything that had been buried for centuries needed expert preservation. Slowly a great mass of something at first unrecognisable appeared. Hanging from the winch, it oozed and dripped globules of mud. The carcass and bones of an animal fell away as it squelched out of the sludge. Wheels and metal outlined the framework of what seemed to be a wagon. Never had they seen the like of something so amazingly preserved. They laid it carefully sideways onto a wooden pallet with coir matting to pad the base. Parts of the outer boards were dislodged, but the metal bolts and boxed compartments were still intact.

 They stood silently in awe of this immense discovery.

Olivia rushed down from the house when she saw what had been brought up.

'Theo, what is it? It feels like you've raised the Mary Rose.'

The gusty south westerly battered at Theo's face. His hair was standing on end. Amidst the noise of the wind, he shouted out.

'This is no ordinary farmers cart.'
He walked around it, pointing to the wheels.

'These wheels, it looks like there were at least four. This was a nobleman's carriage, the amount of iron and bolts. If the interior is preserved, it will be highly decorated.
Possibly a woman would have been conveyed in it. The state of this one side and the twisted bones suggest that this cart and the animals pulling it had a catastrophic end.'

Livia immediately noticed dark cube-like chests strewn across the inner compartment. There were six of a similar shape and one smaller than the others. She pointed these out to Theo.

'What are they?'

They measured, photographed, and scrutinised the wagon

from every angle for the next few hours. They found no skeletons or evidence of passengers, just intriguing boxes of differing sizes. Then carefully lifting the pallet by attaching forks to the digger, they took it to the covered tent area.

After all the recording and photography had been done, Theo turned to Olivia. He was tired, and his muscles ached. Floria was grizzling, but Olivia was still full of energy.

'I need to do some writing and make a stack of phone calls. You take the small casket, clean it up, see what you make of it, any inscriptions you can decipher. I'll put Floria down and be in the study. Take photo's at every stage.'

The wooden shed now came into its own. Olivia carefully placed the small casket onto the workbench on a turntable, examining it from all angles. She wiped it with an acid-free cloth and distilled water. Delicate filigree work of acanthus leaves alternating with olive leaves started to appear. The casket was beautifully preserved, the same as when it was first made and used.

Livia felt a tingling sweeping through her hands and arms. If she had been standing, her knees would have given way. What would the interior, opened, reveal to her? She gingerly prised the lid to the casket. Thoughts swept through her mind, this fine casket. Who had been the custodian of it centuries ago? Who had been the last person to have opened and closed it? She felt a strange quickening in her heart. Her breath was shallow and laboured. The lid lifted, and she propped it against a book pile behind the hinge. Inside was a dark sticky cloth wrapped around something small but weighty. Olivia's senses returned. She knew she had to photograph every stage of her discovery. Her hands were filthy, and the camera shook in her fingers, but she took photographs from every angle she could. Then, carefully prising the sodden cloth away, there before her eyes was an exquisitely engraved golden stylus. She measured the length from point to its flat, wedged end, approximately fifteen centimetres. It was a piece of fine craftsmanship, expertly made. Olivia traced her fingers along the shaft and read the words.

'Carissime et Pomponia filiae
cogitationes tuae scripto ferrea'

It was as if they had been inscribed that very day; it was so clear.
Her knowledge of Latin immediately deciphered the meaning.

'My dearest daughter Pomponia. May your thoughts go down in
writing
and endure.'

She moved her fingers over the delicate acanthus and olive
leaf engraving and then back gently across the words.
Was this a gift to the young girl Pomponia from her father?
The name Pomponia, to Olivia, was a name she had come across
before. Pomponia. Drumming her fingers on the desk, her eyes
saw the row of encyclopediae above her head. She reached out
and flicked through until she came to the heading;
Pomponia Graecina, she read:

Wife of Aulus Plautius, the general who led the conquest of
Britain in 43AD. Noblewoman, daughter of Gaius Pomponius
Graecinus and his wife Asinia, related to the Julio Claudian
dynasty of emperors. Pomponia was known to mourn the death
of her cousin Julia Livia, granddaughter of emperor Tiberius,
killed by the imperial family. Very little is known of her later life.

Looking intently at the stylus, she spoke softly:
'Pomponia, was this really yours? What sort of a woman did
you become? What did you write? What happened in your life? '
Olivia shivered and looked around her.
'Were you here, Pomponia?
What have I got in my hands? Is this your writing tool?'
Olivia was frozen to the spot. Her whole body shook, her
teeth chattered, and she felt as though she was going to faint.
She could not move from her chair. Gradually, slowly, regaining
her composure. She took deep, deep breaths. There was no way
that she could leave this casket in the site shed that night.

This potentially was one of the most significant finds of Roman antiquity, and if the small box contained this, what would the other six chests reveal?

Olivia wrapped the casket and its contents into a large cotton cloth. She picked up her camera, turned off the light, bolted the door, and slowly walked back to the house. Theo was upstairs with Floria, singing softly to her.

Olivia could wait. A few minutes or hours were nothing compared to the two thousand years Pomponia's Stylus had waited to be uncovered.

CHAPTER 16

.....We question our purpose, our part and our place
In this vast land of mystery suspended in space,
We probe and explore and try hard to explain
The tumult of thoughts that our minds entertain.....
Helen Steiner Rice
The Mystery of Life

Exeter, on the Estuary and Topsham 1981

Olivia paced up and down in her study, excitedly waiting for Theo to put Floria to sleep. She thought ahead to the opening of the other caskets. What possibilities lay ahead? Clothing, jewellery, and household items. The gold stylus suggested finding tablets. Would there be fragments to uncover? Olivia looked feverishly through all the numerous books that Theo had in his study. There was a series on ancient scrolls and wooden artefacts and their preservation methods. She read and became thoroughly engrossed, not noticing when Theo entered the room.

'You okay Livvy? Well....any news?'

Olivia spun around in the chair.

'Theo, you are not going to believe what we have. Just look at this. I cannot believe it.'

Olivia removed the white cloth revealing the casket, carefully opening it and showing Theo the gold stylus. Her hands trembled as she handed it to him. Theo took it over to the anglepoise, looking at what Olivia said.

'These words Livia, come on what do they mean?'

Livia blurted out.

'My dearest daughter Pomponia. May your thoughts go down in writing and endure.'
Don't you see Theo? It's remarkable. She was the wife of General Aulus Plautius, who conquered Britain.'

Olivia's eyes misted over.

'She could have been here. Here on this land!'

Theo scraped his fingers distractedly through his unruly curls.

His eyes narrowed.

'I need to get in touch with my old professor Dan Forden at the university in Pittsburgh. They have a specialist department in preservation. He will be able to call on the contacts we need. The top priority now is conservation.

He took a deep breath.

'What have we unearthed? What is in the other boxes?'

Late that night, Theo went to the covered tent. The temperature had dropped, and the wind battered the canvas sides. His torch flickered over the black structure, casting elongated shadows on the billowing tent walls.

He had an important task that night. He was preserving history, binding the limbs of broken shafts, encasing a fragile carcass. Slowly and methodically, he wrapped the cart in layers of silicone mylar film, then covered these with cellocast resin bandages.

The slow process enabled him to give it a steady, measured examination, systematically noting the gigantic size of the project. To him, it was like fulfilling a dream, the past coming to life. His fingers felt numb as a biting wind swirled around the tent. After three hours, he finally stood back, cold, tired, but exhilarated. Walking back to the house, the freezing air caught his breath. For the first time in his life, he was elated by a howling south-westerly wind.

The following day the phone did not touch down for two

hours, as Theo called all his contacts for urgent help with the conservation. Finally, he stretched out his stiff right arm and replaced the receiver. Immediately it rang out. Looking at it with annoyance, he reluctantly picked it up.

His mother's familiar voice rattled away.

'Ive been trying for the last hour Theo. How are you all? Darling Floria? Olivia? Is everything okay? I'm so excited had to call. I want to come over. Now. To see you all. I can't wait until Ben's free. Theo are you listening honey?'

Theo was tired, his head full of dates, times, names and appointments. He couldn't focus on his mum's stream of chatter.

'Hi Mom. Look, good to hear from you. I'm up to my neck in a big project and all the admin and red tape to sort out. Can I put you on to Livia? Speak soon.'

Theo handed the phone to Olivia, raising his eyes and pointing at it whilst mouthing 'my mom'. Olivia smiled and readily took the phone.

'Hi Sophia, how are you? I hope you received the recent photos we sent. The ones where Floria is in the play-pen in the garden with her bucket and spade.'

'Yes, she is just gorgeous.

We're so far away, though, and I'm missing all the precious moments.'

Sophia sighed.

'We are all very well at the moment.

Now, Ben and I have been having a long discussion. I have a plan. I've recently taken early retirement from the school, and well, Olivia, I can't wait until next July before we come.

So, if it's possible and okay with you two, can I come before Ben and stay over for a while? It sounds like Theo's got some big project on? How about I help out with Floria? It would be a dream for me, my first little grandchild, we could bond, you know, she would get to know me and then when I call in the future she would recognise my voice. I understand if you need time to discuss this, but I'm ready and waiting. I could book a flight this weekend.'

Olivia's thoughts quickly assimilated what Sophia had just said. This could be the perfect solution, Sophia at their house, helping out with Floria. Livia smiled as she thought of her delicious baking and home cooking. It would give Livia time to concentrate on the Roman find with Theo. With the added bonus of granny getting to know her granddaughter. Olivia's mind was made up as she said:

'Sophia, it sounds like a fantastic idea. It would be special for Floria to have her Nonna's attention. Definitely a lovely thing for you both to be together. Could you come on your own?

Did Theo tell you we have an archaeological project on the land surrounding our house? Roman artefacts, the most incredible find.'

She replied:

'Well, I know my Theo, and I could tell there was something pretty big going on work-wise. He did seem a bit, well, distracted. I didn't think he was hearing what I was saying. That's one of the reasons I knew I would get more sense out of you, Olivia.

So you've dug up something in your own back garden?

Well, you are going to need me there. You will have to be on hand alongside Theo, and you need me to share the load, helping with Floria. I could cook and give a hand with the big house you've got.

So is it a yes? Do you need to clear it with Theo, honey?'

'Oh, Sophia, you just come. Yes, It will be wonderful if you're sure Ben will cope without you?'

'Well, that's settled. Ben will be fine at a European conference next month, tree conservation. Somewhere in Scandinavia, he might even get a weekend in your neck of the woods, so to speak. He's positively pushed me to phone you today.

I've missed seeing you all. I will get off this line and straight onto the airline booking office and get back to you as soon as I can confirm the date and time. Speak soon.'

Livia cradled the phone in her hands, smiling to herself. Should she tell Theo or keep it a big surprise? She felt elated but nervous. Her larger-than-life mother-in-law. She remembered liking her, being pleased to see her big personality, and how she affectionately hugged her boys and still treated them as babies. They had barely spent a few nights and days together since the first meeting. Life was going to be very interesting over the next couple of months in more ways than just the arrival of Mamma Sophia.

Theo installed coolers in the site hut, keeping the temperature at fifty degrees Fahrenheit, and humidifiers kept the air dry. A welcome atmosphere for the preservation work to begin.

The first casket brought out swayed precariously in the hoist as it was gingerly lifted. Its top was darkened, beaten silver and decorated with acanthus and myrtle leaves. After gentle levering, the lid creaked open. Dark gooey mud oozed out. Below this layer was another more ornate casket slotted inside the outer casing.

The air was electric as cameras clicked and whirred. Everyone silently leaned forwards and peered into the dark mass. Suddenly the young helpers, Mel and Jackie, squealed out loud. Their outburst gave a sense of childish rawness to an eery atmosphere. The dim light and howling wind only added to the chill they all felt.

As the mud was removed, Theo raised his hand.

' If we force it, this box will disintegrate.'

He was undecided as to whether to try to open it from within its outer casing or use special tools to open up the sides of the silver outer box. The decision was made to open up the sides and, if necessary, rebuild it afterwards.

The inner casket slowly emerged as a soft murmur rippled around the room.

However old gold is, never can its lustre be dulled. Two

thousand years of dark concealment made no difference to what shone out that day in all its glory of intricately beaten gold and iron clasps. The gold gleamed, and the iron blackened like jet stone. As the lid was opened, what appeared before their eyes were like a pirate's treasure trove. A tray filled with jewellery, amethyst and emerald rings, a gold necklace and bracelets of pearls. Torches flickered, and the cine camera whirred, panning across the sparkling gems.

Theo gently eased the tray out of the case; it was dry, though fragile. The wooden outer frames looked distinctly like a book. There beneath were darkened black writing tablets. The wax had long ago perished, but underneath, etchings had been scratched onto the wood and slate.

He removed the first tablet to reveal five more similar ones. He delicately bound them with the same materials he had covered the wooden cart and placed them individually in packing cases. The work of deciphering would be long and laborious. Theo remembered an archaeological discovery in 1973 of wooden sheets of Roman writing from the time of the Roman occupation of the north of England. These tablets were rigid leaves impregnated with ink and had been photographed using infrared cameras to enhance the writing. However, Theo was sure that these would have been layered with wax at one time. Therefore the imprint on the wood would be from the metal stylus. This would need another technique to view the Latin script.

Sophia arrived that weekend and immediately took over the care of Floria. She whispered Italian songs in her ears and fed and bathed her as if she had been her own daughter.

Meanwhile, Theo and Olivia became totally engrossed in their work. Some of the tablets were examined and photographed using different levels of angled light bringing out the words engraved onto the wooden surface where the wax had been. The text came alive from the photographs. Livia pored over the prints. Slowly the scratchings of words began to make sense, the text became legible, and it could be separated into individual pieces of literature.

The first writings were about the beauty of the landscape, with short sentences and childlike descriptions of valleys and olive groves. The sunsets, the birds, the flora and fauna, were all mentioned in great detail. Olivia stumbled across the name of a villa. It appeared the family travelled from Rome with all the slaves, carts and belongings each spring to the Villa Julian, which looked across towards distant hills.

From the original find of the golden stylus, Olivia was convinced that the writer of these tablets was Pomponia Graecina. A woman related to the ruling families of Rome. Olivia was familiar with the writings of Tacitus. She knew that he had written about Pomponia. The wife of the Roman general Aulus Plautius Silvanus, who had conquered Britain in 42 or 43 AD. A few sentences written by Tacitus referred to her being tried and released by her husband following an accusation of being part of a foreign superstition. Suetonius mentioned a son named Aulus, who had been executed by Nero. Nero accused Aulus, the younger, of having been the lover of Nero's mother.

Livia told Theo all the clues she was discovering.
Almost too scared to hint at the enormity of their findings. They would sometimes just sit and stare. Theo would catch a glimpse of the fear in Olivia's eyes, then reassuringly stroke a hair from her dishevelled face and say.

'This is the big one, honey. It's such an unknown. Together we can do this.
We are dealing with written words directly from a female living at the time before the conquest of Britain!'

Olivia was intrigued that here were the words of a woman, yes, educated and of the noble families of Rome. A few scholars of Roman history had made references to women, but always through the eyes of men, and these were men of scholarly background speaking nothing of the lives of slaves and those less fortunate than themselves. Pomponia by contrast had insight and deep feelings for her surroundings and ordinary people. She expressed what she was feeling and felt the sufferings of those around her. It was not just some literary poem of fanciful life and love, but there was a real woman who related events as they happened around her for good or bad. She appeared to have friendships with her slave girls. They confided in her, and she in them.

Every waking moment of Olivia's life was taken over by the life of this person, Pomponia. Each day, more and more revelations were revealed. She learned the names of her slave girls, the experience of when she first met her future husband, the plight of her slave girls and their relatives, and what had happened to them. The young girl also had fears and spoke of mysteries she could not understand. Pomponia poured her heart into her writings and always recorded the good and the harmful incidents. Throughout the reports, Livia sensed Pomponia had to conceal what she was writing. She spoke of powerful men that she was afraid of. Not her father or her husband and brothers, but there was someone she did not name that frightened her. The recorded visit to her grandmother at the imperial palace with her cousin Julia had been entertaining, reading about the music and dancing. Then Pomponia had written the warning words from her grandmother to take care of what she wrote and what she said. The closer she was to the emperor, the more danger there was to herself and her children.

A chill ran through Olivia. More questions were raised in her mind. What had happened to Pomponia? What and whom was she afraid of? Livia was desperate to see inside the other caskets whether any additional documents could reveal more. Olivia started to build up a file of information. She saw in her mind's eye a girl with high ideals, hopes and a seeker of truth. She found herself imagining and re-reading passages, 'the life of my family at their summer retreat in the foothills a days journey from Rome. My stylus swiftly moves across my scrolls'

She stopped abruptly as the words 'a days journey from

Rome' jumped out of the page. Where could this be? Excitedly she measured a circle around her map of Rome. Roughly twenty to thirty miles would be the distance of a day's journey by carriage from Rome.

Her circle reached as far as Frascati in the foothills of the Alban Hills to the southeast. Olivia retrieved her black notebook and started to make quick notes. As she looked back through the previous pages. The bullet point referencing the metal bauble found at Nonna Francesca - inscribed with Villa Julian, Gracaen - Tiberius. These all started to connect together. Pomponia Graecina, she had mentioned Villa Julian. She would have lived during the reign of Tiberius.

Where had she seen these words before? In the book given to her by Monte. The Victorian explorer. He had found a tomb somewhere in the hills. What had he seen inscribed?

Olivia skimmed through her notes. There it was. She had noted what had been inscribed:

"I gave voice to with my stylus.
Pom¦. Graeci ¦.of Au¦. Pla¦..ius.'
Was this a tomb? The hand of a noblewoman of Rome.

The Pom could stand for Pomponia. Then the Graeci could have been originally Graecina, her family name. The Au and Pla, her husband, Aulus Plautius? Where had Pomponia's family lived during their summer months? What was the connection? Had Pomponia lived here in England as well as in Rome and Frascati? If she were such a prolific recorder and writer of events, was there more of her work to be discovered? She needed, urgently, to speak to Sophia and learn more about Nonna Francesca and her childhood in Italy.

While walking by the Quay together the following day. Livia had her opportunity to broach the subject of Sophia's childhood and the land around their home in Italy.

'Sophia I would love to hear more about where you grew up in Italy.'

'Well, my family lived outside Rome in the region of Frascati. My grandparents had lived there all of their lives. In fact, for generations, we had farmed the area. We had vineyards and olive groves, delicious wine and olive oil. There were clear freshwater lakes to swim and play in.

When I was nine, just before the second world war, there was so much poverty in Italy my father decided to emigrate to America with me. My father sent money from America to my mother. He worked very hard in the construction industry. I would return to visit my mother each year. She never came to America. Papa helped educate Theo's uncle Ernesto Gambocelli, which enabled him to become an archaeologist. Theo visited as a young boy and was hooked on the ancient world of dust and antiquities. Ernesto lives near Rome, too. We still have many relatives there. You met a few in Rome?'

She paused:

'Theo tells me you met my formidable mother. Ahh, fiercely independent.'

Sophia's expression altered to closed and brooding. Quickly she changed the subject away from Nonna Francesca.

'I haven't returned for many years, but it would be interesting to visit the area again around Frascati, I believe there was a small chapel built for the Gambocelli family, many of our ancestors were buried there in the foothills.'

Livia was keen to hear more of the family histories, but something Sophia said had resonated with her about the foothills, the vineyards, the olive oil, the short distance from Rome, and rural life. It sounded familiar. Pomponia described her summer journey from Rome to their villa in the rolling hills, mentioning hidden lakes where she had been swimming as a child. Sophia noticed that Livia had disappeared into her own world, and Floria was grizzling; the sound was getting louder. She touched Olivia's arm gently and said.

'Livia, honey?'

Olivia shook her head as if returning from a reverie. She looked up at Sophia, then vaguely at Floria. She gasped and put her hand to her mouth.

'Sophia, you speak of Italy, the family estates around Frascati. There's an incredible connection, I'm sure. The family of the Graecinas and Frascati. It's a known fact that the families of Rome built their summer villas in that region.

Oh, Sophia, I'm sorry, I'm getting so distracted again. You've been an absolute brick. You are marvellous. Theo and I couldn't have done even one per cent of what we've done the last six weeks if you had not been here. I know I haven't been the best hostess, but this talk of Frascati, that's the modern name for the ancient area of Tusculum where the Roman nobility built their country villas! Could Pomponia have walked through those hills and valleys? Your mother showed us an old bronze bauble. The words Villa Julian and Tiberius were inscribed on it.
I have an old book by an early 19th-century Victorian explorer who discovered a tombstone somewhere in the Alban hills with a worn-out part inscription in ancient Roman Latin. It speaks of a stylus, then P Graeci and A and P ius. It's all connected!

I have to decipher more of her writings to pinpoint where she lived in Italy before she came to England.'

That night Sophia and Olivia sat companionably with a bottle of wine, looking out over the estuary, talking of the discovery and possible connections with their Italian family. Sophia smiled to herself and said:

'You know I'm going to telephone Mamma. I think it will be interesting to tell her what you've found. I always call about this time each week.'

After the usual stream of Italian chatter around health and family. Sophia spoke of Olivia's findings. Nonna Francesca gasped and stopped talking. Her breathing became laboured.

'Mamma, are you still there? Are you okay?'
Olivia jumped out of her chair. After a few seconds, they heard her mother say:-

'Put me onto Olivia, I need to speak with her.'
Olivia took the phone to her ear.

'Nonna Francesca are you alright? We were so worried when

we didn't hear you speaking?'

'Bah, it's nothing. I, too, have to gather my thoughts together. Just because I'm old doesn't mean I'm speechless.

Now listen carefully. You don't have to speak.

I tell you, there is a connection here on this land with the Graecina family and the Plautius family. The broken trinkets I showed you when you came are nothing compared with what's in the barn. Stones are inscribed with names, parts of statues, garden ornaments and pottery. I have it all catalogued. I have kept it quiet. Too much bureaucracy and nosey authorities around once it's public knowledge. Over the years, as we have farmed the land, we have unearthed a lot. The family have not been here enough to take an interest, but it's all here, Olivia. There must be so much more too.

I am an old woman I can't physically do anymore, but you and Theo could. It's all here, Olivia, the clues to what's under this soil.

Now I don't want a load of busybodies, bureaucrats and officials to know about this. I will keep it safe for you, my log, locked in the armoire. I have two keys, one on my person and the other I will send to you. You come and carry on the search if anything should happen to me.

Now put my daughter back on the phone, and she can arrange the delivery.'

Olivia stood dumbfounded for a few seconds. She swallowed hard and then, wide-eyed, shaking her head, handed the phone back to Sophia.

The arrangements were made with Sophia trying hard to prise out of Francesca more details, but none were forthcoming. The conversation ended abruptly as the Italian line went silent.

Sophia raised both hands in a questioning shrug, looking enquiringly at Olivia, who spoke.

'She knows about her land. There is a connection between the Graecinus family and the Plautius family. She's collected evidence and wants me to have her log.

Oh my, this is far-reaching. What have we started?

As usual, the postage across Europe from Italy took some weeks. Olivia concentrated on more of the deciphering work as more caskets were opened. Then one day, she was enjoying the prose of Pomponia, mentioning her gardens and building another villa. The name of Columella sprang out of the writing. Even her husband, Aulus, had taken time to enjoy his company. He had been invited to help them with their bees and husbandry.

The writings described her leaving Rome and sadness her boys would remain as she travelled to Brittania. The sea and the land of ancient times were beautifully detailed, along with animated discussions with her slave girls. Long passages portrayed her eventful travels across Britain to the west, finding gold, and the marriage of her slave girl to a chief's son. Then the writing began to alter in its tenor. Pomponia sounded weak. Her written strokes became clumsy.

Olivia scrutinised the words carefully.

Was Pomponia ill? Her last words were.

'I must return to my husband and the army.'

The writing stopped abruptly.

Olivia now had to get seriously down to reading the works of Columella as it was all starting to fit into place. Even her jewellery became more meaningful as she deciphered that the name of Columella was inscribed on the gold. Aunt Geraldine confirmed that the pieces had been found at the lake Avernus site near Puteoli. Maybe Columella had had a villa near there.

The more Olivia uncovered, the more she realised the
strong connections there were with Pomponia,
Columella, their site at Exeter and the land near Frascati.
The work in Exeter had to be thoroughly researched
before they went anywhere near Nonna Francesca's
findings and log, however tantalising it all seemed.

CHAPTER 17

Time present and time past
Are both perhaps present in time future,
And time future contained in time past..........

Time past and time future
What might have been and what has been
Point to one end, which is always present.
No 1 of Four Quarters
Burnt Norton
T S Eliot

Exeter, on the Estuary and Topsham 1981

Nonna Francesca's key and a thick packet of handwritten Italian letters finally arrived. Olivia had only time to read the first few pages. Where it appeared to be recipes and gardening plans, and diagrams. The writing was neat but faint, and it would take a few days of effort to wade through it all. She put it all carefully away as the present Archeological work of preservation, conservation and deciphering took precedence. The whole process was like unveiling a new world of treasures to Olivia. The jewellery found was nothing compared to these shreds of sentences conveying emotions and most profound feelings, all carefully put down by the hand of Pomponia. They became alive as friends writing from another part of the planet, yet with experiences and day-to-day activities like her life as a woman.

   After two months of work, the press had gotten wind of a

significant Roman find in the area around Exeter, ancient Isca. The confidentiality of the discovery had so far been kept, but as more and more scholars and specialists became involved in conserving these precious items, the word spread wider. Theo now had to employ a full-time secretary to take all the calls that were coming in each day. Olivia was buried in the lost world of Pomponia and slept, dreamt and breathed the life of this woman with whom she felt a great affinity. Constantly moved by her writings, Livia thought Pomponia had been brought to life as an actual living, breathing woman, like herself. She gained courage and insight from the stories. Weeping when Pomponia grieved, she was taken over daily by the emotions of this person who, by now, had become her closest companion. She dreamed of her and felt the pains of her illnesses and losses. Olivia was transported into another world. Her waking moments were in the company of someone more alive than those around her. Reality started to slip.

Sophia had been more than happy to spend the previous two months getting to know her delightful little granddaughter. For the first couple of weeks, it had been a novelty to wake when Floria woke at night, rock her back to sleep and happily dress and feed her in the mornings when Theo and Livia were already working on the dig. Little Floria was totally besotted with her grandmamma, as Sophia was with her. Sophia enjoyed all her unique time with Floria, and little Floria started calling her Mamma. Sofia found this highly amusing, but after a month of all the work and time she had spent with Floria, Sophia, in all her wisdom and knowledge of watching the progress of her son and daughter-in-law with their preoccupations, was concerned at Olivia's degree of obsession. Sophia recognised the possible complications ensuing when she eventually returned to America.

The arrival of Geraldine was precisely what was needed. After a few days in her company, Sophia took to this indomitable woman and felt she could speak to her, knowing how much she loved Olivia and Theo. Together they devised a plan, a slight distraction that would help Olivia to come back into the real world and connect again. Geraldine suggested a small charity exhibition party of Olivia's Roman jewellery, one or two of the found artefacts, and a fragment of the deciphered writings. As added fun and attraction, everyone invited would dress in costume from the Roman era. The money raised could be donated towards a scholarship for a student to study archaeology at the university. It would be great publicity for the gallery and a good distraction for Olivia from the intensity of her work.

With Theo so engrossed in the continuing cataloguing, Olivia cautiously welcomed the plan. The seed of the idea was left with Livia. Geraldine with Sophia began making arrangements before returning to Missenden after promising to be back for the exhibition party.

Livia had not spent much time with her old friends for so long, but now they all rallied around. Tristan, Alice, Jason and Tati threw all their efforts into helping. Secure tempered glass cabinets were made. The electronic security system already attached to the Picasso paintings was extended to surround the new exhibits.

A clean-up was in progress a week before the exhibition. When suddenly, the glass doors burst open. All eyes turned as a tall, elegant woman swept in. She was dressed in a scarlet figure-hugging mini dress, wearing dark sunglasses with her hair swept back behind a black chiffon scarf. The impact was dramatic. Made all the more so by the contrast of the dusty, jean-clad group preparing the gallery. She scanned her audience, then, removing the sunglasses, narrowed her eyes towards Olivia, saying:

'Hello, my darling sister. I just had to come down to support you for the coming party. When word got around of the most fantastic discovery you and your gorgeous husband had made.'

Imogen moved forward towards a startled Olivia, leaning in to air kiss on both cheeks. Carefully keeping her clothes from coming near the dusty Livia.

'I'm staying for a few days at Gung Ho, don't want to be any inconvenience to you all. Besides I have a few house guests arriving tonight. You know friends and famous, they will be such an asset to your little exhibition. Help to boost the publicity. '

Imogen scanned the studio, her eyes alighting on the new cabinets where the exhibits were to be housed. She moved over to them, gliding her gloved hand along the dusty tops.

'I can see there's still some work to be done. I won't detain you. I can help when everything is settled in its place.'
She pointed towards the cabinets and fixed her eyes on the Picassos.

'This is where they will be? Next to the Picassos?
Make sure the lighting is good, Olivia. So important, I do know about these things. Lighting is paramount.
Well then, I will be off. So much to do before my guests arrive this evening. It will be such fun to see everyone in costume.'

Just at dramatically as she arrived, she left with a faint trace of her perfume wafting through the air. They all looked at Olivia in silence.

'That was my dear older sister. So sorry for the sudden arrival. I had no idea she was coming. I wonder if Aunt Geraldine has either. Ah well, any publicity will be good for the gallery.'
Livia started to laugh out loud.
'I'm not too sure who these 'friends and famous' will be though.'

Imogen returned to Gung Ho as a large delivery of food and alcohol arrived along with her five guests. One of them, the tall, bearded, handsome man, stuck closely to her. He showed her photos of the Picassos and quizzed her surreptitiously over the security system installed. Imogen was in love, she craved the attention he gave her and feigned interest in anything he was interested in, and as the wine flowed freely, her tongue loosened. Her photographic memory could recall all the details, the complete layout, security and position of the paintings. Her boyfriend, whom she knew as 'Ian St Ledger', wooed and wheedled around her. She basked in the undivided attention he gave her.

On the evening of the party, guests began to arrive dressed in their draped togas. The women copied the richly clad noble women of Rome decorating their necks and arms with sparkling jewellery. Imogen, along with her friends, radiated elegant Roman opulence. Her friends Diana and Carmen looked as though they had stepped off the cast of a production of Ben Hur. Their costumes were obviously from very exclusive hire companies. The male partners stood tall, acting out their Roman roles. One was a centurion, another emperor Nero, and the other a gladiator with a full leather mask covering his face. Imogen moved around the packed gallery laughing and entertaining. The tall gladiator followed her, his right arm encircling her waist. Olivia thought how confident she seemed, able to draw a crowd around her wherever she went. As the evening continued, Theo chinked his glass with a metal pen. Three bell-like sounds echoed through the room. The noise of voices subsided as all eyes fixed on him. He pulled Olivia towards him.

'A few words of thank you for coming this evening to support the charity for a student to study my favourite subject.'
He smiled as he continued.

'Its been a long, tedious, exhausting but amazing time of our lives. The uncovering of a significant relic of Roman times. Not only the objects themselves but reading the thoughts and words of a woman living through tumultuous times and having the courage to write and preserve her viewpoint has been unprecedented in archaeological history. I want to thank all the team that have worked tirelessly with us, all the experts that have helped. Our relations that have been our ardent supporters. Its been now hundreds of people along the way. There's still an immense journey ahead. Olivia and I can't thank everyone enough.'
He then turned to Olivia.

'She won't want me to say this but.... I'm going to anyway.

This lady here, my wife, my partner in all things, the cleverest decipherer of ancient Latin. You are the best. Biggest thank you, my love.'

Olivia buried her head in Theo's toga, hugging him through gulped sobs. All the weeks of work and intense concentration suddenly overwhelmed her. If Theo had not been holding her tightly, she would have collapsed. He waved his free hand to the audience, whooping and clapping. The colour-themed lighting flashed on and off, and conversations burst out again. Corks popped, and glassed were filled. A couple of ice buckets crashed onto the floor, and ice spilt out. Imogen was splashed in the commotion. She turned to shake out her drapes as she looked around for her 'Gladiator.' By now, she was unsteady on her feet, her speech slurred.

'Where is Ian? Darling where are you?'

The friends with her supported her arm as she wobbled. Diana and Carmen looked around the room. The gladiator was nowhere to be seen. They signalled to their two companions, who quietly ushered Imogen towards the door. By now, she was semi-conscious, making no protest at being taken from the party.

Olivia hardly noticed the departure of the six from London. She was tired now. So many people had wanted to talk to her. So many questions, photographs, flashing lights and the hubbub of noise. Her head was spinning. Suddenly there was a shriek from the rear of the gallery. Sophia was shouting out. Someone stopped the changing lights and put the overhead spots on.

The case containing the Picasso paintings was empty!

Theo rushed towards it, shouting for all to step back.

'Don't touch anything, keep well back. Someone telephone for the police. Please everyone stay where you are.'

Within fifteen minutes, the police sirens and flashing blue lights appeared. The casements were cordoned off, and everyone there was searched, including clothing, handbags and pockets, all to no avail. After two more hours of questioning and dusting for fingerprints, everyone was allowed to go home. Sophia and Geraldine went back with Olivia to her house. Geraldine immediately went into the study and closed the door. They could hear her talking on the telephone. After some time, Geraldine emerged.

Olivia was exhausted and tearful.

'Aunt I am so sorry. Where did I go wrong? The security system was updated. Why didn't any of us see them being stolen? Why didn't the alarm go off? The only people that left before the theft was discovered were my sister and her cronies.'

Geraldine raised a stern face towards Olivia. She silently narrowed her eyes and gritted her teeth together. The seconds passed, her fingers tapping lightly on her knees.

'You are not to worry, Olivia. Remember I told you I had my own safeguards in place. The Picassos are secure. The thief will be caught presently. Tomorrow we will go to see your sister at Gung Ho. It will all become more transparent in the morning. For now, we all need a few hours of sleep. It will be dawn soon.'

The once immaculate path to Gung Ho was strewn with litter. Two large black plastic bags bulging with rubbish leant against the front bay window. The front door was slightly open. As Geraldine pushed it further, she gasped. The hallway was marked by muddy footprints, and banging and crashing could be heard from upstairs. Olivia followed Geraldine through. The kitchen looked like a third-world squatter's den. Empty bottles and glasses scattered across the centre worktop, and greasy splatters up the back of the cooker stained the tiles. Cigarette butt ends, foil and various dubious straws and papers were piled up on china saucers. No wonder the door was propped open. An oily, smokey odour filled the air. A sharp gust of wind slammed the front door when they opened the back door. The noises from upstairs stopped. An angry voice shouted out.

'Ian is that you? Where have you been? What's going on?'
A furious red-faced Imogen appeared over the bannisters. Geraldine said.

'Stay here Olivia, I will deal with this. Don't touch anything until I get down.'

Olivia retreated into the garden and sat on one of the sun loungers trying to concentrate on the beautiful calm estuary and the many birds going about their business swooping and diving. What had happened to the paintings? What were her aunt's safeguards? Was Imogen involved with her friends in the theft? Her heart sank as she contemplated the scandal and furore that would come about if this were so.

Geraldine came out into the garden, with Imogen following behind. She strutted forward towards Olivia, dark glasses covering her eyes as she tossed her head backwards defiantly. Geraldine carried a large polythene bag containing two wine glasses, one covered in red lipstick.
'Sit down here Imogen and do not move until I return.'
Geraldine pointed to the chair opposite Olivia. She glared ferociously at Imogen, who slightly cowered, but slumped down into the seat.
Olivia watched as Geraldine marched back into the house. They heard her speaking on the telephone.

Imogen looked at Olivia, taking her sunglasses off her eyes, revealing a livid bruise on her right eyebrow. Livia gasped.

'Whats happened Imogen?'

'Don't stare so! It's all your fault. How was I to know that my boyfriend was a fraud? Ian wasn't even his real name. Aunt keeps banging on about his past. Related to some devious family or other. Didn't you see him? Why didn't you say something? Now look at what's happened. You're to blame. Always been the favourite, protected, and shielded. Little miss goody two shoes. Always buried in the past with your old relics. I've had to forge my career and use my contacts and acquaintances to pay my way. Aaargh, you make me sick! Look at my face too. He hit me.'
She started to whimper, which rose to a sob and gushes of

tears.

Olivia had a sick feeling in her stomach. Who was the man with her at the gallery function? What was Imogen talking about?

At this moment, Geraldine appeared, addressing Imogen. 'Right young lady. You are to remain here. The police are coming, and this evidence will be given to them. You will make a statement of the facts, Imogen. No lies or dramatics. Full description of 'your boyfriend'. The so-called Ian St Ledger, who I am very sure is, in fact, Sebastian Routledge. Our old friend Inspector Brockett has on file the fingerprints taken from your jewellery Olivia all those years ago, which were never identified. Yes, they are still on record and will no doubt prove to be an identical match with what is on this wine glass and the casement at the gallery.

Olivia shook her head, running her fingers through her hair and said.

'This is just too awful. All that's happened. What has been going on here. The state of this house. Imogen's face. The paintings too Aunt, how will you get them back.'

Geraldine narrowed her eyes, pursing her lips together angrily, looking at Imogen.

'I will explain later.'

The police from Exeter CID arrived and took Imogen and the bagged evidence with them back to the station. Olivia and Geraldine followed in their car. Everyone gave their statements. It seemed to take forever as they waited around in the stuffy Police station rooms, sitting on long vinyl-covered benches in the draughty corridors. Familiar memories of her days waiting outside the headmistress's office at Lady Clara Grammar returned to Olivia. Thoughts of Ranjit, carefree summer days, rambling with Ruby, the old house, all the projects and mysteries she had recorded and tried to solve. Her mind wandered, then abruptly she returned to reality as she saw the familiar large form of her old ally Inspector Brocket ambling towards her. He walked now with a slight stoop, and the independent eyebrows seemed much more wiry, bushier and whiter than she remembered. His expression changed and softened as he recognised Olivia, shaking her hand and inviting her into one of the airless little interrogation rooms. He laid a thick manilla file on the table in front of them. Explaining matching up fingerprints from her jewellery with the ones on the wine glasses and casements at the gallery. He had questioned Sebastian Rutledge over previous unsolved incidents, and he had always got away with his crimes. Brockett leaned in towards Olivia and smacked his hand on the files in front of them.

'We've got him this time, good and proper. Our young, clever clogs thought he could pull off this stunt. And when we get him and the paintings, that will clinch it.

Your Aunt's a very wise old bird.'

He paused, scratching his chin.

'She had the paintings marked with a chemical dye so that when they were removed from their glass frames it attaches itself to skin and gets under the finger nails, causing a nasty blister as well as staining the reverse of the paintings and the persons fingers.'

That's not the best of it, though.

They're copies. Not the originals. 'Aunt Geraldine' has those safely stashed away somewhere.'

Olivia shook her head from side to side smiling.

'My Aunt. She's a genius. That explains the printed labels on the back of them. The warning not to remove the backing card. Who would have thought.'

The Inspector gathered up the file and ushered Olivia to the bench where her aunt was waiting. There were just a few more formalities to complete, and then they could take Imogen away. Fortunately, no further investigation was made into the possession of questionable items at the house, and neither Imogen nor Geraldine wished to press any formal charges for any other crimes.

The drive back to Gung Ho was long and silent. Imogen sighed and fidgeted in the back seat. She slunk into the house and raced up the stairs, returning in a baggy shirt and old dungarees. Ready to help with the clearing up. Quickly stuffing as much as she could away into the rubbish bags. They worked as a team; the windows opened, and the clear salty fresh air blew from the estuary, quickly returning the calm fragrant atmosphere to Gung Ho. Geraldine and Livia, at last, flopped into chairs as the final bags were placed outside. The hard labour must have chastened Imogen, for she didn't sit down immediately but made hot mugs of tea for them all. Devoid of her makeup and designer clothes, her flushed face and reddened hands almost looked normal. For once, hard work and a long day at the police station seemed to have affected Imogen. Sitting down, calmly sipping her tea. She coughed nervously and whispered.

'I can't go back yet. So much scandal. I've been taken for a ride. Such a fool I've been.'

Olivia looked long and hard at Imogen. Was this a chastened new Imogen? Or was this one of her most extraordinary acts of pathos?

Imogen's eyes brimmed with tears as they overflowed and trickled down her hollow cheeks.

Olivia was moved with pity. The great and glamorous Imogen. All the stuffing of self-importance appeared to have gone. Just a woman bruised and shamed. Her sister, after all. Despite what had gone on. She placed a hand on her shoulder and kissed the top of her head.

'Ahh, come on Sis'. That shiner of a bruise, it will calm down. You just need a few days to recuperate. The skins not broken, you will have no lasting scar. You're welcome to come and stay with us if you like.'

Aunt Geraldine quickly stepped in.

'Come on, my dear, now. You will get over this little incident. Hopefully learn a lot of lessons from it, Imogen.

You should stay here at Gung Ho for a few reflective days. Just until the bruising has died down. Rest out in the garden. I will get some groceries delivered, and Mrs Groves can pop in daily to keep an eye on the housework. You get to bed now. Have a hot bath, and I will bring you cocoa and warm toast. An early night tonight, that's what you need. I'm staying over tonight, and we will see how you are in the morning. Come on off, you go.'
Imogen didn't protest but meekly followed Geraldine up the stairs. Livia went to hug her, but she just brushed past her and climbed the stairs.

Peace and tranquility gradually returned as Olivia drove home with a massive sigh of relief. She did not want Imogen in her home with a mood of irritability and spiteful words spewing from her mouth. Their part of the Exe was where the treasure had been found. Not just materially but something more valuable. Turning into their lane, she smiled, slowed the car to a standstill, and pulled over onto the grass. Looking up at her house at the end of the long drive. She realised it was starting to settle into its surroundings. The original old vines and creepers were winding their tendrils around the stonework. The newer wooden window frames had mellowed into the tones of the weathered oak door. The young branches of trees brushed against new walls. They were claiming it as their own. Even the wildfowl rested on the roof at times. Recalling when she first saw Rivertree House, which also had appeared to be claimed by the trees, nestled and cradled in their boughs. It was happening here. Their house was owned by its surroundings. If she closed her eyes and listened. She heard the swish of the birds landing on the Exe, imagining a sound heard many centuries ago, paddles of oars dipping in and out. The trees creaked like a straining ship carrying her noble friend across the waters away from the sunken treasure she had left behind. Olivia whispered. 'Thank you Pomponia.'

CHAPTER 18

‘O Call back yesterday bid time return’
William Shakespeare

On the Exe

After two days of recovering at Gung Ho, sleeping and sunbathing, Imogen's natural restlessness returned. She lay in the sun, watching the waders paddling and ferreting around in the sandbanks. Slowly the seed of a new idea began to sprout in her mind. Stretching out, she sat up. Her fingers gently caressed her brow; no longer did it sting. Looking into her makeup mirror, she spoke out loud.
'So Imogen Hadleigh. No permanent damage done.'
Smiling into her mirror, she posed, pouting her lips and half closing her sultry eyes.
'A new phase, I think, darling. Fame comes in so many different ways.'

She ran into the house and picked up her diary and address book. Making herself comfortable by the hall telephone, she began her new project.

From supposedly unknown but well-informed sources, word soon got around that the actress Imogen Hadleigh had been assaulted. She then helped the police apprehend a mysterious 'international art thief' involving members of a notorious London gang. Imogen remained at Gung Ho to receive all the journalists that wanted an interview. Her photo started to appear in local and then national newspapers. Her agent in

London was inundated with new parts for her to play. Then just as quickly as she had appeared, she returned to London. Her fame was secured for the present.

Geraldine despaired and quickly got her lawyers onto Imogen to ensure she didn't commit any libellous statement that would damage the case. The serialisation of her story was stopped in the tabloids. Imogen was annoyed, though only briefly, having already secured a long-term contract for one of the soap operas appearing each evening on the television. Olivia kept well away, hoping the publicity would not descend onto her peaceful part of the world.

Inspector Brockett visited the gallery and informed them of the progress in retrieving the paintings and catching the thief. He confirmed that the three sets of fingerprints were identical. The original ones from Olivia's jewellery, the prints on the casements at the gallery, and the wine glasses from Gung Ho were all one and the same person. However, no trace of the missing Sebastian Routledge alias Ian St Ledger could be found so far. Inspector Brocket sometimes said these cases took years to solve, and the thieves would be caught only when the painting emerged for sale or trade. He chuckled to himself.

'You know that aunt of yours, placing a dye on the paintings. That thief will have purple fingertips for quite some time.'

He started laughing heartily and took out his handkerchief to wipe his eyes.

'Best of all, though, she had swapped them for copies. Ahhh, a woman after my own heart. There is a lot more to her than meets the eye. I have even heard a few whispers about her former career during the war. All hush-hush, mind you. Daresay, we will only get to the bottom of some of this.

Well, Olivia, I had best be off now.

I hear you and your husband have been busy in the archaeology field. I've had a bit of interest myself over the years. My wife and I have been on a few tours of Pompei and Rome.'

He paused, his independent eyebrows lifting up in different directions enquiringly.
Olivia put her head to one side and smiled.

'Inspector another time I would love to show you what we have dug up. I think we could have a lot to talk about together. We are only just starting. Firstly here on the Exe. Also, we're uncovering exciting new information that traces history back to Italy and Theo's family land near Frascati. We must arrange a time for you and your wife, Inspector, to come for dinner.
He held out his hand and warmly shook Olivia's.
'Och lass. Its Hamish. I think you could call me by my first name. Its been a pleasure to meet up again, and I will definitely take you up on that return visit to see some of the treasures you've dug up. Well, I will be off now. I will keep you informed of any progress as and when we hear anything.'

The excitement of the exhibition, theft of the paintings, police investigation and Imogen's notoriety all took some weeks for life to settle down again. Olivia gradually restarted her research into the significance of her Claude Acte jewellery, Columella and links with Pomponia and the family estates in Italy. The wall of her study started to look like a police investigation board. Photos, maps, copies of written phrases from textbooks, and the works of Columella and Pomponia's deciphered writings were pinned onto the walls. Then any links were pegged with coloured cords and small notes stuck to the string. The book from the Victorian explorer was key to discovering more about where Pomponia may have lived and died near Frascati.

Bringing to life the words and writings of Pomponia from the bog and sandy swamp of the marshes was a painstaking task for Olivia. For many hours, she pored over scraps of sentences in the ancient Latin cursive script. It was a gigantic task of piecing small fragments of scattered years of life and experiences, all gradually joining together as a masterpiece of literature and priceless historical records. Pomponia came alive to Olivia, and as she entered this courageous woman's mind, she observed the similarities of thought, emotion and activity between them. As Olivia deciphered more of the works they had discovered from the mud, she realised that Pomponia must have had a life upon her return to Rome. Then one day, she found amongst the writings of Tacitus a mention of Pomponia, Book XII. She read it rapidly:

'32 1 There was also passed a senatorial decree, punitive at once and precautionary, that if a master had been assassinated by his own slaves, even those manumitted under his will, but remaining under the same roof, should suffer the penalty among the rest. The consular Lucius Varus, sentenced long before under charges of extortion, was restored to his rank. Pomponia Graecina, a woman of high family, married to Aulus Plautius — whose ovation after the British campaign I recorded earlier— and now arraigned for alien superstition, was left to the jurisdiction of her husband. Following the ancient custom, he held the inquiry, which was to determine the fate and fame of his wife, before a family council, and announced her innocent. Pomponia was a woman destined to long life and to continuous grief: for after Julia, the daughter of Drusus, had been done to death by the treachery of Messalina, she survived for forty years, dressed in perpetual mourning......'

Olivia was thrilled to read her very own Pomponia had returned from Britain, but here was something else. A trial, a solid relationship with Julia, the daughter of Drusus and murderous treachery by Messaline. Her heart started to race. Could there be another forty years of writings by Pomponia to be discovered? Indeed she would not have kept silent when she returned to Rome. She must reply to the letter from Chiara Fortuna again. They had been corresponding for some months now, and Olivia was sure the Fortuna family archives had much more information to help uncover more of Pomponia's life near Frascati.

Olivia closed her eyes, and the tears started to roll down her cheeks. What trials had she undergone upon her return to Rome? Pomponia, the woman, brave, courageous and loyal friend.

Reflecting back through the years of her own young life. The friends that had come and gone were Mandy, Ranjita, her old headmistress, the girl's Harmony and Suzi from the Chinese restaurant and their father, Mr Manchu. Where were they all now? What had become of them? She thought of Imogen. Did she really know what she was thinking? Did she ever need a friend or a sister to talk to? Olivia had always turned to her father and mother, feeling their care and warmth. Imperceptibly these people had directed and steered her through her young days.

Then there was the considerable role Aunt Geraldine had impacted on her person. For the first time in her life, it was as if Olivia realised how much past chances, or maybe not chance, but even chosen and directed moments, had shaped her life. Her past flew out before her. She saw events in depth she had never focussed on before. People and their words flashed in front of her mind in three dimensions. She felt a burning need to know how they all were. Pomponia had stirred in her subconscious an aspect of individuals from her past that she needed to know about. Where were they all now?

The personal writings of Pomponia so far revealed her younger years. The latter years of Pomponia's life were shrouded in mystery. There must be more to uncover.

The exhausting enormity of the task and responsibility to reveal accurately the writings of Pomponia weighed heavily upon Olivia. Not only was she privileged to have the translation job but also the interpretation of events and life of Roman women, the ordinary woman, the slave and now this noble woman Pomponia Graecina. She sighed as she dabbed away her tears. Her thoughts flew towards her steady, reliable Theo.

Olivia stood up, glancing around at the array of cross-referencing, coloured strings and notes plastered on her wall. Her brain felt like a mishmash of all these thoughts. She had to get away from it. She closed the door to her study and saw the light on at Theo's desk. He had his back to her as she entered. Feeling her hands on his neck, he swung round and drew her onto his knee. She lay her head on his shoulder and, sniffling, tried to tell him how she was feeling. The overwhelming magnitude of the task and how her own personal need to seek out past friends and know them more deeply had been ignited. Her brain was sparking off in all different directions, from the translation work, the interpretation, the human aspect of emotions, and the actual story of the life of Pomponia and the women she had written about. Sophia had added another element to Livia's thoughts, what about the history of the families that had lived in the area surrounding Frascati? She raised with Theo the possibility of further discoveries in the lands that the Gambocellis owned around ancient Tusculum. Could there be a connection with where Pomponia had built her summer villas? Were there more of her later writings to be found in Italy? Livia seemed to get more and more excited as she spoke with Theo. He listened and advised but could see she was sinking into a quagmire of irrationality, with the scope of the workload and the emotional side of her attachment to the words she was revealing. Theo decided she needed another woman's intellectual brain and emotional support on this matter. She needed direction and mental stability, and he knew exactly who was the one to help out. After some time, he put his finger to her lips. Stroking her hair, he picked her up in his arms and carried her along the landing, gently placing her in their bed. Even before he had turned the light off, she was sleeping soundly. He set plans in motion for the arrival of his friend and mastermind, Geraldine Spitzer.

To Olivia's surprise, Aunt Geraldine telephoned the

following day to say that she was over at 'Gung Ho' for a couple of weeks and desperately needed good company and intellectual stimulation. Could Olivia come over as soon as possible? Olivia in her heightened state of awareness and emotional sensitivity, dropped all her work and was there the same day.

Theo took himself off to his continued work with the Roman antiquities. He was never without the phone ringing for interviews, and now a special TV crew were trying to arrange a documentary of the discovery. He was relieved to see Geraldine take care of Livia. Sophia was more than happy to take charge of little Floria, and now that her husband Ben was with them, they both were enjoying the luxury of total involvement with their first grandchild.

As soon as Geraldine saw the physical state of Olivia, her wild-eyed look, the unkempt hair and the fact that, opening the door, she burst into tears, Geraldine immediately took charge. She ushered Olivia into the garden with a large box of tissues and pushed her into one of the sun loungers under the giant parasol. She gave her a liberal dash of gin and topped this up with a dash of tonic water, ice and lime. Insisting they just sit for five minutes and savour the beautiful view and their delightful drinks without talking. All Geraldine said to Olivia was:

'Now, my dear. Deep breaths of this fragrant air, open your eyes just to the clouds and listen for one bird's song at a time. Let it sweep over you, all this beauty.'

Livia lay quietly on the lounger. Her tense body had felt edgy and restless, slowly relaxed. She tried to concentrate on the birdsong as her aunt had suggested, and as she listened, her heart beat loudly in her chest. Her head and ears were pounding with the sounds. Her breathing became laboured, then quickened. She leaned forward, grabbed the chair's arms, and gasped for breath. Her aunt could see what was happening. She just held her hand and said:

'You feel like your heart is going to leap out of your chest don't you Olivia? It won't my darling. Just let it keep on beating as loud as it likes. Let yourself keep on breathing also as much as you like, take deep breaths, through your nose, of this wonderful salt and seaweed-scented air. That's it, let all these strange feelings come over you, don't fight them. Let them sweep over you and you go with them. You have a strong heart Olivia.'

As Livia sat there, a wave of deep sadness swept over her as her breathing slowly returned to normal and her racing heart returned to its quiet, steady beat. The tears came as she cried softly, she lay back, and the tears trickled down her cheeks. The sun was shining brightly, but under the parasol, Livia shivered as her power and energy left her, making her feel fragile and cold. Aunt Geraldine found a soft alpaca shawl and wrapped this around her shoulders.

'Oh aunt I'm so sorry, I'm such a wreck. What's happening to me? I feel so feeble and weepy.'

'Olivia my dear, you are exhausted physically and emotionally. When was the last time you had a complete night's sleep? I mean from a reasonable hour to a reasonable hour, say 10.30pm to 8am?'

'I can't remember, I'm not sleeping well at the moment. When I do get off, my sleep is fitful, full of dreams, vivid scary things happening to me, Floria screaming out, people shouting at me. Even horrible things, drowning, the house on fire. All of the work I've done going up in flames. I haven't wanted to tell anyone, I'm frightened. Am I going out of my mind?'

'No, Olivia, you are not going out of your beautiful mind. Your body is telling you that it's exhausted. It's a mechanism that comes into play when you go through, say, trauma, overexertion of mind or body, also extreme grief and loss can bring the symptoms on. Following this, you don't take time to regroup, rest and find something totally different to relax with. It's a bit like a record stuck in the groove. You become obsessed with one thing, and it digs deeper and deeper until you can't stop yourself from going round and round on the same obsession. We have to physically nudge it to the next groove with a record. With ourselves, we might just need a little help for a while. Believe me, Olivia, I've been there. I know from experience that enthusiasm and passion for a belief, cause or occupation can quickly become an obsession that takes over everything. We stop eating regularly, miss sleep, and then can't sleep. The body then reacts with a panic attack, which you have just experienced. Don't be alarmed if it happens again, now or over the next few days or weeks. Just allow yourself to let it happen, even say to yourself, 'come on then, old heart, beat as loud as you like, and breathe as deeply as you like. Oh yes, and if the breathing gets too shallow, just grab a paper bag and breath into it for a short while, the carbon dioxide of your own breath will restore normality. Say, 'I do not have a heart attack, and I don't have a brain tumour, so you just carry on until you've finished,' works every time.'

She continued after a moment's hesitation.

'Now, Olivia, my dear girl. You will stay in this lounger for one hour, resting and thinking only of the sounds and sights you see around you. Nothing else, is that clear? I am going to prepare some lunch for later. I will telephone Theo and tell him you are staying with me for at least two days. You will rest entirely from all your work, and we will talk. I will listen, and you will tell me all. We will gently knit together your frazzled nerves, and as always, Olivia, we will set a strategy in place. For all your discoveries and the new awakenings that this has stirred up within you.

Do you remember all the cataloguing we did together when you were a young girl? Yes, well, that is a life lesson, Olivia. We need to catalogue your life, we will prioritise, will make lists, and we will take action where necessary. Olivia, my darling, none of us can do everything perfectly. We make mistakes, and sometimes we have regrets, but I have learned never to procrastinate. We rest when we need to, and then we take action. You will now relax, recuperate, and then you will enjoy the work to come.

I will help you come to your own conclusions, and when you feel able, you will begin again. This discovery is exciting, Olivia, but it is not the only thing in your life. Once you have recorded everything, you may find that it will lead to further enquiries and unanswered questions, so this is just the beginning, Olivia. You must take a day at a time. Today you rest.'

Olivia looked at her aunt and wanted to giggle and cry simultaneously for the first time in weeks. She could see a person who knew what she was talking about, a woman of experience, depth and wisdom. Geraldine's practical manner and non-judgemental but reassuring words gave Livia a child-like trust. Yes, everything was in hand now. She would be all right. Even the mammoth enterprise of bringing the works of Pomponia to life. Then contacting all her friends from the past, re-invigorating old friendships, planning for the future, setting right old wrongs, and recognising her own limitations, all these thoughts were settling into places she could deal with, slowly, one by one. No rushing, no cramming, gently taking time to enjoy life with people she loved and that loved her. She sank back into the soft shawl and closed her eyes, thinking only of the sounds and touch of the golden sun and breeze which swept over her hands and already sleepy body.

Geraldine sat in the kitchen after she had prepared a light meal. So many thoughts to contemplate. Her fingers felt for the envelope in her pocket. She took it out again. The thick creamy paper with gold embossed letter heading. Was this the new lead that they were looking for? Who was this man, Christian Rosenburg? What was the gallery in New York? Had the Picasso's passed through his hands? She re-read the phrase.
'Up until now We did not know of the existence of the your two paintings by Picasso. My client has two already and I have a great interest in seeing the two that you have. I would like to arrange to meet up. My son is visiting England in the fall. ...'

The old familiar pain deep inside twinged. Memories of her acquaintance before the war in Paris flitted through her mind. The Rosenburg name was not unfamiliar to Geraldine. She folded the letter again, returning it to her jacket pocket. Were answers still hidden in her past?

Olivia's few days with her aunt brought a feeling of lightness to her life. Her perspective shifted. It was as if the estuary's waters had lightly trickled over her furrowed, dented mind. Smoothing and washing away the jagged lines and moods of anxiety. Geraldine, too felt refreshed. She had grand plans to set in motion herself.

Olivia returned to Theo, Floria, Pomponia and their home amidst the curlews and bullrushes.

Sofia's stay with them was nearing its end, and she had decided to take one more look at the gallery, and a particular piece of sculpture Justin had been working on. The morning air was light and balmy. The sparse clouds seemed to scoot along the bright blue sky. Sophia stopped and stared up. She put her hand on Olivia's, resting on the pushchair.

'This is really something to remember. A Devon sky, that deep blue, it glows behind those white and grey clouds. I feel inspired to paint again.'

As they drew close to the gallery, Sophia pointed at the new display in the window.

'That is the piece I was thinking about. I do hope its not sold yet.'

Justin moved shyly towards them as they entered. Sophia immediately began examining the completed new wire sculpture of the two oystercatchers flying in synchronisation. She looked at it from all angles. She gently touched its distinct black and white markings and spread her arms, measuring the wingspan. A few minutes passed quietly as Sophia paused. She decidedly spun around on a rather startled Justin, who jumped back and turned bright red.

'Now Justin, I want this piece of art. I love it. I know exactly where I'm going to place it at home. Something to remind me of this beautiful estuary, the people I have met here, and the adventures I've had. It's so lifelike. It has your individuality stamped across it. It will look fabulous at Rivertree, in the garden, near the river.

So, how much?'

Justin was taken aback by her directness and had not even priced the piece. He looked embarrassed, but as always, Tati, totally attuned to his ways, stepped forward and negotiated an acceptable sum with Sophia. Even venturing to increase the value by an amount she knew reflected the true worth of the artwork.

Tati was a tremendous asset to the gallery and her husband. Natural friendliness, enthusiasm and newly found confidence prompted a cautious buyer to be persuaded and become more than happy to purchase there and then.

The deal was done, and shipping directions were all sorted. Sophia said her goodbyes to Justin and Tati, assuring them of a welcome if ever they wanted to visit Pennsylvania and take a look at the sculpture's placement at Rivertree. Both Justin and Tati grinned, unsure of what this bighearted American lady meant. Slightly embarrassed, Tati invited them to have coffee and cake and enjoy the views outside across the Quay.

Livia felt relaxed and contented as she looked down at Floria in her enormous sun hat, shielding her face as she slept in the pushchair. At last, Livia was starting to unwind and switch off from the cares and life of her new friend 'Pomponia'. She felt a calm reality about life here in Exeter and recounted how fortunate she was. Her life was good, not perfect, but the people around her mattered. Theo, her best friend, her almost ideal daughter, her newly appreciated mother-in-law. Sofia had become a good friend. Olivia realised what an unselfish, sensible woman she was. Unaware of the practical, gentle steps Sophia had taken to bring her back to the reality of her life. Her own natural warmth and affection swept over her as she reached a hand across to Sophia and squeezed her hand, saying.

'I just want to say a big thank you. You have helped me so much the last couple of months. I remember you saying you hoped to bond with your granddaughter. Yes, you certainly have, she loves you, but Sophia, I do too. I think we will always be friends.

We're going to miss you so much when you return. We must make plans to visit each other soon. We will come to you next, it's a promise.'

CHAPTER 19

'I count myself in nothing else so happy as in a soul remembering my good friends.
William Shakespeare
Richard II Act 2 scene 3

'Curlews' on the Exe

Over the next few months, life for Olivia fell into a gentle rhythm, each day editing and compiling her translated notes into book form. The findings from the Exe were only a start. So many questions kept coming up, unanswered. This brave woman Pomponia, what had become of her life when she returned to Rome? There was much more to learn about Pomponia. What were the connections? Pomponia, the places she had visited and Theo's family. It was a story so tantalisingly close, nearby within reach.

As work on her new friend Pomponia and the Exe moved along, nagging memories of her old friends kept flashing into her mind. Looking out on the damp rising mist over the Exe in the early mornings, her thoughts became like that swirling fog. Persisting, they were like loose straggly threads, unattached and frayed. They were rolling around like vapour whipped up into thunderclouds inside her brain. The mire of questions unanswered about her old friends. She had to get clarity and some semblance of peace.

Her thoughts were ragged ends of torn moments which needed mending and knitting together. Livia tried to think of what Aunt

Geraldine would now say to her.

Mandy was amazed to hear from Olivia. The younger voice of her oldest friend echoed back in her mind. The years of distance disappeared within thirty seconds. They laughed and recounted those early days together at school. Mandy even remembered that last day when Olivia had had tea at their house. She giggled as she related the chipped garden ornament as Livia had kicked up the stones.

'My mum was livid.'

She paused.

'It's so long ago now. The house, the garden, Dad's beloved cars, being worried about what people thought of us. It was all so pointless.

Both my parents have died. First, Mum had breast cancer. Then Dad went to pieces soon after she died. He went into a sort of melancholy, deep sadness. I was married by that time to Tony. We had the twins tiny and did what we could, even living on the same road. I still wonder if I could have done more. I was busy and exhausted trying to set up the dance school. Then one day, I found him. In his garage, he loved that old Jag.

Mandy gulped, and her voice went quiet. Olivia's heartbeat quickened. The seconds passed by in silence.

'Ah, well. As some say, 'life goes on. The dancing school is a success with all the mums who believe their little princesses will be ballerinas. I've grown plump and reasonably contented.

Now come on, how about you? What's all your news?'

A potted version of recent events brought lots of 'wows' and 'ahs' from Mandy. Even as Olivia spoke, it didn't sound like her own life. She surprised herself with how many exciting things had occurred over the past few years. Mandy was an excellent appreciative listener and encouraged Olivia with intelligent questions. In the background, a bell started buzzing.

'I've got to go, Olivia. That's the business line. Tony's sales and my school, it's all go. But please, please keep me up with what you find in Italy. I haven't enjoyed such a diverting

conversation with a real adult for ages. Promise to keep in touch.'
Olivia smiled to herself, whispering,
 'Thank you, Aunt Geraldine. You made me do it.'

The call to Ranjita took a little more effort and time. At first, a person answered who spoke no English at all. There were many shouting and banging sounds in the background, then a crackling, and the line went dead. After two more attempts, a child answered. She spoke soft lilting English.

'My auntie is not here today. I love my auntie. She is so kind to me. I have the lovely books she has given me. There are pictures of places I want to see. Flowers I have not seen here in my village. My name is Kuljit. What is your name, ma'am?'
'Hello, Kuljit. My name is Olivia, and I am a great friend of your auntie. We went to school together. When can I telephone to speak with her:.'
'Well, she will be home tonight, I think.

Olivia quickly calculated the time difference and said she would call in four hours.
'Thank you for speaking to me, Kuljit. I will call again this evening. Do you have a clock or watch nearby?.'
'Oh yes, ma'am, There is the big clock here. It chimes on the hour.'
'Well, Kuljit, do you think you could watch out for it when it chimes at 7 o'clock tonight? Because I will telephone then, and if you could get your Auntie Ranjita to be near the telephone, I could speak with her.'
Olivia heard soft footsteps; the phone rattled.
'Yes, ma'am, I can see when it will be 7 o'clock. I will be here with my Auntie.'

Finally, the long-awaited phone call with Ranjita happened. The years and miles between them disappeared. Ranjita had become a self-assured, confident Barrister. She was championing the rights of young women in Amritsar. She had no children, but the young girl, Kuljit, was her niece. As she spoke, the inflexion in her voice showed her love for the young girls nearby. She was helping make a difference in their lives.

'Olivia, my work here is making headway. It's early days, but we have great plans. My husband and I plan to visit Europe soon. We need more investment in our school to start building work next year. We've formed a Trust for women's education and already have some famous names attached to it.'

She laughed.

'It's quite funny. The Bollywood female stars are all keen to help us. It's their new thing. They have lots of money and want women's drama and film education to play a major part in the school.'

She chuckled again.

'I never thought I would be mixing with this glamorous crowd. I think we might get your sister involved too?'

The hour they spoke together evaporated the years and miles of distance between. Jockeying back and forth, they talked and joined up all those frayed, jagged edges like jigsaws that clicked satisfyingly into place.

A purposeful phone call the next day from Aunt Geraldine, along with all the family news, intrigued Olivia. Her aunt was thinking of taking a trip to New York. She was vague with Olivia and said she was following exciting leads that followed the trail of other missing artwork and past unanswered questions she had.

'I've had a letter from the Rosenberg Gallery in New York, and I'm meeting up with a young man in London next week. Can't explain more at present but will bring you up to speed when I know more.'

Geraldine's voice sounded excited. When Livia tried to press, nothing was forthcoming. Geraldine, however, was more than happy to pass on the phone number of Mr Manchu.

He cried as he spoke of his two daughters with pride. Suzi and Harmony had made their separate ways in life. Harmony was setting up more restaurants with him, and Suzi played table tennis for the England team in the forthcoming Olympics. Mr Manchu had translated his favourite Chinese proverbs into English and promised to send her a copy of his book when it was published.

'Miss Olivia, do not forget there will always be a special meal for you and your family here at my restaurants. Send me a copy of your book too. We can learn from our ancestors much that will help us in our future. The stones are not dead when we read what is inscribed. You must continue in your investigations. This woman you have discovered may have wisdom for our times.'

While Livia was contemplating and delaying getting in touch with Imogen for a couple of days. The phone rang. Imogen's familiar voice gushed and giggled.

'Darling, I have to come down to see you this weekend. I am ecstatic with happiness. I have some fantastic good news to share. I feel like a new person. I have to tell you my news in person. You will be thrilled.'
She whispered huskily down the phone.

'Livia, it's life-changing. See you Friday night?'
The phone clicked and went dead.
The call was intriguing but, as always, anxiety-inducing. Olivia held the handset at arm's length, quizzically half expecting Imogen to suddenly waft out of the mouthpiece. Her elder sister had the knack of speaking as if everything she did was of great credit to herself, and everyone would be delighted to hear of her hair-brained escapades. Friday night was awaited with curiosity and trepidation.

In her usual dramatic way, Imogen descended, her silver sports car screeching up the gravelled path. A tall, handsome, fair-haired man stepped out of the driver's side and opened the passenger door, offering a hand as Imogen awkwardly wiggled out from the low seat. Olivia, open-mouthed, stared at her sister and the sizeable rounded bump protruding from her tummy. She certainly had life-altering news for them all.

Imogen clung to the arm of the young man. Tottering forward on her high heels, she introduced him.

'This is Captain Shaun Ferguson. My husband .'

Theo looked at Livia. He saw her shocked expression and speechless open mouth. Quickly taking charge of the situation, he moved forward and shook Shaun's extended hand.

'Welcome, I'm Theo, and this is Olivia. Come on in.'

Those few seconds Theo gained for Livia gave her the needed time to gather her thoughts. Her natural warmth and affection swiftly returned, along with her newfound resolve to set matters straight with friends and relations. Theo walked ahead with Shaun, and Olivia took hold of Imogen's arm, kissing her cheek warmly. Responding immediately, Impy threw her arms around Livia. She burst into tears. Through her sobs, she gasped. 'My darling. I had no idea how wonderful this feeling would be. You never told me. This, this having a baby.'
She closed her eyes, smiling serenely as her arms cradled her tummy.

As they sat and Imogen chattered away. The whole story of the whirlwind romance came out.
Shaun had met Imogen at a party in London. Immediately they fell in love, marrying very quickly. Imogen insisted out of necessity, as Shaun was taking up his new job in the West.
She looked excitedly at Olivia.
'We are going to be near neighbours, Olivia. How the children will bond!'
Shaun was a handsome man with an open, slightly shy smile and bright blue eyes. The 'Captain' part of his introduction was that he was an airline pilot working for British Airways. The 'life-altering' news for Impy had been she was going to have a baby, and the 'life-altering' news for Theo and Olivia was that Shaun and Imogen were going to move to Exeter as his work was now based at Exeter airport. There was going to be a lot of bonding going on soon.

Just as quickly as the couple had arrived, they left. Imogen was in a hurry to be at their temporary accommodation. She had so much to do over the next few weeks before their new house was found. There was furniture to be bought and the nursery to organise. Breathlessly, Imogen pleaded with Olivia to spend a day the following week helping her shop and plan. She laughingly agreed. With the departure of Sophia, a hectic day with her sister would be interesting and diverting.

Olivia's life was altering. Each day new challenges appeared. Then the biggest surprise, tinged with sadness, arrived. The news came that Nonna Francesca had died. A long letter came from her Italian lawyers requesting Theo and Olivia attend their London offices. There was paperwork to be sorted out along with bequests she had made. Theo spent a long time in Italian conversations on the phone. The old familiar running his hands through his dark locks reminded Livia of those early days at Rivertree as she watched him pacing the floor. His Italian flowed as his gestures grew more like his mother's. At one point, he threw his hands in the air, almost dropping the phone.

'Ve bene, ne parliamo domani!'

His face looked thunderous as, uncharacteristically for him, he slammed the phone down.

She put her hand on his shoulder and waited.

'Italian bureaucracy, it drives me crazy. My grandmother was a very old lady. She died in her sleep. But no, there is to be an investigation into the cause of her death. The funeral cannot take place immediately. The lawyers in London themselves cannot understand what's happening in their Italian branch. We may have to fly out there sooner than the funeral date. I was hoping that we could all go as a family for the funeral,
There's something else too.'

He paused, turning towards Olivia. He stroked her cheek, brushing away the strands of hair falling over her eyes. She waited, searching his eyes for clues. He took a deep breath.

'The house and estates were all left to the family in Italy.

Apart from a tract of land that Nonna entailed to me and a barn with all its contents. The lawyers need to figure out what to make of the bequest. They have started to inventory the house and the barns, but the specific barn bequeathed to me is entirely empty.

There's something else too. Nonna bequeathed explicitly to you the Armoire chest. My Nonna, bless her soul. Was a wily old bird, But there's more to this. Don't you remember her sending the key to you for the armoire where she had stored documents of her relics? I think we need to find out what's in those Italian letters that came with the key. She may have hinted at where all her stuff was. At the moment, we keep all this to ourselves before we have to start involving any authorities. '

Olivia's heart quickened. Was this her opportunity to get to Italy and uncover more of Pomponia's life along with what Nonna Francesca had discovered? Would she be able to find the tomb mentioned in the old book? Could she find out where Claudia Acte had lived? What was the relationship to Columella?

'Theo, let's go. I'm ready whenever you are.'
He noticed the feverish excitement in her eyes.
'I know you, too, have your investigations and questions unanswered, my love.
What have we started, Olivia? So much we've uncovered. There's much, much more. I feel it in my bones.'

He drew her to him, and taking her hand, they walked together through the open glass doors down the bank out towards the water. They sat on moist springy grass amongst the tall swaying bulrushes.
The estuary before them glinted flat and still. The now-familiar curlews waded in the mud amongst the reeds. Theo pointed out that the only difference between the male and female was the female tended to have a slightly longer curved beak. He laughed and said maybe she was more inquisitive and better at digging

than the male as he pulled Livia closer to him and kissed the end of her nose.

He was proud of all the digging she had done, probing, and the treasures she had unearthed from the ancient writings.
He then said:
 'You know we've never given this house a name. There will be much more digging and turning over the soil around us. How about we take the name 'Curlews' for the house? We want to make the lake eventually here; this will be their home too. You and I are like a couple of curlews, poking around and tossing out what we find. There is still more searching and a lot of unanswered questions. There are more secrets to uncover. Curious mysteries have come to light.
What do you think, my love - 'Curlews'?'

 'I like that, Theo, 'Curlews', we will help them to not just survive. I want them to thrive and be safe.
We won't stop digging, wading, lifting up the soil, and bringing out the treasures.'

She placed her cheek next to Theo's and noticed the faint curlew prints in the sand. The wind stirred the reeds, whispering as it swayed them. The seed pods drifted in the breeze, alighting near and far. Such minor events with far-reaching effects. The evening sun was setting behind them as it stretched its light across the water. It seemed to have no end.
How far would they travel tracking, unearthing, and revealing?
Their quest together had only just begun..........

ABOUT THE AUTHOR

Philippa Varney

I live and work in south Devon with my architect husband, Steve. We have a great family, two clever creative sons. Two beautiful and gifted daughters-in-law and four gorgeous, fun grandchildren. We previously lived in Berkshire, and I have been involved with interior and garden design development, having worked in the creative field for the past 25 years, training in silver smithing, jewellery design and CAD.

As far back as I can remember, I have loved to cosy up and read a good mystery or historical life account. Sometimes as many as four a week! It's always been a delight to read and be read to.

I recall my mum introducing me to Georgette Heyer, Dickens and Christie. Then I discovered Forster, Wilkie Collins and Dumas. What adventures for the mind and soul. Widening out to modern-day authors, my mind has become a fertile ground for writing my stories. They have been buzzing around in my head for years.

Coming to Devon has been inspirational, and I no longer procrastinate. I just now write! The rich history of this county and archaeological finds have sparked so many stories that need to be told. The more I have researched and delved into accounts and facts about the people, events from the past and this area, the more I have come up with fantastic plots and fictional tales.

Mixing true factual accounts and real places with events that may have happened has been exciting and enjoyable.

Come with me on the trail of the ancient Romans to modern-day spies, intrigue and secrets discovered by my characters. Family sagas and mysteries are uncovered and answered in this series of books, travelling through time from AD14 Rome to modern-day Exeter and Topsham. My first book in this series was Pomponia's Stylus, and the second is Olivia's Isca Whispers.....

The third will be....

the story behind Aunt Geraldine's past and what continues to plague her life. What did happen to her during World War II? Where has Archie disappeared to?

What will happen when she visits New York? Is there more to be discovered by Olivia and Theo in Italy? What did Nonna Francesca leave behind for Olivia and Theo?

The next book in this series will start to untangle their lives and mysteries......

Look out for short story book coming soon...

and young adult book of fun and time travel. 'Trotters might fly'

You can hear these books being read to you on

Youtube - PhilippaVarney

If you are enjoying this book let me know.

email: pjvarney@gmail.com